STARBORN

THE FLAXFIELD

QUARTET:

VOLUME FOUR

Starborn

TOBY FORWARD

WALKER
BOOKS

First published 2013 by Walker Books Ltd

87 Vauxhall Walk, London SE11 5HJ

2 4 6 8 10 9 7 5 3 1

Text © 2013 Toby Forward

Illustrations © 2013 Jim Kay

The right of Toby Forward and Jim Kay to be identified as the author and illustrator respectively of this work has been asserted by them in accordance with the Copyright, Designs and Patents Act 1988

This book has been typeset in Historical

Printed and bound in Great Britain by Clays Ltd, St Ives plc

British Library Cataloguing in Publication Data:

a catalogue record for this book is available from the British Library

ISBN 978-1-4063-2046-6

www.walker.co.uk

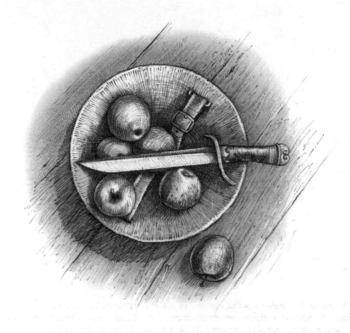

*All that is necessary for the triumph
of evil is that good men do nothing.*
Edmund Burke

This book is dedicated to all those
who don't stand by and watch.

Flaxfold died on a Friday,

which was a shame, because she was the person Sam needed most. She died in the same room where Sam had found Flaxfield dead. Except that the old man had died in his sleep, an afternoon nap, and Flaxfold had been killed in the first battle of a war.

It was the same kitchen, the same house, the same day, only more than a year later.

Either way, they were both dead now, and Sam was left to deal with it on his own again.

First, there was the kitchen. Sam didn't know where to start.

"It doesn't matter where you start," Flaxfield had always told him. "As long as you do the first thing."

"What's the right first thing to do?" Sam remembered the question. He was always asking the old man questions.

"You'll know when you've done it," Flaxfield told him.

Sam looked around at the mess. The floor was littered

with the bodies of dead beetles, the shards of the smashed bodies of kravvins. The rushes and sweet herbs were stained with the slime and pus that burst from the creatures when they split open.

Where to start?

Sam took his staff in both hands and grasped it high above his head, level with the ground. He drew in a deep breath and held it. Mist poured out of both ends of the staff, curling down, rising up, billowing out. White mist, cool and clean. It wrapped itself round Sam and flowed out, filling the whole room. Every small space, every crevice, every tiny gap filled with the mist.

He waited until all was still and the cloud had come to rest. Slowly releasing his breath, he crossed the room and walked out through the door into the garden. He slid his hands over the staff, bringing them together at the end. The mist followed, a trail of cloud. No longer white and clean, it was stained yellow and green. Sam whipped the staff round and pointed it up to the sky. The mist curled after the movement and spiralled away, dragging the slime and debris with it. A whirlwind of filth and death.

Sam watched it disappear, leaning on his staff. When it was clear, he made his way back into the room.

"It's clean now, at least," he said.

He ignored Flaxfold's body. There were others to deal with and he sorted them first, just making them straight and seemly.

"Next?" he said.

Next was the furniture. Chairs were scattered and the table was broken. It leaned lazily on its side. Smashed pots and broken windows. The wall next to the kitchen range had a wide gap in it. The range itself had twisted and buckled. Sam righted the table, found the broken leg and made a mending spell. He put the chairs back into place around it. The small things took a lot of time and were picky to deal with. He mended them one by one, putting each in its proper place as it was finished. All the time he kept his eyes away from Flaxfold and the other bodies.

The gaping hole in the wall he filled with smoke and watched it blend together and heal.

He enjoyed mending the kitchen range. The metal was pleasing to work and it soothed him.

After a long time, too soon, all was complete. Sam looked for something else to mend, something new to tidy. Nothing. All was done. Only the bodies remained.

He went outside. The light was failing. Clouds covered the moon and stars. A soft drizzle dampened the grass. Starback nuzzled up against him, his rough skin pleasant against Sam's legs.

Sam sat on the wet ground with his back to the wall and cried so hard that it made his throat hurt.

He was thirteen years old. ‖

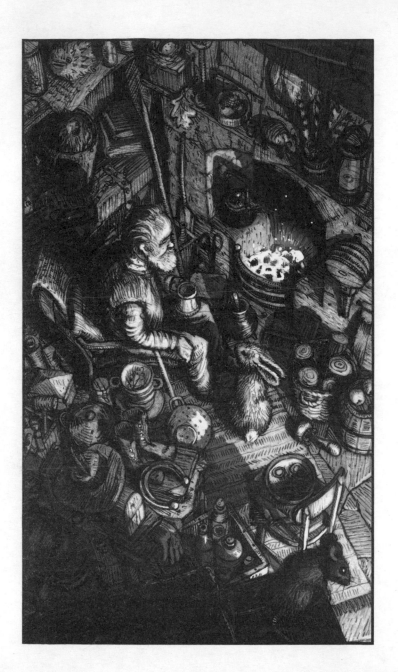

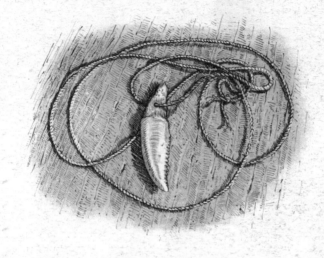

Part One

STARSEEKER

In the Deep World

it is never night. Far underground, guarded by secret doors and passageways, the sun never shines and the light never dims.

"I want to see the stars," said Tadpole.

"They're nothing special," said his father. "You'll see them one day."

"I want to see them now."

"That's your trouble. You always want everything now."

Megatork smiled down at his son, to take away some of the sharpness of his answer. Roffles are, for the most part, kind sorts.

"I've been twelve for over a year now," said Tadpole, who didn't give up easily, "so I should have been Up Top."

Megatork stroked the neck of the memmont which sat next to him. Tadpole waited.

"You know why you can't go," he said, at last.

"No."

"Seventeen," said his father. "Seventeen roffles killed. In one week."

"I'll be careful."

"We're all careful. They were careful. Roffles have to be careful Up Top. You know that. It doesn't matter how careful you are, you're not going, and that's that."

Tadpole sat down on the floor next to the memmont and put his arm around it. The creature nuzzled up against him and Tadpole felt comforted by the soft fur, the solid yet graceful bulk.

"What's changed?" he asked his father. "Why is it danger-ous now? More dangerous?"

"I'm not supposed to tell you. I promised your mother I wouldn't."

Tadpole jumped up.

"If you won't tell me, I'll go Up Top and find out for my-self."

It was a challenge. Tadpole measured his breathing while he waited for an answer.

"Come outside," said Megatork. "Walk in the garden with me."

Where his mother wouldn't be able to hear. Tadpole pressed his lips together in tight triumph.

The memmont loped behind them, snuffling at scents on the path.

"Since Flaxfield died," said the older roffle, "things have been getting worse Up Top. You know about Flaxfield?"

Tadpole nodded. Of course he did. Every roffle did. You learned about Flaxfield the way you learned about how to tie a knot, or the proper way to lift a roffle pack on to your back, or how many ten times seven is.

"Flaxfield kept things in order Up Top. More or less. Or when they went wrong he put them right."

"Did you ever meet Flaxfield?" asked Tadpole.

"No. I never did. I wish I had. It's too late now. He died the best part of two years ago. It was like taking the keystone from an arch. All the other stones lose their support and tumble against each other and then the whole building falls."

Tadpole had a secret about Flaxfield and he came very close to telling his father then, but he hesitated a moment too long and Megatork carried on with his story.

"Death has been busy amongst the people Up Top since then. And in new ways, cruel ways. Villages destroyed. Whole populations killed. Kravvins, creatures never seen before, with blank shiny faces, more beetle than man, have ripped through the countryside. They kill and carry on, red and ruthless."

"Where do they come from?" asked Tadpole.

His father shook his head. "You know how stories grow," he said, "and how many stories answer one question. All I know is that people say that Ash made them."

"Ash?"

They reached the end of the garden and looked back at the house. The memmont circled round, looking for things to tidy. Tadpole looked up at the never-dark sky above them.

"Isn't there anyone who can stop it all?" he asked.

His father put his arm around him. "Not you," he said. "So you'll stay down here, in the Deep World, until it's safe to go up again."

"When will that be?"

He had never seen such a look of sorrow and regret on his father's face.

"Perhaps never," he said, and walked back to the house.

Tadpole shut his eyes tight and tried to conjure up the image of a black sky, peopled with stars. It was no good. The light was too strong for his eyelids.

He tickled the memmont's ears.

"Let's go and see Delver."

Megadelveradage's house was famous.

"You can come in, young Tadpole," said the old roffle. "But leave your memmont outside."

"Sorry," said Tadpole.

The memmont sulked away and curled up under a tree.

Going into Delver's house was like stealing food from a hungry person, or kicking a wounded dog. It felt wrong. Tadpole's skin prickled every time he walked through the door.

Yet he loved it there.

"Apple?" offered Delver.

"Yes, please."

"Help yourself."

It was an old game between them.

"Where are they?" asked Tadpole.

"If you can find one, you can have it."

When Delver sat down his armchair leaned to one side.

His house wasn't dirty. No roffle could live in a dirty house. But it was untidy. Tadpole started to search for a bowl of fruit.

"Tell me about magic," he said, lifting a fanned pile of old papers with black handwriting and red drawings. No apples there.

"Why is it always magic with you?" asked Delver.

"You've seen magic. Tell me about it."

"Again?"

"Again," Tadpole insisted.

He looked under the table. There was a hat and a saucepan, but no apples.

"Try behind the cupboard," said Delver.

Tadpole shook his head. "No," he said. "I've been tricked like that before."

"Suit yourself."

"I'll do without," he said.

"Sit down, then," said Delver.

Tadpole looked around for a chair. There were plenty. It was just that none of them had any space for a roffle to sit. Piled high with Delver's stuff.

"Try that."

Delver pointed to his leather roffle pack.

Tadpole smiled and shook his head.

"Go on."

"I can't."

"Go on."

Tadpole started to clear a pile of books and plates from a chair. A rabbit hopped out and landed with a gentle splat. It turned a sleepy, accusing face to Tadpole.

"Go on." Delver kicked his pack with his toe. The leather was hard, dry, and smooth, worn to a deep shine. A squashed barrel in shape.

"No one sits on a roffle pack, except the roffle who owns it," said Tadpole.

"Have you got one of your own?"

Tadpole shrugged. "You know how it is," he said. "No one goes travelling any more."

"Sit on that one, for now. I don't mind."

Tadpole pushed it into place, flat end up, and sat on it, roffle-fashion.

"Please, tell me. Magic."

"If you were a wizard," said Delver, "you could just clap your hands now, and the apples would rise up into the air, spin round and round, turn blue and gold, silver and red, come tumbling down into your lap, ready to eat."

Tadpole shivered with pleasure.

"And you've seen that?"

Delver smiled. "How many times have I told you?"

"But that? The apples. You've seen that?"

Delver thought for a moment.

"Not exactly that. But things just like it. That's small magic," he said. "The sort of thing a village wizard would do. A proper wizard does more than that."

Tadpole pulled his chair closer.

"Why is there no magic in the Deep World?" he asked.

"Ah, now that's a good question."

Tadpole waited. Delver didn't say anything.

"What's the answer?" he asked, at last.

"I don't know."

Tadpole stood up and started to tidy the table.

"Stop that."

Tadpole straightened the papers, cleared some pens and a couple of small clay pots.

"Don't."

Tadpole grinned. Tidying Delver's house was like throwing things around anywhere else.

"I like all this jumble," said Tadpole.

He stopped tidying and sat down again.

"I lived a long time Up Top," said Delver. "Too long for a roffle, really. When I came back everything looked too neat, too tidy. This reminds me of happy times, when I was a young roffle, like you."

"I'm going to go Up Top."

"No. Not now. It's finished. It's all death and danger there now."

"I know about the kravvins," said Tadpole.

"Do you, now?"

"I don't care. I've got to go. I've got to see the stars. I've got to see magic." Tadpole clenched his fists. "You understand. You've been there. You know what it's like. I have to see it."

"I've been there," said Delver. "But I wouldn't go now. Not with the things that have happened. Not now the kravvins are there."

"Can't the wizards get rid of the kravvins? Can't they use magic?"

Delver looked more serious than Tadpole had ever seen him.

"Magic isn't like that. It's not that simple."

Tadpole surprised himself with the fierceness of his reply.

"Tell me, then. Not just nice stories about magic. Tell me the truth. How does magic work? Why can't I do it? What's wrong with roffles that they haven't got any magic? Tell me, or I'll go Up Top and find out for myself."

Delver put his finger to his lips.

"Hush. I'll tell you all I know."

Tadpole settled himself on the roffle pack and waited while Delver gathered his thoughts. It was surprisingly comfortable.

"This is a secret story," said Delver. "I'm not supposed to know about it."

"How do you know, then? Who told you?"

Delver wagged a finger.

"You listen, and you don't speak. Or I won't tell you anything. Understand? Good. It's the story of Smokesmith.

Long ago. Before memory. There was no magic Up Top. And then there was a blacksmith. He made swords and shields, axes for war, chainmail and visors. The best ever seen. Molten iron, mixed with charcoal. It gleamed. It cut. Arrows and spears bounced off it. He hammered it to a perfect shine. One day, he made a mirror. Beaten steel. Smooth as sleep. The first mirror there ever was." The old roffle's voice dropped to a whisper. Tadpole had to lean in to hear him. "When the first person looked at herself in the surface of the mirror, the magic burst out."

"What happened? Sorry. I'll shut up."

"The mirror was locked away. That's all I know. It was never seen again. Magic was loose by then."

Tadpole breathed out slowly.

"What about that apple?" said Delver.

Tadpole looked around the room. Too many places. Too much stuff. He'd never find it. He reached out and picked up one of the small clay pots from the table.

"You like that?" asked Delver.

"What is it?"

"I got that from Flaxfield's kitchen."

Tadpole nearly dropped it.

"Careful."

"Really?"

"Really."

"You met Flaxfield?"

"Shake it," said Delver.

It rattled.

"Have a look."

Tadpole tipped it upside down and a tooth fell out. A length of cord had been threaded through a hole drilled into the root. Delver held out his hand for it.

"This is a dragon's tooth."

Tadpole smiled.

The old roffle tossed it to him.

"How do you know?" asked Tadpole.

"See how big it is."

Tadpole weighed it in his palm.

"You can have it."

"Is it magic?"

"Tie it round your neck."

"Did Flaxfield give it to you? What was he like? Did you see him do proper magic?"

"This little clay pot had dried herbs in it," said Delver. "Smell."

Tadpole put it to his nose and breathed in the dusty aroma.

"Have that as well."

"Are you sure?"

"What do I need with it? Is there anything else you want? Have a look. I brought back lots of things from Up Top."

Tadpole felt embarrassed.

"I didn't come to take your things," he said.

"I know. What about that apple? Look behind the cupboard."

Tadpole, feeling foolish, decided to play the game. He bent

and looked, and there they were, piled on a shallow dish.

"Told you," said Delver. "Bring the whole thing."

It was surprisingly light.

"Tip them on to the table," said Delver. "That's the way. Help yourself. Now, what do you think of the bowl?"

It wasn't a bowl at all. There was a strap inside. Tadpole turned it over.

"What is it?"

"What do you think? Put your arm through."

It was black, light, thin and very hard. And very shabby and wretched-looking. Tadpole didn't want to, but he slipped his arm through the strap and lifted his hand.

"It's a shield," he said.

"There's a knife as well, somewhere. Where did I put it?"

The roffle looked around as though searching for something. Tadpole waited.

"Help me look," said Delver.

"Where is it?" asked Tadpole.

Delver smiled.

"Can't fool you, can I?"

Tadpole smiled back.

"You know where every single thing is in here," he said.

"Perhaps I do. Try the little drawer in the table."

And there it was.

"I'm not allowed to have knives," said Tadpole.

"Just pass it to me."

Tadpole picked it up. As his hand closed over the handle he

had a sense that it had been shaped to his palm. It belonged to him. He handed it to Delver.

"There's a story," said the old roffle. "This knife and that shield were made by the same blacksmith who made the first mirror, time before knowledge."

"How did you get it?"

"Just picked it up. Like I just picked up the story."

"You said it was a secret story."

"It is. But, if you'd ever been Up Top you'd know that people forget about roffles. Because we talk in our Up Top voices they think we're a bit stupid. They say all sorts of things they wouldn't want us to hear, if they were thinking about it."

Tadpole sat on the pack again.

Silence licked round them and Tadpole didn't know how to make a sound again. At last, Delver said, "Roffles don't do magic. Never have."

Tadpole answered him quickly, too quickly. "I know. I just want to see it."

Delver waited.

"How did you know?" asked Tadpole.

"When I was a young roffle I wanted to do magic," he said. "You're not the first. And when I saw it, Up Top, when I saw what it could do, I wanted it more than ever."

"That's it," said Tadpole. "I've got to see it."

"Seeing it makes it worse," said Delver.

"It can't."

"It does. You just want to do magic yourself more than

ever. But," he added, "it's better to see magic and not do it, than never to see it."

Tadpole jumped to his feet. Delver held out his hand for silence.

"One day, you will go Up Top," he said. "But you have to wait until the kravvins are gone."

He lowered his hand but Tadpole didn't answer.

"Anyway," he said, "you'll need a roffle pack when you go, and you may as well have that one."

"I can't."

"There's no other way of getting one now, is there? Go on, take it."

Tadpole started to lift it.

"Wait. You may as well put that thing in there." He pointed and Tadpole lifted the lid and put the shield in, without looking inside. "And tuck the knife into your belt. You never know when you might want to peel an apple. But you'd better not let anyone see you've got a pack. They might jump to conclusions. Go on now. Before I change my mind."

"Thank you. I promise that—"

"Shh. No promises. Just remember. I'm telling you very clearly. Understand. You must not go Up Top until the kravvins are all gone and your father gives you permission. Is that clear?"

"But…"

"What?"

"You gave me your pack."

"And I've told you not to go. Right?"

Tadpole grinned.

"Right."

"Get out, then. And come back and see me soon. All right?"

"I will."

"And take that memmont with you, before it creeps in and makes a tidy of my things."

The memmont was asleep under the tree.

"Come on home," said Tadpole, stroking him awake. "I want to show you something."

The creature looked at him as though it understood what he had said and followed him into the house.

"Look at this," said Tadpole, opening the door and letting the memmont in with him.

Tadpole had been working secretly in the box room, trying to make it like Delver's house.

The memmont sprang on to a broken wardrobe and started to straighten the door on its twisted hinges. The creature's slender fingers were strong and they bent the metal back into shape as though it was pastry dough. Before Tadpole could stop him the memmont had ordered the doors so that they hung straight and it was rummaging inside, sorting piles of old sheets and blankets, broken toys and boxes of screws, empty bottles, a paperweight, a comb with missing teeth.

"That's enough," said Tadpole.

He spoke sharply and the memmont cast a reproachful look over its shoulder.

"Sorry," said Tadpole. "Stop that now and come here."

The memmont forced itself away from the wardrobe, but not before it straightened one last pile of papers and an old hat.

Tadpole stroked its neck. It sat next to him and licked the back of his hand.

"You can't always be tidying," said Tadpole.

The memmont blinked and put its head to one side.

"I mean, I know that's what memmonts do, and it's good. But not here. Not now."

Tadpole, not for the first time, felt how difficult it was to make himself understood. If his mother and father didn't know what he liked and what he thought was worthwhile, how could he expect a memmont to?

"Sometimes it's good for things to be tidy," he said. "But not everything. And if this place was tidy…" He paused and looked at the closed door. "If this place was tidy, then anyone could find what's in here, couldn't they? I like things to be jumbled sometimes."

The memmont moved a sly paw to one side and straightened a drawer in a scruffy desk.

"I saw that," Tadpole warned him. "No more tidying."

He gave the memmont a friendly scratch on its head.

"I'm going to show you something," he said.

He moved the memmont aside and opened a little cupboard in the kneehole of the desk that it had just tried to tidy. He drew out a box, big enough to hold two two-pound loaves of bread. Leaning against the desk, he put the box on the floor in front of them and opened it.

"I found these in here," he said, "a couple of months ago."

He opened the box. The memmont's busy fingers darted in and, as fast as a flea's leap, the contents were all in order and arranged ready to read on the floor.

"No. Stop it. I mean it."

The memmont nuzzled its nose against Tadpole's neck. He laughed.

"No. Really. Do you know what this is?" he asked. "Of course you don't. No one knows. Only me."

There were five big notebooks, with stiff covers. There were loose pages, covered in writing and tied with blue string. There were other pages with exquisite ink drawings, sometimes just one to a page, others where the whole page was covered with pictures woven into each other so that there was no empty paper to be seen.

Tadpole ignored the loose pages and opened the top notebook.

"This belonged to Megapoir," he said to the memmont, which looked back at him as though it understood. "He was my great-great-something-grandfather. I don't know how many greats." He put his head close to the memmont and whispered, "He knew Flaxfield. He was his friend."

He showed the memmont the pages, covered with closely written notes.

"This is his diary. And these—" he showed it the loose papers — "are letters from a friend Up Top. A wizard. Called Waterburn."

Tadpole looked at the locked door again.

"And there are directions," he said. "To Flaxfield's house. From here."

He snapped the book shut and put it back into the roffle pack with the other books and papers, except for one, which he folded and put into his pocket.

"I'm going there," he whispered. "To Flaxfield's house. Now."

The memmont stood up and followed him to the door.

"You stay here," said Tadpole. "I'm just going for one hour. Well, perhaps longer. I don't know what time it is there. But I'm going to Flaxfield's house. There won't be any danger there. And I'll wait until it's night."

He slung Delver's roffle pack on to his shoulders, and, making his way to the front door, walked out into the light.

"Stay here," he said.

The memmont sat and looked up at him. Tadpole felt he needed to explain.

"I just want to see the day turn to night. To see the sky go black. To watch the stars come out. That's all. And I want to see magic. I'll be back before anyone knows I've gone. Now, stay there."

He walked past the Up Top door three times, looking as though he wasn't interested in it, to make sure no one saw him go through. When he was sure that no one was looking he opened it and stepped through, as fast as he could, and kicked it shut behind him. Or nearly shut. He didn't notice the memmont slip through. And the memmont, which knew just how important it was to keep the doors closed, folded its fingers over the handle and closed it with a soft, secret swish.

Tadpole consulted his paper and took the passageway to the left, then up and round a corner and left again. And there it was. As near as that.

"It can't be," he said. He checked his paper. "As close as this, all the time."

It seemed right, so he folded the paper, put it away and opened the door. It was thick and wide and solid, so he braced himself to push hard, and was taken by surprise when it moved as easily as the door to the pantry at home.

"Right," he said, and stepped through, round a gloomy bend and was, all at once, Up Top.

It wasn't dark, so there were no stars. He was standing at the corner of a house, with a garden, a fence where the ground sloped down to a river. He could smell fish cooking. He moved slowly, quietly, round the corner and found himself face to face with a monster.

"Kravvins," he said.

He tried to run back but the creature was too quick for him and seized his arm, holding him fast. ‖

Tadpole shouted again,

as loudly as he could.

"Kravvins!"

The creature's hand bit into his arm. Thin fingers folded tight. Its face was almost human. It was cross-hatched with ridges and furrows, raised white skin seared through dark-red flesh. No lips, not really, just a line for a mouth. The eyelids barely met when the creature blinked. Thin straggles of hair fringed a blue scarf tied tightly on the head, knotted at the back.

Tadpole grabbed his roffle pack and swung it at the creature. He tripped and fell against it and a hand closed over his mouth, choking his cries.

A man came round the corner of the house.

"What have you got there?" he said.

After the man, a boy. And a girl. And two women, one old, one of an age that didn't disclose itself.

"It's a roffle," said the monster.

Tadpole bit the fingers and the hand jumped away.

"Kravvins!" he shouted. "Help. Kravvins."

The hand jammed back down on his mouth.

The boy came and put his face close to Tadpole's.

"It's all right," he said. "If she lets you go will you promise not to shout?"

She?

Tadpole looked at their faces. It seemed as though the man was trying not to laugh. The old woman was looking over Tadpole's head at the creature, a trace of apology over her face.

Tadpole nodded.

The hand came away.

He scuttled forward, dragging his pack after him. He looked around and the creature had pulled a scarf round its face, leaving only the eyes in sight.

"I'm so sorry," said the old woman.

The creature walked past her and into the house.

"Why did you do that?" said the boy.

Tadpole remembered to answer with a roffle question. "Why does a horse hit a hammer on an acorn?" he asked.

"Oh, stop it. My name's Sam. What's yours?"

"Tadpole."

"Come on, then. Follow me. And forget that roffle talk."

Tadpole followed them in.

It was Tadpole's first meeting with Up Top people and he knew it had not got off to a good start. He liked the house.

His first Up Top house. Bigger than a roffle house, but people were bigger than roffles, so, what else? He liked the room, a kitchen, fragrant with the scent of fresh fish, and furnished as a comfortable parlour as well.

The old woman gave Tadpole a hard look, though not without some kindness.

"This lady is called December," she said, indicating the monster. "And I'm Flaxfold." She pointed to the girl. "This is Tamrin." The girl scowled. "This is—"

"Don't bother," the man interrupted her. "He's not staying long enough to get acquainted."

"He's called Tadpole," said Sam.

"Tell me your name now," said Tadpole, standing in front of the man and glaring at him.

Flaxfold laughed.

"Serves you right, Axestone," she said. "Come on, let's eat."

No one introduced the other woman, and she said nothing.

They all sat round the table. The boy offered to cook for December.

"No. I'm not hungry. Thank you."

"I caught eight," said Sam. "Just in case."

"No. I ate on the way."

Tadpole didn't believe her. She still had her scarf wrapped round her face. The Axestone person stared at him. The slim woman looked as though she might smile. The Flaxfold poured a drink and handed him the beaker.

"Just in case there's a roffle," she said.

"Eh?" asked Sam.

"You caught eight, just in case, and here he is." She gestured to Tadpole. "So you'd better cook it for him."

"No, thank you," said Tadpole. "I'm not hungry." He didn't want to eat where he wasn't welcome.

"All right," said Sam. He sat down next to December. A ripple of alarm went through Tadpole when she put her hand on Sam's and squeezed it. He couldn't bear the thought of her touch. And he was starving. He shrugged his pack from his shoulders and sat on it, roffle-fashion. Light to carry, perfect to sit on. He looked at the trout by the pan and at the plates on the table with the heads, tails and bones of the fish on them. He looked at the crusty bread, the yellow butter, the apples.

The big man laughed and poked Sam in the ribs.

"Ask him again," he said.

"What?"

Tadpole wished more than anything in the Deep World that he had never ventured Up Top. He almost thought he'd rather have been killed by kravvins than have to endure the embarrassment of this kitchen and these people looking at him and laughing at him.

Flaxfold rapped her knuckles on the table.

"Enough," she said. "December, dear. I'm so sorry this young roffle upset you, but it really isn't his fault, I think."

The woman nodded, her face still covered.

"We're your friends," she went on. "We're used to you. This poor thing can't have been Up Top before. Have you?"

Tadpole shook his head.

"You see? He had no idea. Sam, look after him. There's a good lad."

"I'll cook three," he said. "Waterburn's here. He'll be with us in a minute. And December will have one, won't you?"

She looked at him.

"Please," he said.

She loosened the scarf from her face and let it fall away. Tadpole looked at the wrecked features.

"I was burned," she said to him. "Long ago. Other than that, I'm just as these others. Not a kravvin."

"I'm sorry," said Tadpole. "You frightened me."

"I know."

Waterburn appeared in the doorway.

"Is that trout?" he asked.

There were hugs and handshakes, kisses and smiles. Tadpole watched them, feeling left out again. He noticed that Waterburn and December were shy with each other and wondered why. They hugged longer but said less to each other.

"Who's this?" Waterburn asked, at last.

"He's not staying. He's just a roffle," said Tamrin.

Tadpole had had enough of being treated like an intruder.

"Who's a bigger pig than a donkey, and what does it want going round a shoemaker's shed?" he said.

When they all laughed he turned as red as riches and made a step towards the door.

"Whoa," said Waterburn. "Stop there. Please." He took

Tadpole's hand and shook it. "I'm pleased to meet you," he said. "You know my name. Please tell me yours."

Tadpole relaxed, and felt the pleasure of the man's greeting. The girl made an unpleasant noise and turned away.

"Don't mind her," said Waterburn. "It's a while since I saw a roffle, and it does me good to meet you."

Now the slim woman came over and put her hand on Tadpole's shoulder.

"Eloise," she said.

Tadpole couldn't look at her. He just nodded.

By the time the introductions were made the fish was cooked and they set to. Conversation faltered, then. The ones who had eaten first chatted to the others. Tadpole felt that they were just finding things to say before they got down to something serious. This was a meeting, not a party. He had worked that out. And some of them had travelled a long way to be there. So it was important.

Like every roffle, Tadpole loved his food. But, even though the trout was delicious, he found it hard to give it his full attention. He wanted to know what was happening.

When the meal was done and the table cleared and the dishes washed there was an uncomfortable silence. They all looked at each other and then they looked at Flaxfold. Tadpole knew that it was her house now. It was her meeting. She should start. They expected it.

"Flaxfold," said Axestone. "Time to start. You're in charge."

"No," she said. "Sam is. And Tamrin."

"First," said Axestone, "we need to say goodbye to the roffle."

He stood and made a movement to show Tadpole to the door. Tadpole gripped the sides of his barrel.

"Can't I stay?"

"Of course not." Axestone seemed to be used to taking control. "Thank you for visiting. It's been a pleasure to meet you. Now, if you'll just say your goodbyes and find your roffle door you can go home."

"I can't."

"What?"

"I can't go yet."

"Why not?"

Tadpole couldn't go because he had never had such a sense of an important occasion. Something was happening here, something he didn't want to miss.

"Why can't you go?" asked Axestone.

Tadpole remembered that he had to disguise his speech Up Top.

"Why can't a mouse boil a windmill?" he asked. Not the best reply, a bit simple, but the most he could manage in the rush. Everyone laughed — even, for the first time since he had seen her, December. And when she did, some of the horror of her face melted and he saw something of beauty in her.

"Don't laugh at me," he said.

Flaxfold shushed them.

"I'm sorry," she said. "But you see, every single one of us here is a wizard. This is Flaxfield's house."

"I know it is."

"Then what did you expect to find but wizards? So your roffle talk's no good for us. We know you only do it to fool us poor Up Top folk. There's no need for it, Tadpole."

"So it's time to go home," said Axestone. "We'll send word when it's safe to come again. You should never have tried it. You might have got yourself killed, but you got away with it this time."

"I can't go back. Not yet."

"You have to," said the big man.

Tamrin spoke quietly.

"Why not, Tadpole?" she asked.

He gave her a grateful look and before he could stop himself from telling the truth, though it sounded stupid as he spoke it, he said, "I haven't seen the stars."

A silence covered them. Tamrin broke it.

"Is that why you came here?"

He lowered his head.

"Yes."

"I caught eight fish," said Sam.

"And there are eight places laid at the table," said Eloise.

"And," said Waterburn, "there's always a roffle, isn't there?"

"Yes," Flaxfold agreed. "There's always a roffle, and it looks like it's you, Tadpole," she said.

"So I can stay?"

He beat his fists on the side of the barrel.

"Just a moment," said Axestone. He took Tadpole's hand and made him stand up. "We've come here today," he said, "to make plans."

"I know. Well, I guessed."

"Don't interrupt."

Tadpole flinched at the reprimand.

"Don't be harsh, Axestone," said Eloise. "There was never a roffle in the history of the world who didn't interrupt."

Axestone looked into Tadpole's eyes.

"I don't think that every one of us will live beyond the work we're planning today. If you stay with us, you might not. Do you understand?"

Tadpole looked steadily at him. "Seventeen roffles were killed in one week," he said. "I understand."

"Do you? You were frightened half to death by a woman just now. How will you manage when you see a real kravvin?"

"Enough," said Flaxfold. "Tadpole. What we're about to do is very dangerous. We're all in danger and we have great magic. You have none. If you stay, you'll put yourself at risk. Are you prepared to do that?"

Tadpole didn't answer straight away. He remembered the Deep World, the safety of home. He thought of his father's warning. Going back down seemed a very pleasant thing. Perhaps he should leave them to it.

"I think, after all..." he said. Axestone smiled, and Tadpole pointed to him. "I think I ought to ask a question first. If you fail, if you lose and the kravvins win, will they stop here?

Or will they get down into the Deep World and come for us next?"

Sam whistled. A long, slow whistle.

"He's right," said Tamrin.

"Yes," agreed Flaxfold. "And we never even thought of it."

"Well?" said Tadpole.

"I don't know," said Axestone. "Not for certain. But if you want my opinion, yes. If they win they'll come for you. They'll swarm all through the Deep World."

"Then I'll stay," he said. "Start your meeting."

"Hello, what's this?" said Axestone.

The memmont had slipped through the door and was tidying the dishes away into a cupboard. ||

Tadpole made up his mind

not to say anything in the meeting at all.

"Are lots of people Up Top wizards?" he asked.

"Don't interrupt," said Axestone.

"Sorry."

Sam and Tamrin sat side by side at the table. The others gathered round.

"If Tadpole's with us we have to help him to understand," said Eloise.

Axestone growled something.

"Not everyone is a wizard," said Flaxfold. "Not many people. You've just happened to come to a special house on a special day."

"Thank you."

He tried to listen to the meeting, but there were so many things he couldn't follow that he gave up. He looked around at the kitchen. He liked the cooking range and the rushes on the floor, and the scent of the herbs that rose up when you trod on them. He liked the door half-open into the pantry, with hams hanging from hooks in the ceiling and a wheel of cheese with a damp cloth over it to keep it cool and fresh. He liked the way the wood of the furniture gleamed with polish and age. He liked the rows of plates and mugs and dishes on the dresser.

"What do you think you can do to help?"

He liked the way the ripples in the glass of the windows muddled the afternoon sunlight.

"Anything? Nothing? No help at all?"

Tadpole looked at the others and they were all looking at him.

"What do you think you can do to help?" asked Waterburn again.

"What did you say your name was?" asked Tadpole.

Axestone banged his fist on the table.

"I'm sorry," he said. "This isn't going to work. It really isn't. We can't let him stay. He'll get himself killed and he'll get all of us killed."

"Perhaps you're right," said Flaxfold. "We can't risk letting him get hurt. I'm sorry, Tadpole."

"Waterburn?" said Tadpole. "Is that right?"

"Yes. Why?"

"Are lots of people called Waterburn? Is it a common name?"

"Only me," he answered.

Tadpole hopped off his barrel, lifted the lid and, taking

care that no one could see inside it, he found a folded piece of paper. He handed it to Waterburn.

"What's this?"

"Look."

Waterburn opened it up. He stared at Tadpole and back at the paper again.

"What is it?" asked Sam.

"Where did you get this?" asked Waterburn.

"Let me have a look," said Tamrin.

"Who gave you this?" Waterburn said.

It was the map from the Deep World to Flaxfield's house.

"That's got your name on it," said Tadpole. He put his finger on the paper. "There."

"Where did you get this?" repeated Waterburn.

"I've got letters as well," said Tadpole. "Letters from someone called Waterburn that are years and years old. So there must have been someone else called that. A long time ago."

"No," said Waterburn. "Only me."

"No," Tadpole insisted. "They're very old. Very, very old."

"A long time ago," said Waterburn, "when I was about the same age that you are now, I had a friend who was a roffle. That's when all this trouble started."

"What trouble?" asked Tadpole.

Axestone clattered his chair back and strode across the room.

"I give up," he said. "Have you been paying any attention to what we've been saying?"

Tadpole lowered his eyes and shook his head.

"Why should he?" asked December. "Everything here's so new to him."

"If he doesn't understand..." began Axestone.

"He will," she said.

She extended her arm to Tadpole, and he knew that she knew he found her frightening, repellent. "Will you walk to the river with me, and I'll explain some of it, not all?"

Tadpole hesitated and he saw that she knew why.

"Yes, please," he said.

He put his arm out. They linked arms. He didn't mind. No, not just that. He liked linking arms. She smiled.

"Follow the stars," she said.

"What stars?" Tadpole put his head out of the door and looked up at the sky, blue and bright.

Axestone barked out a laugh.

"Cabbage," said December. "Do you think we could have some stars, please?"

Tadpole looked for someone new. Cabbage?

Waterburn moved ahead of them. He bent his arm, flung it out, as a farmer scatters seed on the field, and a shower of tiny stars burst from his opened palm. They fell in a line, a path of stars, glittering in front of them. Waterburn walked ahead, flinging stars as he went. Tadpole grinned until he felt his face would fall in two.

Magic. Real magic. His first ever sight of it.

And it was stars. Just as he had wished for. Later it would

be dark, and he'd see other stars. He couldn't stop himself. He jumped and laughed.

"Come on," said Waterburn.

December and Tadpole followed.

"Tread softly," said Waterburn, "for you tread on my dreams."

Tadpole looked over his shoulder at the house, and a small, grey cat followed them, licking up the stars as it came.

At the riverbank Waterburn flung one last handful of stars into the water, where they flashed silver and gave themselves to the current. The cat stopped at the river's edge, lapped up the last of the stars on the grass, looked at the ones on the water, turned, walked away, sat in the green shade and licked its paws.

"Why did you call him Cabbage?" asked Tadpole.

The three of them sat together looking at the sunlight weaving the ripples on the water.

"We're very old friends," said December. "Since we were children. That was what he was called then."

"Why?"

"And we both know the person who had that map, and the letters," said Waterburn, before December could answer.

"You can't have done. He was my great-great-ever-so-many-greats-grandfather. Hundreds of years ago."

"Wizards live a long time," said Waterburn. "Longer than roffles."

"Too long, I think, sometimes," said December.

"Perhaps you're right."

"You knew Megapoir, my ancestor?"

"We did. But we called him Perry then. He was my very best friend. And I saw him every year until, well, until he wasn't there to be seen any longer."

"He was a great roffle," said December. "A hero Up Top."

"A hero?"

"Not famous," said Waterburn. "But he did great things, and we're all in his debt."

And December explained how, when she and Waterburn were children, they had both been apprenticed to wizards.

"I was Flaxfield's apprentice," said Waterburn.

"Were you? What was he like? I wish I'd met him. Were you his apprentice as well?"

"No," said December. "No. But I met him. I was apprenticed to an old, dying wizard called Slowin. He stole my name, my real name, and he stole my magic."

Tadpole wanted to ask a question. December stopped talking and waited for it.

"Is that...?" he said. He stopped.

"Go on."

"No. I've forgotten what I was going to ask."

December drew the scarf around her face and looked away. Waterburn put his hand on Tadpole's shoulder.

"Don't," he said. "Don't tell lies. It's never good."

Tadpole looked over December's shoulder at Flaxfield's house.

"Look," he said.

He pointed. The sun was past its highest point now and something with huge wings hung over the rooftop, dark against the fading day.

"It's a dragon," he said.

"It's Starback."

"Really a dragon?"

"Really. You'll see a lot of him."

Tadpole looked at Starback over December's head, turned away from him.

"I'm sorry," he said. "Please. I was going to ask if that was why your face is like that. But it seemed rude."

She didn't turn back when she replied.

"But it wouldn't be rude to ask me. It was unkind not to."

Tadpole thought about this.

"Yes," he agreed. "I'm sorry. Please don't look away."

"There was a fire. Not an ordinary fire. Magic fire. It nearly killed me. Cabbage here found me. And he took me to Flaxfold. If it wasn't for them I'd be dead."

Questions bubbled up in Tadpole's mind and appeared on his face. He couldn't stop himself from asking them.

"Couldn't they have used magic to, well, you know—"

"Ask me," she said. "You have to ask."

"Make your face better?" he splurted out.

"Good boy. Never avoid something difficult if it's important."

She drew back her scarf further and sat upright, head, neck

and shoulders bare. The scarring and damage didn't stop. It covered her, disappearing in the yoke of her dress.

"All over," she said. "I am burned like this everywhere. And it's all right. It took so much magic even to save my life. No magic I know of is strong enough to make me any better than I am."

Tadpole looked steadily at her and thought there was something beautiful in the puckered skin, the smooth patches.

"Slowin," he said. "What happened to him? Is he all burned?"

December shrugged herself back into her scarf and flinched as though he had hit her.

"We'd better go in," said Waterburn.

"No," said Tadpole. "No. I want to stay outside. I want to see the stars. It's why I came here."

"It won't be dark for a while yet."

"Still. I'll come in later."

Tadpole had seen Tamrin walking down from the house, and he wanted to see if she would talk to him. ‖

Tamrin walked down to the river

and took off her shoes and socks. It was cool on the bank under the alders. She dangled her feet in the current, watching the patterns on the water.

Tadpole wanted to speak to her, but she seemed so perfectly alone that he hesitated. He put his hand to the trunk of a willow that stood away from the water. Pushing, he slanted a roffle door half-open, stepped in and watched her.

A bee blundered against her shoulder. It bounced off and hovered round in front of her face. She smiled.

"Yellow and black," she said.

She held out her left hand, pursed her lips and blew on the bee. It circled down and settled on her palm. She stroked it with her right forefinger. The striped body was fat, furry, pleasant to touch. She folded her left hand, with the bee inside it, blew into the space between her thumb and finger and opened it again.

She was holding a tiny, perfect yellow and black striped cat, no bigger than an acorn.

It sat down and licked its paws.

She stroked it again. The fur was softer now. The cat turned its face and licked her finger.

Tadpole nearly fell out into the open. He caught himself just in time and kept back.

He followed her gestures, opening and closing his palm, blowing into his empty hand.

It looked so easy, so natural. He had to be able to do it. Now that he was Up Top. There was magic everywhere. There must be enough for one roffle.

A shadow slid along the grass and covered the cat.

"Room for two?"

Tamrin didn't look up.

"Hello, Waterburn."

"Are you waiting for me?" he asked.

"I don't like having a lot of people around," she said.

"Can I sit with you?"

She shuffled along as though space was in short supply. He sat a little apart from her.

"What are you doing?" he asked.

"Yellow and black."

"Of course."

He leaned over and looked at the cat.

"What's next?" he asked.

"I'm a bit stuck. I can't think of many things that fit those colours."

"Shall I?"

"If you like."

He snapped his fingers. The cat grew wings, lengthened, its legs growing slimmer and its neck longer. It spread the wings and flew up into the air in front of Tamrin's face, just where the bee had hovered.

"Tiger-dragon," said Waterburn. "Very rare. Not full size, of course."

Another dragon. Tadpole held his breath. First day Up Top, and first dragons. It had to be right.

The dragon perched on Tamrin's shoulder and nuzzled against her neck. She wriggled.

"How big's a real one?"

"About the same size as a donkey."

It ran down her sleeve and fell off, opened its wings and flew round. Tamrin held out her hand again and it settled there.

"I like it."

"They're good company," said Waterburn. "You should learn from it."

She scowled at him.

"See what I mean?" he said.

She was caught now. The more she scowled the more she put herself in the wrong, but she was too stubborn to smile.

Tadpole was pleased to discover that Tamrin was moody and unpleasant to everyone, not just him. These two were clearly old friends, and she was being really rude to him.

"Find something else," said Waterburn.

Starborn

"I can't think of anything. I only chose yellow and black because it was a bee."

"Have a think about it."

She studied the dragon.

"That roffle at the house," she said.

"Yes?"

"He shouldn't be here."

Tamrin turned her hand over and over and the dragon crossed from palm to back and then to palm again.

"Are we going to die?" asked Tamrin.

"Eventually."

She frowned.

"You know what I mean," she said.

"You mean is this fight going to kill us?"

"Yes."

Waterburn lay back and looked up at the sky.

"I don't see why it shouldn't kill us," he said. "Whole villages are being killed. Lonely travellers. Families on farms. There was even a group of merchants with twenty donkeys, travelling to the city to trade. Every single one of them was slaughtered by the kravvins, men, boys and donkeys. The kravvins fell on the bodies, gorged themselves and left all the merchandise lying by the side of the road."

Tamrin folded her fingers over the dragon, shook her fist, and when she opened it she was holding a pansy, with a black face against a bright-yellow rim.

"Very good," said Waterburn.

"I don't want to die," she said. "Not yet."

"Perhaps you won't."

He stood up.

"I'm going inside," he said. "Talk to the others. It's been a long time."

Tamrin blew on the pansy. Its petals fluttered and when she stopped blowing they curled over and formed themselves into a bee. It buzzed into the air, circled her head once and flew off across the river.

"I'm not going to let them kill me," she said. She stood up and faced Waterburn. "I'm going to kill them."

He put his arm round her shoulder and walked her up to Flaxfield's house.

"I'll do the same," he said. ||

The river ran softly

past the tree and Tadpole's hiding place. The roffle stayed half-in half-out. He had seen magic. He had seen dragons. He had met wizards. It was enough for one day, for one visit, for a first experience.

And yet, he hadn't seen the stars.

But neither had he seen a kravvin.

He could stay a little longer, wait till night, see the sky alive with stars.

Or he could go back now. Back to the Deep World. To home and safety.

To a telling-off, of course. Unless they hadn't missed him. But there was no chance of that. Even less chance that he could go back and hold his tongue and not tell the others what he had seen.

If he stayed, just one night, even just an hour into the night, he would have seen everything.

Except a kravvin.

What if he stayed, saw a kravvin, and didn't live to see the stars?

Half-in, half-out. He hesitated.

A black beetle ran up the tree trunk, close to Tadpole's face. He paused in his thoughts to look at it.

He liked beetles. Glossy, hard, like jewels. Who would think that under those curved cases were delicate wings? And who would think those wings strong enough to carry that hard body?

Tadpole smiled and let the beetle drop on to his shoulder and crawl down his sleeve. He held out his arm for the beetle to use as a platform for flight.

A hand smacked down, hard, on his arm and grabbed him, pulling him out of the roffle door.

The beetle span off and splashed into the river.

Tadpole fell, only to be hauled to his feet. The hand hurt like fire. He kicked out and his legs flew up, turning him upside down. He hung suspended in mid-air.

Twisting his head to one side, he saw Sam's face, glaring at him.

"Let me go," Tadpole shouted.

Sam let go. The pain eased. Tadpole braced himself for the fall, only to find that he remained in the air. He struggled to right himself, like a swimmer turning to find the surface. There was nothing for his hands to push against and they flailed uselessly.

"Put me down."

Sam put his face close to Tadpole's. "You shouldn't be here. Go home."

"Put me down."

The leather thong that Delver had given him fell loose and dangled beneath his downturned head.

"What's this?" Sam closed his hand round it.

"It's a dragon's tooth."

"What?" Sam was laughing.

"It's a dragon's tooth."

Sam let the tooth fall, and it hung, swinging, out of Tadpole's sight.

"Dragons don't lose their teeth. Don't you know anything?"

Tadpole's anger and fright gave way to shame. Delver's gifts, his treasures, were just junk after all.

"That's some old memmont's tooth. I'll show you dragons' teeth."

Sam stepped back and raised his arms.

Tadpole began to swing in the force of a rushing wind. He caught a glimpse of blue and green as a wing fanned his face.

He squirmed, trying to get out of the way.

The wing clipped his cheek. The rush of air ceased and Tadpole found himself looking into the gaping mouth of a dragon. He could smell the smoke, feel the hot breath, see the red tongue, forked and flickering.

"See the teeth?" said Sam.

Sharp, white and ranged in perfect order. The teeth were nothing like the yellow stump tied round Tadpole's neck.

Shame fought fear and Tadpole relaxed, hanging, up-turned and defeated.

The dragon backed away, revealing Tamrin, walking towards them.

"What are you doing?"

She clapped her hands. Tadpole, buoyed up by warm, supportive air, turned upright and floated to the ground.

The dragon hovered, just above the height of a roffle's head.

"It's so beautiful," said Tadpole.

Tamrin and Sam stood side by side. When they spoke Tadpole found it hard to tell which was which.

"You shouldn't tease him."

"He asked for it. He shouldn't be here."

"He didn't know."

"They've been told. All the roffles have. They know how dangerous it is."

"Do you think Ash will know he's here?"

"We should send him back now. Push him through the roffle door."

"There was a beetle. On his hand."

"I saw it."

Tadpole wished he could work out which was speaking. The girl hadn't seen the beetle. She wasn't there.

"What about the memmont?"

"That'll find its way back. They always do."

"He'll only come back if we push him out."

"How do you know that?"

"Look at him. He's one of those meddling roffles."

"Perhaps it was just a beetle. You know. A beetle."

Tadpole interrupted.

"I'm here, you know. I can hear what you're saying."

They ignored him. As he looked at them, the dragon moved down and back, spreading its wings wide. It hovered over them so that they seemed part of it, folded under its wings. For a moment, Tadpole had the impression that the boy and girl were not speaking at all, but that the words came from the dragon.

"He'll have to go back."

All at once, Tadpole knew what he had to do. It wasn't about magic or stars any longer. It was about doing something.

"You can both shut up," he said.

"He'll get in the way."

"We'll always be having to rescue him from something."

"He'll put us all in danger."

"That's enough," said Tadpole. "I'm staying. And anyway, who are you? Which of you is speaking?"

The dragon rose up, flapped its wings, tilted and flew off, coming to rest on the roof of the house.

Tamrin and Sam looked at each other. They both shrugged. Both turned away and walked towards the house, leaving Tadpole alone, as though he didn't matter. ||

The memmont strolled

along the waterside, pretending to gather leaves and twigs. Tadpole knew it was just coming to make sure he was still there. He reached down and let the memmont rub its back along the palm of his hand.

"It's not the way I thought it would be," he said.

The memmont rubbed against his legs.

"For one thing, all the books say the Up Top people like roffles and make them welcome." He came right out from under the shade of the tree and looked up at the sky, the sun low now and casting long shadows. "Mind you," he added, "I suppose it's different when you're dealing with wizards."

He hoisted his roffle pack on to his back and made towards the house.

"All that fuss about a beetle," he said.

The memmont trotted after him. A breeze ruffled its fur and Tadpole had to turn his head to one side to avoid a swirl of dust. They were at the corner of the house now. He looked up.

"Look," he said. "Black clouds. I'd forgotten about them."
He stopped and stared. "It might rain. Think of that. Rain."

"That's an old memmont," said Flaxfold, making Tadpole
jump. "Sorry. I didn't mean to startle you."

The memmont left Tadpole's side and rubbed against
Flaxfold. She scratched its ears. "Rain is nothing new to this
one," she said.

"No. But it is to me. Is it really going to rain?"

"Heavily. Come on in. We need to talk."

There was none of the companionable ease in the room
now. No food. No chatter. Everyone was waiting for Flaxfold.

"Sit down," said Sam. "Tell us about the beetle."

Tadpole settled himself on to his pack.

"Are wizards better or worse than other people Up Top?"
he asked.

"None of your roffle riddles here," said Axestone. "Answer
the question."

"It's not a riddle. It's a proper question," said Tadpole.
"Is a wizard worth a whisker or does a wizard want a wallop?
That's a roffle riddle."

It was the sort of cheek that would have got him into trouble at home, and he tensed himself for an angry outburst,
perhaps even a bit of painful magic. Axestone looked ready to
give him some when Eloise laughed.

"Good for you," she said. "Stand up to him."

Tadpole saw the others smile as well, even Tamrin.

"Because," he said, "all the guides about Up Top say how

welcoming everyone is. Do you know that?"

"We gave you a meal," said Axestone. "A nice trout."

"Better a dish of cabbage with friends than a fat trout without a welcome," said Tadpole. "And that's not a riddle, either."

Flaxfold looked at the others. Sam had the grace to look embarrassed. Tamrin glared. Axestone shrugged his big shoulders. Waterburn put his hand to his mouth and coughed gently.

"I think Tadpole's right," he said. "And I apologize."

"No," said Tadpole. "Not you. You've been kind to me."

Flaxfold touched the roffle's arm.

"Patience," she said. "Up Top, it's the ones who don't need to apologize who are first to do so."

"That's stupid," said Tadpole.

"It is. But it's the way things are. And sometimes we just have to accept that."

"I don't want anyone to apologize. I just want them to be kind to me. That's all."

"And we shall," she said. "All of us. In our different ways. Won't we?"

Some of them nodded. Eloise, most of all, smiled. No one disagreed.

"What we'd like, please," said Flaxfold, "is for you to tell us exactly what happened with the beetle."

"I don't understand. Why? What's special about a beetle?"

Sam joined in. "There's such a lot you don't know. You'll just have to pick most of it up as you go along. But take it from me, beetles are a bad sign. All right?"

Tadpole thought about this.

"All right," he agreed. "Tell me the three most important things I have to know." Sam started to speak, and Tadpole interrupted him. "I know about the kravvins," he said. "Three other things."

Axestone stood up and stamped his feet. Tadpole thought he was angry at first, then he saw he was laughing.

"What are you laughing at?"

"Not at you, young roffle. Not at you."

Tadpole looked at Flaxfold for help.

"Stop it, now," she said.

Axestone sat down. "I'm sorry," he said. "I'd forgotten how nice it is to have a roffle around. Especially a clever young one."

"Carry on, Sam," said Flaxfold.

"First, then," said Sam, "is the enemy. Ash. Ash wants to kill us. And she's getting stronger. So far, we've been defending ourselves. That's not working any more. We have to attack."

Tadpole nodded. His father had told him Ash was the cause.

"Second," said Sam, "there's the mirror. And third is the beetles. The mirror is—"

"Just a minute," said Tadpole.

Sam scowled at him. "Don't interrupt. The mirror—"

"No. You can't decide the three most important things. I have a say, too. And I want to know about you and her."

He pointed at Tamrin, who scowled back at him.

"No," said Sam.

"Yes."

It was Flaxfold, as usual, who intervened to calm things down.

"Why are you asking?" she said.

Tadpole was shaking. He couldn't decide whether it was fear, or anger.

"At the river," he said, "they were talking to me. And I couldn't tell which was which. The voices came from both of them at the same time. And it wasn't like proper talking. It was like..." He hesitated, looking for the right way to say it, looking for a way to understand it. "It was more like thinking. More like the things I say to myself when I'm trying to work something out. It was—"

Flaxfold held up her hand for him to stop.

"It was like—" he said.

"Very good," said Eloise. "I've watched them. It's just like that."

"It's nothing to do with him," said Tamrin.

Tadpole saw that she was blushing. He felt ashamed. He still wanted to know, but he felt he had done something wrong, gone where he shouldn't go.

There was a long silence. Tamrin held his gaze for a while, then she looked away. Sam watched her.

Tadpole looked from Sam to Tamrin and back again. Tamrin's eyes were fixed on some object in the corner of the room. She was shutting out everyone.

"I'm sorry," said Tadpole. "I wish I hadn't asked. Please, forget it. Tell me about the mirror instead."

Sam laughed. Eloise looked as though she might cry. Flaxfold put her hand on Sam's shoulder. Waterburn looked at Tamrin. Axestone folded his arms and waited.

"I wish people would stop laughing," said Tadpole. "Is that what you do Up Top? Is everything a joke?"

Eloise was the first to answer.

"We're all very old friends, here," she said. "We're comfortable together. And now, you're here. And you're a stranger. I want to make you welcome. But you unsettle us. You make us shy. We're a little embarrassed. And so we laugh."

Tadpole smiled.

"We do that, too," he said. "Sorry."

"And we've embarrassed you, as well," she said. "So I'm sorry, too."

No one else joined in, and the silence folded round them again.

Tamrin's voice was very small when she finally broke the silence.

"Tell him about the mirror," she said.

She kept her eyes averted.

Sam didn't answer.

"The mirror made the magic," said Tadpole. "Is that what you mean?"

"Well," said Sam, "if you know that…"

"That's all I know. Smokesmith. The first mirror. The

first magic. That's all. Please, tell me the whole story."

Flaxfold spoke softly. "He can't do that," she said. "I'll tell you one thing. See if Sam tells you another. The mirror that made the magic is in this house."

Tadpole felt as though he had been lifted from the floor and was floating.

Sam said nothing. It was Tamrin who spoke.

"The mirror made me," she said. "And Sam. The mirror made both of us. Except there's not both of us. There's only one of us. Do you understand now?"

Tadpole nodded. He didn't understand at all. He had had enough now. It was all so different. Different from the Deep World. Different from how he had imagined Up Top.

"I'm going home now," he said.

"You can't," said Sam.

Tadpole stood up and hoisted his roffle pack on to his back.

"You can't stop me," he said.

"I can," said Sam. "If I want to. I really can. But you're not going back. You know things you can't take home with you. Not yet."

Tamrin moved to stand next to him.

"You came to fight Ash," she said. "You'll have to stay now."

Then both voices merged.

"There's always a roffle."

"And this time, you're the roffle."

"You don't have a choice."

Tadpole stepped back, raising his hands.

"I do have a choice. And I'm going home."

His sleeve fell back from his wrist and a beetle dropped to the floor.

There was a quick movement of chairs and feet. They all stood and prepared themselves.

"What?" said Tadpole. He let his hand fall. Another beetle dropped from the other sleeve. And another. Seven. Eleven. Seventeen. They were pouring from him.

"It's Ash," said Sam. "She's attacking."

Tadpole was covered with beetles. They washed over him and streamed down to the floor.

"They're killing Tadpole," said Tamrin. ||

Tadpole discovered what the power of magic

could feel like.

The crawling beetles made him feel sick. He fell, squashing the ones beneath him. They burst, covering him with a wet stink.

He rolled away from them, only to squash more. They bit and scratched and he had the sensation that they were burrowing into him, under the skin.

He opened his mouth to scream and they poured in. He spat, writhed and choked. They were in his hair, his clothes, even in his shoes.

Something slapped his face.

"Open your eyes!"

Another slap. Harder.

"Open them!"

Terrified that beetles would swarm in and burrow into his eyes, Tadpole squinted. Tamrin was standing over him. She slapped him again.

"Look at me!"

He opened them wider. She slapped him again, harder than ever.

"Keep your eyes open!"

Tadpole hated her. He kicked out. His foot smashed into her ankle and she staggered.

"Don't be stupid. Look at me. Do it."

He looked and she slapped him again.

There were no beetles on his face now. None in his hair.

"Give me your hands."

She grabbed them, lifted him to his feet and he kept rising, floating above the ground again. She shook him. A flash of pain tore right through his body. The beetles dropped to the floor and exploded. Tamrin let go of him.

"Are you all right?" she asked.

He coughed. A beetle fell out of his mouth and burst in mid-air.

"You need to get out," she said. "Follow me."

It was a pointless order. His feet were still above the floor, still above the beetles. He was dragged through the air after her by her magic, not by any action of his own. He stared at the room.

He had expected magic to be light, and joy and — well — magic.

This was not.

The beetles were the advance guard.

They had shocked Sam and the others, taking them by

surprise. Eloise draped her cloak over them in sweeping movements, and they shrivelled and died under its touch. Axestone was smashing at them with his staff, killing them, but taking longer about it. Waterburn had made an invisible barrier between himself and the beetles. They crawled over it and around it, but they couldn't break through. The old wizard was watching them, thinking, planning. Sam used fire. Flames streamed from him. From the palms of his hands, his eyes, his mouth. The beetles sizzled and popped under its heat.

Flaxfold stood alone, in the centre of the room. She allowed the beetles to crawl over her. She made no resistance, put up no fight. Tadpole thought she should be covered, should disappear under a mask of black, scurrying legs and shiny bodies. It didn't happen. They climbed and fell, slipping from her as though she was made of polished marble. She was ignoring them, her eyes fixed instead on the door. Tadpole turned to see what it was she was staring at.

"Oh, no," he said.

Tamrin stopped dragging him and looked back.

"What?"

"Kravvins?" asked Tadpole.

Black, blank faces stared in at the windows. They peered over the shoulders of a figure who stood in the doorway. They pressed against each other, ready. The second wave.

"Worse than kravvins," said Tamrin.

"What's worse than kravvins?" asked Tadpole.

Tamrin was looking at the doorway, her eyes following Flaxfold's stare.

"Smedge," whispered Tamrin, in a voice so small that Tadpole only just managed to hear her. "That's what's worse."

But the figure in the doorway heard. He turned his head, saw Tamrin, and smiled.

Tadpole had never been so terrified. He looked for a roffle door. Of course, there could be none in Flaxfield's house. He wanted to fold in on himself until he wasn't anything at all. He would rather not be than have to look on that smile.

The figure stepped forward, into the room.

The kravvins froze. Time seemed to stop. Tadpole held his breath. The beetles started up again, scattering in all directions. They poured out of the doors and windows.

"Smedge," said Flaxfold.

He looked at her.

"You haven't changed," he said.

Tadpole tried to work out in his mind what it had been about the smile that had so terrified him. What it was about the figure that even now caused him to want to be anywhere else.

He was a boy. Just a boy. About Tadpole's age. Slim, and neat, in school clothes that looked as though he had just put them on. No creases or stains. No scuffs or marks.

"You have," said Flaxfold. "Since the day you were made here, from slime and from wild magic."

"The filth and stinking waste of wild magic," said December.

Tadpole had forgotten her. She had been out of sight when

the battle with the beetles was being waged.

She stepped into the centre of the room, opposite Smedge, but not close to him.

"I remember you at the beginning," she said.

Smedge stared back at her.

"Do you remember?" she asked.

She slipped her shawl back, leaving her face and neck and shoulders completely visible, the scars and burns.

"Do you?" she said.

She put her hand in front of her, palm towards Smedge.

Rain was falling hard now, battering the windows. It ran down the faces of the kravvins waiting outside, glistening and slick.

"Remember?" she said, her palm towards him.

Smedge became as smoke. He remained the same at first, though the edges of him rippled and Tadpole could see through him.

"Remember," said December, and it wasn't a question, it was a command.

The rain beat harder. The room was dark, whether from clouds or oncoming night Tadpole didn't have the experience to know.

Smedge lost shape. He was melting. The clothes dripped off him. His face twisted and changed. Tadpole stared as the boy, no longer a boy, became, by turns, the ugly reflection of a dog, a ferret, a toad, a slug, until he was all shapes and none, a green mess of slime that stank and oozed.

December still held her palm out. Tadpole saw that she was shaking with the effort. A blue vein rose, pulsing, in her neck. Her feet were planted firm to keep her balance. Smedge began to bubble and smoke. She was destroying him.

"Kill!"

"Bite!"

"Eat!"

The kravvins began to chant.

"Kill!"

"Rip!"

"Eat!"

They beat their feet on the ground. The house trembled.

"Kill!"

In unison they bashed their shiny bodies against the walls.

"Eat!"

"Stab!"

The rain hammered. A flash of lightning and an immediate crash of thunder ripped the sky. The kravvins surged in, chanting.

Sam swept his staff round and scythed through them.

Axestone leaped on the nearest and tore at him with his bare hands. Kravvins smothered him, and one punched a sharp arm straight into the wizard's chest. Axestone grabbed the creature by the throat and snapped off its head before he fell, and the kravvins surged over his body. In death, he repelled them. Something covered him, with a shimmering haze. The kravvins stumbled back and turned their attention elsewhere.

They barged into December. She lost her balance, put her arms out to recover it. As soon as her palm was deflected from Smedge the pool of ooze stopped bubbling. December tried to fix him again with her spell. Kravvins jostled and attacked her. She needed all her attention to defend herself.

Tamrin pulled Tadpole up the stairs again.

"You have to get out," she said.

The kravvins were winning. Eloise had fallen. A kravvin crouched over her corpse, and plunged a hand forward to rip into her. The haze engulfed him and he lost his arm. Shrieking, he ran back, leaving Eloise in a flickering glow, which faded as softly as it had arrived.

She and Axestone lay alone, islands of silence in the tumult of the attack.

Sam was cornered. Waterburn seemed to be trying to escape through a window. December had given up the struggle to kill Smedge and was battling to stay alive. Flaxfold occupied the centre of the room. Smedge was reforming. Rising from the slime.

Flaxfold brushed aside the attacks of the kravvins. She slapped them with the flat of her hand and they broke like clay models filled with pus. She waded through them to deal with Smedge.

"In here," said Tamrin.

She threw open a door on the top landing. Tadpole hung back, hating what he was seeing and unable to stop looking.

Flaxfold was on top of Smedge now. She leaned over the

gathering shape. Kravvins smashed at her. They jabbed their sharp arms. They shouldered her, trying to push her away from him. Their arms snapped. She stood firm. She stooped to bind Smedge with a spell. And, as she opened her mouth to speak the words, he shifted shape into a spear and plunged into her face.

Flaxfold staggered back, scattering the kravvins. Smedge pushed through, into her mouth, until he was invisible. She clutched her throat, her face. She made a savage noise of gulping and coughing, and fell, cracking her head on the floor.

Tamrin shrieked, "No!" and gripped Tadpole's wrist so tight that he cried out in pain.

Sam tried to run to Flaxfold. The kravvins swarmed at him, blocking his path.

Flaxfold twitched. Lay still. Green smoke poured out from her eyes, her ears, her nose, her mouth. It streamed up, hung over her head and regained substance.

"Get in there," said Tamrin. She hurled him into the room. "And get away. Escape. And remember, it's up to you now. You've got to fight this for us. You need to stay alive."

The last thing Tadpole saw, as Tamrin slammed the door on him, was the shape of Smedge reappearing beside the fallen Flaxfold. No longer a boy in uniform, he was armed and armoured, in black leggings and jerkin, boots and a mail tunic.

And Tamrin was hurtling towards him. ‖

The room was as silent

as sunlight.

Tadpole knew that the battle was still boiling outside. Here, behind the closed door, there was no trace of it.

There was a table, and chairs, and he stumbled across, sat down and put his head on his arms.

He was shivering. His dinner was high in his throat. His roffle pack bumped against the tabletop. He slipped it from his back and it fell to the floor, rolling to a halt by the slammed door.

When he was able to lift his head and look around, he thought first of the memmont. In the confusion and fear he had lost it.

He decided that whatever happened, however much danger the creature was in, and however much Tadpole ought to look after it, he just couldn't open that door.

"I'm sorry," he said. "I hope you're all right."

Memmonts were sensible, timid creatures, and Tadpole felt it was likely that it had slipped back down a roffle hole.

Unless a kravvin had reached it first.

No.

Don't think that.

Look at the room.

It was lit by good candles, as though prepared for some-one. The scent of the beeswax was pleasant and went some way to comforting him. The glow of the flame was reflected in the window. It was full dark already outside. Tadpole could see nothing of the garden, or the river, or the sky. Only the sound of the branch of an ash tree scratching and tapping the window told him that there was anything beyond the room itself.

As for the room, it was small enough to be cosy, large enough to be comfortable. With books everywhere. On all the walls, in piles on the floor and the table.

A small fire burned in the grate, giving more light, and a cheerful heat.

Tadpole stood and went to the fireplace. He touched his fingers against the blue and white pottery propped up against the wall. It felt old, as though it could remember other days, other people in this room.

He crossed to the window and looked out. The rain lashed down. The tree swayed in the wind. The sky was black with cloud.

"No stars," he said. "Still no stars."

He leaned forward to look down, fearful of seeing an army of kravvins carrying off the remains of his new friends. He smiled, surprised to think of them as friends, even though their welcome had not been generous.

He hitched his pack on to his back, stood before the door. He put his ear to it.

Silence.

He put his hand to the handle.

Drew back again.

Listened.

Put his hand back.

He turned the handle.

Slowly.

The door opened a little. Still no noise. He stepped back and opened it wider.

And he looked at a different landing, a different staircase, a different house. Tadpole stepped out of the room, keeping the door open and his hand on the handle, ready to run back in if danger appeared.

He heard voices, below. Friendly, cheerful voices. And laughter. And footsteps coming upstairs.

He darted back into the study and closed the door.

The room was the same. The sky was still dark. The ash tree tapped the window.

He turned the handle again and stepped out.

A field of kravvin heads turned. A hundred identical, blank kravvin faces stared up at him. And one face, human again now, and smiling. Smedge. Tadpole looked for the others. He caught a glimpse of Sam and Waterburn, still fighting for life.

Smedge smiled at him.

Tadpole froze under Smedge's look.

"Come here," said Smedge.

His voice was soft, inviting.

"Come and see us."

Tadpole came further out.

"No," shouted Sam. "Get back in."

He raised his staff over his head and howled. The kravvins fell back. Smedge whirled round and screamed a spell.

The window burst inwards, scattering glass over the kravvins, shining shards filling the air.

And the dragon flew in, head back, throat open, screaming with one voice with Sam.

Tadpole slammed the door shut and ran to the other side of the room, banging his leg on a chair.

He waited there, braced for a fight, sure that the kravvins would break in and flood over him.

Silence again.

He crossed to the door and put out his hand. This time, he noticed that the door had two handles, one on the right, one on the left.

He tried to remember which he had turned the first time.

He took the left one and moved it round slowly.

The door opened.

He listened.

Silence.

He opened it wider.

It was the other landing, the other staircase.

Tadpole remembered Tamrin's orders, to escape, to get away.

He closed the door behind him, fearing the decision. He tried the door. As he had expected, it was locked. No going back.

Well, here he was. There would be roffle holes outside. If he ever got outside again.

Following the stairs down, he found himself in a wide corridor with rooms leading off on either side. He went into the room the voices were coming from. As soon as he entered, the talking and the laughing stopped.

Faces stared at him. Four men at one table. Three leaning against a counter. A woman alone. Three more men at a corner table. It was an inn.

"Roffles, is it?" said a man at the counter. "Nothing good ever came of roffles."

"Least it's not a kravvin."

"I don't know which I like least, roffles or kravvins."

"Then you've never met a kravvin."

There was laughter again.

"No one ever met a kravvin and lived to tell. Not close up."

"Anyway, I don't want roffles here."

"They're bad luck."

"That's why they stay away these days."

"Here, you. What are you doing Up Top?"

Tadpole turned and made to leave the room. The man at the table nearest the door seized his arm.

"No you don't," he said. "What's going on? Are you lot spying for the kravvins?"

"Have you done a deal?"

"Hold him there."

"Come on, what are you up to?"

The woman stood up. She was taller than Tadpole had first thought, slim and determined. She put her hand on the man's shoulder and squeezed.

"Ow. What are you doing?"

"We're leaving, now," she said. "Let him go."

His grip tightened on Tadpole's arm. Her grip tightened. Tadpole saw the strength of her fingers. The man yelped. He released Tadpole.

"Come on," she said. "Time we were on our way."

She steered Tadpole back into the corridor and through the front door.

"Don't go bringing roffle spies back here," someone shouted after them.

She smiled at Tadpole.

"People are afraid," she said. "They're not bad. Don't worry."

The rain was coming down hard. Tadpole stood with his face upturned and let it fall on him.

"What are you doing?" she asked.

"Rain. My first rain." He wiped his face with his hands. "It's cool, and soft."

"Get used to it," she said. "What's your name?"

"What's a name for a bad apple in a barn full of bees?" asked Tadpole.

"You can forget that," she said. "Roffle talk's over. So are a lot of things. I'm Dorwin. Sometimes 'Winny' for short. What's your name?"

"Tadpole."

"Good name for someone who likes to stand in the rain. Come on, Tadpole. We've got a long walk."

She took the handles of a cart and walked off. He stayed where he was.

"It's come with me, go back in there, or set off on your own," she called over her shoulder. "But I've been waiting for you."

Roffles love a puzzle, and Tadpole couldn't resist finding out why she'd been waiting for him. He trotted off after her.

"How did you know I was coming if you didn't know my name? And where are the stars?"

"Covered with cloud. The rain's set in. You won't see any tonight."

Dorwin pushed the handcart along with no show of effort. She was strong, used to work.

"How did you know I was coming?"

"I didn't know it was a roffle."

"What?"

"A roffle. I wasn't expecting a roffle."

Tadpole found that rain made walking harder. The road was muddy. He slipped and squelched. The wheels of the cart skidded and dragged. Dorwin pushed on, easy strides and confident that she wouldn't fall.

"Can we slow down, please?"

"Sorry. Is that better?"

Tadpole settled into an easier pace. He waited for Dorwin to tell him why she had been waiting. She didn't speak.

His feet were getting heavy. The mud clung to them. His legs ached.

She still said nothing, just pushed the handcart relentlessly on.

"I've never been in the dark before," he said.

"What's that?"

Tadpole spoke louder. "I've never been in the dark before."

"How do you like it?"

Tadpole thought about this.

"I'm not sure."

Dorwin slowed down.

"Do you mean you've never been Up Top before?"

Tadpole didn't answer.

She stopped walking. Lowering the handles of the cart, she turned to see him.

"Look at you," she said. "You're exhausted."

Tadpole looked down. He was muddy up to his knees. His clothes were crumpled and unkempt. His roffle pack was slipping from one shoulder and looked as though it would fall off at any moment.

"Have you?" she asked. "Have you been Up Top before?"

He shook his head.

She knelt so that her face was level with his.

"How old are you?"

"Thirteen."

She put her arm around him.

"You were in Flaxfield's house," she said.

"Yes."

"That's why I was waiting," she said. "For someone to come from there. I wasn't expecting you, though."

He nodded. "The girl sent me. Tamrin. She told me to come here."

"Was there trouble?"

"Yes."

"Was it awful?"

He nodded, not able to speak without trembling at the memory.

"Come on," said Dorwin. "I'm sorry I was unkind."

He shook his head.

"What do you want to do?" she asked.

"I want to go home. Back to the Deep World."

Dorwin paused.

"All right," she said. "We can do that." She looked around. "Here you are." She walked to an elm near by and indicated a roffle door.

Tadpole was puzzled. "You can see that?" he asked.

Dorwin nodded.

"Are you a wizard?"

"No," she said. "But I can see them anyway. Most people can't."

Tadpole hesitated. "I want to go home," he said. "I want to see the stars. I want to help my friends, the ones I met at Flaxfield's. I want to be far away from the kravvins. I want to do what Tamrin said. I don't want to let her down."

"You can't do both," said Dorwin.

Tadpole sat on the muddy road, his pack still on his back. He shrugged when it bumped against the ground. "I forgot I had this," he said. "I should go back. I can't help."

"All you have to do is walk through this door. You'll be safe then."

"How long for? How long before the kravvins come to the Deep World?"

"Perhaps soon. Perhaps never. There's a lot to do here first."

Tadpole leaned against the cart.

"Are you going to fight?" he asked.

"It's where I live. I have to fight."

He hauled himself up, using the handles of the cart.

"I'll stay," he said. "Long enough to see the stars, anyway."

Dorwin came and put her hand on his shoulder. "Come on," she said. "You can ride a little way." She pulled a covering from the cart and made a space for him.

"I'll walk."

"I'll get there sooner if you let me push. You're slowing me down."

He allowed her to bundle him in. He curled up, head

resting on his barrel, and fell asleep. The cart rocked and bumped. He dreamed he was flying, on clouds in a stormy sky. The motion soothed him. Stillness, when it came, jerked him awake.

"Are we there?"

"Not yet. We'll rest here for the night."

He pushed back the cover and looked up at three faces: Dorwin, a man and a woman.

"He's only a boy," said the woman. She bent down and put her arms around him. "And he's cold, and wet."

Tadpole struggled and freed himself. He clambered out of the cart. It was a house, alone, with wide windows and an old oak door. The rain had eased, but Dorwin stood, drenched and tense, controlling her shivering.

"I should have walked," he said. "I'm sorry."

"We'll sort you both out," said the woman. "I'm Mrs Martin, and this is Mr Martin. Come on in."

Before Tadpole knew what had happened he was sitting, wrapped in a huge towel, in front of the fire, with a bowl of stew, a chunk of fresh bread.

Mrs Martin seemed to think that Tadpole's bowl had something wrong with it, because every time he managed to get it half-empty she filled it up again. After three refills he put his hand over it.

"No more," he said. "Thank you."

"Don't you like it?"

"It's lovely. Really. Thank you. But I'm getting full."

"Call yourself a roffle," said Martin. "I've seen roffles eat us out of bacon."

"Ah," said Tadpole. "That's different. That's breakfast."

He scraped his bread round the bowl to soak up the last of the gravy and noticed a nose and eyes emerging from round the side of a dresser.

He sprang to his feet.

"It's a memmont."

The creature came towards him, and lowered its head for him to stroke. Tadpole looked overjoyed, then disappointed.

"It's not the one I came with," he said.

"No," Mrs Martin said. "He lives with us."

Tadpole shook his head. "There are no memmonts Up Top any more. Not since the problems."

Martin clicked his fingers at the memmont. It looked at him, turned away and settled at Tadpole's feet. Martin laughed. "Hasn't seen a roffle for a long time," he said. "Anyway, there aren't many memmonts Up Top, that's true. But we always have one."

"You're a weaver?" said Tadpole.

"I am. And proud of it."

Tadpole had lots of questions and would have asked some of them if he hadn't fallen asleep asking the second one and if they hadn't taken him up to bed.

In the morning he tried to eat them out of bacon, but Mrs Martin had more than enough for them all. His clothes had been washed and dried overnight. He still hadn't asked his questions by the time that Dorwin told him to get his barrel and get ready to go.

"This is good," he said to Mrs Martin. "Thank you."

She hugged him.

"Always welcome, Tadpole. Any time."

The memmont nuzzled against him.

"Up Top isn't so bad," he said. "Here, anyway. I like it."

"Thank you."

The morning was clear and fresh.

"If it was dark we could see the stars," said Tadpole.

"And if I was Tuesday I'd be a barber," said Martin, who had appeared in the doorway.

"And if you had a hat for a horse and hare for a hop you'd be a roffle," said Tadpole.

They laughed.

"Goodbye," said Martin. "Remember, roffles are always welcome here. Especially you."

He held out his arm and offered Tadpole the length of cloth that was draped over it.

"Take it," he said.

"What are you doing?" asked Dorwin.

"None of your business," said Martin. "Go on, Tadpole. Take it. It's yours."

Tadpole took the dark-green cloth and held it out. "It's a cloak."

"It is. All one piece. I sat up all night weaving it."

"You can't do that," said Dorwin.

Martin didn't look at her. He smiled at Tadpole. "Look, here." He took the selvedge and showed Tadpole. There was a small memmont woven right into the fabric. "To remind you of the Deep World."

Dorwin started to speak again, and Mrs Martin interrupted. "We won't keep you here, though we hate to see you go."

Before Tadpole could stop her she had given him a kiss.

"It'll keep the rain off," said her husband.

"I'll help with the cart," said Tadpole.

Dorwin kissed Mrs Martin, seized the handles and pushed off. "We'll be quicker if I do it," she said.

Tadpole waved goodbye and trotted to keep up. His new cloak felt light and cool, and even hung properly over his roffle pack.

"How far is it?" he asked.

"We'll be there by midday, if we don't meet any kravvins or takkabakks."

"What's a takkabakk?"

"As bad as a kravvin. Though they stay nearer to home. They don't wander far."

"Is there a plan?" he asked. "And how did Flaxfield's house turn into the inn? And how do you know about that? And can someone go back from the inn to Flaxfield's? And what about the others? Are they all right? And who is Smedge?"

Tadpole didn't ask all of these questions at once. He was finding it hard to keep up with Dorwin, so his breath came in short bursts. The road was dry now, and easy going. The cart travelled well over the ground.

"Are you going home or staying?" asked Dorwin.

"I'm going to stay," said Tadpole.

"How did you make up your mind?"

Tadpole thought about this. Sleep restored his courage. And the good stew. And the breakfast. He felt braver now the rain had stopped, though he wanted to stand in the rain again. As long as he didn't have to travel in it. And Tamrin. She was only a girl, only his age. And, even though she was some sort of magic thing with Sam, Tadpole thought that if she could fight kravvins, he could.

They turned a corner, came out of a line of trees and Tadpole saw a house, outbuildings and a column of slender smoke.

He stopped.

"It's all right," she said. "We're there."

Tadpole hesitated.

"It looks like a forge," he said. "Like a blacksmith's."

"Of course it is. What did you expect? Come on."

Dorwin agreed to let Tadpole go up to his room as soon as they arrived.

"My father will want to meet you," she said.

"I need to rest," said Tadpole. "My head hurts."

She showed him a small room upstairs. It was simple, plain, comfortable. The bed was soft. The window looked out over fields and a stream. The chair was not too high for a roffle to sit in without discomfort. There were flowers in an earthenware jug and a small table with a marble top. It was all as neat and clean as a roffle room. Tadpole sat in the chair and rummaged in his roffle pack. He brought out the guide to Up Top. There was a list of topics. He had not read them all, but he knew which one he wanted now.

Up Top ~ A Guide for Roffles

BLACKSMITHS
Blacksmiths came before magic.

Before magic, the most wonderful thing Up Top was the fire in a smith's shop. Fire melts metal. Fire wraps hard iron round in its arms and gentles it to a willing, moving thing. Fire fills iron with the power of change. And change is magic. And magic is change. In the arms of fire a lump of iron can become a plough, a hook, a brooch, a knife.

The very first fire, in the very first forge, came from the Deep World. After that, the lessons learned, other fires were lit in other forges. But only one forge kept the roffle fire. It never goes out, day or night, and it's always attended by a roffle.

By mistake and by luck, by accident and by experiment, the smith learned that charcoal, added to the iron, heated and folded, heated and folded, would make stronger, sharper, brighter metal.

And so, the first reflections appeared. In the bowls of spoons. In the blades of knives. On helmets and shields. Rounded, broken, imperfect reflections. Until one smith beat the iron flat, polished it and perfected it, first on a shield, and then, better, flatter, on a mirror, made for a king.

It was from a smith's forge that the Up Top people first saw what they looked like when they looked at themselves. The image bounced back at them, doubled and different.

It was a blacksmith who first brought magic into the world, by the mirror, but that is a story that should not be written down, so I won't say any more about it here.

If, by a smith, magic first came into the world, and all the good that magic can do, so, by a smith, came all the evil that magic can work, too.

Smiths bring good and ill and it is wise to be wary of them until you know them well. They work with fire every day, so they know that it is a good friend and a terrible enemy. Daily, they look into the forge and see the power of fire. Daily, they take metal, drawn from the earth, and make it bend to their hands.

Without smiths there would be no ploughs, no harrows, no scythes, no shears, no seedtime, no harvest.

Without smiths there would be no swords, no knives, no spears, no arrows.

Without smiths there would be no magic, no spells, no double-sight, no looking back.

Roffles and good smiths know each other and work together. If they can.

If you need help Up Top, you can usually trust a smith. Usually.

It's different when you're dealing with wizards, of course.

It seemed to Tadpole that his ancestor could have been more helpful. That was the problem with this guide. It gave a roffle a lot of useful information, but it raised as many questions as it answered.

For instance, how was a roffle to know the difference between a good blacksmith and a bad one?

Dorwin had been kind to him. That was good. He wanted to trust her. But he was uncertain. She had scooped him up, like a tickled trout, and brought him here. She had even, when he dawdled, put him into her cart to get him here.

He read the page again. It was no help. And another thing: Dorwin had hardly answered any of his questions. Even the wizards were better than she was, and they hadn't told him half enough.

Dorwin looked nice. Tadpole remembered Smedge and shuddered. Smedge had looked nice, standing in the doorway, neat and tidy in his uniform, until he had looked in Tadpole's direction and smiled at Tamrin. Looks were no guide.

After all, think about December.

He read the page a third time, and was near the end when he heard heavy footsteps on the stairs. Closing the book quickly, he put it back into his roffle pack, shut the lid, hopped out of the chair and sat on the pack.

A knock at the door. Three raps, followed by a pause and a fourth.

"Yes?" said Tadpole.

"Are you hungry?"

This was a bit of a stupid question. Roffles are always hungry. Tadpole decided to play a trick.

"No, thank you. I'm not."

"If you're not hungry, you're not a roffle. And if you're not a roffle, you're not welcome here. You're some creature come to do us harm."

Tadpole cowered from the voice. Deep, resonant and calm, it should have soothed him, but the words promised danger.

"And if you've come to do us harm, then I'd better harm you first."

The door flew open and Smith stood framed in it. He was broad and tall, sleeves rolled up to show thick arms. The scent of smoke flowed from his leather apron. He held a short hammer in his left hand.

"Are you hungry?" he asked again.

"Starving," said Tadpole.

Smith laughed.

"I thought so. Come and eat."

Smith stood aside. Tadpole hoisted his roffle pack, dodged past him and scooted downstairs. He was sitting at the table, next to Dorwin, before Smith was halfway down.

Smith laid the hammer on a dark-oak chest and sat at the head of the table. He carved a rib of beef with a long knife that was so sharp it passed through without pause or sound.

"Eat some greens as well," said Smith.

Greens were not Tadpole's favourite food and he took only a little.

Smith ignored him after that and spoke to Dorwin as though Tadpole wasn't there.

"I wasn't expecting a roffle," he said.

"No," said Dorwin. "I thought it was a mistake, at first. Perhaps he'd just popped up from some roffle hole I hadn't spotted. Then it was clear. He had come from Flaxfield's, through the study."

"It seems wrong. I was expecting one of the wizards."

"Yes. Or, if things went badly, a kravvin."

Smith took his time to chew a large piece of red beef.

"No, not a kravvin. I doubt they could come through the study. But Smedge."

"Yes."

"Or," he said, "worse thing, even Ash herself."

"But it was a roffle."

Tadpole found it irritating that they were ignoring him and he ate with a sullen air. It did mean that he was learning things, though, so he kept quiet.

"That was what made me decide it was right," said Dorwin. "It was so unexpected that it had to be right."

"Did you wait for anyone else to come through?"

"No. There was ill feeling at the inn, so I set off quickly."

"Good." He cut more meat and put some on Tadpole's plate without asking if he wanted it.

"Have another batter pudding if you take more greens as well," he said.

"Thank you."

Tadpole took the biggest batter pudding from the dish, and the smallest possible spoon of greens.

"Did he tell you what happened?" asked Smith.

"No. And I didn't ask him. He was too frightened. Too shocked."

"I'd rather hear him tell it himself, anyway."

"Yes. But he did say it was awful. And he said that Tamrin told him to fight."

"Tamrin said that?"

"Yes. That was how I knew I could trust him."

Tadpole pointed his fork at her.

"You didn't think you could trust me?" he demanded.

"Don't point your fork," she said.

"Sorry." He lowered it. "Of course you can trust me. I didn't know if I could trust you." Tadpole gave a sideways look at the smith as well.

"And you really don't think you can trust me, do you?" said the man.

Tadpole looked down. "No," he said.

"Stay like that," said Smith. "It's good protection."

"So I shouldn't trust you?" asked Tadpole.

"Not until you've got good reason. No."

Tadpole looked at Dorwin for help. He didn't know what to do, what to say.

"He's right," she said. "Generally. But, you know, sometimes, you just have to make up your mind about a person. How do they seem? Is there anything we can do that will make you trust us?"

Tadpole thought about this. He reached into his jerkin and took out the tooth on the thong. He handed it to Smith.

"What's this?" he asked.

Smith looked at it, turned it over in his hand, sniffed it.

"Who gave it to you?"

"A friend."

"Do you trust him?"

This wasn't an easy question. Delver had given him a tooth, said to be a dragon's tooth, which it wasn't. So, he'd let Tadpole down. But did Delver know it wasn't?

"Well?" asked Smith. "Do you?"

"Yes."

"What was it given to you as?"

Tadpole blushed. This was getting worse.

"I don't want to say."

Smith tossed it back to him.

"I don't see how I can help you, then."

Tadpole caught it, and let it dangle from his fingers. "You tell me what it is," he said.

"We both tell. All right?"

"All right."

"You say first."

"He told me it was a dragon's tooth," said Tadpole. "Is it?"

Smith waited. He looked at the tooth again.

"Not Up Top," he said.

He watched the disappointment cross Tadpole's face.

"But who knows what it is in the Deep World?" said Smith.

"What?"

"It may be a dragon's tooth down there."

"That's not possible. Things are what they are," said Tadpole.

"I don't think so."

"No?"

"Things are what people think they are. That's not the same. And things are different in different places."

Tadpole pushed the tooth across the table, away from him.

"Don't do that," said Dorwin.

"It's junk."

She took the tooth and hung it around Tadpole's neck.

"It was a gift, well-given, by a trusted friend," she said. "That's better than a dragon's tooth."

"Now," said Smith, "are you ready to tell us what happened, in Flaxfield's house?"

Tadpole felt himself grow dizzy at the memory. He wanted to go to sleep. If he told Smith, he would be sharing a secret, and that would help the big man, if he was Tadpole's enemy, if this was all a trap.

He tried to remember the exact words of the guide to Up Top.

"All right," he said. "It was like this." ||

Once Tadpole had started

to tell Smith and Dorwin his story he found that they were surprisingly good listeners. He had expected interruptions and questions. None came. The big man paid close attention to all that Tadpole said. He frowned sometimes. He smiled when Tadpole told them about hiding in the tree and the argument with Sam and Tamrin.

"They're so odd," said Tadpole. "I don't see how two people can be one person."

Smith didn't answer, so Tadpole carried on with the story.

Dorwin went pale when she heard about Axestone falling under the attacks of the kravvins. She cried when Tadpole said that he thought Flaxfold had been killed.

"I don't know, though. Not for sure," he said. "I've never seen anyone die."

He found that he didn't have words that could describe how he felt when he saw Smedge smile.

"How can a smile be worse than an angry face?" he asked.

He told them everything that had happened since he had stepped out into the daylight Up Top. Right through to the moment he walked into the inn parlour and saw Dorwin.

"That's it," he said. "Everything. And there's so much I don't understand, so many questions."

Neither Smith nor Dorwin spoke.

"I want to know about Flaxfold. Who she is. And Sam and Tamrin. And where the dragon fits in. And the other wizards, the grown-up ones. Why aren't they in charge? And what's Smedge? He looked like a decent sort of boy, and then he was all sorts of horrible animals and then just slime. And another thing: Ash. What's her part in this?"

He beat his fists on the table and confronted their stares.

"You know, don't you? Don't you?"

"Yes," said Smith. "I think I have a pretty good answer to all of the questions."

"Tell me, then."

"No."

Tadpole stared at him.

"What?"

"I said, no."

"I told you everything. Everything that happened. You promised me you'd tell me things."

"I don't think so."

"You did."

"No. You thought I said that. What I said was that I would help you."

Tadpole banged his fists again.

"Answering questions will help me. I need to know all about things. I don't know what anything is. Not Up Top. It's all strange and new to me."

Smith didn't seem to mind that Tadpole was shouting at him. He answered again, as calmly as before.

"I don't think so. No. I don't. But I will help you. In my own way."

"What way's that? Doing nothing? I trusted you."

"And you were right to do so."

Smith pushed his chair back and stood up. "Come to the forge with me," he said.

"No. I'm leaving."

"You'll like the forge."

Dorwin smiled at Tadpole. "Where will you go, if you leave?" she asked.

Tadpole waved his arms. "Anywhere. Nowhere. I don't know."

"Will you go back to the Deep World?"

He hesitated. "No. Not yet. I want to help."

Smith came around the table and put his arm across Tadpole's shoulders. It felt good. For the first time, nearly, since arriving Up Top, Tadpole felt as though someone could look after him.

"Come and see the forge. You'll get ideas there. You'll know what to do next, where to go. I promise."

Tadpole allowed Smith to lead him out and to the forge.

✠

Tadpole saw the forge and the furnace and he stopped in the doorway and stared.

"It's roffle fire," he said.

"In you go," said Smith.

Tadpole approached the furnace with a look of wonder. He held his hands out to the fire. The coals burned with a low intensity. The heat was sleeping.

"It is, isn't it? Roffle fire?"

"Well, if you don't know, I don't know who does."

Tadpole hesitated. He put his hands closer. He scooped them together and rubbed them on his face, like a thirsty man scooping water from a spring.

He didn't turn around to look at Smith. "Do all blacksmiths use roffle fire?"

"No. Not all."

"How many?"

"It's the best fire there is," said Smith. "Gives the truest metal, the sharpest steel."

Tadpole didn't want to move away from the glow of the coals.

"It's like being home," he said. "I can smell the Deep World. How did you get the roffle fire?"

Smith stood next to him and rested his hand on Tadpole's shoulder.

"I've never been to the Deep World," he said. "All these years, working with roffle fire. All these years, with I don't know how many roffle workers here. Lads, just like you, learning the trade. All that time, and I've never been to the Deep World."

"Would you like to?"

"Very much."

"Why don't you? People did, in the old days. You could."

"You take me there," said Smith. "When all this is over, take me and show me your world."

"I don't know. Perhaps."

"See? It's not as easy as you think, is it?"

"No. I mean, you'd be very welcome."

Smith squeezed his shoulder. "Never mind. Let's talk about other things. First off, have you got a weapon?"

This was an embarrassing question. Delver's knife was still tucked into Tadpole's belt. If the dragon tooth was a fake, how poor would the knife be? And the scruffy shield?

"No. No, I haven't."

Smith led him to a closed cupboard, fastened with a lock on a sturdy hasp. He unlocked and opened it.

"Oh," said Tadpole.

"What do you think?"

Tadpole surveyed the weapons, arranged on narrow shelves and supports, like spice jars and ladles and spoons in an ordered kitchen.

Swords and daggers, an axe and three maces. Tadpole touched his fingers to a short blade, halfway between an Up Top sword and a knife, perfect for a roffle. There was a weapon that looked like something for harvesting, with a curved blade. Shields and mail. It was a war chest.

Smith grimaced. "I don't usually make these things. But

we've been expecting trouble."

"It's arrived," said Tadpole.

"And so have you," said Smith. "That's not a coincidence. When you walked through that door from Flaxfield's study, you walked into a war."

"I walked away from one," said Tadpole. "I left them to die."

"You did as you were told. That was the right thing, then. Now, you have to make up your own mind. Do you want a weapon?"

Tadpole reached out and took the short sword. He didn't know how to hold it.

"Be careful."

He turned to answer Smith, swinging the sword as he did so. The blade flashed in the forgelight. Smith stepped back, just in time to avoid the edge of the blade slashing his face.

"Sorry." Tadpole let his arm fall to his side, and the sword nearly cut through his thigh.

"Are you sure you want that?"

Tadpole raised his hand, slowly, very slowly, watching where the sword went.

"I'd feel safer if I had a sword," he said.

"Would you? Would other people be safe? And would you take your fingers off?"

"I'd learn. I'd get used to it."

"I know. I'm not saying you won't. You'll need some practice, though, before you go. I can teach you some things."

"I don't even know where I'm going yet."

"You will."

The sword was already growing heavy and Tadpole looked for somewhere to rest it. He didn't want to put it back into the cupboard, for fear of never having it again. He pushed his cloak aside, as though to fix the sword into his belt.

"What's that?" asked Smith.

Tadpole tried to hide Delver's knife under the cloak.

"Oh, it's just a bit of junk. I can leave it here. Make room for the sword."

"May I see?"

"It's nothing."

"All the same."

Smith was persistent. Tadpole handed him the sword and felt bereaved when it was replaced in the cupboard. He gave Smith the knife. It looked so old and shabby and clumsy after the elegance of the sword.

Smith took it over to the forge and examined it in the light of the fire. The blade seemed to ripple in response to the pulsing coals.

"This is a good knife," said Smith.

Tadpole watched him weigh it in his hands, test the edge of the blade with his thumb. Just a touch brought a small line of blood to the surface.

"Sharp. Balanced. A well-shaped handle. Tempered to perfection."

Tadpole was looking at the knife as though he had never seen it before. He remembered how much he had liked it on first taking it in his hand. Remembered how ashamed he became of Delver's gifts when the tooth was mocked.

"Where did you get this?" asked Smith. His face was hard. His voice had taken on a different tone. Tadpole felt himself to be accused.

"I didn't steal it."

"I didn't say you did. But someone came by this in a strange way. Where did you get it?"

"The friend gave it to me."

"The dragon-tooth friend?"

"Yes."

Smith's face relaxed. He laughed. "Your friend seems to have had a habit of picking things up," he said. "Perhaps he put it into his roffle pack by mistake and forgot to give it back."

Tadpole couldn't accept this excuse. "I don't think so," he said. "I think he meant to have it."

"I think he did." Smith handed it back to him. "And now it's yours."

The knife felt so good in his hand. The sword had been extra to him, an unpredictable extension of his arm. The knife felt like part of his hand.

"Is it all right to have it?" said Tadpole. "Should I try to give it back to its owner?"

Smith worked the bellows and the embers gushed out fire.

"It must have been a long time ago," he said. "Perhaps the real owner's dead now. Best you should keep it. You never know when you might need something like that."

"What about the sword?"

"Best leave that where it is, eh?"

Tadpole cast a longing look at the open cupboard, the range of weapons. He put the knife back into his belt.

"A knife isn't much of a weapon," he said.

"Depends on the knife. Depends on who uses it. Depends on the enemy."

A shadow fell across the floor and Dorwin appeared in the doorway.

"I've packed you a meal," she said. "For the journey."

"Where am I going?"

"That's up to you," said Smith. "Here." He led Tadpole to the door. "I don't know who's alive and who's dead," he said. "But Waterburn lives at the college, that way." He pointed. "December, she lives among the miners, and you'll find her if you go that way." He moved his arm and pointed again. "And, if you follow that road, you'll come to Boolat and the castle."

"What's there?"

"Ash is there," said Dorwin.

"And someone's got to kill her," said Smith. "Before she kills us all, and magic makes slaves of the rest."

"Will a knife kill her?"

"No. Not even a good knife like yours."

"I liked December," said Tadpole.

"That way."

"And I liked Waterburn, as well. What about Sam and Tamrin? Where are they?"

"Best leave them to themselves."

"And Smedge? Where's he?"

"If we knew that," said Smith, "we'd be better able to defeat him."

"What is he?"

"You'll meet him again one day. Ask him yourself."

Tadpole didn't move. Within his sight there were six roffle holes. He could go through any one of them and be home in no time.

Smith looked at the roads.

"You want answers to your questions, don't you?"

"Yes."

"You think that if you know all about it, you'll be able to work it out, make a better choice. Well, you won't. For some reason, you've come into this war from the Deep World. You've got new eyes, new thoughts. You need to learn about this as you go along. You know Ash is the enemy. She's the cause of all this. You know Smedge is her agent. I'll tell you this one thing more. Long, long ago, Flaxfield and December and some others sealed Ash up in the Castle of Boolat. She's been struggling to get out all this time. She made the monsters you've seen. She's breaking down the spell from the outside. Soon, she'll be free, unless we stop her."

Tadpole shuffled to make his roffle pack comfortable.

"I've heard about the college," he said. "I'll go that way."

"I'll walk the first part with you," said Dorwin. "Then I have other things to do." ‖

Part Two

STARSAVED

Canterstock College, huge, grey and grim,

rose up above the roofs of the town. Tadpole had to stop and stare and look in his roffle pack for the guide to Up Top. He sat down with his back against a large rock and looked again at the page about the college.

Up Top ~ A Guide for Roffles

THE COLLEGE FOR WIZARDS

Canterstock College is one of the most beautiful buildings in the whole of Up Top.

The stone glows in the sun. Think of honey. Think of the soft folds of sand on a warm shore. Think of the finest cloth, dyed to look like yellow iris in blue water. Think of the sky at sunrise. None of these is as warm, as golden, as lovely as your first sight of the stone of Canterstock College.

With spires and turrets, arched windows and wide,

welcoming doors, it is a palace of learning. Kings have been proud to live in less lovely houses.

The teachers there are gentle and wise. They show the pupils the right ways of magic and turn them aside from thinking of how to use it for their own gain.

Pupils are admitted when they are very young. Only those who keep the baby-magic magic which so many are born with but which so many of them lose.

The college principal is a leader, a friend, a ruler and a servant. She directs and encourages. Her own knowledge and experience are the besetting virtues of the whole college.

Sometimes, a pupil is expelled. Never for not paying attention or for not being clever enough. The world needs village wizards who can make a good-enough spell, just as it needs village carpenters who can make a rough table, but not a throne for a king. No, pupils are only expelled when they show that they do not know how to use their magic for others, not for themselves.

The corridors are bright with the glow of floating globes. The rooms are wide and spacious.

The laboratories are home to every herb and substance. Fire and ice, smoke and scent, feathers and fish, diamonds and dung, all are needed for the uncovering of new spells and the weaving of old ones. There are pupils who, having entered the laboratories as children, never leave them. They love the place so much that they spend all of their lives there, learning and teaching, discovering and, *sometimes, hiding things away that are better not shared.*

The hall is a place of laughter and talk and food and friendship.

The gardens, contained within the walls of glowing stone, are bigger than the vastest deserts, with endless paths and trackless groves.

But the heart of the college, its brain, its blood, its muscles and its strength, is the library.

The great wizards do not attend the college. They are apprenticed, but the college is the nursery of many good men and women, wizards who are as needful to a town or village as is a doctor, or a baker, a midwife or a teacher.

To enter Canterstock College is to walk into joy and wisdom, life and learning.

"It can't be the right place," he said. "I've taken a wrong turn."

Except that there hadn't been another turn. The way had led him, without choice, straight here. No other road had led off. And, only a few hours ago, he had passed a roadside stone post which said, *Canterstock and College 3 miles.*

The town crouched round the huge building as though cowering beneath its contempt. Tadpole shouldered his pack and walked on. If it wasn't Canterstock at least it would be a place to stop and eat. And someone would be able to direct him to the right road.

Two guards crossed their pikes and barred his way as he

approached the gate of the town. He stepped back. They confronted him with unfriendly faces. Perhaps they weren't guards? They wore no uniform, just the working clothes of labourers. And they were dirty, but he supposed soldiers might be dirty as well.

"Am I allowed in?" he asked.

"What do you want?"

"Is this Canterstock?"

"Where else could it be?"

"Is it or not?"

Their arms had grown tired of holding their pikes. They stood at ease and rested, one on his pike, the other against the gate.

"'Course it is."

Tadpole didn't like the way they laughed at him. And he didn't like the look of them.

"That can't be the college, though," he said. "It's grey and nasty."

"Hear that? He thinks our college is nasty."

The one leaning on the gate scratched his chin. "Well, he's right, there. It is nasty."

"Not for him to say, though, is it? Cheeky roffle."

"I thought roffles weren't Up Top any more."

"That's right."

They were growing angry.

"He's a spy. For the kravvins."

"Look. Roffles don't wear cloaks like that."

"He's some new sort."

"Take hold of him."

They were slow, not expecting Tadpole to resist. He side-stepped them and walked into a roffle hole he had spotted just by the left upright of the gate.

"Have you got him?"

"Where is he?"

Tadpole watched them from the safety of the roffle door. They were clowns. Stupid. While they were searching he slipped out, through the gate, and was in the town.

And a miserable, dirty town it was. Dog mess and rotting vegetables on the streets. Shops boarded up or half-empty, no goods in the windows. Tadpole crossed a market square and found himself at the gates of the college. Grey walls, not honey-coloured; at the base, green with moss and mould. Water overflowed the blocked guttering and spilled down the walls, bruising them with slippery stains.

The big gates were locked, with a small wicket giving entry. He stepped through it and looked around a quadrangle. Grass grew in every crevice. A cold wind seemed to blow, making a shrill noise. Tadpole huddled his cloak tight around him against the wind.

"Who's there?"

A thin, pointy man came out of the porter's lodge and stared straight at Tadpole.

"Who's there?" he asked again.

He looked left and right and back at Tadpole.

"What's that noise?" he said.

Tadpole began to answer. Before he could speak, the man shrugged. "Just the wind," he muttered. He went back into the lodge.

Tadpole moved to the side of the quad, to avoid being seen by anyone else. There was something wrong with the porter.

He found a door and went inside.

The corridors were lit with floating globes, just as the book had said. These, though, were not bright. They hung, yellow and dim, throbbing, like the nests of some stinging creature, ready to burst. Tadpole, short though he was, ducked to avoid bumping his head against them. He peered through the grimy window of a classroom door. Eight pupils at desks, scattered in a room made for thirty, listened to a fat teacher who seemed to be telling them off. Tadpole couldn't hear what he said. A sign on the door said, *Dr Duddle*.

He followed the corridor. More classrooms. More empty desks. More teachers looking angry or tired. And the stink! Tadpole gathered his cloak and put it over his nose and mouth to try to cover the smell. Things rotting, dying.

Stairs led up. He wound round, hoping the smell would be less as he rose higher. It was no better.

The light was worse up here. There seemed to be no classrooms, and the doors didn't have windows in them. Studies? Bedrooms? He moved quickly, afraid to knock, afraid to try a handle. Turning a corner he saw a bigger door, with an arched top and a worked-iron loop for a handle. It was cold. He put his ear to the door. Was there a noise? A rustling, perhaps? Or a murmur?

Better not try it. He took his hand from the iron ring and it fell, making a sharp clang. Before he could move away the door opened.

"Come in."

There was no one there. Tadpole backed away. His roffle pack bumped against the opposite wall with a thud.

"Come in. And be quick. And shut the door after you."

At least the smell disappeared when he shut the door. There was still no sign of whoever had spoken to him. But the place was marvellous. A room like a drum, round and tall and endless above his head. Gallery after gallery, one above another, out of sight. And every one of them covered with books.

He was alone. At least, there was no one else to be seen.

"What do you want?"

Tadpole stepped back. He looked in all directions.

"If you don't tell me, I'll throw you out again."

The voice was very near. Perhaps it was from someone behind a bookcase? Tadpole moved to his left and brushed against something.

"Watch where you're going."

Tadpole coughed to mask a sick feeling, and hoped he wouldn't throw up. Was it Smedge?

"What's the matter?"

Tadpole backed away.

"I'll throw you out. You're wasting my time."

Tadpole tried to move sideways to the door to escape.

Something stirred overhead in the galleries. The sound of trees, before the rain starts and the wind lifts up their leaves. A whispering, that resolved itself into speech.

"He can't see you."

"What?"

"He can't see you."

Tadpole had reached the door. As he had expected, it was locked. Did all doors Up Top lock themselves as soon as you went through them?

"You can't open the door. I let you in. You have to ask me to let you out."

The air was thickening around the voice.

"Please let me out," said Tadpole.

"To the stink? To the dirt? To Frastfil and Duddle? To those dunces and liars and frauds? Is that what you want?"

"I want to get out of here, please."

"Very well." The voice was coming from a shape, now, something like a man. It approached him. "Out you go. To stink and Smedge. To Duddle and dirt. Out you—"

"What?" asked Tadpole.

He moved away from the door to make room for the man shape. Tadpole could see right through him.

"I'm letting you out."

"You said Smedge?"

"Yes."

"Aren't you Smedge?"

There was more noise from the galleries. Tadpole looked up and the light was rippling there, the shadows of clouds.

The shape disappeared.

The galleries laughed.

Tadpole grabbed the door handle. It was still locked.

The shape formed again. More like a man. Tadpole could only just see through him.

"Smedge? You think I'm Smedge?" He waved his hand and the whisper of laughter from the galleries ceased.

"I'm sorry. I've never been Up Top before. And I saw a boy who was there and then he wasn't there. And then he was other things."

"Always other things," said the man. "Never really a boy. All right. No harm done."

Now that Tadpole could see him properly, the man was real. He was old. Older than Tadpole thought possible. Not frail. Not infirm. Just old. As trees are old. Old, as rocks and lakes are old.

"My name's Tadpole."

"Is it? Nice for you. Are you going to be a frog tomorrow?"

The man thought that was a very funny question and laughed at it for a long time. Tadpole, who had heard it lots of times before, thought it was less funny, or not funny at all, really, and he was glad the galleries didn't laugh either.

He scanned the galleries for any sign that there might be people up there, to make the noise, to speak to the man.

There was only the play of light and shade.

"You're supposed to tell me your name, now," said Tadpole.

"Am I? Why?"

"It's what people do?"

"Is it? It's been so long, I don't remember what people do."
He became slender again, against the light, and started to disappear.

"Don't go."

"Eh?"

"You're fading again."

The man made an effort and reformed.

"Are you a ghost?"

He disappeared.

"Where are you?"

Tadpole had grown used to the man. His eyes had adjusted to him. Although he had faded away, he left a disturbance in the air wherever he went. Tadpole followed him.

"I can see where you are."

He moved.

"You're by the door."

Moved again.

"By the picture of a dragon."

Again.

"In front of the table. Behind the table. Stand still so I can talk to you."

The whispers of laughter from the galleries returned.

The man materialized and glared up at them.

"Don't call me a ghost."

"I'm sorry."

"What's a ghost?"

Tadpole hesitated.

"Come on. It's not a trick question. And it's not a hard question. What's a ghost?"

"Someone who's died and come back to haunt somewhere."

There was a sigh from the gallery. The essence of sadness. It went straight through Tadpole's heart and he wanted to cry. He had to brush the edge of his cloak against his eyes to keep them dry.

"What's that?" asked the man. He came and touched Tadpole's cloak. "A roffle. In a Cloude cloak?" His fingers found the selvedge and he looked at the memmont woven into it. "No doubt about it."

"It's not a Cloude cloak, whatever that is. Mr Martin wove it for me."

"Martin?"

"Yes."

"Ah, well. I never thought to see the like." He gave Tadpole a long stare. "And now you're in my library."

"Your library?"

"Of course." He put out his hand. "Jackbones. Librarian of Canterstock College."

As Tadpole shook his hand there was a murmur from the galleries. Jackbones looked up and said, "Formerly, librarian of Canterstock College."

"What are you now?"

"I am, as you see," he said. And he seemed very pleased with this as an adequate answer.

He walked off and started to tidy some books on the round table. Tadpole watched him, to see if his feet touched the floor, or if he drifted along above it. Jackbones walked normally. Tadpole waited for him to say something else. Jackbones seemed to have forgotten him.

There were stairs, wrought iron, circling up into the galleries. Tadpole put his foot on the bottom step and looked up. Second step. The gallery rustled. He changed his mind and moved away, bumping into a stool. Jackbones put books back in their places on the shelves.

"Aren't you going to ask me why I'm here?" said Tadpole.

"Do you want to tell me?"

"Yes."

"Then I don't need to ask, do I?"

Tadpole put his pack on the floor and sat on it at the big table. Jackbones looked over his shoulder at him and carried on stacking books. Tadpole waited. Jackbones sneaked another look. Tadpole smiled to himself. He had won. Jackbones was curious. It wasn't long before the man edged his way back to the table. He was a little like a squirrel, or a bird — some wild creature which advances and then retreats, wanting to be near, not certain whether it's safe.

He slid the books on to the table and sat down.

"I'm looking for Waterburn," said Tadpole. He was amazed

at the reaction. Jackbones jumped to his feet and rushed around the table. He seized Tadpole's throat and shook him.

Tadpole fell back, grabbing Jackbones' wrists.

The noise from the gallery increased. Jackbones had leaned Tadpole back and the roffle was looking straight up into the never-ending rows of books.

"Where is he? What's happened to Waterburn? Have you hurt him?"

Tadpole pulled the hands from his throat. Jackbones was thin, had little strength. It was only the suddenness of his attack that had overpowered Tadpole. He took care not to hurt the librarian as he pushed him away. One by one, then more and more, faces appeared in the galleries. Tens, and hundreds and thousands, leaning over the rails, looking down at them.

Jackbones looked up at them and looked away.

"Who are they?" asked Tadpole.

Jackbones grinned. "They're not there."

Tadpole looked again. The faces didn't move. They were silent.

"I can see them."

"Not there."

"I heard them."

"Not there."

"You saw them. I watched you."

"Not there."

Tadpole moved into the centre of the room and looked up.

"Who are you?" he asked.

Jackbones moved to stand beside him. He leaned in and whispered, "Do they frighten you?"

"You can see them."

"Do they? Do they make you quake with fear? Do they make your stomach roll and your head grow dizzy?" His whisper was a snake, a sandslip, a secret in silk. "Do they speak to you of silence and pain?"

Tadpole shivered. They did. He wanted to look away, and his eyes wouldn't leave them. Jackbones stroked cold fingers on Tadpole's cheeks. "And you heard them?" he said. "Do you hear them now? Do you hear their promises, their lies? Do you?"

"Jackbones, leave the boy alone."

Jackbones gripped Tadpole's arm. "She's not there. Don't look round."

So, of course, Tadpole looked round.

The spiral staircase to the first gallery creaked. First a foot, small and slender in a soft leather shoe, then a dress, green and blue and shimmering, then the whole figure, a woman, of no age and all age. She paused, looked at Tadpole, stepped softly down and stood a little distant from him.

"Welcome to our library," she said.

Tadpole couldn't answer.

"She's not there."

"Jackbones, you're forgetting about Waterburn."

The librarian closed his eyes and shook his head. "I did," he admitted. "I forgot him. When you all looked down." He took Tadpole's arm again. "Have you hurt him? Where is he?" He looked at the woman. "Springmile, make the roffle tell me where he is."

The woman moved across and removed his hand with gentle fingers. She led Tadpole to the table and sat next to him.

"Tell me," she said. "Tell me about Waterburn. Please."

Jackbones sidled round and sat, two chairs away from them.

"Is he alive?" asked Springmile.

"I don't know. Perhaps."

Jackbones howled.

"Shh," she said. "Time to grieve when we know if it's needed. Now, Tadpole, please tell us what you know."

"You know my name?"

She nodded. "In the library, we hear what happens."

He looked up. The faces were silent, listening.

"Please," she said. "Will you tell us what brought you here and what's happened to our friend?"

Tadpole began to feel like a travelling storyteller, repeating his tale at every stop he made. He gave them the same account that he had given to Smith, and he thought about how to add the part about visiting the forge.

He was interested to see how the way he told it changed a little from last time, and the way that the new part about the smith was changing the first part.

Springmile listened quietly, looking at him all of the time. Jackbones couldn't sit still. He squirmed and wriggled, twitched and jumped, clenched his fists and made fierce grimaces as the different parts of the tale unfolded. At one point, when Tadpole described seeing Smedge arrive, Jackbones stood up, pushing his chair back and shouting, "No!" He grabbed an inkwell and threw it into the room. The ink sprayed out, and each drop, each splash, became a spinning ball of spiked iron. They crashed into the walls, the books, the door, the floor. Some of them flew right up into the galleries above. And when they hit, they exploded, sending shards of jagged iron flying out. Tadpole ducked as one sped round his head and dug into the tabletop.

Springmile went to Jackbones, rested a slender hand on his shoulder and helped him to sit down again. She ran her hand over his head, smoothing his hair. She made small, comforting sounds with no words.

"I'm sorry," said Jackbones. "Smedge. You know?"

"Yes, I know."

Springmile flung out her arm, scattering a shower of silver-green leaves of willow over the library floor. They blew into every corner and fell on to the shattered iron fragments. Springmile waited, then blew gently and the leaves fluttered away, taking all traces of the sharp metal with them, leaving no trace of the damage or the explosions.

She sat down again.

"You were saying," she said. "Smedge appeared, and the kravvins were with him." ||

When Tadpole reached the point in his story

where Flaxfold fell, impaled, the galleries gave a universal sigh of loss.

"You're sure?" said Springmile.

"I saw it."

"She might have lived."

"With magic, I suppose. I don't know what magic can do."

"She's dead," said Jackbones.

"I think she is," Springmile agreed. "I feel it. It's in his story. It's true."

"So, it's over," said Jackbones.

"Perhaps soon. Not yet. Please, Tadpole, tell us the rest."

He finished his story.

"And the porter didn't even see me come in the gate," he said. "Is there something wrong with him?"

"The boy's a fool," said Jackbones. "We should take it off him."

"I'm not a fool. And you're very rude."

The galleries were amused.

"I'm just new here, Up Top. I don't understand everything. It doesn't make me a fool."

"It doesn't," said Springmile. "And Jackbones is sorry."

"He hasn't said sorry."

"And he probably won't. But he is, all the same."

Tadpole looked across the table. Jackbones looked away. Truth to tell, he did look sorry.

"Did you want to be seen by the porter?" Springmile asked.

"No. I was trying to hide."

She touched his cloak. "No roffle has ever worn a Cloude cloak before. You'll have to get used to it. But it has its uses."

"You mean I was invisible?"

She smiled.

"But you can see me."

"You're not hiding from me. And, besides, you're in my library."

"What else can it do?" he asked.

"All in good time, Tadpole. First, we have to make plans. Let's just be clear about what you are saying. Eloise and Axestone are dead? Killed by kravvins?"

"I think so. It looked that way. But, you know, magic..."

"It's best if we think the worst. And Flaxfold. She seemed mortally wounded?"

Tadpole found himself growing unsteady at the memory of Flaxfold, attacked and defeated. He wiped his eyes with the edge of his cloak.

"Careful with that, boy," said Jackbones.

Tadpole gathered his courage and his calm. "I don't see how anyone could live after that. Why do you keep asking me? I've told you already."

"Because we won't believe it," said Jackbones.

For a moment he was more solid than ever he had been, then he wavered and Tadpole could see right through him again.

"We must believe it. But Sam and Tamrin, December and Waterburn? All safe?"

"They were all alive when I was pushed out. That's all I know. But it looked bad. They were losing. Until the dragon arrived."

"Starback. Starback. Starback." The name rustled round the galleries and up and down, the whispering of a breeze-blown forest.

Springmile stood up. "You came here to find Waterburn. I think that means he lived. You have to find him. You and Jackbones together."

"Just a minute," said Tadpole. "I don't have to do what you tell me."

"No."

"And I'm not leaving my library," said Jackbones. "And I'm certainly not going anywhere with a roffle."

"You have something you want of us," Springmile said to Jackbones. "And you have to earn it." She linked her arm through his and drew him to the foot of the stairs.

"Years ago," she said, "more years than it's good to remember, you did a wrong thing."

"For the right reason," said Jackbones.

"Yes. The right reason. And it was brave."

Jackbones tried to take his arm away from her. She held him tight.

"So you fade away, but never die," she said. "You are denied the Finished World. Denied the right to join us." She looked up the winding stair. "I can take you there," she said. "I can lead you. But you have to earn it."

"Not with a roffle. That's flat," he said. "I won't do it."

"And this doesn't even seem the right place," said Tadpole. "How do I know this is even Canterstock College?"

For this first time since he had met her Tadpole saw a puzzled look cross Springmile's face.

"What else could it be?"

"A trick. I don't know. But it's grey and filthy and it feels wrong. The real college is warm and the colour of honey and full of life and joy."

The galleries made a long, sad, withdrawing roar. Tadpole looked up. The faces drew back. The galleries emptied. He was alone with Jackbones and Springmile.

"What do you know of Canterstock?" she asked.

Tadpole stood so that she could not see inside his roffle pack while he took out the guide book. He opened it at the page about the college. "Look."

She looked at it. She turned to the title page. "This is a curious book. Where did you get it?"

"Is it right?" he asked. "Is that what the college is like?"

Jackbones seized the book. "Where did you get this?"

"It's mine. Give it back."

They struggled. Jackbones had found new strength. His body grew solid. He was winning the tussle. Tadpole had to let go of the book or it would rip in two and Jackbones would have the greater part. He stopped pulling and ran at the man, tipping him over. Jackbones fell across the back of a chair, and he snapped. Tadpole regained the book and wriggled away. He looked in horror at the librarian.

"I've killed him," he said. "Oh, no. I've killed him."

Springmile helped him to his feet. She put her arm around his shoulders. "Nothing so kind as that," she said. "Watch."

Jackbones opened his eyes, saw his broken back, sighed, pushed himself to the left, until he was more or less straight again. He breathed deeply. He gave Springmile a reproachful look and hauled himself to his feet, using the chair that had snapped him.

"He was dead," said Tadpole. "He was."

Jackbones scowled at him. "If only you could kill me," he said.

"You two must be friends," said Springmile. "You are to go and find Waterburn together."

"What about the book?" said Tadpole. He clutched it away from Jackbones' reach.

"The book is right," she said. "The college was just like that. But it has changed. As you see. As we all have. As you shall. Some change is for the better. This is for the worse."

"What happened?"

"Frastfil happened," said Jackbones. "And Ash happened and Smedge happened."

"And why aren't you dead?" said Tadpole.

Jackbones turned away. Springmile put her finger to her lips.

"He can't die?" said Tadpole. "How?" A look of hope came over his face. "Perhaps the others can't either. Perhaps they mended, too."

"He can't die here." she said. "Who knows about what happens outside? But the others can. When we took it away from him it was a punishment, not a reward."

"I don't understand," said Tadpole.

"No. No, you don't, boy."

Tadpole gave up. "But what happened to the college?"

"You can talk about it as you go," she said. "Time is wasting."

"I'll go alone," said Jackbones. "I'll leave the library, but not with a roffle."

"Tadpole," said Springmile. "Will you let Jackbones see your book again?"

"No."

"If he promises not to touch it, will you?"

"Will he promise?"

"Yes. Jackbones, do you promise?"

"Why should I?"

"Because you need to see this book."

The librarian turned back again.

Springmile leaned over and looked at the book. "Where did you get it?" she asked.

"It's mine. My great-great-something made it."

"And this is his name?"

"Yes, but he was called Perry, Up Top."

Jackbones moved as fast as a snake strikes. Tadpole swung away from him, protecting the book.

"What name?"

"You must promise not to touch it," said Springmile.

"I promise. Now let me look."

Tadpole didn't move.

"He keeps his promises," she said.

Tadpole allowed him to see the book. Jackbones read the page about the college with a mocking smile on his face that faded and was replaced with a look of grief. "That's it," he said. "That's how it was. I'd forgotten. I'm so used to it as it is." He sighed. "Perry?" he said. "You're descended from Perry?"

"From Megapoir," said Tadpole. "Yes. He knew a lot about Up Top. That's why he made this guide."

"Do all roffles see this?"

"No. Only me. I found it."

"All right," said Jackbones. "I'll go with the roffle. We'll look for Waterburn."

"Thank you," said Springmile. "Look after him."

"What?"

"Tadpole. Look after him."

Something happened to Jackbones. Every last trace of transparency left him. He was quite solid now.

"I shall," he promised. "Let me get some things."

Jackbones disappeared through a side door. As it opened, Tadpole glimpsed a sort of stock cupboard-cum-sitting room. When Jackbones emerged, he wore a cloak, like Tadpole's, and he supported himself with a staff, the same height as himself. A murmur overhead made Tadpole look up.

The faces had returned. And they looked different: eager, expectant. The sound became a buzz of excitement. Springmile smiled.

"You look uncomfortable," she said.

Jackbones wriggled.

"It's been a long time," he said.

"You'll soon get used to it."

"Come on, lad," he said.

Tadpole didn't move.

"One foot in front of the other is the usual way," said Jackbones.

The galleries made a ripple of laughter. Jackbones looked up. They smiled down at him.

"Don't think I won't be back," he said.

Their faces grew solemn, silent.

"You may not be back," said Springmile. "Not this time. Tadpole, are you willing to go with Jackbones?"

"I don't know."

"Why not? You need help."

"He attacked me. And..." Tadpole thought what to say. "He's odd. He's not real. I'm sorry. I don't want to be rude, but he is. And he doesn't like me. He doesn't like roffles. I don't trust him."

Tadpole felt ashamed, saying this, but he felt it was right. He had to say it. He was shaking.

"Jackbones?" said Springmile.

The librarian sat down, wrapping himself in his cloak.

"You're right," he said to Tadpole. "I'm sorry. It's been a long time. I don't speak to many people. These ones—" he gestured up at the galleries — "don't appear often. You brought them out."

He held his staff with both hands and leaned forward. After a while he continued. "Roffles," he said. "Roffles." He shook his head. "No offence, but they're not easy. All that riddling talk. Not that you do that. I met a bad roffle, once. It put me off them."

Tadpole started to object. Springmile touched his shoulder and motioned him to be quiet.

"But I had a friend who was a roffle," said Jackbones. "A long time ago. He used to visit someone I knew. Boy called Cabbage."

Tadpole couldn't stop himself interrupting now. "Cabbage is Waterburn," he said.

The galleries sizzled with astonishment. Even Springmile stepped back, amazed. Jackbones stood up. He held out his hand. "Come on," he said. "If you know that, then we'll have to work together. You're in this very deep. Come on. The roffle I knew, he was Cabbage's friend, Perry. Yes, that's right. I'm as old as that. Older, in fact. Let's get going. And I'll tell you all sorts of things about those two."

Tadpole started to say goodbye to Springmile, but she had already left and he saw her dress disappearing in the turn of the stair. He looked up. The faces withdrew and, in an instant, the air was filled with white petals of blossom, tumbling down and covering the table, the floor, Jackbones and Tadpole.

"Let's go," said Jackbones, opening the door. "Brace yourself for the stink."

It hit them like a shower of rotting fish guts. Tadpole covered his nose with his cloak.

"No, don't do that." Jackbones stood tall and breathed in deeply. "Fill your lungs. Don't flinch from it. You'll never beat something if you're not willing to put your hands round it, not willing to take it on on its own terms. Breathe in, boy."

Tadpole took the cloak away from his face and breathed, half-filling his lungs before he choked and retched.

"You'll get used to it," said Jackbones. "Come on." And he strode away, a complete man. Tadpole had to trot to keep up with him.

"Where are we going?"

"We'll look in at Cabbage's kitchen, for a start. See if he's there."

"Why would he be there?"

"Why wouldn't he?"

Another voice joined in.

"Why wouldn't who be where?"

"Eh?" said Tadpole.

Jackbones had wrapped his cloak around his face. Tadpole could still see him and he wanted to laugh. The librarian made a sign for him to be silent.

"Why wouldn't who be where? And who are you? And what are you doing here?"

It was a cheery, tall man with a thin face, and a beaming smile. He was the most welcoming and friendly person that Tadpole had seen since he arrived Up Top.

"We're looking for..." Tadpole began. He saw Jackbones shake his head, and his answer dried up.

"We? Who's we?"

The cheery man looked around. He looked directly at Jackbones and didn't see him. Jackbones raised his eyebrows.

"I mean, I ... I mean, I'm looking for..." He wondered what he should be looking for and had an idea. "I'm looking for the principal of the college."

"And you've found him." The man wagged a teasing finger at Tadpole. "Or, perhaps I should say, I've found you."

"You?"

"None other. I am Professor Frastfil, the principal of Canterstock College." He looked as proud as a pointed roof. "And you are a roffle."

"Yes."

"Come along with me and tell me what you want here, in this splendid palace of learning, the finest market of magic there ever has been."

Saying this, he waved his hand, whistled and the walls of the corridor began to sprout branches. Dead, rotten branches, with the sullen remnants of leaves, hanging from the twigs. They stank of stagnant pond water, and as Tadpole brushed against them they snapped and fell.

"What a brave show," said Frastfil. "Such ... such— " he searched for a word — "such autumnal splendour."

Jackbones, dancing ahead of them, pushed his fingers into his mouth and pretended to gag. Tadpole couldn't stop himself laughing. He tried to turn it into a cough, not to annoy Frastfil. But the man beamed down at him. "It delights you? Yes?"

It made him feel sick. "Oh, yes. It delights me."

"Splendid." Frastfil jingled loose change in his pocket and beamed wider than ever. The cheeriest person Tadpole had ever met. And so pleased with himself and his sad magic and his stinking college. It was all very different from the guide to Up Top.

"I wonder," said Frastfil. He stopped and looked at Tadpole. "You look like a roffle. That's for sure. But you don't speak like a roffle." He became fierce all at once. Fear and anger fought for dominance on his face. "Speak up, boy. What are you? Are you a roffle?"

"Is a party for punches a pot of palaver?" asked Tadpole.

"That's it," said Frastfil. He made a little dance and beamed and beamed, and jingled his money. "That's the roffle talk. Well, you can stop it now. It makes me dizzy."

Jackbones tapped his head and let his tongue loll out and crossed his eyes, to show Tadpole what he thought of Frastfil's intelligence.

Tadpole really did fall into a fit of coughing this time. By the time he'd finished and recovered they were at the door of the professor's study. Jackbones slipped in and sat down in the most comfortable armchair. Frastfil sat behind his desk and tried to look important. Tadpole stood in the centre of the room.

"Now," said Frastfil. "Why were you looking for me?"

He rested his hands on the desk and looked at Tadpole for an answer. It would have been impressive for a young roffle on his first trip Up Top, if the study hadn't been quite so nasty. The desktop was covered with so much stuff, and all of it dreadful. A pile of old papers had worms in it. Purple slime bubbled up out of the top of an inkpot and spread over the pens and nibs and rulers around it. There was a rat, eating a dead squirrel, lifting its face and looking at Frastfil, as if to give a warning that he wasn't prepared to share his dinner with the principal.

"Speak up. We haven't got all day." Frastfil's changes of mood came all at once, with no warning.

The rat looked at him again, stroked bloody paws across its whiskers and carried on eating its dinner. Jackbones poked out his tongue and waggled it from side to side, sticking a finger up his nose at the same time. His cloak slipped to the side and Frastfil turned his head in that direction.

"Is that...?" he began.

Jackbones flicked the cloak back into place.

"What?" said Tadpole.

Frastfil shook his head. "Nothing. I sometimes think I see things, just out of the corner of my eye. You know?"

In some ways it was like Flaxfield's study: walls of books, and little jars and pots and feathers and strange implements. In the most important way it was entirely different. The books were mouldy and mildewed, their spines broken, pages falling out, foxed and frayed. The carpet was greasy. The walls were damp. And a thin layer of green slime covered many of the surfaces.

"Ah," said Frastfil, beaming again, plunging his hands into his pockets and jingling his loose change. "Ah, yes. A scholar's study. You've never seen anything quite like it, eh? The finest place in the world." He leaned forward and lowered his voice. "I don't mind telling you that when I took over this college it was in a pretty poor state. Not the great and wonderful place it is today. Oh, dear me, no. It was run down and failing. I made it what it is today. I changed everything."

"He did," said Jackbones, standing up. "He did. I admit that. He destroyed Canterstock, almost single-handedly, with his stupidity, and weakness, and vanity, and laziness."

"What's that?" asked Frastfil.

"Just the wind," said Tadpole.

"Ah. Yes. Now, be quick with it. What did you come here for?"

"Tell him," said Jackbones, "that Ash sent you."

"Ash sent me."

It was as though Tadpole had run him through with a spear. Frastfil's hands flew to his chest and he gasped.

"Tell him she's started the fight, the war," said Jackbones. "Tell him he's needed for the battle, and that the college will see blood before the week's out."

Tadpole repeated this.

Frastfil screamed. He tried to stand, fell back and fought to get his breath.

"Tell him she expects him to be brave," said Jackbones.

Tadpole told him.

Frastfil nodded. He recovered his breathing. "Are you," he said, with a sly look, "are you on our side?"

"Leave him," said Jackbones. "Open the door. We've got better things to do."

Tadpole followed Jackbones out.

"Come back!" Frastfil ordered him. "Come back."

Jackbones kicked the door shut.

"Let's find Cabbage," he said. "If he's alive, he'll enjoy hearing about this."

"That was fun," said Jackbones.

He let his cloak fall aside and was clear to all now. Not that there was anyone but Tadpole to see him. Sometimes he was solid. Sometimes, as they walked along, Tadpole could see through him still. But he was a different Jackbones from the librarian.

"What's wrong with him?" asked Tadpole. "Why was he grinning all the time?"

"Wants you to like him. Come on. My word, I feel remade. I should have left that library years ago."

He bounced along ahead of Tadpole, thwacking his staff against the corridor walls and setting them booming. The globes overhead shivered and looked about to burst like boils.

"Won't someone hear us?" asked Tadpole.

Jackbones stopped and the roffle ran into the back of him. There was a bit of a tangle, and once Jackbones had sorted it out he said, "Quite right. Should have thought. Quietly does it." And he advanced with an exaggerated air of stealth that made Tadpole giggle again.

When Tadpole spoke again, he kept his voice to a whisper. "When Frastfil came, was the college the way it is in the book?"

"Oh, he was a very young man, then. And not at all promising. His grandfather or uncle or someone had been a very great wizard, or I doubt poor little Frastfil would ever have been made even a master here, certainly never the principal. No one believed that a relative of that great man could be as useless as Frastfil."

"That seems stupid."

They were going downstairs, circling narrow stone steps, Tadpole's roffle pack banging against the walls.

"Way of the world," said Jackbones. "Way of the world. Here we are."

They were in a basement passageway, with racks of uniforms and books and equipment, and a counter for a storeman to stand behind.

"This is where Waterburn lived. Lives."

"What? This place?"

"What's wrong with it?"

Tadpole couldn't find a way to explain that a great library was a fitting place for a wizard, but that an underground storeroom wasn't. Jackbones saw it in his face.

"Don't be fooled," he said. "The person makes the place. The place doesn't make the person."

"I don't understand."

"If a doctor works in a cowshed, is he a cowman?"

Tadpole liked this. Roffles are trained in riddles from a very early age.

"Is he healing people or milking cows?"

Jackbones clapped him on the shoulder. "Good lad. Healing, of course."

"Then he's a doctor."

"If a cowman sets himself up in a doctor's house, is he a doctor?"

"Can he heal people?"

"No. But he can milk a cow if you bring it to him."

"Then he's not a doctor."

"You've got it. You can put a fool like Frastfil behind a big desk, but he'll still be a fool. If a great wizard like Cabbage chooses to work in a storeroom, then he'll still be a great wizard. And you should find out why he's there, rather than think he's wrong."

"Why is he here?"

"Always questions with roffles, isn't it? Now, let's see. It isn't easy to find where he lives."

Jackbones felt his way along the black wall opposite the shelves. Tadpole followed him. In the dim light it was difficult to tell, but he couldn't see anything different about any part of the wall. Jackbones stopped a couple of times and felt more carefully, then moved on.

"It's well hidden," said Jackbones.

"What are we looking for?"

"A door. You won't find it."

This made Tadpole look even more carefully.

They reached a dead end.

"I've missed it," said Jackbones. "We'll have to turn back and try again."

At least the walls were dry and free of slime. Tadpole followed, leaving a bigger space this time between himself and Jackbones. Not long after they'd started the second time, he found a place he remembered. It was a spot where the air seemed not to circulate, and he lingered there.

"What are you doing?" asked Jackbones.

"Sorry. Coming."

Tadpole moved on.

"No. What were you doing?"

"I'm sorry. I wasn't being lazy. It's just that there's a place back there where the smell isn't so bad."

"Where? Show me."

Tadpole retraced his steps. "Here it is." He took a deep breath of the cleaner air.

"Good lad. Stand back."

Jackbones struck the wall with his staff and muttered something. Where the wall had been, a curtain hung.

"We're in," said Jackbones.

He went through and Tadpole followed.

The stink melted away like frozen piss from a jakes in the sun. A few steps took them to a door. Jackbones knocked and went in without waiting to be invited.

For a moment, Tadpole thought it was another of those rooms like Flaxfield's study, that existed in two places at the same time. He thought he was in Flaxfold's kitchen again. Another glance told him that it was not the same room. The likeness was one of stone floor and oak beam, big table and bunches of fresh herbs, of plates and spices, pots and candlesticks. It was comfort and welcome and work and companionship.

"Is this how all wizards live?" he asked.

"Cabbage loved Flaxfold," said Jackbones, as if that ought to do for an answer.

"Perhaps he died with her, in her kitchen."

"I don't think so."

Jackbones moved around the room like a dog looking for

rats. He trod lightly, held himself alert, ready. His eyes travelled over everything, giving it a general view. He let his gaze rest on a few things before he searched again. Sometimes he cast a shadow. Sometimes the light poured through him, leaving no mark.

"That's different," he said, pointing.

"How do you know?" asked Tadpole. The room was so full of interesting things it was hard to see how one difference could stand out.

"Oh, I came here a lot, in the old days. I helped him to set it up." Jackbones crossed to a bookcase that held as many curios as books. "This is new," he said.

Tadpole trotted over and stood on tiptoes to see. Jackbones lifted down a small, clay model of a cat.

"May I hold it?"

"Here you are. Don't drop it."

Tadpole cradled it in his hands. It was light, delicate, made with a sure hand that formed the clay into simple lines that captured the image perfectly.

"It's small. I thought it would be a kitten when I saw it up there."

"No. It's an old cat."

The bones of the hips were visible beneath the skin. The face carried years in its features.

"Put it on the table. Careful."

Tadpole pushed aside a book and a cup and made room for the cat. Jackbones held his hand in the air over the cat's head.

He flexed his fingers and stars showered down, shimmering their slow way to the table and covering the cat.

A pink tongue appeared between the brown clay lips. It licked up a star. The eyes opened. The cat blinked. It lapped another star, and another.

"It likes to eat stars," said Jackbones.

"I know. I saw it before."

"Did you?"

"Waterburn fed it. He made them. How can you do it?"

The cat sat up and shook itself. It licked its fur, finding more stars to swallow. Standing up, it teased a star, lifted its paw delicately to its mouth and popped it in.

"May I stroke it?"

"You can try."

Tadpole reached out a hand and touched the cat. There was nothing of clay about it now. It was all fur and eyes and teeth and tongue. He smiled. The cat paused, looked at Tadpole, hesitated, jumped up and landed in his arms.

"He likes you, child of Megapoir."

Jackbones hadn't spoken. Tadpole looked for another person in the room. It was empty.

"Who's that?"

The cat patted Tadpole's cheek with a soft paw. It licked his nose. The tongue was rough, as a normal cat's. The tingling that it gave was quite new. Touched by starlight.

Jackbones shook his head. "I've never seen anyone — anyone — hold Cabbage's cat before."

Tadpole felt very proud. The cat snuggled up to him and purred.

"If his cat's here, that must mean Cabbage is here, too," said Tadpole.

The cat jumped out of his arms, licked a last star from the table and vanished.

"There's your answer," said Jackbones. "He's not here."

"We can look."

"I've looked. He's not."

"What about the cat? Is it Cabbage, telling us he's all right?"

"Perhaps. Or saying goodbye."

"What do we do now?"

"We keep looking."

The door moved. Tadpole stepped nearer to Jackbones. A nose appeared. For a second, Tadpole rejoiced that the memmont had found him. The nose was followed by a grey-brown face, drooping ears and a dog, half-in, curious, and not a little frightened. Tadpole sighed. The memmont would be safe enough. Probably. Meanwhile the dog stayed half-in, waiting to see how it would be received.

"That you, Tim?" said Jackbones.

The dog came in and stood next to him, not touching, his head down. Tadpole put out a hand to stroke him and the dog flinched and backed away.

"I won't hurt you," said Tadpole.

Tim let him put his hand on his neck and stroke a little.

"Whose dog is he?"

"No one's. He was Sam's friend, once. And Tam liked him. Then Smedge—"

Tim twisted his head round and started to howl.

"Sorry," said Jackbones. He stroked Tim. "Smedge hurt you, didn't he? Do you want me to see if I can make it better?"

Tim pulled away and cowered. He dropped his head lower still, bent his legs and shivered.

"That dog's been whipped," said Tadpole. "Who would do that? Who would hurt an animal? That's terrible."

"I started to tell you," said Jackbones.

Tim howled again, ran to the door, left the room, and came back in again instantly and looked at them. He ran out again. Back in, looking. Out. In. He yelped.

"He wants us to go with him," said Tadpole.

"Clearly."

"Go on, Tim," said Tadpole. "We're following."

"I don't think that's a good idea," said Jackbones.

But Tadpole chased after Tim. Jackbones followed, faster still and pushed past Tadpole.

"Hey, watch out. I nearly fell," said Tadpole.

Jackbones looked over his shoulder at Tadpole and snarled. It was a face of such anger and hate that the roffle stopped. He gasped for breath. The effect of the glare had been like a punch in the stomach. Was Jackbones on the side of the enemy, after all? Had he used Tadpole to find out what was happening?

Tadpole wrapped himself in his cloak for comfort. When he looked up again his worst fears were realized. Jackbones was standing looking straight into the placid, smiling face of Smedge.

There was no way out. The passageway leading to the stairs was blocked by Jackbones and Tim and Smedge. And Jackbones had spread his arms and placed his hands on each wall. Tadpole couldn't even see Smedge any longer.

"I thought you'd left the college," said Jackbones.

"Why should I do that?"

"Why have you come back here?"

"This is a strange sight, Jackbones. Out of the library? Have they had enough of you at last? Did they throw you out?" Smedge was taunting him.

"They left me no choice," said Jackbones. "I had to leave."

Tim's nose poked underneath the hem of Jackbones' cloak. Big eyes looked at Tadpole.

"Is that so?" said Smedge. "And you look, well, shall we say, more solid. Are you returning to the world? What are you doing down here?"

"I came to talk to Waterburn."

"That's interesting. So did I."

"He's not there."

"You won't mind if I pass, then, and look in his kitchen."

Tadpole saw Jackbones move, not aside, but bracing himself to prevent Smedge from coming through.

"You won't be able to do that, Smedge. You know you won't. Waterburn's room is locked."

"You went in?"

"Of course."

Tim scrambled under the cloak and came and curled up at Tadpole's feet.

"Then perhaps I can go in. I have magic, too."

"I don't think so. Who do you think taught Waterburn how to lock a door?"

Tadpole heard surprise in Smedge's voice. "You?"

Jackbones became completely transparent. Tadpole could see through him as clear as through glass. And there stood Smedge. The schoolboy. Neat. Tidy. Combed and washed. His face as innocent as a child's. It was more frightening than Smedge the animal, Smedge the mixture of predators. The disguise was worse than the reality. Tadpole pressed against the wall, to hide, knowing it was no protection. Smedge looked at him and Tim.

"Here, boy," he called. "Come to me."

Tim stood and cowered. Tadpole wanted to reach out and touch him, for comfort. Something told him not to. The moment passed and Jackbones was a barrier again.

"Let me have my dog," Smedge demanded.

"He'll go where he wants," said Jackbones. "He'll find you if he wants to."

Tim pushed himself against Tadpole's legs.

"Where have you been?" asked Jackbones. "While you've been away."

"I had a message to take for Professor Frastfil."

"To Boolat?"

Tim whimpered.

"A message," said Smedge.

"Anything exciting happen while you were away?"

"What sort of thing?"

"Oh, there are kravvins and takkabakks on the loose. People have to be careful these days."

Smedge laughed. "I can take care of myself," he said. "I'm not afraid of them."

"You'd better run along to Frastfil, then. Tell him you're returned."

Jackbones lost solidity again and Tadpole saw Smedge. The mask of innocence slipped and Smedge's face contorted. Not to a different shape, but as the heat from the ground in summer affects the sight. His face shimmered, revealing a malign intent. He recovered quickly, gave a polite smile and turned to go.

"We'll meet again, Jackbones," he said. "Are you planning to leave the college?"

"Report back to Frastfil, Smedge," said Jackbones. "He'll be pleased to see you, I expect."

Tim didn't move. Jackbones waited until Smedge had gone before lowering his arms. Tadpole stood next to him.

"Why couldn't he see me? Was it my cloak?"

"No. I made a blocking spell."

"But he's got magic, too. Couldn't he see through it?"

Jackbones knelt down to stroke Tim, and his face was level with Tadpole's.

"I'm an old wizard," he said. "A sly old wizard. And I've learned more magic than Smedge will ever know. He's got the strength of youth. But I've got the tricks of age."

"Will he come back?"

"I don't think so. He knows he can't get into Waterburn's. Not now. He was hoping it had been left open."

"Is that a good thing?"

"I don't know. If he'd seen Waterburn die, Smedge would think the seal was broken. But if he thought that Waterburn was here, wounded and weak, he might want to carry on the fight. Kill him before he could recover."

"Couldn't you kill him? There and then? While he was alone?"

"Kill him? You take a light view of life, young Tadpole."

"I didn't mean..."

"Have you ever killed anyone?"

Tadpole squirmed.

"I thought not. It's not that simple, killing."

"Smedge isn't a person, is he?"

"No. No, he's not."

"So you could kill him."

Tim was excited. Tadpole didn't know whether he was frightened, or had heard someone coming, or whether he knew what they were saying. And, if he knew, did he want to protect Smedge or did he want them to kill him? Up Top was really very confusing.

"I don't know," said Jackbones. "He's something special,

and I don't know if I could kill him. Even if I wanted to."

"Don't you want to?"

Tadpole really thought now that Tim wanted Smedge dead. He was capering round and whimpering.

"I want to get on," said Jackbones. "And find out who lived through that fight at Flaxfield's. I want to see Cabbage again."

"And where is he, Cabbage? If he's not in his room."

Jackbones looked down.

"Do you know, Tim?" he asked.

The dog leaped up and ran to the stairs. He stopped and looked back at them.

"Perhaps he does," said Tadpole.

"Only one way to find out. Come on."

Tadpole hung back.

"Smedge said Tim was his dog. Can we trust him?"

Tim's face came back round the stair. His tongue lolled out.

"What choice do we have?" asked Jackbones. "Come on."

The porter didn't even come out of the lodge, as they crossed the quadrangle. Tim panted. Jackbones did the seeing-through-him thing again and Tadpole nearly laughed when he finally realized what it reminded him of. Frogspawn. Transparent, but with specks of something here and there.

Frogspawn and Tadpole. He choked back a laugh and Jackbones gave him a warning stare.

Tim led them through the town, back to the gate. He

slipped through first and sat waiting for them to follow. Tadpole, now that he knew what he was doing, wrapped himself in his cloak. Jackbones stayed solid and just gave the guards a curt nod. They weren't so bothered about people leaving.

The sky was grey and low. A fine drizzle settled on them, jewel-dusting the shoulders of Tadpole's cloak. Jackbones led them on, his staff bruising the path.

When they were clear, Tim sat down, lifted his hind leg and scratched his ear. He looked up at them, expectantly.

"Where now?" asked Tadpole.

Tim turned his head to one side.

"Come on, boy," said Tadpole. "Take us to Cabbage."

"You'll have to do that, lad," said Jackbones.

"I don't know where he is."

"No. But neither does Tim. Do you, boy?"

Tim gave a doggy grin.

"He just wanted to be out and away."

Tim ran in circles round them.

"See? Away from Smedge and college."

"Does it rain a lot Up Top?"

"What do you think?"

"No."

"No it is, then."

"What shall we do?"

"Walk with me," said Jackbones. "Follow the road. See where the way leads."

"Really?"

"Why not?"

Tadpole found himself shouting at Jackbones. "This isn't right. It isn't right, at all. I came Up Top just to see the stars. Just to — hey, where are you going?"

Jackbones had set off. Tim sat waiting.

"I'm talking to you," shouted Tadpole.

Jackbones carried on walking. Tadpole ran to catch him up.

"We can't just go anywhere. Listen, I came to see the stars."

"You said that."

"I came to see the stars, and to see some magic. And I wanted to know what it was like Up Top. Just for a day. Just until the kravvins were all gone and it was safe to come up properly. I couldn't wait. That's all. I came because Up Top is beautiful and strange and different. But it's horrible. It's killing. And rain. And clouds. And I mean I like the rain. It's lovely. And the clouds are, well, I love the clouds because we don't have clouds in the Deep World. And I love the bigness of everything and the way the sky never ends. But it's all wrong."

He stopped and Jackbones carried on.

Tadpole shouted at the top of his voice. "It's all wrong. It's not what I want. I want to see the stars."

Jackbones stopped and looked over his shoulder.

"I want magic," Tadpole shouted. "For me. I want to do magic."

He covered his face with his cloak, slipped his roffle pack off his shoulder, sat on it and started to cry.

Tim pushed his face under the cloak and licked the back of

Tadpole's hand. Jackbones came back along the road and laid his hand on the roffle's shoulder.

"Go away," said Tadpole. His voice was muffled by the cloak.

Jackbones walked away.

"No. I didn't mean it. Come back, please."

Tadpole lifted the edge of the cloak and looked. Jackbones waited.

"I'm sorry. I didn't mean go away."

Jackbones held his staff in both hands and leaned on it as he replied, "Say what you mean, Tadpole. Always say what you mean. Frastfil lies. Smedge lies. Ash lies. Don't slip into that. Even by saying what you feel, rather than what you mean."

"I don't understand."

"Take Frastfil. He never meant to tell lies. But under his leadership the college got worse and worse. He could see it, but he didn't like it. So he pretended to himself that everything was all right. He pretended to other people that it was all right. He convinced himself that Ash is good, so that she would help him. In the end, he couldn't tell the truth from a lie. So just say what you mean."

Tim licked Tadpole's face, and he was glad to have the tears disappear without having to wipe them away himself. It was as though he hadn't been crying at all.

"Shall we walk on?" asked Jackbones.

"Where to?"

"We'll see."

Tadpole nodded.

Tim ran ahead, darting back to lick Tadpole's hand again before running on.

"I'm sorry I shouted."

"No need to be. Shouting clears the head. And at least I know what you want, now. I'm sorry that Up Top is such a disappointment."

"It's not."

Jackbones smiled at him. "No?"

"No. Yes. I mean..."

"Say what you mean."

"If I'd seen the things I wanted to see first, then I would like the other things better."

"Everything?"

"Not Smedge. Or the stink in the college. Or Frastfil. Not them."

"Or the kravvins?"

"That's it," said Tadpole. "That's just it. The bad's mixed in with the good. That's what I don't like."

They walked together in silence for a while. The drizzle was turning to hard rain. Tadpole wanted to ask where they were going.

"Jackbones?"

"Yes."

"The woman in the library?"

"Springmile?"

"That's the one."

"What about her?"

"She said that you did something wrong."

"Yes."

"What was it?"

They walked in silence again.

"I wish I'd met Flaxfield," said Tadpole.

"Ah, he was a great man. A great wizard. Do you know, things were getting bad before he died, but since then, it's worse, much worse."

"What was he like?"

"He was like a town. Like a country. There was so much to him, so many aspects. You think you know a place and then, you turn a corner and there's a street you've never seen before, a house you've never visited, a row of shops selling goods you never imagined. That's what Flaxfield was like."

Tadpole didn't really understand this.

"Was he kind?"

"Kind? No."

"No? Why not?"

The road was getting more difficult. Puddles and mud slowed them down. Tadpole's feet grew heavy and clumsy.

"He was gentle. He was fair. He was honest. That's better than kind."

Tadpole stopped.

"What's the point?" he said.

"The point?"

"What's the point of just walking? We don't know where we're going. Have you any idea where Cabbage is?"

"None at all."

"So let's stop. I'm tired."

Jackbones waited.

"Well?" asked Tadpole.

"What do you want?"

Tadpole shook his head.

"Remember you said, back there, that you want to be able to do magic?"

"I was just shouting."

"Tadpole. Say what you mean. Remember?"

"Yes."

"You just have to learn that roffles don't have magic. Never have. I can help with magic, if that's what you want. Is it?"

"Yes." Tadpole spoke with such fierceness that he surprised himself. "Yes. Use your magic. Take us out of here. Get us warm and dry. I'm fed up."

"All right. Where shall we go?"

"To Waterburn."

"I don't know where that is. Think again."

Tadpole closed his eyes and pictured Flaxfold's kitchen. He made sure that Smedge wasn't there. Axestone and Eloise were dead. Waterburn was struggling. Tadpole clenched his teeth. His hand went to the knife in his belt. He closed his fist around it. Starback swooped in. December was crushing kravvins. December? Tadpole opened his eyes.

"What about December?" he asked.

"What about her?"

"I think she might have got away. Not been killed. Remember?"

"Yes."

"We can go to her. Where does she live?"

Jackbones rubbed his hands with pleasure. "There you are," he said. "I told you."

"Told me what?"

"Told you that if we just followed the road, we'd know where it led. It leads to December."

"Can you get us there?"

"It's many days away."

"With magic?"

"With magic, no time at all."

Tim jumped up and down and barked, wagging his tail. Tadpole would have wagged his if he had one. He just had to make do with jumping.

"Where does she live?"

"At the mines," said Jackbones. "Let's go."

The pleasure drained from Tadpole. He stood still.

"The mines?"

"Yes. Are you ready?"

Up Top ~ A Guide for Roffles

THE MINES
Do not go to the mines.

The barrier that prevents magic from coming into the

Deep World is very thin in the mines, and it gets muddled.

The miners are special men. They're hard-bodied, strong and determined.

They live in darkness most of the year. Without them, there would be no kettles or pans, no iron stoves or ploughs. They provide the metal for swords and shields, knives and spearheads. Theirs is the life that gives comfort and strength to others. They work in darkness so that the rest can prosper in the light.

And they guard the boundary between Up Top and the Deep World.

Long ago, roffles helped in the mines.

They didn't dig for the ore.

They watched over the work. They cleared away debris from roof falls. They could squeeze into places too small for men, and rescue buried miners.

And when the miners died, their Finishings were deep below ground. Roffles carried them on their last journeys. Special roffles. Roffles who had given up the everlasting light of the Deep World for the everlasting darkness of the mines.

These roffles spoke little. They forgot their riddles and their roffle talk.

When the wild magic broke through into Up Top, the roffles left the mines. It became too dangerous, even for them.

The wild magic seeped into the mines and made trouble.

Explosions ripped through the tunnels. Fire raced through, consuming everyone. The flames became burning wolves, chasing men and consuming them.

Roof props snapped and turned into poisonous snakes. Miners raced deeper underground to escape them and died, hewing agony out of the rock.

For years the mines were not worked.

As the wild magic died down and was locked in Boolat, the miners returned, but the roffles didn't.

The magic is still muddled in the mines. And now it is malicious. It lurks, weakened, but ready to strike.

The miners live with it. Sometimes, they die from it. Always, they are aware of the dangers. But the mines are their life. And the mines are the life of everyone Up Top.

The first magic came from a mirror.

The mirror came from metal.

The metal came from ore.

The ore came from the mines.

Where magic began, magic runs wild.

Where magic began, magic destroys.

Where magic began, who knows what can happen?

Stay away from the mines.

Tadpole shrugged at the straps of his roffle pack. It helped him to think.

"Do you think she's there?" he asked. "She might have died."

"They all might be dead," said Jackbones. "We don't know. If she's alive, that's most likely where she'll be."

"Does she live in a mine?"

"What do you think?"

"How would I know? It's Up Top. Anything could happen."

Jackbones smiled, more to himself than to Tadpole. "Sorry. Of course it is. I keep forgetting how new this is to you. No, she doesn't live in a mine. She lives in a village where the people are miners. That's all."

"Why?"

"Because people need a wizard. To help them. Someone for when babies are born. For when people die. Someone to bind broken limbs. To make soothing potions and salves. December does this for the people in the mines."

Tadpole sniffed. "It doesn't sound like wizard work."

"Much of it isn't. But there's magic needed as well. And she does that for them."

Tadpole looked around him. The evening was shuffling in, taking possession of the fields and the lane. The rain was steady, indifferent. He looked up at the darkling sky.

"There'll be no stars tonight," said Jackbones.

"You can get us there quickly? By magic?"

"With your help, I can."

"Why do you need my help?"

Jackbones took his staff and held it out to Tadpole. "Take it."

Tadpole grasped the staff, and the two of them were joined at either end of it.

"Side by side," said Jackbones.

They stood, grasping the staff in both hands, like beasts harnessed for the plough. Jackbones started to chant, his voice low, soft, almost beneath hearing. As Tadpole looked, a gatepost began to glow. A gap in the hedge joined it, their lights reflecting back. A tree stump. A boulder at the field edge. All glowed.

"Stop it," said Tadpole. "Stop it. You can't."

He tore his hands away from the staff and jumped clear of Jackbones.

"What are you doing?" he demanded. "That's not allowed."

"You want to go somewhere warm and dry, where there's food and a bed?"

"Not that way."

"I found the way in. Now you have to take me."

"I can't."

"You said you'd help."

Jackbones lifted the staff and the glowing returned, each one a roffle hole, an opening to the Deep World.

"I can find them by magic," said Jackbones. "And, if I want to, I can go in. But I can't find my way around. Very few Up Top people can do that."

"No one can. Only roffles. Stop it. Stop them glowing. People mustn't see them."

"Which one shall we use?"

"None of them. We can't."

Jackbones moved to the tree stump. He put a foot inside the roffle hole. Once he had made sure he was in and couldn't lose it again, he rapped the staff on the ground. The glowing entrances faded and were gone. No sign of any way into the Deep World.

"Come back," shouted Tadpole.

Jackbones turned his back and disappeared. Tadpole ran after him.

Jackbones was waiting just inside. There was a tunnel, with branches leading off. Along one of the paths there was a door. The others led away. It was gloomy, damp, unwelcoming.

Tadpole stood very close. He put himself between Jackbones and the door.

"You've made a mistake," he said. "I don't know how to do this. You have to be taught. If I went through the door I could find my way home, probably. At any rate, someone would help me. But I can't just find my way to the mines. I've never done this before. You know that."

"I do. And I know something else. I know you've got a guide."

"You can't see that." Tadpole sat down on his roffle pack and crossed his arms.

Jackbones walked away, along one of the tunnels. He came back and walked towards the door. Putting his hand to it he pushed. The door moved open a crack. Light tumbled in. He held the door ajar, not looking through it.

"I could take you a different way," he said. "Up Top. Fast. The trouble is, magic leaves a trail. There's a lot of magic about at the moment. Bursts of it. Too many to notice. But if I used the magic I need to get us to the mines, it would be noticed. It would lead Ash to us. It would send Smedge to us. And kravvins. And takkabakks. I can't risk it."

Now that Jackbones was a distance from him, Tadpole stood up and opened the roffle pack. He took out the guide book.

"There are maps," he said. "And diagrams. I think I can understand them."

"Do you know," said Jackbones, "at every big moment in Up Top history, for as long as anyone can remember, there's been a roffle, helping out?"

"Has there?"

"You're that roffle, now."

Tadpole looked at the map, not trusting himself to look at Jackbones.

"I'm just an accident," he said. "I shouldn't have come Up Top."

Jackbones kept his back to the door. His face was dark, his head framed by the light. "No accidents," he said. "Can you see a way to the mines?"

"I wanted to find one through the tunnels, but I can't. They're all near the surface and the same as the roads above them. The only fast way is into the Deep World itself and out through another door."

"Lead on."

"I'm not allowed to. It's forbidden."

Tadpole closed the book and put it away. He shrugged. "There's nothing I can do. I can go to the mines alone. But I have to leave you here."

"What good would that do?" asked Jackbones. "You heard Springmile. We have to go together."

"Up Top people aren't allowed down there any more. It's not like the old days. I'm not allowed to take you in."

"Then we may as well forget it," said Jackbones. "You go home. I'll go back Up Top and see what I can do." He came to Tadpole and held out his hand to shake. "Goodbye, Tadpole. It was good knowing you. I'm sorry I was wrong."

"Wrong? What do you mean, wrong?"

"I thought you were the roffle. The one who's always around when we need one. I thought you had a job and a reason to come to us Up Top. I thought you were someone, not just an accident."

Tadpole glared at him. He wanted to hit him. He wanted to make a magic spell and turn him into a centipede. He slung his roffle pack on to his shoulders, barged past Jackbones, knocking him to one side, and almost ran to the door to the Deep World.

"Come on," he called. "Don't dawdle."

Tadpole threw the door open and walked out of sight. Jackbones smiled and followed.

"Close the door behind you," said Tadpole.

Jackbones closed it and looked around at the Deep World.

After the never-ending light of the Deep World Tadpole felt a strange pleasure in stepping out into the damp night of the village by the mines.

He breathed deeply and looked up at the cloudy sky.

"Darkness is as beautiful as light," he said.

"It is," said Jackbones.

"Nothing ever really goes wrong in the Deep World," said Tadpole. "Not the way it has here."

"Let's hope it stays that way. It's a long time since I was there. I'd forgotten how beautiful the light there is."

Tadpole stared at him. "You've been to the Deep World before?"

"I'm a very old wizard, lad. There's not much I haven't done."

Tadpole shook his head. "You could have told me."

The roffle door was at a street corner. Rows of small houses ran away in four directions. Smoke from chimneys rippled above the rooftops. Tadpole could hear voices of people talking, children laughing. Lights cast shadows on the curtains.

"Where are we going? Have you been here before?"

"I have. Long ago. But I remember."

Jackbones led him to a house near the end of a row. The lights were out. There was no smoke from the chimney. Tadpole strained to hear at the door. All was silence.

"Not here," he said. "It's a wasted journey."

Jackbones put the palm of his hand to the door. Tadpole was growing impatient. He took the door handle and twisted it.

"Locked," he said. "Empty. And it's still raining, and I'm tired."

Jackbones rapped his staff on the door. Three knocks.

Evenly spaced. The handle grew warm. It turned again in Tadpole's hand, moving of its own purpose.

"In," said Jackbones. "Quickly. Come on."

He pushed Tadpole's back. The door opened and he stumbled in. Jackbones slammed it, quickly, silently, the wood making no noise as it struck the frame.

The fire was stoked up and burning well. The lamps gave a warm and welcoming glow. A man was curled up on a bed, his back to them. From an armchair near the fire, December looked up and tried to smile. She raised her hand to Tadpole. Her face and neck were uncovered. The shawl was over her knees. Her smile, through the wasted lips, was a mixed miracle of pleasure and pain.

"You found me," she said.

Tadpole strained to hear the soft words.

Jackbones touched her shoulder as he passed and went and sat on the edge of the bed.

"He's not dead," said December.

"No. But he's as close as you can get to it," said Jackbones.

"I'm sorry I can't offer you any food," said December. "I'm very tired."

Tadpole didn't know what to do. He had never seen grown-ups helpless before.

"I don't mind," he said. "I'm not hungry."

December managed a smile. "Not hungry?"

"Well. A little."

"If you can find food, you're welcome. Perhaps if I..."

She tried to stand. Jackbones, looking over his shoulder, clicked his fingers and she slumped back into the chair. Tadpole ran over to her and took her in his arms. Her destroyed skin seemed to him now more like the pages of an old book, or the dry surface of a warm garden, not ugly, but having a character all of its own.

"Leave her," said Jackbones. "Let her sleep."

He turned the man in the bed and Tadpole saw Waterburn's face.

"Cabbage," whispered Jackbones. "What have you done to yourself, lad?"

He was no more a lad than December was a girl. His face was contorted into a grimace of fear. His hair had half-gone, burned off or ripped out on the left side of his head. His eyes were open, staring, not seeing.

Jackbones cradled him.

"Is he really alive?"

"In a way."

"Can you make him better?"

Tadpole wanted to sit down. It seemed disrespectful, so he stood, his legs tired, his damp clothes clinging to him. The heat from the fire made them smell.

"I can keep him alive, I think. Perhaps even strong enough to walk. Whether his mind will return, or whether he'll ever make magic again, I don't know."

Jackbones laid Cabbage back on the bed, straightened his arms and put a pillow under his head. He stood, shrugged off his cloak and banged the tip of his staff on the floor.

The whole room rang out with a booming shudder.

"People will hear," said Tadpole.

"No. December sealed the room. No sound. No light. No smoke escapes. Stand back, now."

He took a burning coal from the fire with his hands.

"Careful," said Tadpole, forgetting about magic.

"Right back," said Jackbones. "Over there."

Tadpole stood by the door. Breeze stroked his cheek through the door jamb.

Jackbones stood before December, the burning coal in his hand. Tadpole looked on in disbelief.

"What are you going to do?"

"I'm not sure," said Jackbones.

"You don't know?"

"I know. I'm not sure if I should do it."

"Then don't," said Tadpole. "Put the fire back."

Jackbones paused, moved to return the coal to the fire, and, at the last moment, dropped it into December's lap and stepped away.

December flared up like a blazing torch. The flames embraced the ceiling and splashed patterns over the walls. Tadpole pressed himself against the door and drew his arm over his face to shield him from the heat. Peeking over his arm he saw Jackbones, standing firm in front of December. The flames spilled over him and he withstood them, as a sailor faces down the sea spray.

Tadpole screamed at him to stop, to put it out. Jackbones watched her burn. He moved away, ignoring Tadpole, and stood over Waterburn. Tadpole couldn't move. There was no water, nothing to put out the fire. The heat kept him pinned to the door. He thought his own clothes might catch light any moment. He put his hand to his head, to check if his hair was burning.

Jackbones leaned over Waterburn, putting his hand to the wizard's forehead.

"I don't know," he muttered. "I don't know."

The door shook. Tadpole was caught between the blaze and the danger of an intruder.

"Jackbones," he shouted, over the roar of the fire. "Jackbones."

"Shh. Not now."

The door shook again, and something hard rapped at it.

"You have to listen."

Tadpole could hear the harsh, metallic rattle of the kravvins. In his mind's eye he saw their blank faces. He could hear their brittle chanting. Kill. Eat. Kill.

Jackbones waved his request away.

The door shook and the handle turned.

"The spell's broken," he shouted. "The door's opening."

There was nowhere for Tadpole to go. Fire in front of him and attackers from behind.

The door pushed him aside and he stumbled to his knees.

✠

Tadpole fell to the floor. His cloak covered his head. His roffle pack banged on his back. He hurt his wrist, putting his hands out to break his fall.

The door slammed behind him. They were in the house. And he was helpless. His only hope was that the cloak stopped them seeing him and he could crawl away. Perhaps go for help. But could he leave Jackbones alone to fight them?

He kept perfectly still, hoping they couldn't see him.

"You don't think that cloak makes you invisible, do you?"

He knew the voice. It hurt to move. His knees were banged. His wrist sent stabs of pain when he steadied himself with his hand.

"Come on. Up you come."

A strong hand lifted him to his feet. The cloak was tangled over his head. He swept it aside.

"That's better. Are you all right?"

Smith stood like a tree, looking down at him. He was wet from the rain. His sleeves were rolled up and he held a short, heavy hammer in his left hand.

"Took some getting that door open," he said. "Good spell," he called across to Jackbones.

"Not mine. December made it."

Tadpole looked at the armchair. The blaze had given way to a steady fire. The flames didn't reach the ceiling now. December was a candlewick, glowing in a raindrop of fire, but not consumed. Sometimes it seemed as though her skin was smooth and healed. Then the flame flickered and it was puckered and stretched and scarred.

Smith stepped over to her. As he moved away, Tadpole could see that Tamrin had been hidden behind him. Something made him pleased to see her.

"You're alive," he said. The pleasure rushed to his face, and, despite the terrible sight of December burning and Cabbage lying stricken, he found he was smiling a broad smile of joy.

"Of course I am," she said. "What did you think? Did you think Smedge could kill me? Even for a roffle you don't know much, do you?"

Tadpole looked away. He felt that Tamrin was still glaring at him. It was impossible to look at her now. Smith put his hand into the flames sweeping round December. He touched her cheek.

"She's cool," he said.

Jackbones sighed and almost smiled. Tadpole understood that the wizard had been waiting for some sign that he had done the right thing.

"Let the flames die down completely," said Jackbones. "It's the only way."

"What about Cabbage?"

"I can't think. I don't know what to try."

Smith joined him and they looked down on Cabbage together. Tamrin went to December and sat on the floor next to her. She slipped her hand into the woman's.

Tadpole just wanted to walk out and close the door behind him, find the nearest roffle hole and go home. He didn't belong here. They all knew what to do, and he didn't. He tried to pretend that he wasn't there.

"You found us," said Jackbones.

"No," said Smith. "We weren't looking for you. We came for December. And for the mines. And we hoped that Cabbage would be here as well. Tamrin came to me after the fight."

"She's all right?" asked Jackbones.

"I'm here," said Tamrin. "You can ask me."

"I can see that you're here," said Jackbones, "but I didn't think you wanted to answer questions. Not after the way you spoke to my friend."

"What friend?"

Jackbones didn't bother to answer her.

"Tamrin was shaken badly," said Smith. "But not hurt. Not too much."

"What about Sam? Did she say what happened to him?"

"I'm here," Tamrin said again. "I'm here. All right? And I was there. I saw it. If you want to know, you can ask me."

Jackbones spoke softly. "Tam, we know you're upset."

"I'm not upset. I'm angry."

"We know you're upset, but that's no reason—"

"I'm. Not. Upset. Understand?" Her face was red and she gripped December's hand. "I'm angry. That's all."

"Stop shouting. Please."

"Then stop saying I'm upset. And stop staring at me. And you, roffle — what are you looking at?"

Tadpole looked away again. He couldn't meet her eyes.

Smith nodded to him and half-smiled. Jackbones spoke to Tamrin again.

"It's all right," he said. "Why don't you come and help us?"

Tadpole thought that something had happened to her. At first, there was no answer. After that, a noise, like a chicken having its neck pulled. He looked at her. Her face was lost in tears. She moved her lips but no words came.

"Look after her, Tadpole, will you? We're busy," said Jackbones.

"What? Me?"

"Go on."

Smith and Jackbones leaned over Cabbage again.

Tadpole moved towards her.

"Go away," she said.

He stopped and waited. She put her hands to cover her face.

Tadpole sat on the other side of December, on the floor, so that he was the same height as Tamrin. The flames had gone from December's body, and only the last few crowned her head.

"I've been frightened ever since I arrived," he said. "I was most frightened when the kravvins were attacking."

Tamrin kept her face covered, her head half-turned.

"I wanted to fight. I wanted to help. I was too frightened to do anything. I was so glad when you pushed me out through the door. And I was grateful and relieved at the same time. And ashamed. Ashamed to leave you."

"It's all right." Her voice was muffled. "You had to get out."

"And now Waterburn's dying. Cabbage. And I like him more than anyone. He was kindest to me."

December's hand moved and touched his head. She stroked him. He looked up. Her face was as ever. Her lips smiled. Her eyes were bright again, and her touch was strong. The flames had all gone.

"He was always kind," she said. "Always." She looked down at Tamrin. "And you, Tam, you were kind, too, before the trouble at the college."

"Well," said Tamrin. "Kind doesn't get you anywhere."

December stroked Tamrin's cheek. She sat up in the chair. "It was kind of you to come and help me."

"We need you to fight with us."

December looked across at Cabbage.

"You two," she said. "Leave him alone."

"He'll die if we don't help him."

"He'll die if you do. Come away. Let these two try."

Jackbones kept his back to her. "He was my apprentice. I taught him. I gave him an example. If he dies now, it's my fault."

"He's not been an apprentice these long years," she said. "Come away. That time's past. Your time's past. It's time for these two. Stand aside and let them near."

Jackbones stood and put his hands to his back, stretched his shoulders and moaned. "Aches and pains. Leaning over's no good."

"Then stand up and move away."

Jackbones did as he was told, and Smith joined him.

"You're a nuisance again, now you're better," he said. "I should have left you."

"To die?" Her voice was pleasant in its mockery.

"You don't know how sweet that sounds," said Jackbones.

December stood and steadied herself. She put her arms around the librarian. "Perhaps you'll get your wish," she said. "Soon."

Tamrin was already at Cabbage's bedside. She motioned for Tadpole to join her.

"What did you like best about him?" she said. "Think."

"He was kind to me."

"What else?"

Tadpole thought. The rain danced on the window.

"He made stars for me," he said.

"Right. That'll do."

Tamrin put her hands on Cabbage's cheeks. She bent over him and blew on his closed eyes.

"Vengeabil," she said. "Old storeman. Vengeabil. There's a roffle here who wants stars."

She blew again. A small star came from her lips and hovered over Cabbage's face.

"It's all I have," she said. "I'm tired. I was hurt."

The star flickered. It looked tired, too.

"Come on," she whispered. "Let's have stars."

Tadpole saw a movement, under Cabbage's head. The corner of the pillow lifted and the old cat peered out. Eyes, whiskers, a nose. It pushed forward. The ears followed. Its eyes were fixed on the star. It wriggled free and came and sat on Cabbage's chest. The star hovered. The cat leaped and licked it up. It landed back on Cabbage as light as mist. It looked at him, waiting.

"Come on," whispered Tamrin. "Come on, Vengeabil."

The cat lifted a paw and patted Cabbage's face. He made no response; his breathing was shallow and fast.

"There's a roffle here, wants to see you," said Tamrin.

The cat put out its tongue and licked Cabbage's cheek.

"Nothing," said Tamrin. "It's no good. I've tried. Sorry."

The cat moved away and pushed its face under the pillow. Tamrin started to stand up.

"Wait," said Tadpole. "Look."

A star fell on the cat's tail. It twisted its head back and saw it.

"See," said Tadpole. "A star."

The cat whirled round, chasing its tail. The star clung to it.

"Careful," said Tamrin.

Another star. And another. They fell softly from above the cat, sprinkling it with light. The cat jumped and caught them, darted and pawed them, licked them up from the bedspread, from its fur, from Cabbage's cheeks.

"Yes," shouted Tamrin. She wrapped her arms around Cabbage's neck and hugged him.

"You'll strangle him," December warned her.

Tamrin let him go and she hugged Tadpole instead. He

put out a hand to push her away, thought better of it and hugged her back.

December slipped past them and sat by Cabbage. She stroked his cheek and murmured to him. Tadpole couldn't catch what she was saying. It was half-speech, half-song.

The cat finished the stars and, without warning, dissolved away.

"Is he all right now?" asked Tamrin. "He must be. He made the stars again."

"Not quite," said December. "But better. Much better. You did a good job. Now eat. There'll be food if you look."

Tamrin was suddenly sick-looking. Her excitement died. Her face was grey. Her hands shook. Tadpole tried to touch her shoulder. She moved away, with an apologetic shrug.

"It's costly, magic," said December. "She'll be all right soon. Give her time."

"Help me with this, lad," said Smith. He had found eggs and butter, bread and fruit. "You cut the bread. Can you do that?"

Tadpole gave a clear and rather impertinent signal that cutting bread was no problem for a roffle, and Smith tossed a chuck of butter into a pan he had put on the range. It hit the metal and sizzled. Smith broke eggs into a bowl, whisked them with a fork and poured them into the pan.

Soon, they were sitting down to bread and butter with scrambled eggs. December had lifted Cabbage, and he lay on the bed, supported by her, and taking a little of the eggs and trying to speak.

"Not yet," she said. "You were hurt most of all. You'll take a little longer."

"Tomorrow," he managed to say.

"Maybe tomorrow. We'll see."

Tadpole found a space between mouthfuls to speak to Jackbones. "You're not eating," he said.

The man played with some eggs on the end of his fork. He raised it to his lips, paused and lowered it again.

"I'm not hungry," he said.

"But you need to eat," said Tadpole.

Smith spooned some more eggs on to Tadpole's plate.

"Eat up," he encouraged him. "Bedtime soon."

"But we've got lots to do," said Tadpole. He watched Jackbones push his plate away.

"First, we sleep," said Smith.

Tadpole and Tamrin argued most, but it was soon clear that the older ones were as tired as they were. There was a neat bedroom upstairs, where Tamrin and Tadpole took a small bed and a couch. Smith managed to get comfortable in an armchair. The last thing Tadpole remembered before falling asleep was the rain running down the window as he looked, unsuccessfully, for stars through the cloud. When he woke, the night had fled and a clear, blue sky promised a better day.

Tadpole was first down in the morning. December was asleep on the bed and Cabbage had started to make breakfast. He opened his arms and let Tadpole crash into him.

"I thought you would die," he said.

"Not this time," said Cabbage. "Thank you for helping me."

"It was Tamrin."

"And you, I think. Here, do you like bacon?"

"Does a dog sing acorns when the sun is green?" asked Tadpole.

They laughed.

"That's a yes, I suppose," said Cabbage, tipping bacon and mushrooms on to a plate, which he put before the roffle. "Make a start. The others can catch up."

Between mouthfuls, Tadpole tried to get the wizard to talk.

"Why do wizards have so many names?"

"Well, I've only got three. A nickname. A proper name, and Vengeabil, a name for hiding in the college. That's not so many, is it? You've got two."

Tadpole had to admit that this was so.

"And, please, tell me all about what happened after I left the house."

"Eat your breakfast. Time for that when we're all gathered."

"Do I smell bacon?" asked Smith, coming down the stairs.

The sunshine outside, the food, the company, the breakfast table filling up, and December and Waterburn both recovered, all raised Tadpole's spirits, and he was happy as the meal drew to its close. Up Top was turning out to be more exciting than he had expected. Now that he felt part of it, he began to enjoy himself, even the sharp, seasoned tang of danger.

He watched Jackbones carefully. The man played with his food again, and again he pushed his plate away without eating.

The table cleared, December and Waterburn and Tamrin told their story.

"The fight was terrible," said December. "There was no end to the kravvins. It's easy to kill them, but they keep on pouring in. In the end, tiredness and the battle against pain defeat you."

"And Smedge," said Waterburn. "His magic is like a sickness that lives inside you. He probes and pierces. He finds weaknesses you never knew you had, and then he strikes."

"But how could he kill Flaxfold?" asked Smith. "She's..." He struggled for words. "She's the most ... I mean, she *is* magic."

There was silence.

"It was Flaxfield," said December, at last. "Without him, she's weakened. We never noticed. She hid it well. But it was there. It was Flaxfield's death that opened the door for Ash and Smedge. Smedge knew that. I think that's why they attacked her there."

"Where she seemed strongest," said Cabbage.

"Exactly. In her own home. In Flaxfield's old house. His absence is greater there than anywhere else."

"So the kravvins made her weak and Smedge struck home," said Cabbage.

Tamrin banged her fist on the table. "And we'll strike

back," she said.

"All in good time," said Smith. "What happened next?"

"There is no 'next', really. It all seemed to happen at once," said Cabbage. "Axestone fell. Killed the same way."

"Eloise fought bravely," said December. "But they picked her off."

"It was Starback," said Tamrin. "Starback turned the struggle our way. Once I'd got Tadpole out of the way, Starback drove them back."

"I was badly hurt," said December. "I escaped, with Cabbage."

"You saved my life," said Cabbage. "If you hadn't got me away, they were killing me."

December shook her head. "I saved myself," she said. "And brought you with me. I ran away."

"I chased Smedge," said Tamrin. "I was going to kill him. I will kill him."

"But he got away?" said Smith.

There was no need for an answer to this.

"Where's Sam?" asked Tadpole. "What happened to him?"

The others all looked at Tamrin. "I don't know. I can't hear him." She dragged her sleeve over her face. "I'm alone," she said. "Completely." ‖

Smith seemed too big

for December's small room. He paced as much as he could while the table was being cleared. He lifted the curtain and looked out into the street. He put his ear to the front door and listened.

Tadpole could see that Tamrin was getting annoyed. Smith kept walking too close to her and she had to move her feet out of the way every time he passed. Not that she could complain. If she'd helped to do the dishes she wouldn't have been in his way.

Jackbones sat on the edge of the small bed in the corner.

Tadpole sat on his barrel and watched. He waited until the clatter of washing-up had finished and then he asked, "What are we going to do now?"

No one spoke. Smith stopped pacing.

Tadpole looked at them in turn. "Well?" he asked.

They stared back at him.

"Are we just going to sit here?"

"We're waiting," said December.

"What for?"

"I'm not waiting," said Smith. "I'm going out soon. It's why I came here."

"Where are you going?" asked Tadpole. "And what are you waiting for?" he asked December.

"I'm going down the mines," said Smith.

"And we're waiting to be told what to do next," said December.

And there was silence again.

Tamrin behaved as though she had never seen Tadpole before. She didn't look at him or pay him any attention. Cabbage gave him an encouraging smile. December sat and stared into the fire.

"Jackbones," said Tadpole.

The old wizard started, as though he had not been paying attention. Tadpole noticed that the wall behind Jackbones, hung with a tapestry, was visible through the man's body. Jackbones gathered himself and was solid again.

"What is it?"

"You brought me here. What should we do now?"

"I don't know. I was just looking for Cabbage."

Tadpole crossed and shook the man's shoulder.

"What's happened to you? You were better yesterday. Now you're like you were in the library."

"It's all right," said Cabbage. He took Tadpole's hand and led him away. "It's been a long time, Tadpole. He'll be all right."

"I'll get going, then," said Smith. "Will you wait here?"

"We'll see what happens," said December. "Take care."

"Come on, then, lad," said Smith, and he laid his hand on Tadpole's shoulder.

"What?"

"We're off down the mines."

Tadpole sprang to his feet, pulled his roffle pack away from Smith and hoisted it on to his back.

"I'm not going there," he said.

"You have to. I need a roffle. It's the mines."

"No. I can't." He looked to December for support. "I don't have to, do I?"

She didn't answer.

Tamrin snorted. Tadpole glared at her.

"What's the matter with you?" he said.

"You may as well go now. It'll save time," said Tamrin.

"I don't understand," he said. "If it's up to me, then I'm not going."

Tamrin turned to the others for help. "Doesn't he know anything?" she asked.

Cabbage's face was stern. "Be kinder, Tam. Remember how hard it is to learn." He relaxed and smiled. "Gentle teachers are best. Remember?"

Tamrin blushed. She spoke to Tadpole with a softer manner. "It's your choice," she said. "But it's not for you to choose. Sometimes, things choose you, you don't choose them."

December, who had been uncovered the whole time that Tadpole had been in her house, drew her shawl around her face and looked deeper into the fire.

"What happens if I accept it?" he asked.

Tamrin began to answer and he interrupted her. "I'm asking December," he said.

December tightened her shawl at her neck. "If you accept what has chosen you, then you accept whatever it brings," she said.

"And if I don't accept it?"

Her reply was a long time coming.

"Then you're just another roffle," she said. "And you could have stayed at home, in the Deep World."

Tadpole felt sick.

"No," said Cabbage. "No. You're not just that. You're our friend. You're my old friend's family. You'll never just be another roffle."

"I can't go there. I'm not a mine roffle," Tadpole said to Smith. "They were special."

"You're a roffle," he replied. "And in an emergency, you'll do. Anyway, I'm off. I have to go. If I can't have your help, I'll have to make do without it."

He swung the door open and walked out.

Tadpole didn't know what to do. He shuffled his roffle pack on his shoulders, straightening it.

"Are you going?" asked Tamrin.

"I don't know."

"Do you know where the mine entrance is?"

"No. Will you come with me if I go?"

"No."

"Please."

"No. It hasn't chosen me."

Tadpole looked to the others for help. December kept her shawl tight around her face. Cabbage shrugged.

"Jackbones," he said. "Will you come, please?"

"Of course." He stood, took a moment to steady himself, and started to move.

"No," said Cabbage. "I'm sorry, Tadpole. You'll go with Smith or not at all." He gently helped Jackbones to sit again and put his arm around his shoulders.

"If you wait, you'll never find the way," said Tamrin.

Tadpole left, closing the door behind him. The road was empty, save for the figure of Smith, walking with purpose and long strides. The houses stretched in both directions, all the same, small, neat and silent.

"Wait for me," Tadpole called.

He raced after Smith and caught him up just after the man had turned to the left.

"I'm coming with you," he said, trying to catch his breath.

"Yes."

Tadpole wasn't happy with this answer. He would have liked a thank you, or a word of approval.

They made their way in silence. The mine lay a little way beyond the village boundary.

"Will there be kravvins?" Tadpole asked as they reached open ground.

"Tell me if you see any," said Smith, which wasn't the sort of answer Tadpole wanted, either.

He trotted alongside. There was a mingled manner in the big man. Tadpole found him daunting, a person who might be dangerous. But that was also a comfort to the roffle. He felt the danger would be to other people.

They reached the mine entrance all too soon. Tadpole stopped and looked at it, preparing himself for the darkness. Smith made no pause at all. His strides carried him into the black space framed by the rough wooden props.

"Please," Tadpole called. "Give me a moment to get ready." He waited. Nothing happened. "Please?"

Smith reappeared.

"It's best just to go in," he said. "Don't think about it."

"But why? Why are you going in? It's dangerous. What do you need to go there for? And why do you need me?"

Smith came out again and stood next to Tadpole. Together they looked into the darkness.

"I need iron," he said. "For my work. This is where it's mined."

Tadpole shook his head.

"I'm a roffle," he said. "Remember? I know all about slippery answers and riddles. Tell me why you're really here."

"For iron."

"There's iron at the forge, waiting to be worked. I saw it."

"There is. But there's iron and iron. It's different from different parts of the mine. And I need a different sort of iron."

Tadpole took a moment before he answered. It seemed an honest reply.

"What do you need it for?"

Smith started to move again. "Are you coming in with me or not?"

"I suppose so."

"Lead on, then."

"What?"

"I don't know where to find it. Only the roffles know that."

Tadpole could have stood on his barrel and pummelled the man's head.

"But I'm not a mine roffle. I don't know what to do, where to go, where to look."

"Off you go," said Smith. "I'll follow."

For a reason he didn't understand, Tadpole did as he was told and walked into the gaping entrance. ‖

Wooden rails led into the mine,

to carry the trucks bringing out the ore. Tadpole followed the lines until the light died and it was no longer possible to see. The walls seemed to press in on him, the roof to lower. He stopped.

"I can't go any further."

"Why not?"

"Why not? Because I can't see, that's why not. It's dark."

His voice bounced back at him.

"What did you expect?" asked Smith.

"We can't go any further."

"We must. I need the iron."

Tadpole slammed his roffle pack to the floor and sat on it and folded his arms.

"Well, you lead, then. I can't. I can't even see you."

He waited for Smith to reply. And waited.

"I said, 'You lead'," he said again.

The roof timbers creaked. The air whispered past his face.

A sound like rats, or cockroaches, scratched along the floor. He lifted his feet, just in case.

"Are you still there?" Tadpole called.

His voice bounced back again, distorted, now.

"This isn't funny," he said. "I'm going back out."

He moved his feet, feeling for rats. Getting down from his barrel, he pushed his toes around, looking for the rails. Now that he had left them, they were hard to find again. He reached out for a wall, to get his bearings. His hand found a corner. He stooped, followed the floor away from the wall with his hands and got hold of a rail. It was a cross-piece. The track divided here.

"Which way?" he said.

A rat ran over his hand. Tadpole jumped up and tripped over his pack. His shin banged against a rock and he shouted out. He grabbed his pack, hoisted it up and pressed against the wall. More noises now. Murmuring. Kravvins? Some creature of mine magic?

"Please," he whispered. "Please, Smith. Are you there?"

Tadpole's head was against the rough stone of the wall. He heard rustling. And voices? Or was it laughter? He wrapped his cloak around him.

For long minutes nothing happened. He was too fearful to speak, too frightened to move, too anxious to stay still. He tried to work out whether the breeze had come from deeper in or from the entrance. It must be from the entrance. And the voices? If they were voices. Which way were they? He had to move away from them, towards the breeze.

Feeling his way along the wall with his hands, he began to move. At least it was dry.

His confidence began to return. He moved with more certainty. The breeze grew stronger. Perhaps it was a trick of his eyes, but he thought there was a little light. He stopped, turned his head. A shape to his left, brawny and tall.

"Smith," he said. He kept the anger out of his voice, stopped himself from shouting at the man. "What are you doing? That's a mean trick. Why didn't you answer?"

The light grew, and Tadpole saw that it was coming from him. His cloak was glowing. With every breath he took it glowed brighter. The mine had opened up. He wasn't in a tunnel any more, but a cavern, wide and high. He was pressed against just one wall. The light was not strong enough to pick out the roof or the further wall.

But it did show that the man was not Smith.

He was as tall as Smith, and as menacing. A shirt with sleeves rolled up showed thick arms, strong wrists. The skin was patterned with black lines. He held a short pick in his left hand.

"Roffle." The voices Tadpole had heard whispered out a gathered sigh.

Tadpole secretly put his hand to his belt and grasped his knife under his cloak.

"Knife," they whispered. The voices had faces. Rows and rows of them. All men. They gathered behind the man who towered over Tadpole. The roffle and the big man stood alone in a space at the entrance to the cavern. The crowd formed a semi-circle, facing them. Tadpole could turn and run, into the darkness. He stepped back, and bumped into Smith, who was concealed round the corner.

Smith placed his hand on Tadpole's back and sent him staggering into the cavern. He stopped himself hardly a foot away from the man.

The voices laughed, and Tadpole remembered the throng that gathered in the galleries high above him in the library. Like them, these figures held back. They shimmered, and their faces came and went. Only the man at the front was clear, solid. Too solid. Too clear. Too big. And with a short pick, the handle in his left hand, the head weighed in his right.

"Roffle," the voices said again.

Tadpole looked up at the big man.

"Does a squirrel make a meal of a seven-stoned peach?" he asked him.

"Does a roffle bring a Smith to the Finished Mine for a joke?" said the man.

"Smith. Smith. Smith," sang the soft voices.

"Come in, Smith. Stand by your roffle," said the man.

Smith emerged from the shadow. They faced each other, level height, level gaze, Smith's hammer and the miner's pick in opposite hands.

"This is Tadpole," said Smith. "He led me here."

"He knew the way?"

"You know my name, and his," said Smith.

It was a challenge and an invitation, not a request.

"I'm Bearrock."

"Bearrock," sang the voices, deep and steady. "Bearrock, the miner."

"The roffle led you here?"

"He didn't know what he was doing," said Smith.

"You did?"

"Yes."

"Why did you follow, then?"

"To see you."

"Me?" Bearrock raised his pick.

"All of you."

"All of us," they chanted.

"No one leaves the Finished Mine," said Bearrock.

"No. I know."

"Hey," said Tadpole. "What's going on? What's the Finished Mine? And why does no one leave? I'm not staying."

"So why did you follow, Smith?"

"I need iron."

Bearrock smiled. "There is iron in plenty where you come from."

"Excuse me," said Tadpole. "What do you mean? What's the Finished Mine?"

"It's where miners go, after their Finishing," said Smith.

The faces disappeared. Only Bearrock remained.

"Finished," whispered the voices. "Finished."

Slowly, the figures returned, their faces looking towards Tadpole.

"It's where the first iron was ever mined," said Smith. "The iron that made the mirror."

"Just the mirror?" asked Bearrock.

The way he asked made Tadpole know that he was mocking the smith, that he already knew the answer.

"Other things, too," said Smith.

"Other things," they whispered.

"Long ago," said Smith. "And now, I need more."

"The iron is here," said Bearrock. "But you can never take it away. You've come too far. You should have asked us to bring it to you."

"Too far," they whispered.

"Those days are gone," said Smith. "I need it now."

"No one leaves the Finished Mine," said Bearrock.

"No one has," Smith agreed.

"The iron will be no use to you. You can't take it away from here."

"I need it."

"Then come and take it," said Bearrock.

He took Smith's arm, and, to Tadpole's amazement, Smith allowed him to lead him away, deeper into the cavern, towards the centre, beyond where the light of his cloak shone.

"Stop," he shouted.

Smith looked over his shoulder. "You did well," he said. "Go back."

"You said I can't."

"You're a roffle," said Smith.

"Roffle," they whispered.

"Go back," said Smith. And he vanished into the darkness beyond sight.

"Go back. Go back. Go back." The whispers grew and swelled to a shout.

Tadpole grabbed his cloak, turned and fled. In the light he could see the many twists and passageways in the mine-working. It was a network of low, narrow tunnels. He didn't stop to think or guess or try to remember. He just ran, taking any turning at random, until he saw daylight ahead. His cloak dimmed. He slowed down. By the time he was a few paces from the mine entrance no light came from him at all. He paused at the opening, looked out, with cautious eyes. Seeing it was clear, he stepped out.

Instantly a sheet of blackness fell over him. Strong hands grabbed him, and pinned his arms to his sides. He tried to call out. Whatever had smothered him soaked in the sound and nothing came out. A foot kicked the back of his knee and he fell to the floor.

"Kill."

"Eat."

"Girl."

"Eat."

"Kill."

Kravvins all around him. They clicked and scurried.

Tadpole shuddered as he imagined their legs crawling over him, stabbing him, their blank faces and their hard mouths.

"Gone."

"No. Here."

"No. Gone"

"Kill."

"Gone."

"More kill."

"There."

"Kill here."

"Girl."

"Gone."

Fewer voices. Less scratching.

Tadpole had ceased to struggle and lay still in the darkness. The hands still gripped him. Painful fingers dug into his arms. He wanted to call out in protest. Fear and the smothering darkness prevented him.

"Kill."

The kravvins sounded distant now.

"Eat."

He strained to hear them.

The last of the voices faded. The clicking and the scratching ceased. The hands relaxed. Tadpole wriggled.

"Wait. Quiet."

He stopped.

"Shh."

A blade of light cut through the darkness. His arms were

free. He pushed at the covering.

And saw Tamrin.

She pulled her cloak away from him and stood up. He staggered to his feet.

She put her finger to her lips.

"This way. Come on."

She led him round and over the mine entrance. They settled behind a mound of big rocks.

"What's going on?" he asked.

"I was waiting for you. I hid us under my cloak."

"What's happening? Where are the others?"

"Follow me," she said. "And make sure you're properly covered when we get close."

They climbed the hill behind the mine opening and skirted round to a high point overlooking the town.

"Cloak," said Tamrin.

They wrapped themselves securely and she moved closer to the houses.

Kravvins swarmed everywhere. There were bodies in the streets. To the other side of the town, kravvins chased escapers, stabbing and falling on them to devour them. Houses blazed. Fires leaped from roof to roof.

"Where are the others?" asked Tadpole. "Cabbage?"

"They fought off the kravvins. December's house was the first target. I escaped from the back to get you while the others protected the front. When I was clear, they counterattacked." Tamrin's eyes shone with joy. "You should have seen the magic. It was fierce. Of course, kravvins are like ants. They don't care how many of them are killed. They keep coming at you. But it gave December and the others time to raise the alarm. They drove as many of the people as they could out of their houses and into the countryside."

They looked down at the devastation and slaughter.

"Those that are left were too slow," she whispered.

"Can't you do something?"

"If I tried, they'd come at us again. No. You and I need to get away."

"Who's that?" asked Tadpole.

"Where?"

He pointed.

A tall woman stood at the edge of the town, directing the battle. She motioned to the kravvins where to go, when to strike, how to find stragglers. She strode up and down, her long grey gown flowing out behind her, the breeze lifting her hair.

"That's Ash," said Tamrin. "No. It can't be." Her face was a mask of pain. "She's locked away. Sealed in." Tamrin's hand went to her throat and she clasped a metal pendant on a leather cord.

The woman in grey paused. She lowered her arms and looked around her.

"She's looking for us," said Tamrin. "Hide."

She pulled Tadpole to one side and they ducked behind more rocks, flat on their faces. Tadpole was winded and he grazed his cheek. More Up Top unpleasantness.

They peered over the edge. The woman was looking away from them. The kravvins had stopped ransacking the town and gathered around her, waiting. She divided them into cohorts and sent them out, searching, hunting.

"She's looking for us," said Tamrin. "We have to get out of here."

She scrambled away, keeping low.

"Wait," said Tadpole. "Look."

Ash flickered and lost her edges. For a moment her face was a dog, mouth wide, jaws slobbering. In an instant she was herself again.

"It's Smedge," said Tamrin. "It's not Ash."

"Then why...?"

"I don't know."

The Smedge-Ash creature turned its head in their direction and sent a cohort of kravvins their way.

"Time to get out," said Tamrin.

Tadpole and Tamrin didn't stop until it was nearly night. The sun, long hidden behind cloud, touched the horizon.

"Can we stop, please?" asked Tadpole.

"Soon. We need to be sure."

"It's ages since we started off. We haven't seen a single kravvin. They're not following."

Tamrin slowed down. "You're probably right. But we need to be sure." She stopped and listened. The evening crept towards them across the fields, following the sinking sun.

"Where are we going to sleep tonight?" asked Tadpole.

"Roffles," said Tamrin, and she smiled. "If it's not your stomach it's your sleep."

Tadpole sat down on his pack, glad of the rest.

"What's wrong with that?" he asked. "You can't live without food or sleep."

"True. But you shouldn't live for them."

Tadpole might have taken offence earlier, when she was being surly. Her tone was different now, lighter, and friendly.

"So, where are we going to sleep tonight?"

"We'll have to rough it," she said. "Your cloak will keep you warm, and the trees will cover us. And—" she stopped Tadpole from speaking again — "before you ask, I'll catch us something to eat. You won't go hungry."

Tadpole looked up at the sky. It was dark enough now. No stars. The cloud gathered overhead.

"This way," said Tamrin. "We'll need water as well."

Cutting across a hay meadow, she followed the slope of the ground until it led them to a small stream.

"This should do," she said.

Tadpole was delighted with the ease and speed she showed in getting their dinner.

"You'd better make the fire," she said.

"Oh, I'll watch what you do," said Tadpole.

Tamrin crossed her arms and stared at him.

"Are we starting to be friends?" she said.

Tadpole nodded with enthusiasm.

"Then don't treat me like an Up Top fool. Get some sticks

and bigger wood, find the roffle fire in your pack and get it blazing. Come on."

"Sorry."

"That's all right."

He kept an eye on her while he prepared the fire. She picked low-growing leaves and brought them. She took out a knife and dug into the damp earth by the side of the stream, finding roots, which she placed on the leaves. Last of all, she made her way back into the hay meadow and stretched out on the ground, her arms in front of her.

Tadpole washed the roots in the stream. While his back was turned he heard a squeak and a snap. Tamrin came back with a rabbit, its head dangling to one side.

"You've got a can in that pack as well, have you?" she asked.

Tadpole admitted that he had.

They sat together by the fire. Tadpole boiled water in the little can. Tamrin skinned and gutted the rabbit, throwing the innards, the skin, feet and head into the stream. They chatted while they worked.

"Will the others be all right?" asked Tadpole.

"They should be. It's the townsfolk who need to worry. The ones who survive have nowhere to live."

"When can we join them again?"

"I don't know. We're not going to try. They'll do what they have to do, we'll do what we have to."

She sharpened a stick and drove it lengthways through the rabbit.

They held an end of the stick each and turned the rabbit over the glowing coals. The scent of roasting drifted up. Small drops of fat fell on to the fire, making it blaze and fade.

The rabbit, the roots, the leaves and some fresh water from the stream made an excellent dinner. By the time they were finished, Tadpole's face glowed with grease and pleasure.

They settled down for the night on the margin of the fire's warmth. The orange glow streaked Tamrin's face, and Tadpole was comforted by her presence.

"No stars, still," he said.

"They're up there. You'll see them."

"Not tonight."

"No."

Silence gathered round them. Then the noises of the night.

"Are we safe?" asked Tadpole.

"How do you know I wasn't asleep?"

"What if the kravvins come?" he asked.

"They're not silent things," she said. "We'll hear them coming."

"Are you sure?"

"Listen."

He listened.

"What can you hear?"

"Nothing."

"That's right. Do you know why?"

Tadpole felt that he was being lectured, so he didn't answer.

"It's because you're jabbering," she said. "You scare the animals away. As long as you're quiet, they'll start running again. And you'll hear the night. If the kravvins get near, the first thing you'll hear is the silence. Good night."

The silence returned, and then the scratching and rustling.

"What's happened to Sam?" asked Tadpole.

Tamrin sat up.

"Are you going to talk all night?" she asked.

"I can't sleep."

"Let's walk, then."

They walked along the riverbank.

"Nobody tells me anything," said Tadpole. "Every time I ask, they say, 'Find out for yourself'."

"What do you want to know?"

"Ash. Who is she? Why is she dangerous? Why can't you or the other wizards just go and beat her?"

Tamrin thought about it for a moment. The moon tried to escape the net of cloud. Tamrin stopped and took the pendant from under her jerkin.

"Look," she said. "What is it?"

"A dragon's head. With fire blazing from its mouth. Is it Starback?"

"Look at the neck of the dragon."

Tadpole's face drew close to Tamrin's as he examined the pendant. He could feel her breath on his cheek.

"What is it?" he asked. ‖

Tamrin stepped back

and the pendant dropped from Tadpole's fingers.

"It's a seal," said Tamrin. "Years and years ago Flaxfield and some others sealed Ash inside the Castle of Boolat. Since then, she's never been able to escape. So, she works through others. She's made the kravvins and the takkabakks to go out and kill and terrify people. She uses Smedge. And she uses that fool Frastfil and others in the college. She's trying to destroy all magic except her own."

"I heard about her being locked up," Tadpole said. "But who is she?"

Tamrin walked on. An owl swooped low over the water and disappeared into the tree on the opposite bank.

"It's a complicated story," she said, at last.

"Tell me. I'll follow."

Tamrin raised her arm and made a throwing movement with her hand, like flicking something away. A shower of blue petals rushed out and hovered over the water. Iris petals, with yellow throats and black scribbles. They showered down on to the surface, making it bright with beauty in the night.

"An old wizard, tired, weak, greedy and dying," she began. "His name was Slowin. Took a girl as his apprentice, and, when the day came to sign her indenture, he stole her name. Stole her magic. Her name was Flame, and, instead of giving it to her when she signed her indenture, he stole it for himself."

"What was the girl called?"

Tamrin frowned.

"Roffles," she said. "Never just listen."

Tadpole hung his head. She nudged him and smiled. "She was known as Bee, then," she said. "That was when the wild magic broke out. It fell as fire. Slowin was transformed by it. His old self was burned away, changed. And he became Ash. Young, beautiful and a woman."

The last words were almost silent and Tadpole had to strain to hear them. Tamrin clicked her fingers and the petals sank beneath the water. She was invisible again in the new darkness.

"The girl?" asked Tadpole.

"The girl was burned, too. She nearly died. Flaxfold saved her life."

"December," said Tadpole.

"December."

Tamrin turned from the path and pushed into the undergrowth, hacking obstructions out of the way with her staff. Tadpole followed.

"There was a fight," she said, over her shoulder. "December

sealed Ash inside Boolat. December, and Cabbage, and Flax-field, and Dorwin together. They all did it." She stopped, turned, looked at Tadpole and said, "And Perry. The roffle. He was there. He was one of the group that defeated her, and sealed her away. Wizards and humans and roffles together. They did it."

"My ancestor," said Tadpole.

"Of course." Tamrin took out the seal. "And this is it. This is the very seal they used. All those years ago."

Tadpole touched it again. He saw that the base was carved into the shape of a bird.

"This is what Ash wants," said Tamrin.

"How did you get it?"

Tamrin started to hunt around for something, chopping away with her staff.

"Flaxfield was the keeper of the seal. He gave it to Sam. Now we keep it."

"What do you mean? If Sam keeps it, how can you?"

"She thinks that if she can break this seal then she'll break free of Boolat."

"And can she?"

"I think she can. The sealing spell is weakening, though. And I think we need to take the seal and renew it."

"And you'd do that? You'd go to Boolat?"

Tadpole almost managed to keep the fear out of his voice.

"I have to. Sam and I, we're the ones Flaxfield trusted to do this. That's why we have the seal."

She stopped hacking and called out, "Found one."

"Can you do it on your own?" asked Tadpole.

Tamrin pulled branches away from a low bush. She smashed into it with her staff, stripping away twigs and leaves.

"Hawthorn," she said. "Small and strong and reliable. That's the one. Here. Cut the twigs off with that knife of yours."

She had found a straight shoot. He flicked away the leaves and twigs. Perhaps not quite straight, now he could see it properly. He put one end on the ground. The branch was not quite as high as he was. About up to his nose.

"Give it here."

Tamrin took it back, pushed her way clear of the woods, and regained the riverbank.

"We should have more time, really," she said. "Shouldn't rush." She looked at Tadpole. "Still. Got to get on."

She put down her own staff and took the hawthorn branch in both hands. Bracing herself, she drove it down into the ground, the effort showing on her face. Her lips were tight, her eyes screwed shut. The branch sank slowly down. Tamrin dropped to her knees, pushing it in, until just about a hand's breadth remained above ground. She drew back, panting, the sweat dotting her forehead.

"Get your cooking can," she said. "Fill it with water."

Tadpole found the can in his pack, knelt on the bank and scooped up the water. He handed it to Tamrin.

"No. You do it. Pour it over."

"How?"

"Just do it. Anyhow."

Tadpole poured the water over the end of the branch. It pooled in a dip that Tamrin had made with her fists. The end of the branch grew round. It sucked up the water. Tadpole watched as it formed a sphere of polished wood, amber-coloured, smooth and glossy.

"What's on it?" asked Tamrin.

"Nothing."

"Look more closely."

Tadpole peered at the branch.

"Stars," he said.

"How many? How big?"

"Tiny. So small. And thousands of them."

"How do you know they're stars?"

Tadpole laughed.

"All right," she said. "Stand back."

Tadpole moved away slowly, never letting his eyes leave the branch end. Tamrin had to elbow him out of the way.

She took hold of the moulded end of the branch and pulled. She braced her legs, straightened her back and tugged. The effort was even greater than before, but the branch stayed where it was. Not an inch. It was wedged tight in the earth.

She stood back, her breath loud with labour.

"I can't move it," she said. "Come on. We need sleep if we're going to travel tomorrow."

She walked away.

Tadpole stayed staring at the end of the branch. It seemed

as though the stars had gained strength and light. They gleamed in the darkness of the wood.

"You'll get lost," Tamrin called. "Better follow. I'm not going to wait."

Tadpole started to follow her. He stopped, looked back. The stars had dimmed. He followed again. Again he stopped. For a second he couldn't see where the end of the branch was. He stared into the gloom. A tiny light blinked at him. He ran across to it, seized the rounded end and pulled.

And he nearly fell backwards on to the ground. The branch came out as easily as a fish from a stream. It span into the air, crashing through the lower branches of trees and sending down showers of leaves and twigs. Tadpole held his breath and hoped that the falling debris would turn into stars. They fell to the ground as bits of tree. The branch clattered down after them. Tadpole picked himself up, rubbing himself where he had landed with a thump, and grabbed the branch.

"You got it, then?" Tamrin stood next to him.

Tadpole examined the branch. Its time underground had stripped the last of the small, sharp edges. The bark was smooth and glossy. The end, where the water had soaked in, was the size of a roffle's fist, comfortable to seize and hold on to.

"Try it," said Tamrin.

He leaned on it. It didn't bend. He took it in both hands and swung it round, smacking into the trunk of a tree. It was as hard as flint.

"It's a wizard's staff," Tadpole whispered.

"It's a walking staff," said Tamrin. "And there's a handy club on the end, if you want to hit a kravvin. You can use it to hack away at stuff if we're walking through overgrown places."

"Will it do magic?"

"Try it."

"How?"

"Come on," she said. "Time to sleep."

Tadpole followed. The going was a lot easier with something to lean on, to swing, to hack away with. Secretly, he tried to make it pour stars out of the tip, or to light up in the dark, or to make streamers. None of these worked. Still, it was a good staff and he was glad of it.

Tamrin refreshed the fire and they lay again in its glow.

"Good night," she said.

The night noises returned, comforting and close.

"What's happened to Sam?" asked Tadpole. "Do you miss him?"

Tamrin's voice was different when she finally said, "Go to sleep, or I'll send you to sleep and you won't like that."

"Sorry." He waited for her to answer. There was a question he had been avoiding, and now he had to ask it. "Are we really going to Boolat tomorrow?"

"I am. You'll have to do what you want." ‖

Part Three

STARBEGIN

Sam's throat still hurt

when he woke up.

He braced himself to look inside the house. Flaxfold, Axestone and Eloise. All dead. Killed by Smedge and his army of kravvins.

He stepped away, back into the early sunlight. Shadow of dragon wing swept across the grass. Sam didn't need to look up to see Starback, circling overhead.

"That's it," he said. "Stay up there. Keep away. Nothing but death and ending here."

He stiffened his shoulders, took a deep breath and went back inside the house.

Busy. Keep busy was the way.

Eloise first.

Flower-like in death, she was slender, light and fragile. Her blue-green robe flowed down as Sam lifted her in his arms and carried her out of the house and down to the riverbank. He laid her softly on the wet grass.

"The time for Finishings will be later," he promised. "If I live to do them. For now, the sky and the water protect you. The grass hold you. The air sing to you."

He stood for a moment, waiting. When the sunlight shifted through the trees she seemed to disappear into the background. Green of grass. Blue of water.

Without warning, a tiny arrowhead of colour flashed along the river. Sam smiled.

The kingfisher veered round, flew past again, over Eloise and back to the water. It dived in. A mushroom of spray marked its path. And then it was out, a fish thrashing in its beak. Sam nodded, stooped, touched Eloise's cheek, and left her.

Axestone was heavy. Without the aid of magic Sam could never have lifted him. He scooped up the big man, like a lamb, and carried him, further than Eloise, into the wooded area beyond the garden. It was hard going, even with magic, and Sam was sweating and panting when he cleared the first stand of trees and found an open space.

"You always were a burden," he said, letting the older wizard rest on stones and mast. He smiled at him. "Sorry," he said. "Not a burden. But heavy. You were always heavy. Good cheese is heavy. Iron is heavy. And stone and sorrow."

The quick rustle of dead leaves indicated another presence. Sam caught a glimpse of grey fur, bright eyes, a red tongue.

"Lie heavy on him now, till I return to Finish him," said Sam, looking up at the wide, green branches overhead.

He moved away, paused at the edge of the clearing and

watched the wolf break free of cover, trot in a circle round the edge before coming to rest at Axestone's feet, where it sat, patient, looking.

"Flaxfield dead first. All of Flaxfield's apprentices being killed," said Sam, as he returned. "One by one. The seal weakens."

He had put if off for long enough, and now he must do it. Starback still wheeled round in the sky, tireless, vigilant. Sam shielded his eyes against the sun and watched for as long as he could, before duty drew him in and he looked down at Flaxfold's body.

He had straightened Eloise and Axestone before he slept. Flaxfold he had left as she fell. He sat cross-legged on the floor next to her. There was no mark on her body. Whatever Smedge had done to kill her he had achieved by a sly, probing magic. Killing her from inside out.

Sam touched the back of his fingers against her cheek.

"So cold," he said.

Her grey hair had fallen across her face. He brushed it away, and tucked it behind her ear, as he had seen her do a thousand times.

"I don't know where to take you," he said. "Eloise needed the river, and Axestone the bare ground in the woods. But I don't know where to take you."

He wrapped his cloak around himself and looked at her a long time.

"I tidied the kitchen," he said. "It's all just as it was. As though the fight never happened. As though you're going to bake more bread."

His voice failed him and he put the cloak around his face.

The clock on the wall ticked away the time. Sam cleared his throat.

"Anyway," he said. "I can't leave you here. Look at you."

He moved her arms to her sides, straightened her legs so that she lay on her back, orderly and correct.

He closed his eyes and he was above the house, high in the sky, circling round and round.

The rushing air soothed him. The dip and veer and rise restored him. He felt the ache in his wings from constant flight, and the pain cheered him. The river threaded below him, blue on green, wet on dry.

He was thirsty. Laying back his wings he dived, spearing the air and plunging into the water. Twisting like an eel he surged through the water, mouth gaping, taking in refreshment, and he broke the surface again and flew up. Droplets exploded from him, sparkling in the sunlight. He flapped his wings, sending showers of silver down. He circled the house once, then glided to the topmost branch of the highest tree, folded his wings and looked down on the tiny figure of Eloise.

Sam opened his eyes and was back in the kitchen, sitting by Flaxfold.

"Come on," he said. "Let's make you comfortable until I know what to do."

He carried her upstairs, as she had once carried him when he was tiny and sick. He kicked open the door of her room and laid her on the narrow bed. Sunlight welcomed them, drenching the room with its warmth and brightness.

Flaxfold's room was as bare as the rest of the house was filled with things. A bed and a chair. A small chest and table. A jug of freesias on the table. A bookcase, no bigger than a garden gate.

And the mirror.

Sam had known it was there, but he never came into this room.

It dominated the space. It was the size and shape of a door, hung on a stand so that it could be tilted forward and back. Sam tried not to look at it.

It was the mirror of story. The first mirror ever. The mirror that had brought magic into the world. It was dangerous. It had a power and a history of its own.

Ash had tried to use it to break free of Boolat. For a moment she had managed to step through it to freedom. Sam and the others had rescued it, and now it was here. Hidden in Flaxfold's room. They were afraid that if ever it was unveiled Ash would break through again and she would have won.

It was kept covered. Covered with a cloth to stop it reflecting. Covered as a hawk's eyes are covered before the hunt. Hooded and weakened, but ready, as soon as the blind is slipped, to rise and kill.

Sam brought the chair next to Flaxfold's bed and sat with his back to the mirror.

"I don't know why I'm talking to you," he said. "I know you can't hear. But there's no one else."

The hair had fallen loose again on the journey to her room and Sam again tidied it behind her ear.

"Tam's gone," he said. "I don't know why. After the battle, or even during it, she disappeared. I can't hear her any more. I can't be her. It's like ... I don't know what it's like."

He looked through the window at the sky.

"I think they came for the mirror," he said. "And the seal. I think Ash wants them both. Tam's got the seal, so that's all right. But what if they regroup? We drove them away, but we didn't kill them all. And Smedge is still alive. I think."

He stood up and crossed the room to the mirror. He stood in front of it, testing himself. Daring himself to be there.

"If they'd killed Smedge, they'd have come back and told us," he said. "Wouldn't they?"

He wrapped himself in his cloak.

"I think I've got to go to Boolat," he said. "I've got to take the fight to Ash. But I don't know how. The others have gone. Eloise and Axestone dead. December and Waterburn wounded. Tam nowhere to be found. And a roffle," he remembered. "Poor Tadpole. Caught up in this."

He turned to face the body of Flaxfold.

"The thing is," he said. His voice grew louder as he spoke. "The thing is, if Flaxfield hadn't died we'd have been stronger. He shouldn't have done that." He was shouting now. "Just when we needed him. And then, you promised me. You promised I could be your apprentice. And look at you." He was screaming at her now, the tears flowing down his face. Tears of rage as well as of grief. "Look at you. Dead. You can't expect me to do this all on my own. Can you? Can you?"

He stamped on the floor, made his hands into fists and beat them against his sides.

"Look at you. Just look at you. Dead. You've no right to die. No right. Look at you."

He stumbled back, stepped against the mirror and fell. He reached out his hands to save himself. They caught hold of the fabric covering its surface. He tried to let go of it. Too late. He fell, banging his head against the wooden foot of the mirror stand. The cloth fell on top of him, blinding him. He clawed it away and kicked himself clear.

The light from the window struck the polished surface and reflected back on to Flaxfold's body on the bed. Sam looked at it. His kick had sent the mirror round so that it was facing her directly. She was reflected full-on in it.

The light from the window flickered and was consumed by a greater, a brighter, light from inside the mirror itself.

"No," said Sam. "No."

The mirror shook and a sound like a huge branch breaking in a storm shattered the room.

"No. Get back."

Sam leaped to his feet and grabbed his staff. He pointed it at the mirror, ready to fight magic with magic.

Another crack, louder than the first, hurting Sam's ears.

And a rush of wind, too strong to withstand. Sam was blown back against the wall, his staff spinning away from him.

And a figure, tall, grey and slender, stepped through the mirror and into the room. ‖

The grey figure ignored Sam

and crossed the room towards Flaxfold. Sam, still stunned, crawled towards his staff. He was half-blinded by the flash, half-deafened by the noise. He fell to one side, bumped against the wall and threw up. Or, rather, nearly threw up. He hadn't eaten and all that came was bile. It burned his throat and made him cough.

"Ash," he tried to call. "Ash."

He tried to focus. The grey figure stopped, halfway to Flaxfold. It turned and looked at him. Sam couldn't make out the features.

"Come on," he coughed, the words hurting as much as the bile. "Come here. Leave her alone."

The figure strode towards him, hand outstretched.

Sam lunged forward and fell on his face, his hand just touching his staff. His fingers sought it, and it slid away, beyond his reach. He was finished, powerless.

The figure leaned over him, put its hands under his

armpits and dragged him to his staff. Sam's hand closed over it. He felt a new strength, a new power. His throat still hurt. His ears still sang. His eyes were still dazzled, but he could stand. He dragged himself free of the hands, backed against the wall, raised his staff and pointed it at the figure.

"Sam."

Sam paused.

"Sam."

The grey figure took hold of Sam's staff. It moved it to one side and down.

"Sam."

Sam closed his eyes. Bright flashes of yellow and white and blue carried on behind his eyelids. A hand covered his face. "Sam. Hush."

The lights dimmed. The ringing faded. The hand pressed against his face, warm, a little rough, large enough to cover the top half.

"Sam."

Sam took hold of the wrist and moved the hand away. He opened his eyes. Clear sight now. No flashes and confusions.

"Flaxfield?"

"Who else?"

Sam backed away.

"You're not Flaxfield."

"Sam."

"Get back. Get out. Get back through the mirror."

Sam brandished his staff, ready to fight.

The figure swept its arm back and indicated the broken shards of polished steel, the twisted frame. The mirror was destroyed. It put its finger to its lips and smiled. "Hush. Watch."

Sam watched it turn and walk towards Flaxfold.

"I told you to leave her alone," he called.

He made a barrier spell and threw it into the figure's path. The grey thing walked straight through it and when Sam ran after it to grab it, he bumped into his own spell and recoiled from the barrier.

Helplessly, he watched the figure sit on the chair by Flaxfold's bed. It took her hand, smoothed her forehead and tucked the stray strand of grey hair more securely behind her ear.

Sam beat his fists against the barrier. He stabbed at it with his staff. He kicked and hurled himself at it. He had created his own defeat and Ash, or Smedge, or whoever the figure was, had used it against him.

Now the figure was leaning over Flaxfold. It put its forehead to hers. It took hold of her shoulders and shook them. It leaned back again and turned to Sam with a grim smile.

Sam clicked his mind over and was on the treetop, surveying the countryside, watchful for attack. He leaped from the branch, rose and dived, flying at full speed towards the house. The window to Flaxfold's room was small. Starback folded his wings back and smashed through it, making a sharp turn to avoid crashing into the wall. He flipped upside down, curled round and hovered, upright again, wings spread as wide as the room would allow, breathing smoke and fire.

Sam and Starback watched, with double sight, as the grey figure, holding Flaxfold's hand, helped her from the bed and they stood side by side. Flaxfold and Flaxfield, together.

"Sam," said Flaxfield.

"Starback," said Flaxfold.

And, as the boy and dragon looked, the two figures switched, merged and switched back. For a second they were two people. The next second, two Flaxfields. A moment later, two Flaxfolds. Finally, two people again, as they had been originally.

Sam stepped forward. The barrier melted. He stopped, unsure, feeling foolish, fooled.

"Are you Flaxfield?" he asked.

"Yes," said Flaxfold.

Sam scowled at them.

Flaxfield laughed.

"It's good to see you, Sam," he said.

"Don't say that. What's happening? I don't know who you are."

They switched again, and back again, faster than Sam could keep up with.

"Don't do that. Who are you?"

"We're Flaxfield," they said.

"Flaxfield?"

"Flaxfold."

"I've had enough," said Sam.

He turned and made for the door. It slammed shut as he approached. Sam could feel that there was a strong sealing spell on it, and he avoided making himself look foolish by trying to open it. He kept his back to them.

"Sam," said one of them. Their voices were difficult to tell apart. "Sam, please talk to me."

Sam kept his back to them.

"You're dead," he said. "You both are. This is a trick. I know it is. Go away. Leave me alone."

"We're Flaxfield. We are."

"Prove it," said Sam. He span round and glared at them. "Prove you're not a spell, not a trick, not a trap. Prove it." He pointed to the shattered mirror. "Ash climbed through that once. We beat her back. You're Ash now. Or Smedge. You're not Flaxfield."

They looked at him in silence.

"If you're Flaxfield," said Sam, "tell me about the mirror. Tell me how you used it to get here."

"I'll tell you," said Flaxfield.

"I promise," said Flaxfold.

"But first," said Flaxfield, "I'm hungry. It's not Friday. But I'd like a trout. Will you catch one for me?"

"Please," said Flaxfold.

"How do you want it cooked?" asked Sam. He pointed to the Flaxfield figure.

"Fried. In butter. Dusted with flour and salted. Just as I

taught you. And, at the end of the cooking, sweetened with a few flakes of almond. Please."

"Tell me what's happening," said Sam, in a softer voice. He was staring now at the old man, trying to remember everything about Flaxfield, trying to see if there was anything wrong, anything different. Trying, too, to decide how to feel if this was true.

"I will," he promised. "All in good time. First, we should eat, and meet, and talk about each other."

"You're dead," said Sam. "You both are. Aren't you?"

"We are, as you see," said Flaxfield, "alive."

"And dead," said Flaxfold. "Never forget that."

"I don't understand," said Sam.

"No," she said.

"No," said Flaxfield, at the same time, in the same voice. "No. But let's get some fish while I light a fire in the range. I was hungry the last time you saw me, and I haven't eaten since."

"Why didn't you come back before?" asked Sam, knowing, even before the words were out of his mouth, that there was no answer. And none came. Sam remembered that Flaxfold had always avoided being reflected in the mirror. He started to ask if that was the reason, but couldn't find the right words. So he let it go.

Flaxfield and Sam walked together to the river, a little apart from one another. Starback hovered overhead, watching them, protecting Sam.

"No magic, now," said Flaxfield. "Catch them honestly or we'll go hungry."

Sam nodded. At the riverbank he drew a length of twine from his pocket, attached it to his staff, and, finding a hook behind a fold in his jerkin, made a rod and line. Quick hands caught a hoverfly. He pushed the hook through it and cast his line.

Flaxfield ignored the preparations. He stepped away and up the riverbank to the shade where Eloise lay. Starback watched him from his position high above them both, soaring on dragon's wings.

Flaxfield covered her with his cloak. He produced items from his pockets and laid them by her side. Others he found by foraging in the undergrowth. He climbed the lower branches of a tree and gathered leaves and a length of bark.

When all was done, Sam could hear the sound of an incantation, but not the words. He had hooked his first trout by the time that Flaxfield lifted Eloise, slid her into the water and let her drift away. She neither floated nor sank, but melted away as she passed by Sam's line. The kingfisher darted down, broke the surface, sliced through the water, and Eloise was gone. The bird never emerged, though Sam looked along the length of the stream.

A second fish took the bait, and Sam landed it as Flaxfield disappeared into the trees, in the direction of Axestone.

The third fish was too small and he threw it back. When he had three good ones he scaled and gutted them, sliding the innards into the stream, and carried them up to the house.

The kitchen smelled of fresh-baked bread. The range was glowing. Flaxfold, plump and busy as ever, bustled around, laying places, polishing knives, setting plates and salt and butter, ready for the meal. Sam felt shy with her and put the fish on a marble slab, ready for cooking.

Flaxfold put down a plate, opened her arms and said, "Come, Sam. We're friends."

He hung his head. She walked over, put her arms around him and hugged him. He allowed the embrace, even returning a little of the pressure. When she let him go, he turned away, dragged his sleeve across his eyes and sat with his back to her.

"Ash," he said. "And Smedge. What will we do now?"

"Later," said Flaxfold. "Plenty of time for that later. Now, we need to eat and talk."

Flaxfield's face was grey when he returned. The lines around his eyes were deeper even than when the two of them had walked to the river, just an hour ago. He looked a year older. More. Sam knew the cost that magic took and he said nothing. The old wizard sat opposite him at the table and nodded.

"I'll cook the trout," said Sam.

"I'm doing it," said Flaxfold, and the butter hit the pan with a sizzle.

Flaxfield sliced the crusty bread. He poured water into mugs, passed the butter to Sam.

The trout tasted of the river. Flaxfold had toasted the almonds first, and they were crisp and sweet. The skin of the fish was brittle and salty. She set a plate in the centre of the table for the bones.

Sam couldn't remember when food had tasted better.

He watched Flaxfield eat, and he remembered the day the old wizard had died. No magic could bring back a dead man. Nothing was strong enough for that.

"Did you really die?" he asked.

Flaxfield bit into a hunk of bread and shook his head.

"You didn't?"

"I'm not talking until we've finished eating."

Sam allowed his anger and curiosity to give way to the pleasure of eating. Soon, they were talking of fish and sunlight, the garden, and plans for planting a fig tree and a medlar.

"That bay tree in the pot by the door is looking sad," said Flaxfield. "I'll have to see to that."

"And the handle of the frying pan's loose," said Flaxfold. "I'll look out for a tinker to fix it."

"I can do that," said Sam. "Remember?"

She smiled. "Of course. But it's an apprentice's job. And I think you're past that now, don't you?"

"It's up to any of us to do it until there's a new apprentice," he said. "And I don't mind."

"Later," said Flaxfield. "I'll help you, perhaps."

And the meal passed as though the world was well. Flaxfold stood to clear the table and Flaxfield made her sit again.

"I'll do it," he said.

So Sam ran and drew water from the pump, topped it up from the kettle and washed the plates while Flaxfield cleared the table and dried the dishes.

The sun had lost itself behind cloud and a fine rain dotted the window when all was clear. The old wizard dried his hands, passed the towel to Sam, and, while the boy dried his, he hugged him. Sam remembered the scent of Flaxfield's clothes, the surprising strength of the old arms, the heft and authority of the man.

"It is you, isn't it?" he said.

The wizard unfolded from Sam and sat down at the table. He kicked a chair with his foot to indicate that Sam should sit, too. Flaxfold had not moved since the meal.

They sat and looked at each other.

"That trout was good," said Flaxfield. "Thank you. Now, Sam, is there anything you want to talk about?" ||

Sam gaped at Flaxfield in astonishment,

and when he spoke his voice was louder than he had intended.

"Anything I want to talk about?" he said. "Anything...? What sort of question is that?"

Flaxfold put her hand on Sam's and he shook it off.

"You just turn up, over a year after you died, and you ask me if there's anything I want to ask? And you." He pointed at Flaxfold. "Yesterday you were dead. You were. I know you were. I know when someone's dead, don't I?" He stared at them. "Don't I?"

For a second, they switched and replaced each other. And it was over and they were themselves again.

"And that?" he said. "What does that mean? Switching like that."

"Sam," said Flaxfield. "You, of all people, should know about being two and one at the same time. You and Tam."

"But we're different," said Sam. "We're from the mirror. We—" He stopped and looked at them. Understanding began to print itself on his face. "You'd better tell me," he said. "Just take everything in turn. Starting at the beginning."

The warmth from the range cheered them as the day died and the stories unfolded.

"The mirror," said Flaxfield. "You knew it was the one that Smokesmith made, the one that brought magic into the world, all those years ago."

"Of course," said Sam. "It made me, and it made Tam. It's why we're only one where two should be."

"Or two where only one should be," Flaxfold corrected him.

"Or both," said Sam.

"Or neither," added Flaxfield.

They all enjoyed these games of words and smiled at each other.

"Well," said Flaxfold. "We were the first. Our mother was the very first person to see herself in the mirror. And when one of us was born, the other was reflected."

Sam interrupted her. "Those babies were killed."

"You remember the story," said Flaxfield. "Good."

"And that was so long ago," said Sam.

"So long," agreed Flaxfold.

Sam held up his hand for silence. "If that's right, then you two are the beginning of magic."

"We *are* magic," said Flaxfield. "All magic flows from us."

"Even Ash?"

"Even Ash," said Flaxfold. "That's why Flaxfield died. When Ash stole December's name he twisted magic. He made it wild around him."

"Her," said Sam.

"Him. Her. Slowin. Ash. The same."

"Why are you back now?" asked Sam.

"You saw it yourself," said Flaxfield. "The mirror that made us, remade us."

"And shattered in the action," said Flaxfold.

"This is all too complicated," said Sam.

"Here it is," said Flaxfield. "Simply. Flaxfold and I are one person. And two. We sprang from the first reflection, and we have been the ones who regulate magic for ever."

Flaxfold took up the story. "Slowin distorted that and turned magic in on itself. So Flaxfield, weakened, died."

"And now," said Flaxfield, "we have the chance to end all this. To defeat Ash finally and for ever."

"What about me?" asked Sam.

Flaxfield looked at him with kindly sorrow.

"You should never have been," he said. "The mirror that made you and Tam was hidden away. A chance brought you into being."

"There's no such thing as chance," said Sam.

Flaxfold nodded. "You've learned well," she said. "You didn't choose to be what you are. It chose you."

"So what am I?"

Flaxfield spoke very slowly.

"You are the beginning of a new magic," he said.

"Or the end of magic," said Flaxfold. "We don't know yet. Only the defeat of Ash and the wild magic will show us that."

Sam felt ill. "There can't be an end of magic," he said.

"Everything has its end," she said. "Even us. Even you. Even magic."

"It's late," said Flaxfield. "We should go to bed."

Flaxfold raked the embers in the range and put on more logs, slow-burning wood to keep the fire in all night.

Sam stopped on the stairs. "Just a minute," he said. "The babies. The ones that were made by the mirror. You can't be them."

"Why not?"

"They were taken away by guards to be killed. All the stories say that."

Flaxfield smiled at him. "You know the old stories," he said. "What always happens when men are told to take babies away into the forest and kill them?"

"They don't do it," said Sam. "They give them to a kind woman to look after."

"There you are," said Flaxfield. "Good night."

"Tomorrow," said Sam. "What happens then?"

Flaxfield and Flaxfold stood together. For a moment they merged and there was only one person there. "Tomorrow, we set off," they said. "To Boolat."

Sam woke as dawn was slipping night free. He climbed through his window and dropped the short fall to the ground below.

The grass was wet with dew. Daylight lived on easy terms with night, so the moon was pale in the sky, and the morning star still shone alone with her. Sam wondered if Tadpole was awake and if he had caught his first glimpse of a star.

"Not that one will be enough," he said. "He wants to see the skies covered with them."

He walked down to the riverbank and sat on the edge, watching the water. When he had built up his courage he shrugged off his clothes and dived in. The shock of the cold stunned him for a moment, before he broke free and splashed out. He was a strong swimmer and went upstream, against the current. He flipped over on to his back, lay flat and let the stream take him back to where he had started. The night had full gone, and he stared into clear blue sky, interrupted as he passed under the green ceiling of trees.

Sometimes he thought he preferred swimming to flying. Even for a dragon the air never supports the body as the water does.

He flipped over, swam upstream again, further, faster, till his arms hurt and his breath came in short bursts. This time the drifting back was like a deep, dreaming sleep.

Flaxfield was waiting for him at the side of the river.

"Breakfast," he said, and left him to dress and return.

Morning manners at Flaxfield's were relaxed. Flaxfield was frying bacon while Flaxfold was already eating. At least, Sam thought it was that way round.

"How did you have time to make fresh bread?" he asked.

Flaxfield brought his own plate to the table and started to eat, leaving Flaxfold to answer.

"Are you sure you can't find Tam?" she asked.

Sam nodded. Even relaxed manners didn't allow talking with your mouth full.

"That leaves December and Cabbage," she said.

"If they're still alive," said Flaxfield.

"Yes. And Tadpole. We need to find him."

"Unless he's back in the Deep World," said Flaxfield.

"He won't be," said Sam.

"No?"

"No. He'll stay and fight."

"I thought you didn't like him," said Flaxfield.

"You weren't here," said Sam. "Oh, I suppose..." He looked at Flaxfold. "Do you two know everything that you both know?"

"Is that a real question?" asked Flaxfield. "Does it make sense?"

"Carry on," said Sam. "Forget I asked."

"That's six of us," said Flaxfold. "Is it enough?"

"Enough for what?" asked Sam.

"Enough to defeat Ash," they answered.

"Is that what we're going to do?" asked Sam. "All right. Don't answer. I know it is. I just keep hoping we won't have to. Where do we start?"

"Do we need the seal?" asked Flaxfold.

"Are you asking me?" said Sam. "Because I don't know. I wasn't even there when Ash was sealed in. And if you're asking him—" he pointed his fork at Flaxfield — "you don't need to, because you both know the same as each other."

"Just thinking out loud," said Flaxfield. "We all do it. Even you."

Sam smeared the last of his bread round his empty plate, catching up the juices.

"Tam's got the seal. We take it in turns."

"Then all we have to do is find the others, and her, that makes seven, and we'll set off for Boolat."

"Easy."

They all stood.

"We need the strength of many," said the older ones.

"Where shall we start?" asked Sam.

"Not here. Meet at the study door in half an hour."

Sam let them leave the table. He watched them. All his childhood they had looked after him, taught him, cared for him and loved him. Now, they were leading him into the greatest danger he could imagine.

He went outside and stretched out his arms. Starback landed next to him with a scratch of claws, a scent of smoke and a leathery fold of wings.

Sam put his arms round the dragon's neck and whispered. "I'm frightened," he said. "But I'm proud. And I can't let them down."

Starback waited till Sam let go of his neck. He rose up in circles, as a lark ascends. When he was so high that he was beyond the range of normal sight, he straightened and flew off. ||

Sam didn't know how to tell Flaxfield

and Flaxfold how odd it all seemed. The three wizards, wrapped in cloaks, staffs in hand, faces set for work.

"I've never been in this room with both of you at the same time," he started.

"When you were little we divided the teaching," said Flaxfold. "It was better that way."

"But you left when I was only six."

"I had other things to do," she said. "I came back, though. Didn't I?"

"You'll get used to it," said Flaxfield. "Think how hard it is for people to understand about you and Tam. And Starback."

"This was always my favourite place," said Sam. The book-lined walls, the little fireplace, the blue and white pottery, and the table and chairs held the three wizards companionably.

"If we succeed it will be yours, one day," said Flaxfold.

"I don't want to think about any of that." Sam took the

door handle and walked through into the upper corridor of the inn. "It's wrong," he said.

Flaxfield closed the door behind them.

"We're not going back."

"Listen," said Sam.

There was no noise of conversation. No clinking of mugs, no clatter of knives.

"What is it?"

Sam moved along the corridor. He held up his arm for silence, leaned his head to one side, the better to hear. He beckoned them on.

"It sounds like pigs at the trough," he whispered.

"Pigs are noble animals," said Flaxfield. "These aren't pigs."

"I said sounds like pigs. I didn't say pigs."

Flaxfold boxed Sam's ears gently and rather more sharply boxed Flaxfield's ears. "Stop squabbling, you two."

They grinned at her. She sighed.

"I'll have a look," she said.

She raised her staff and a bubble floated out from the top of it. The bubble drifted away from them, down the stairs. She rapped her staff on the floor and another bubble drifted out and hovered. The three of them gathered around and looked into it.

They saw the downstairs corridor, the doors to the inn parlour, the kitchen, the snug.

"Bodies," said Sam. "Dead, everywhere."

The picture moved on, into the inn parlour.

"Kravvins."

The kravvins hunched over the bodies of the customers. Their hands tore at the flesh. They pushed their faces into the open wounds, gouging and biting, gorging with the pig-like noises.

"We're too late," said Sam. "We have to go back. Look for another way."

Flaxfold shushed him.

"Is it just kravvins?" asked Flaxfold.

The bubble moved on, taking in more scenes of death and feasting.

"No sign of Smedge," Flaxfield said. "Or anything else. It's just a raiding party."

"Just?" said Sam.

"You know what he means," said Flaxfold. "I have a plan." She explained it to them.

Sam listened and backed away in horror. "We can't. That won't work."

"We're going to try it," said Flaxfield.

The kravvins were becoming satisfied with their meal. Scuffles and crashes indicated that they were moving away.

"Kill more."

"Move on."

"Eat."

A noise like laughter.

"Eaten."

"Eat again."

"Eat more."

Flaxfold flicked her fingers at the bubble and it burst.

"They're leaving," she said. "No time to waste."

Before Sam could argue, she ran down the stairs and into the inn parlour. Flaxfield was close behind her. Sam pretended it wasn't happening and ran after.

The kravvins, half-crouched, gorged and alarmed, were overtaken with the speed of the attack.

Flaxfold speared two with her staff and they exploded in a spray of slime. She crashed herself against a third, shouting, "This one's mine. Leave him."

Flaxfield followed her example and stabbed and swung his staff, bursting and snapping the kravvins. Sam ran in and, putting his head down, charged at a kneeling kravvin. He stabbed it in the neck and the creature's head snapped off and went crashing through the window. After the first kill he felt better and set about the others with speed.

"Carry on," shouted Flaxfield. He ran out of the room and took position outside the inn. As the kravvins dived out after him he picked them off, slicing and stabbing.

"None to escape," he called to Sam. "Are you all right?"

"Five left," Sam called back.

Two kravvins burst through the window. Flaxfield swiped them with a flourish, looked through into the room and saw Sam kill the last one.

The last but one.

Flaxfold had one kravvin trapped in a corner. It was snarling and lunging out at her.

"Kill. Eat. Stab."

She held it back with a barrier spell. Sam could see that it was taking all her strength. He stood by her, dripping with sweat and slime, and added his own spell to hers. She relaxed a little and nodded. "Thank you."

The kravvin's attack faded. It still lunged, but less often, less forcefully.

Flaxfield added his own spell and the three of them stood side by side, guarding the creature.

"Can you bind him?" Sam asked.

"Watch me," said Flaxfold. "Stand back."

Sam and Flaxfield moved away. Flaxfold lowered her staff, drew it in the air across the figure of the kravvin. She stood back. The kravvin, free to move, lunged at her and was jerked back. Sam could almost see a thin cord around the kravvin's neck, and another round its ankles.

"Don't forget the mouth," said Flaxfield.

"You do it."

He stood in front of the kravvin. Sam nearly called out when the old wizard put his hand to its face. The teeth were long, sharp and ready. The kravvin twisted its neck, but Flaxfield was faster. He put his hand on its forehead and drew it over its face to its chin.

"That should do it," he said.

The kravvin whimpered, backed into the corner and sat,

huddled and shivering.

"I feel sorry for it," said Sam.

"It would kill you in an instant," said Flaxfold.

"Why do we want it?"

"If we're going to defeat Ash, we need to know everything about her. Everything she has. All her strength. All her weapons. For a start, we need to know if these creatures have any magic. Or even if they can channel her magic."

"Let's get out of here," said Sam. "All this slime."

Flaxfold tugged at the cord and the kravvin hobbled after her. Once outside it rushed at her, only to bounce off the barrier encircling it. It snarled and punched. She tugged again and it followed.

"Where now?" asked Sam.

"You know," said Flaxfield. "Why are you asking?"

Sam hunched up in his cloak and walked away. He could hear that the others had not moved, were not following. He kept walking. He knew it was the wrong way. He slammed the tip of his staff on the road as he walked, stamped his feet, kept his head down. For half a mile he clumped on, waiting to be called back. When at last he turned and looked, they were as he had left them. Almost out of sight. Standing. Waiting.

He walked back in silence, without the stamping.

The kravvin snarled at his approach and flung itself at him. "Kill."

The barrier held. Flaxfold tugged the cord.

"Boolat, then," said Sam.

"Boolat," they agreed.

At the sound of the name the kravvin threw back its head and howled. Flaxfold snapped her fingers to silence it.

"It's calling the others," said Flaxfield.

"No," said Sam. "I think it's afraid." He leaned in to the creature. "Boolat," he whispered.

The kravvin lifted its head again and howled, long and silent under the spell.

"Don't tease it," said Flaxfold.

She tugged the cord to lead it away with them. It fought back, whimpering, but she was remorseless.

They walked in silence until Flaxfold took pity on the kravvin and released the spell of silence. She slackened Flaxfield's spell on its mouth as well, for it seemed to distress the creature, and the barrier was enough protection. For a while its whimpers disturbed them. Sam hated it most. He made a spell that just stopped him from hearing. That cut off all noise and he missed the sound of feet on hard clay, the birds, the rustle of trees and the swish of cloaks. So he tolerated the whimpering until the kravvin had soothed itself with sorrow and walked along with them in silence also.

"There's no one here," said Sam.

"We're a long way from the inn now."

"But travellers," he said. "No travellers. No one working the fields."

"You're right," said Flaxfield. "There should be someone."

The kravvin sniggered.

"It can understand us," said Flaxfold, who had been observing it all the while she led it on. "Every word."

"Be careful," said Flaxfield.

"It can't harm us," said Sam.

Flaxfield moved to walk alongside him, more closely. He lowered his voice. "Usually — until you lost touch in the battle — you know what Tam knows and she knows what you know."

"Like you and Flaxfold."

"Exactly."

"So?"

"The kravvins, and the takkabakks and other things, are Ash's creation. They're part of her. They came from the wild magic. It may be that whatever they know, she knows."

"Then she knows we're coming for her," said Sam.

"She's always known that. She just didn't know when it would happen."

They passed a gate into a field. An old elm rose up in the centre. A ditch ran alongside the field edge. Beyond the ditch, on his side, the body of a man.

Sam shuddered. Not at the dead man. He had seen much of death in his life. A crow perched on his forehead and was pecking at his eyes. Another, on his chest, tore into his throat, the white neck bone gleaming through the red.

Sam kicked out at the kravvin. His foot bounced off the barrier. "You did this," he shouted. "Your kind has destroyed this world."

The kravvin's blank face betrayed no remorse. The

guttural "Kill. Eat." seemed full of a terrible joy.

Flaxfield led Sam away. "It's no more the kravvin's fault that it kills than it's the crow's fault that it feeds on the body. Or the fault of the stoat that it tears the rabbit. It's what it does. It's what it is."

Sam listened and waited before replying. "I know that, really. But it makes me so angry. The death and the pain. The waste. And it makes me angry that things I loved are being destroyed. That the fields aren't safe. The woods and the rivers are overrun with danger."

"I know."

"And the inn. I loved the inn. I have so many happy memories of there. It meant so much to me. And now it's all gone. I'll never forget the stink and slime."

"We have to put it right," said Flaxfield.

Sam thought about this. "We can fight back," he said. "And we might beat Ash. Destroy her. But things won't be the same. They've changed."

"They won't," Flaxfield agreed. "They have."

"What will we do with the kravvin?" asked Sam. "Are we taking it all the way to Boolat?"

"I don't know. It's Flaxfold's idea. She's watching it. Learning about it."

"But you're Flaxfold," said Sam.

"I know."

"You always annoyed me, with your tricky answers," said Sam. "Always."

"I know," said Flaxfield. "I taught you well, didn't I?"

Flaxfold called over to them. "What are you two bickering about?"

Flaxfield nudged Sam, and the boy winked back at him.

"We need to rest," she said.

She tethered the kravvin to a tree and they moved out of its hearing, to sit in the shade of a broad beech. She had brought food, of course, and water in flasks. The kravvin watched them without blinking, never turning aside.

Sam was nearly at the end of a chicken pasty when a sharp scream made him turn his head. The kravvin had caught a rat and was biting off its head. Sam put his pasty down.

"It's the nature of the thing," said Flaxfield.

"That doesn't mean I have to like it."

"No. What do you think?" he asked Flaxfold.

Sam glowered at him. "Don't do that. Just tell me what's happening."

Flaxfold explained. "I've been watching the kravvin all the time we've been walking. I released the spell of silence so that I could listen as well. We've learned all we need to know about it, I think. I'm sure that it's more or less just a thing. Not connected to Ash. I don't think that Ash can see or hear through it. Once they're away from Boolat they just do what they're sent to do, and if they live they go back until the next raid."

"What does she get from it?" asked Sam. "What's the point?"

"Terror," said Flaxfold. "Just terror. And destruction. The more the people fear them and fear her, the easier it will be for her if she ever escapes. All she'll need to do is threaten them with the kravvins and they'll fall into line. She'll rule all of this."

Sam picked up the last of his pasty, thought about it and put it down again.

"Are we taking it with us?" he asked.

"The kravvin?"

"Yes."

Flaxfold looked across at the creature, then back at Sam. "You decide," she said. "What shall we do with it?" ‖

Sam stood up

and walked away from the two old wizards. He looked along the Boolat road, eyes scanning for people, kravvins, anything. It was deserted. They had passed two burned-out villages, some isolated houses, torched and charred. He leaned on his staff and thought. The breeze stroked the hay meadow, and Sam imagined he could smell the scents of grass, the cowslips and clover, bee orchid and fritillary. He walked back, ignoring the wizards, and stood in front of the kravvin.

It had eaten the rat, all of it. Smears of blood glistened on its blank face.

Sam looked down at it and was disgusted.

"You're wrong," he called to Flaxfield. The wizard stood and joined him. "A stoat does more than this. A stoat plays with other stoats. It has babies. It suckles them. A stoat lies in the sun and cools itself in the shade. A stoat feels pain when its leg is caught in a trap. It feels fear. This—" he pointed to the kravvin with his staff — "is just a thing. Let's get rid of it."

The kravvin stared back at them.

"If you're sure," said Flaxfield. "Do it."

"What do you mean, do it?"

"Get rid of it."

"You do it," said Sam.

"What's the problem? You killed them at the inn. And back in the house when they attacked."

"That was to save my life," said Sam.

Flaxfield allowed a silence before he said, "Well, are we taking it with us, or not?"

The kravvin turned its face away. Sam walked off again. Flaxfold was clearing away the scraps from their meal, repacking her bag, getting ready to move on.

"What shall you do?" she said, with a smile.

"Don't try that," said Sam. "You're no different from him. So it's the same person, asking the same question."

"And you still haven't answered it."

"How do I know what to do?" he said. "How can I just kill something like that?"

"But if we take it with us, as we approach Boolat it will grow dangerous to us. It may call others. It may warn Ash. It may grow stronger. We can't take it any further."

"You kill it, then," said Sam.

Flaxfold nodded. "Is that your decision?"

"Yes. No. You decide. Why do I have to?"

"Because you'll be left, when we've gone. We are the past. This is your world, now. Your choice. Kill or not?"

They walked together to the tree and the three of them stood over the kravvin.

"Give the word," said Flaxfield. "Better still, do what you have to do."

"We'll leave it here," said Sam. "Tied to the tree. It can catch rats. It will live. It won't be a danger to us."

Flaxfield's face was stern. "That's a coward's choice," he said. "It's no choice. You're avoiding responsibility. If we take it, at least we can make sure it doesn't hurt a passer-by. It puts us in danger, but it protects others. Or we could kill it now."

"We're not going to kill it. I'll bind it tighter here. I'll put a spell round it to keep people away, let small animals through."

Flaxfold took his arm. "So, you'll let the kravvin kill a rabbit, but you won't kill the kravvin. Is that the decision?"

Sam busied himself with the spell. The kravvin thrashed out at him, trying to grab him. Sam finished quickly and walked off.

"Come on," he said. "We need to get to Boolat."

It was an uncomfortable walk at first. No one spoke. Sam kept apart from the other two, who didn't seem to notice that he was ignoring them.

"You could have killed it," he said, at last.

They didn't answer.

Clouds were beginning to cover the sky. Sam sniffed and recognized the scent of soft earth that comes before rain.

"We'll need some shelter for the night," he said.

"What will you do, if you're face to face with Ash, and you have the chance to kill her?" asked Flaxfold.

Sam walked on, holding a small distance from them.

By the time the light failed it was drizzling again and they were heavy with damp.

"There's a house," said Flaxfield.

"They're all burned out," said Sam. "We can't breathe in them."

"This one isn't."

"It's empty," said Sam. "They'll have run off. Too dangerous to stay here with the kravvins ready to attack at any time."

"It could be empty," said Flaxfold.

"It's odd," said Flaxfield. "The only house not burned out."

"A trap?" she asked.

Sam followed them up the small path to the house. It was slippery with rain. He held back a little, taking stock. Sniffing, there was no trace of charred wood or thatch. Hard to see in the gloom, but the structure looked secure. The roof seemed unharmed. The door was closed, as though someone might be there.

Flaxfold and Flaxfield split up and walked around the house in different directions, checking. Sam sighed, walked up to the front door, rapped hard on it with the end of his staff, kicked it and walked in.

"Anyone here?" he called. "See? Empty. Let's settle in."

A woman's voice said, "Welcome." And a grey figure emerged from the gloom.

Sam backed away. The door slammed, keeping him inside. He swung his staff, banging it against the wall. The whole house lit up, light glowing from the floors, the ceiling, the walls. For a second it was too bright. He had overworked the spell and blinded himself.

The door swung open again. The two old wizards ran in, cloaks flowing out, hair streaming. They shielded their eyes against the light. Flaxfield shouted out a spell and it dimmed, died, leaving the house darker than ever.

"Are you all right?" asked Flaxfold.

"Stand still," Flaxfield commanded, facing the grey figure.

Sam covered his face with his cloak. His eyes were still hurting from the spell. Blue and red lights fought in his eyes. He rubbed the soft, wet fabric over his face, dabbing his eyelids, murmuring cool words of soothing.

"Flaxfield," the woman said. "What's all this fuss? I welcomed you. Now Sam's lit up the night like a lightning storm. Someone will have seen. Someone will come."

"Dorwin?"

"Of course. Who did you think?"

Sam felt a hand on his head. He allowed it to loosen his grip on his cloak, let it fall, uncovering his face. He opened his eyes. The flashes of colour were growing less. He recognized the smith's daughter, tall, slim and wrapped in a grey cloak.

"He thought you were Ash," said Flaxfield.

"Ash?"

"Don't laugh. So did I, at first."

"I wasn't laughing. I was surprised. But of course. It's an easy mistake to make, I suppose. In the dark."

Flaxfold stood at the open front door, looking out.

"Anything?" asked Flaxfield.

"Not yet."

"Perhaps no one saw," he said.

Dorwin stood next to her. "Smith said this was an old place. He said that long ago it had been somewhere that people came for help and for safety. He said perhaps it wouldn't have been attacked."

"It was a healer's house," said Flaxfield. "I remember. We may be lucky."

"What happened to him?" asked Sam. His eyes were recovering. Only a small blue light darted from side to side.

"He was Finished," said Flaxfold. "Long ago."

"But the house still has something of his skill," said Flaxfield. "I think perhaps it's invisible to Ash and her armies. Why are you here, Dorwin?"

"Smith sent me."

"Why?"

"To wait, of course."

Sam knew the answer before he even thought of the question, but he asked it anyway. "Who for?"

"You," she said.

Sam blinked away the last of the coloured lights. "Obviously," he said.

Flaxfield clapped him on the shoulder. "Good lad," he said. "And where is Smith?"

Dorwin told them.

"Why? No one has ever left the Finished Mine."

"He needed the first iron," she said. "To make something."

There was silence, until Flaxfield said, "And we know what magic came from his work before."

"And what mischief," said Flaxfold.

"What is he making?" asked Sam. ‖

Part Four

STARCASTLE

The Castle of Boolat was even more dreadful

than Tadpole had dreamed it could be.

They arrived at night. Tamrin had urged them on, sleeping little, travelling fast, avoiding easy roads, obvious paths, keeping hidden.

"It's nothing like the guide says," said Tadpole.

"It's a false guide," said Tamrin. "They always are. All of them."

Tadpole had grown used to her sharp words and didn't argue now. Or not much.

"It was true when he wrote it," he said. "Not false then."

"What good is that to us?"

They sat on the fringe of a wood, on a slope overlooking the castle.

"I thought castles were built on hills," he said, "For protection. And to look out for enemies."

"It wasn't a castle when it was built. It was a palace. And there was peace. There were no enemies to speak of."

"I wish there was peace now."

"Well, there isn't."

Tadpole looked up at the night sky, still refusing him stars, still cloaked in cloud.

"What are we going to do now we're here? Are we going to attack it?"

Tamrin turned her face to give him a scornful look. Tadpole was already looking at her, with a challenging stare.

" "All right," she agreed. "We can't do that. Not just the two of us."

"So why are we here? And what are we going to do?"

Tamrin waited and watched before she answered. There was a light in the high window of the castle. The rest was in darkness behind grey walls. After a while, when their eyes had adapted to the gloom, Tamrin raised a finger and pointed. "See that?"

"What?"

"Look at the base of the walls. Just in one place."

Tadpole half-closed his eyes, as though that would help. "Is something moving?" He had surprised himself with the speed he had grown used to night. "Something is moving," he said. "What is it?"

"Move your eyes along the wall to the corner. Look there."

Tadpole let his gaze scan the base of the wall to its ending. Creatures appeared now, half-hidden by the darkness, breaking free of the wall and scurrying round to the other side. Smaller than kravvins, about the same height as a roffle, but terrible to look at. Almost a spider, almost a beetle. Horrid with spikes and carried on thin, long legs.

"Takkabakks," said Tamrin. "Don't go near them."

Tadpole ignored this unnecessary advice and pointed at the great gate of the castle. "Is that it?"

"What?"

"That gate. Is that where she was sealed in?"

As he mentioned the seal Tamrin gave a startled, muffled cry and put her hand to her throat. The seal glowed and burned. She held it away from her neck and made a swift spell to hide it and make it cool.

The damage was already done. As a single, many-membered thing the takkabakks hurled themselves towards them. They swarmed up the hill, guided by the seal.

"Run," said Tamrin. "Get away from me."

She pushed Tadpole on the back and sent him spinning away. She turned, ran diagonally down the slope, drawing the takkabakks away from him. Tadpole plunged into the undergrowth. Briars scratched his arms, his face. Tangled roots tripped him. He stumbled on, ever deeper into the wood, losing his sense of direction, flailing at branches. He pushed through a clump of hawthorn and found he had circled round and broken free of the trees. The ground sloped down to the castle. To his left, far away, Tamrin was running ahead of the takkabakks. To his right, very close, a small group of the creatures who had split off from the main body stood ready to pounce on him.

"Waiting for me," he breathed.

The only way to escape was back into the forest, but they were close now and could catch up with him, or down the slope, hoping to outrun them.

He twitched his shoulders to secure his pack and ran as fast as he could, down, towards the castle.

The takkabakks, with a sickening, rattling glee, darted after him. They were lethally fast. He would never outrun them. As he approached the castle the great gates opened, to receive him. The takkabakks weren't chasing him to kill him. They were driving him, herding him.

Tadpole swerved to his left, away from the gate. He ran alongside the wall. The takkabakks were gaining on him. He stumbled, put out his hand against the stone wall to steady himself, and pushed open a roffle door.

Without thinking, he put his shoulder to it and slipped through. He ran a little way, stopped and waited.

The takkabakks rattled and hissed. They scratched at the walls. He tensed himself, ready to run again. The scratching died away. They couldn't find the door. He was, for the moment, safe.

Slipping his pack from his shoulders he sat on it, breathing deeply, trying to recover himself.

"I'll look out later," he said. "When they've gone. And escape."

Something like a damp piece of lace brushed against his cheek, and whispered, "There's no escape from Boolat." ||

The takkabakks were gaining on Tamrin

and would soon catch her up. They clicked and hissed. Their swift legs were sharp on the grass. Longer than Tamrin's, faster. They scuttled ever closer.

Tamrin stumbled and lost ground. She looked over her shoulder. Too late. In a last moment of desperation she flung her arms wide and called out a fire spell, to make a circle of flames around her.

The sky cracked open, lightning slashed across the cloud. Instead of fire, the ground beneath her feet shifted, split and fell.

"Boolat," she whispered.

The wild magic had turned her own into a trap. She was in a wide, round pit, twice her own height. Takkabakks crowded the edge, gazing down, clacking and hissing. She braced herself against the moment when they would swarm over, dropping on to her and stabbing.

She gripped her staff, pointing it upwards to impale the first monster that jumped.

Another crack of thunder. Another bright flash of light. The takkabakks screamed and hissed. One fell over the edge and Tamrin readied her staff to spear it. It turned in the air, landing on its back, legs twitching. Tamrin flicked it aside, ignoring the rancid slime that spurted out. She looked up, ready to spike the next.

There wasn't a next. No sign of them. Only the sound of clacks and screams. Only the boom of thunder. She waited. She couldn't wait. She clambered up the ragged sides of the pit and peered over the edge, ready to drop back down.

Close by, the bodies of dead takkabakks. Further off, the rest of the cohort, scampering off. Overhead, swooping and killing, Starback.

Tamrin scrambled out and stood to watch the dragon destroy the takkabakks. He swooped and rose again, only to swoop once more. Over and over, frying them in his breath, scattering them with his wings, tearing them with his talons. Until every last one was dead.

"Oh, Starback," she breathed. "Where are you?"

The dragon circled higher and higher.

"They're all dead," she said. "No more. It's all right."

Starback straightened, dipped, circled and descended. Tamrin felt the night air beat against her face. The wings holding Starback just above her.

"Come down," she said. "You're buffeting me."

He swerved and settled, folded his great wings and looked into her face.

"So angry," she said. "You look so angry. Different."

She put out her hand to touch him. He flinched.

Tamrin stepped back.

They stared at each other.

"I was you," she said. "Once. Remember?"

Starback made no sign of understanding.

All around them, the bodies of the takkabakks. Far off, just in sight, the vast, vicious bulk of Boolat, hunched in the darkness.

"What happened?" she asked. "How did I lose you?"

She reached out her hand again. Starback permitted her to touch his neck. She stroked her fingers against his scales, remembering.

Lights appeared in the gateway of Boolat. The thud of wood on iron. The ignorant army of kravvins poured out.

Tamrin turned to run. Starback nudged his head against her back. She stopped, turned. He dipped his head and waited.

"Are you sure?" she asked.

The kravvins clashed nearer.

Starback waited.

Tamrin climbed on to his neck, put her arms around him and held as tight as she could.

She recalled the suddenness of the leap into the air, the swiftness of the rise, the gasping fear when the ground swirled round and down. They were high in the sky before the kravvins were twenty paces from the gate, still a quarter of a mile from where Tamrin had fallen into the pit. The blank faces never even saw them rise.

Tamrin pushed her face against the scales and closed her eyes. The night air rushed past them, catching her breath, but it wasn't that which made the tears flow. She rubbed her face against Starback's neck. The night air dried it, leaving it sore and red.

Once, she had flown here in her own strength. Once, she had breathed fire, swallowed smoke. Once, she had rejoiced in the currents and clouds. Now she was a passenger.

She loosened her grip on Starback. They were far from Boolat now and she risked a spell. She sat up, clutched her staff and tapped the dragon's head, making a charm to keep her from falling, however he swooped and dived.

Starback turned and looked over his shoulder. The mouth was still fierce, but the eyes shone with pleasure.

"Still friends, anyway," said Tam. The rushing air grabbed her words and turned them to tiny comets, falling to earth.

Over scarred landscape of ruined fields, damaged houses and barns. Across rivers, dull against the cloudy sky. Starback began to descend. He spread his wings wide, circled round and round, ever lower, towards the broken tooth of a crumbling stone barn.

Tamrin snatched a deep breath and waited for the landing. Soft, easy, the dragon's feet finding the wet earth, taking the jolt. Tamrin sat, silent, slow to leave the dragon. He wriggled and she sniffed.

"All right," she said. "I'm going."

She slid off, her cloak billowing up, her staff steadying her. She stood a while, getting her land legs back.

"Where have you brought me?"

"To us," said a voice. "And about time, too." ‖

Τhey walked towards her, out of the barn,

Jackbones and December, Cabbage following on.

"We thought we'd lost you," said December.

"No. I'm all right. What happened to you?"

"Where's Tadpole?" asked Jackbones.

Cabbage stood next to Starback. Tamrin studied them. They looked at ease together, the dragon and the old wizard. Part of a different time.

"Come on," said December. "There's clean straw in the barn. A warm bed for the night."

"What happened to him?" Jackbones asked again.

"I'll tell you from the beginning," said Tamrin. "When we're inside."

The barn had no roof. Some of the old timbers remained, and by dragging straw to the walls they had made sheltered beds. Cabbage set about getting more for Tamrin while she told her story.

"Takkabakks?" said December.

"Swarms. And so fast," she said.

"And you're sure Tadpole escaped?" asked Jackbones.

Cabbage stood still, arms full of straw, waiting for her answer.

"I didn't see. But he was running into the woods. There are roffle holes all over there. Easy for him to dive into one. Get safe."

"If he thought about it in time," said Jackbones.

"And if he was willing to abandon you," said Cabbage. "Roffles are very loyal, you know."

"I didn't just leave him," said Tam. "I saved him. Remember?"

"You did," said Jackbones.

"So stop looking at me as though I was a murderer, or as though I just left him to look after himself. I didn't."

December squeezed Tam's hand. "You didn't. Of course not. He's probably home and happy now. Glad to have escaped."

Cabbage plumped up the straw for Tamrin's bed. "He won't be," he said. "He'll be around, somewhere."

"Then perhaps he'll pop out of a roffle hole here, soon," said Jackbones. "Whatever. We can't go looking for him now. And we need some sleep."

He folded himself into his cloak and lay on the straw bed.

The others followed. Tamrin was the last to fall asleep. Lying on her back, looking up into the skies. Dim moonlight struggled to break through. No stars. She listened out for kravvins at first, until the broad shadow of a dragon drifted overhead and she understood that there was no need for a lookout. Her eyes closed. The straw was not as soft or as comfortable as she had hoped. Better than nothing. And she slept.

Last asleep and last awake. The sun was just breaking the horizon. Early start. Cabbage had a fire going. December had caught a rabbit. Jackbones found a stream and ferried water up to them in a bucket he'd rescued from the barn.

"There were plenty of rats to choose from," said December, "but I thought a rabbit would be better."

Tamrin stomped away, pretending to ease the stiffness in her legs but fooling nobody.

"What's the plan?" she asked.

Jackbones slopped water from the side of the bucket and laughed, a crackly laugh. "Always plans, these days," he said. "You used to just daydream around the college, eh?"

"How do you know?"

"Jackbones knows everything," said Cabbage. "Don't ask."

The plan revealed itself when they had eaten and drunk, and washed themselves in the stream. They set off, back towards the mines, in the direction of Boolat. Starback swooped dangerously ahead of them, making them jump back.

"Hey, careful," called Jackbones.

Another start. Another swoop. Starback rose and hovered and turned and flew a little way. He paused, circled and flew again in the same direction.

"Herded and led," said Cabbage. "Better do as he says."

So they followed.

"Does he know what he's doing?" asked Jackbones.

"Of course," said December.

"You know better than to ask," said Cabbage.

It was still early when they saw the smoke from the house. Sam's face in the window. Tamrin felt December's eyes search her out. She felt the woman's sense of sorrow as she saw that Tam had not known that Sam was there.

Tam looked up to avoid her eyes. Starback hovered, dipped, flapped his huge wings, and soared away, too fast to follow. ‖

Tadpole tried to reach for his knife,

and his hand wouldn't do as it was told. He couldn't move. He clutched the top of the roffle pack with both hands and anchored himself to it.

He stared ahead, eyes wide, mouth tight shut.

The lace dangled against his ear and whispered. "Once you're inside Boolat, you never get out."

Tadpole was holding his body so rigid that it hurt. His muscles were stone. His jaw was straining to remain still and not chatter with terror.

"Come on." The fragile membrane trembled against his cheek. "Do you want to see Ash? I'll take you to her."

This unlocked Tadpole. He jumped from the roffle pack, seized his knife, stabbed out at the thing that was tormenting him. His hand met no resistance, yet he felt a damp wisp drag over his wrist. He stabbed again, into empty air.

"That won't hurt me," it whispered.

Tadpole steadied himself by resting his staff on the floor.

Some light penetrated the darkness. There were gaps in the stonework. Mortar had crumbled, but it was dark outside and could not be coming from there. He looked up. High above his head a series of gratings opened, on to rushlight or tallow candles, perhaps. He took stock of his surroundings. The roffle door had led straight into the walls of the castle. Though the passageway was narrow, it was high. Dry enough, here, at any rate, though he could smell damp further off.

"I'm leaving now," he said. "Don't try to stop me."

It brushed his face again. He swivelled his neck, trying to find it, looking for something. It seemed almost possible to make out a shape, thin and insubstantial. "Stay," it said. Now that it spoke and he was waiting for it, he could see it.

It had a face. Small, thin and sad. Tadpole felt the fear pour out of him and he was filled instead with a heavy pity.

"Who are you?" he asked.

The face had a body. Tadpole was growing used to it. It reminded him of something. The face wrinkled up.

"What's the matter?" asked Tadpole.

"Thinking. Wait."

Tadpole used the time to make a more careful examination of it. Him, really. For he was definitely a person. Almost certainly a boy. About his own age.

"Maddie," he said.

"What?"

"I'm Maddie. No, I'm not. Wait."

He wrinkled his face again and thought harder. At last he

smiled in triumph, and Tadpole waited for the answer.

"Who are you?" asked the boy.

"Tadpole."

"Tadpole?"

"Yes."

"Like the pond thing? The frog thing?"

"Yes."

The boy put his hands on his head and Tadpole could see that the bones showed through the flesh. Even the bones were insubstantial, and Tadpole knew why it felt like lace.

"You're not going to be a frog?"

"No. It's a nickname."

"What's your proper name?"

"Doesn't matter. What's yours?"

"Taddie."

"No, it's not. That's just a bit like mine."

"Oh, is it?" His face showed deeper thought. "Mattie," he said. "I'm Mattie." Joy poured over his features and Tadpole wanted to cry.

Mattie leaned in and whispered to Tadpole. He felt the brush of lace against his ear. "No one talks to me," he said. "I forgot it."

Tadpole didn't take his head away, even though the sense of damp lace was unpleasant. He didn't want to hurt Mattie's feelings.

"Tadpole?" said Mattie. "Why do you have a nickname?"

"All roffles do. Our real names are too long."

A sly look came over Mattie's face. "Wizards have different names," he said. "Are you a wizard?"

"I'm a roffle. Roffles can't be wizards."

"Can't they?"

"No."

"Do you know why wizards have different names?"

"No. Why?"

"Do you want to see a wizard?"

"Here?" Tadpole felt alarmed at the thought of seeing Ash, excited that there might be a better wizard. Perhaps Sam had managed to get in. He gave Mattie a cautious reply. "Who is it?"

"Come and see."

"No. Tell me. Is it Ash?"

Mattie rose from the floor and hovered. He weighed nothing at all, or near to nothing.

"Ash? No. A different wizard." He settled back on the floor. "I can show you Ash. Do you want me to?"

"No. Are you her friend?"

Mattie rose again, higher this time, and took longer to get back down. He leaned in even closer and his face touched Tadpole's. "She's bad. I'm frightened of her."

"Why would you show me, then?"

"Come on. See the wizards."

Tadpole had no choice. He half-ran to keep up. Mattie swept through the hidden passageways. Soon, Tadpole had lost track of which way they had come. All he knew was that there were lots of different ways and that they had gone down many steps. The walls were damp now, slimy and glowing with green mould.

Mattie waved a warning hand to Tadpole. He slowed down and crept towards him. Mattie revealed a narrow opening from the passageway in the walls through into the corridors of the castle itself. It was a kitchen.

"Are they real people?" he asked.

"They used to be," said Mattie. "Captured from villages, brought here as slaves. Kept alive by Ash's magic. They live longer than people do usually."

"And they're cooking…"

"Yes. That's right. That's what they're cooking. The takkabakks and the kravvins like it. And it amuses Ash."

"Does she eat it?"

All the rules of kitchens were upside down. Tadpole could see rats running over tabletops and along the floor. Lice and cockroaches scuttled everywhere. They dropped from the ceiling into the vast boiling pans and died with a forlorn whistle. Hunks of rotting meat — from no animal that ever grazed a field or was penned in a farmyard — littered the tables. The cooks, great-muscled men and women with filthy hands and faces, their own flesh rotting on their bones, hacked at the joints, tossed them into roasting pans, speared them on spits. Noise and heat and rush and rot.

"Ash doesn't eat," said Mattie. "Not really. She just likes to see this. She comes down here sometimes to feed her pets."

He tugged Tadpole's sleeve and they moved on. The next gap took them into a small cell. The door was ajar, letting light in from the corridor. There was no window.

"Here's a wizard," said Mattie.

Tadpole couldn't see anyone. Just a filthy heap of straw in one corner.

"There's no one here," said Tadpole.

Mattie drifted over to the straw. He leaned over and pulled it away. An old man, skin drawn tight over bone, lay curled up, like a mouse in a nest.

"Dead," said Mattie. "They all die."

Tadpole stayed back. "He was a wizard?"

"Yes. He came here to save someone, and was trapped. Ash made him take a long time to die."

"I want to go," said Tadpole.

"There's another one."

"Dead?"

Mattie made his thinking face again. "I don't know. I haven't looked for a while."

"How long since you looked?"

Mattie giggled. Tadpole didn't like the sound.

"How long?" asked Mattie. "For ever. Come and see."

He slid back into the passageway. Tadpole thought that they only walked far enough to get to the next cell before they stepped out again.

"Is this a dungeon?" he asked.

"Used to be cellars. Storerooms. No dungeon in the

palace. But they're dungeons now."

This time there was a real person on the heap of straw. Tadpole had never seen anything like him. He was thin — starved thin. But it was his skin that was odd. He was the colour of old, polished oak. And he stared. Not at anything. Not at Tadpole. He didn't turn his head. He made no move. His eyes were fixed on a spot just short of the wall opposite him.

"He doesn't look like a wizard," Tadpole whispered.

Though the man made no sign at all, no movement, Tadpole knew that he had heard, and he felt ashamed, talking about him.

"Hello," he said. "I'm Tadpole." And immediately felt foolish. It wasn't a party.

The man didn't turn his head. His gaze didn't flicker from its invisible object. "Are you?" he said. "And what do you want here, Tadpole?"

"He's a wizard," said Mattie. "I told you."

Tadpole moved towards him, knelt down, so their faces were level.

"I don't know," he said. "I don't know why I'm here. Who are you? What did you do wrong?"

"Let's go," whispered Mattie. "I don't talk to them."

"He doesn't," said the man. "He never speaks. Just flits through and watches."

"He's called Mattie," said Tadpole. "Who are you?"

"I'm Khazib," he said, looking at Tadpole at last. "And I'm going to kill Ash."

Mattie made a high moaning noise and slipped out of the cell, back into the hidden passageway.

"Are you really a wizard?"

"Yes."

"Why don't you just use your magic to escape?"

Khazib put his hand on Tadpole's arm. His sleeve fell back and Tadpole could see his bones through the skin.

"Magic goes wrong in here," he said. "It comes back to hurt you. Unless you're Ash. And then it hurts everyone else."

Mattie's face appeared, through the gap. He was whimpering.

"Your friend wants to go," said Khazib. "Go on."

"What about you?"

Khazib smiled. "I was boasting," he said. "When I said I was going to kill Ash. I don't think I've strength enough for many more days."

"You have," said Tadpole. "I'll come back for you. We'll kill her together."

Khazib took his hand away and looked again into the space between his eyes and the wall.

"Come on," said Mattie. "Please."

Tadpole hesitated a long time before he left Khazib.

Mattie had already moved on when Tadpole slipped back into the narrow gap. The roffle hurried to keep up.

Stairs up, now. The walls grew drier. The air cleaner. It was no effort for Mattie, light as a ghost. Tadpole began to pant with the effort and to sweat. He slowed down.

"Wait."

Mattie carried on.

Tadpole started to move, balanced against the wall with one hand, and sat down on the step. He wiped his sleeve across his brow. It was a bit crowded, with his cloak, his roffle pack and his staff. On the other hand, he was pleased and interested to see that the cloak, rather than making him hotter, seemed to be cooling him.

He looked up the stairs, waiting for Mattie to come back. Air stroked his face, moving up, sucked in from some vent. He put his ear to the wall. Scratching. Takkabakks moving around. And harsh muttering. "Kill." "Eat." Tadpole wondered whether there was anything there for the kravvins to kill, or whether they always chanted like that, as lambs baa and birds sing.

"Mattie," he whispered. "Mattie? I'm frightened. Come back."

He listened again. Did the takkabakks hear him? No difference in the scratching.

"Mattie. I want a drink. I'm thirsty."

For the first time since he had made his way Up Top there was no escape for Tadpole, no way back. No roffle doors up here. Only the steep straight stairs and the stone walls, pressing close on either side. Down was the dungeons. And up? Up, he guessed, was Ash. That was where Mattie was leading him.

"Mattie?" he whispered. "Please. Don't leave me alone. Please." ‖

When no one came, Tadpole decided

he would just stay where he was. For ever if he had to.

Better to die of starvation on the stairs than to be killed by kravvins or to have to face Ash.

He tried making magic again. Just in case. He tapped the staff against the wall, thinking at the same time that he would like to see a window appear. He tried with his eyes open. Nothing. He tried with his eyes shut. Nothing. He tried whispering a spell. "Light, bright, shine tonight — window!" Nothing.

Perhaps it was too ambitious for a start? He pointed the staff down the stairs and, remembering what he had seen the other wizards do, he puffed out his cheeks and blew, thinking hard of stars, tumbling from the ceiling. Nothing.

He leaned the staff against the wall and opened his roffle pack. The inside was illuminated with roffle light. He took out Megapoir's guide book.

He started to read the introduction, but he couldn't carry on. Tears blurred his eyes.

Up Top ~ A Guide for Roffles

INTRODUCTION

Many roffles have returned from Up Top with travellers' tales of what life is like there. It is the way with travellers to, shall we say, forget, become uncertain about such small details as size, number, times, places, people, animals, magic, buildings and other things.

To be short about it, travellers make up as many stories as they tell the truth. Sometimes, they do it because they really do get mixed up. Sometimes, to impress. Sometimes, to frighten. To amuse. To instruct. To warn. To gain profit. To hide opportunities for riches. To send fortune seekers in the wrong direction. For good reasons and bad, they do not always tell the truth.

This guide is an attempt to give a full, true and clear description of what a young roffle will find when he first ventures Up Top.

If I have not actually seen and visited a place, then I only write about it if I have heard the same thing about it from at least three roffles who have been there separately.

For the most part, these are the accounts of my own travels, my own experiences and my own findings. Especially I remember that I once had a friend Up Top, the closest I ever knew.

I give this to my family, in the hope that it will serve them. If you are reading this, then I shall be dead, and you will be about to embark on a great adventure, the most exciting journey a roffle ever makes.

I hope that my guide helps you, and that you remember Megapoir, who went there before you and saw wonders and magic and marvels beyond anything pen can write. Perhaps you, too, will make a friend.

And the stars. No roffle ever forgets his first sight of stars. Of all the beauties of the Deep World and Up Top, nothing matches them. They are the difference between us and the people there. We live with a boundary to our sky. Theirs has none, only the endless sea of lights above.

You will not let me down. You will not let your family down. You will not let yourself down.

Never forget, whatever beauty and magic you see Up Top, however much you love that world and its people, it is not your home, and it is not as lovely as the Deep World, where you belong.

Go well.
Come home.
Be cautious.
Be courteous.
Be courageous.

And never forget to look out for wizards.

He closed the book and dried his eyes. It didn't matter. He knew the words by heart anyway, so he didn't need to read them. He put the book away carefully and looked for other things.

The shield made him think of Delver and the old roffle's cottage with its higgledy-piggledy homeliness. He laid it on the step above him. There was a spare pair of shoes. He put those next to the shield. A handkerchief. He wiped his eyes, blew his nose and dropped it back into the pack. A cheese sandwich wrapped in greased paper. A small flask of water. He put these inside the curve of the upturned shield. He reached down for one more item amongst his travelling kit, leaning over to get to it, and felt the brush of lace against his neck.

Tadpole banged his head on the hard rim of the leather barrel in his speed to get clear. He slammed the lid on, before Mattie could look inside.

Mattie slipped past him and stood on the stair below, looking up.

Jackbones. That's what the boy reminded him of. The old librarian had grown more solid after leaving the library. Mattie had the same gauzy look. Fragile and fading, rotting away. Not as fruit does, but like old cloth or wood, becoming dry and brittle, crumbling to dust.

It was like looking in the mirror. In Mattie's look of deep, never-ending sadness, Tadpole saw himself reflected.

"What are we doing here?" he asked. "The two of us? We shouldn't be here."

Mattie stared back. His face wrinkled and Tadpole recognized the look of the boy thinking. He waited.

"I've always been here," said Mattie.

"No, you haven't. You can't have been."

"I have, though."

"Think," said Tadpole. "What did you do before you came here? Why did you come?"

Mattie took his time. Tadpole thought he wasn't going to answer at all. He put out his hand for the packet of sandwiches, unwrapped it and bit into one half, without thinking.

It was old, getting stale, but the roffle pack helped to keep it fresher than it would have been, so it was perfectly eatable. If you didn't mind. Tadpole didn't.

He had nearly finished the first half when he remembered his manners.

"Sorry," he said. He swallowed the last piece, wrapped up the other half and lifted the top of his roffle pack.

"Aren't you going to share?" asked Mattie.

"I can't."

"Why not?"

"It's roffle food."

Mattie thought about it.

"I came here when I was very young," he said. "Long years ago."

"It can't have been."

"It was."

"You're only a boy now."

"Only a boy?" said Mattie. "Always a boy. That's what happened. All those long years ago."

"Tell me."

"I'm hungry. Aren't you going to share?"

Tadpole slid the top of the roffle pack tight shut.

"Why did you come here?"

"Give me a sandwich and I'll tell you."

"I can't. It's roffle food. I'm not allowed."

"Then I'm not telling."

Mattie began to move away, down the stairs.

"No. Please. Don't leave me alone again."

"Sandwich?"

"I can't. No. Please. Don't go."

Mattie stopped.

"I'll give you something else," said Tadpole.

"What have you got? I saw a book."

Tadpole slipped the flask back into the pack as well, just moving the lid aside enough to make room.

"Let me see the book," said Mattie.

"Look at this." He handed Mattie the old shield. It looked worse than ever in this gloom, battered and useless. "It's not much," he said. "I mean, it doesn't look much, but it's special." And it was an Up Top thing, not from the Deep World, so it wasn't too bad to let him hold it.

Mattie grabbed it. His thin fingers felt all around the edge, stroked the surface, found the strap, and he put his arm through.

"It's nice," he said.

"Are you sure?"

"I like it."

Mattie stood back and tried to make himself look like a warrior.

"Can I have it?"

"I don't think so. It isn't mine."

"If it's not yours you can't take it from me."

"No. I mean, it isn't mine to give."

"Or yours to take."

Tadpole tried to grab it. Mattie dived away, slippery as a promise.

"It's too heavy for you."

"No. Look. It doesn't weigh anything."

Tadpole pursed his lips. It was right. Mattie wasn't weighed down at all by the shield. Now that it was being used, Tadpole began to value it more. He wanted it back.

"You can have it for a little while. Then it has to go back."

"How long?"

"An hour."

Mattie banged his fist against the front of the shield. The thin hand only made a small, tapping sound.

"Come on," he said. He slipped past Tadpole and stood on the stair above him. "But hush. We're going to look at Ash. Hurry."

"Do we have to?"

"She won't see us. If you're quiet."

Mattie darted up.

Tadpole didn't hesitate.

"Wait for me," he whispered. "Don't leave me alone again." ‖

It wasn't far to Ash's room,

set high in the tower that rises over Boolat. Tadpole hoped it would take for ever to get there. In fact, they reached it before he even had time to get short of breath.

Mattie ran with the shield over his head, as though sheltering from rain. Tadpole had to work hard to stop his roffle pack banging against the sides of the narrow passageway, alerting Ash of their arrival.

Mattie waved to him to slow down, take care, creep up.

Tadpole hung back. He clutched his cloak around him, hoping for invisibility. It could still be a trap. Mattie could be leading him to Ash as a victim. Tadpole waited. Mattie beckoned him on. He put his bony finger to his lips. Not that Tadpole needed warning. He edged closer. Mattie stood aside and let him look through a chink in the wall.

It was a circular room, the shape of the tower. Windows all round. And it was high.

There, at last, was Ash.

And she was beautiful.

The stairs had led the two boys higher than the level of the floor of the tower room. They looked down from ten feet above her head. The roof of the room was another fifteen feet above them.

Tadpole drew back and stared at Mattie. Really? That's her? His eyebrows raised with the question.

Mattie nodded.

Tadpole looked again. Perhaps he had made a mistake. Perhaps there were two of them in there and he'd missed one. The room was barely furnished. A table for a desk. A chair. A small cupboard. No bed. No easy chair. No room for another to hide. She was quite alone.

Tadpole looked at Mattie again, for confirmation. Mattie pushed him aside, with a strength that seemed too great for his frail body. He looked through the squint.

"That's her," he whispered.

Tadpole looked again.

Tall, slim, with a face composed in beauty, she paced the room. Her grey gown trailed behind her, light, like silk. Tadpole couldn't look away from her.

Surely she was not what they said?

She crossed the room and looked out through the arrow-slit window. Her long hair rippled in the breeze.

It's different when you're dealing with wizards.

What if it was all a mistake?

The only wizard Tadpole knew about was Flaxfield. And he was dead. These others. These wizards. What if they were the bad ones? Megapoir had warned him, in the guide. He leaned in to the viewing place, drew in his breath to call out to Ash, to tell her to look up.

Something bashed the back of his head and sent him thumping into the stonework. He banged his forehead and bounced off. Mattie pushed him away. He ran at him with the shield, driving him down the stairs, away from the squint.

Tadpole lost his balance and tumbled down, rolled on his side and only came to a halt when his staff jammed into the sides.

"What —?"

Mattie put his hand over Tadpole's mouth. It was like being silenced by a handful of dry leaves, odd but not unpleasant.

"You mustn't," he whispered. "She'll hear you."

"I want her to hear me."

"You don't."

Tadpole looked at the terror on Mattie's face.

"You really don't," said Mattie. "Come on."

With many a backward glance Tadpole followed Mattie until, after a long and complicated walk, they stepped into a bedroom.

Mattie looked shy as they entered.

It was a palace room. Still furnished with rich tapestries on the walls, ornate rugs. There were easy chairs, and a bed, a huge bed, with posts at each corner and a rich canopy over.

Tables and dressers, a wardrobe and a desk.

Once, it had been a room for a king.

Now?

Now, it was dusty and decayed. Where the tapestries were rotting away Tadpole could see the wall showing through. The canopy over the bed tilted where one of the posts had broken, eaten away by woodworm. At Tadpole's home, wood gleamed and shone, scented with the beeswax his father used every other day. The furniture here was dull, dark and lifeless, with white blooms of mould.

"This is my room," said Mattie.

"It's..." Tadpole searched for a word. "It's a grand room," he said.

Mattie sat in one of the easy chairs, in front of an empty fireplace. Tadpole moved to sit opposite him. The chair cushions were black with mould. He hesitated. Mattie swept his thin arm through the air in a gesture of welcome. Tadpole braced himself against the texture and sat down. It wasn't as bad as he had expected, though the musty smell wasn't so good.

"Are we safe here?" he asked.

"Ash hardly ever leaves her tower, except to go to the kitchens and the cells, or to walk in the courtyard. She never comes here."

"The kravvins? The takkabakks?"

Mattie looked stricken. He shook his head.

"They don't come here?" asked Tadpole. "Why not?"

Mattie put his hands over his face.

Tadpole stood up and walked around the room, looking at everything.

"At first," said Mattie, his voice smaller than ever, "when Ash arrived, with her beetles, they swarmed everywhere. Here as well. They killed everyone. Nearly everyone."

Tadpole looked out of the window while Mattie was telling his story.

"I hid. In the walls. I was only a kitchen boy, so no one knew where I went, what I did. They didn't notice me. Then, when it was all over, all the killing, the takkabakks and the other beetles went down to the basements and the lower floors. They like it there. They seem to need to be near to the earth."

"Tell me about the walls," said Tadpole.

"I don't know. I don't know if they were secret passageways for hiding and escape. Or workmen's tunnels to get to places. Or servants' routes. They're just there. They saved my life."

Tadpole sat again, eager, now that Mattie was talking, to hear his story.

"How long have you been here?" he asked again.

"Always. As long ago as I can remember I was a kitchen boy. I may have been born here. Perhaps my parents were poor and sent me here. I don't know."

He slid down in his chair as he was talking, his feet in the ashes of the grate.

"A bad spell set fire to the kitchen. Was burned. Hurt."

Mattie spread his hands over his face, as though feeling for something.

"Everywhere. All my body, burned."

He made a high, keening sound. Tadpole looked around at the door and Mattie stopped. He nodded. Put his finger to his lips.

"Yes. Hush. Yes. Right." He put his hands behind his head and pushed his face forward. "Anyway. I ran away. They sent me away. I don't remember."

"What happened to you?"

Mattie looked up. "A girl," he said. "A wizard girl. With magic. She made it better."

"What did she do?"

Mattie sucked his thumb and played with his ear. He rocked back and forward. "Ssmmch."

"What?"

He took his thumb from his mouth and wiped it on the chair. "So much," he said. "It hurt so much."

"What did she do?"

Mattie put both hands on his ears now and pressed them tight, as though blocking out any argument. "She made the pain a stone. And she ate it. She ate the fire."

Tadpole stared at Mattie. It was hopeless. Whatever this boy-thing was, he was quite mad. He sat back in his chair, all interest in the story fled away. The room stared back at him, decayed, damaged. The thin, rocking figure of Mattie made Tadpole's head spin. He closed his eyes, wished he hadn't, and opened them again quickly. Mattie was looking at him, waiting. Tadpole understood that the story wasn't over.

"What happened next?" he said, to be polite. "Where's the girl now?"

The question started Mattie rocking again. He covered his eyes with his hands.

"Dead," he moaned. "She'll be dead, now. She was the only friend I ever had."

He was so forlorn, so bereft, that Tadpole spoke before he thought. "I'm your friend," he said.

Mattie peeped through his fingers. "Really?"

Tadpole had regretted the words as soon as they were spoken. He felt even worse now.

"Of course," he said.

Mattie was off his chair with the speed of a ferret. He switched round and wriggled to sit next to Tadpole in his chair. There was only just room for them both and Tadpole had to budge up. He felt that Mattie might break if he wasn't careful with him. Snap like a fried piece of bacon rind. Mattie darted back to his own chair, scooped up the shield, put it on his head and wriggled back next to Tadpole. He put his forefinger on Tadpole's chest.

"You're a roffle," he said.

"I am."

Mattie looked as though he had discovered a great secret. "What's it like?" he asked.

"What?"

"Being a roffle."

"I don't know. I've never been anything else. What's it like being you?"

Mattie stopped smiling. He pulled the shield down over his eyes, and his voice was hollow when he answered. "It's horrible."

The rim of the shield was in Tadpole's way. He had to lean uncomfortably to one side to avoid it.

"I'm sorry," he said.

"Doesn't matter."

"What do you want it to be like?"

Mattie moved the shield a little to one side so that one eye showed. "I want a friend," he said. "And I want to be able to run about, outside. I want to see the dead girl, and for her to be alive. I want to say thank you to her. She sent me away. She said I couldn't stay with her." He hid his eyes again. "I wanted to. She could have been my friend."

"But you came back here?"

"I hadn't got anywhere else."

Tadpole tried to think what it must be like, living there, hiding. The stink. The fear. The beetles. Ash in her tower. And Smedge? Did Smedge come here? He was Ash's helper.

"Does Smedge come here?" he asked.

Mattie closed his mouth tight and nodded. He screwed up his eyes.

"I wanted to call out to her," said Tadpole. "I thought she looked better than the others. She's..." He hesitated. "She's beautiful."

"At first sight," agreed Mattie. "Until you've seen her work."

Tadpole needed more space. The chair was not big enough for comfort for two. He stood and crossed to the window. Cloud. Always cloud at night. Never stars.

"The girl," he said. "Was there really a girl? Try hard. I have to know you're telling me the truth about things."

Mattie's voice betrayed his disappointment. "I only tell the truth," he said. "Only. Always. All these years I haven't spoken to anyone. I won't waste words on lies. I thought you were my friend."

"I am. Sorry. I just need to know. Tell me something about her."

Mattie came and stood next to him.

"She was pretty," he said. "And kind. And funny. And I think she was sad. Do you believe me?"

"I believe you."

"Her name was Bee," said Mattie. "Isn't that strange? Bee. Like a bee. Buzzzzz." ‖

Tadpole stepped away from the window

and grabbed Mattie's hand so they stood facing each other.

"This is no good," said Tadpole.

"What?"

"Just standing here, being frightened. We can't do this."

"What else?"

"We've got to fight Ash. We've got to beat her."

He pulled his dagger from his belt and stabbed the air.

"We can't."

"No one else can, can they? We're here. We're inside Boolat. We're the only ones who can do it. Come on. What about it?"

Tadpole's eyes were gleaming in the dark room. The blade glinted.

Mattie waved the shield above his head. His thin legs jigged. He laughed.

"I'd rather die," he said, "than live like this any longer. Die with you."

Tadpole paused. His enthusiasm drained away. He gathered himself again and stabbed the darkness.

"We won't die," he said. "Not this time. We'll kill Ash instead."

Mattie danced again. The sight of the wasted boy's sudden joy robbed Tadpole of his own. Mattie danced around Tadpole and whispered as he passed, "Use magic. It's the only way. The only thing."

Tadpole turned round and round, following Mattie's dance.

"I can't."

"What?"

"Can't use magic."

Mattie stopped. He was breathing heavily. He lowered the shield and held it in front of him.

"You have to." He sniggered. "Do you think you can just stab her, with your knife?" He danced back and mimed stabbing.

"I can't use magic," Tadpole repeated. "I haven't got any."

Mattie stopped stabbing. "What sort of wizard are you?"

"I'm not a wizard at all."

"You look like a wizard." Mattie pointed. "With your cloak. And your staff. Why are you dressed as a wizard if you aren't a wizard?"

Tadpole shrugged. "They were presents," he said. "This is to keep me dry. And the staff was to help me walk through a wood."

Mattie's face showed that he didn't believe him. He put his finger alongside his nose and winked. He moved his finger to his lips and winked with the other eye. "Say no more," he said.

"What do you mean?"

"I won't tell if you don't. Keep it a secret."

Tadpole gave up.

"We could ask Khazib," he said. "He's got magic."

Mattie tried to sit on the roffle pack. Tadpole put his arm around Mattie and led him to the window. Mattie struggled a little, tried to slip away and sit down. Tadpole nudged him aside, flipped the pack on to his back and led him back over to the window.

"Clouds," he said, "but no rain."

The moon was invisible behind the cloud. Only a bright glow over the tops of the trees showed where it was.

"What's that?" asked Tadpole.

"The moon."

"No. Something flew past."

"An owl?"

"No. I don't think so. I don't know. It could have been close, but it seemed bigger, further away."

Tadpole strained to look. The clouds shifted in the night breeze. More shapes drifted and flew. For a second the clouds parted and the moon shone bright, then, covered again, disappeared.

"Something down there," said Mattie.

Tadpole dragged his gaze from the sky and followed the path of Mattie's thin finger. A memmont? Crossing the open ground between the trees and the castle? Tadpole leaned forward.

"It's a dog," said Mattie.

"The takkabakks will kill it."

The takkabakks did, indeed, swarm to it. The dog stopped, half-turned, looked at the castle, sat down and waited.

"No," said Mattie. "It's been here before."

The takkabakks circled the dog, clattering.

"It's Tim," said Tadpole.

Mattie touched his arm. "Is it your dog? Is it following you?"

"It's not my dog," said Tadpole. He thought about Mattie's second question and wondered. "It's someone else's dog. At least, that was what I was told."

Tim ran in, leaving the takkabakks to disperse, back to their business of guarding the castle.

"What does it want?" asked Tadpole.

Mattie came away from the window. He sat back in his chair by the dead fire.

"It comes to see Ash," he said.

"I want to see."

"All right." Mattie stood up. "This way."

Tadpole followed, with more speed and less noise this time. He was growing used to the narrow passageways.

"She's got company," whispered Mattie.

Tadpole looked down into the tower room.

Ash leaned against the window sill. Her arms were by her side. The grey dress fell in graceful folds. The draught lifted her hair slightly, framing the beauty of her face. Tadpole was glad that she was angry this time. It broke the spell of attraction that had made him want to go to her. He couldn't tell at first who she was angry with: Tim, who sat with his tongue out, looking up at her, or Smedge or Frastfil, side by side, standing, listening to her.

"You've wasted time," she said. "Both of you."

Smedge met her gaze. Frastfil was trying to. His eyes kept returning to hers, only to glance away again. Tadpole could see that he was terrified.

Something odd caught Tadpole's eye. Something he hadn't noticed before. The floor rippled.

"I could be free of here now," she said. "If you'd worked harder. Frastfil, what progress at the college? How goes it?"

Frastfil spoke too quickly, the words falling out of his mouth in his terror.

"Well. It all goes well. I've cleared away all trace, nearly all trace, of the old magic ways. New teachers. New teaching. New pupils." He plumped himself up in importance. "And the two troublemakers have gone. Jackbones the librarian. Vengeabil the storeman."

"You killed them?"

She stooped and Tadpole saw that the floor was solid enough. The rippling was the movement of thousands of beetles, crawling over it. She picked one up, snapped it in half, sucked it dry and crunched the shell. Tadpole looked away.

Some of Frastfil's self-importance drained away, and he made the best of a bad job. "No. No, I didn't need to kill them. They left. I drove them out." On the word "drove" he swept his arm forward, fist clenched, demonstrating the action.

Ash crossed the room and put her face too close to his. "You drove them out? With your own hands? You threw them out?"

"Not exactly."

"What, exactly?"

"They left." Frastfil's voice was broken. "I made the college too difficult for them, I suppose. They couldn't stand my power any more. They ran away."

Smedge started to speak. Ash put her hand over his face, her fingers buried in his hair, her palm over his mouth.

"Your power?" she said. "You? Power?"

Frastfil hung his head.

"Where are they now?" she said. "What's happened to them?"

Frastfil's lips moved.

"What? Speak up."

The principal of Canterstock College made a final attempt at dignity. He stood tall and spoke directly to her, as though unafraid. "What does it matter where they are? They've gone. The college is clear of them. Ready for you. Nearly ready. But nothing stands in your way now."

Ash took her hand from Smedge's face and pushed Frastfil away. He tripped and fell, squealing, into the beetles. They crawled over him. He struggled back to his feet, whining and slapping, brushing them away. He regained his feet.

"If you think—" he began.

Ash clicked her fingers and Frastfil's mouth disappeared.

"Tell me," she said to Smedge.

He was dressed as a college pupil when he started his account. By the end of it, he was all in black and grey, a tunic and trousers, boots and leather gloves. A sort of soldier.

"The library was the last stronghold of the old college," he said. "Once Jackbones had gone I set about emptying it. I left Dr Duddle in charge. He's loving throwing away all the old books."

Ash smiled and patted his cheek.

"Good boy," she said. "It will be my own room."

Tadpole remembered the endless rows and tiers of galleries, out of sight, and wondered how they would ever empty them all. How would they even reach them all?

Ash leaned down and stroked Tim. "And you're a good dog," she said. "You'll be our college dog, won't you?"

Tim turned big, trusting eyes up to her.

"New magic," she said. "Wild magic. My magic. I'll be free of this prison. I'll gather round me the best, the most powerful company of wizards ever seen."

She put her hands to her head and pressed. "And I know now," she said. "I know now how to take young magic. I'll never die. I did it once. I can do it over and over again. Canterstock will be my everlasting kingdom."

Mattie touched Tadpole's arm. "It's all right," he whispered. "It can't happen. She can't escape from here. She has these dreams. I've seen them before."

Tadpole tried to smile.

Ash darted forward and slapped Frastfil hard across the face. "Wipe that silly smile off," she said. "Do you think I don't know what you're thinking? Do you?"

Frastfil mumbled.

"What?"

He looked away and mumbled again.

"If you don't speak plainly, I'll feed you to the kravvins," she said.

Frastfil's eyes widened. He flailed his arms about, pointing to his face. Ash looked at him. His mouth wasn't there. Just smooth skin from nose to chin.

"Oh, yes," she said. "Of course. Well, I'll tell you, shall I? You think I'm a prisoner here and can't escape. You think I've never found the seal and I never shall. I'll never destroy it. That's it, isn't it?"

He nodded.

"But I don't need the seal, now," she said.

She nodded to Smedge, who darted out a hand and grabbed the dog by its collar. Tim crouched and whimpered. Smedge kicked him, hard, and Tim's back leg gave way underneath him.

"Don't break anything," said Ash.

Smedge pulled the collar harder and Tim slid towards him, his claws scraping the floor.

Tadpole gripped his staff, finding it difficult not to call out and tell Smedge to stop torturing Tim. The dog hung its head and waited for the next kick.

"Enough," said Ash. "Send him away."

Smedge put his face to Tim's ear and whispered. The dog listened, shaking, and bolted off as soon as Smedge released his grip on the collar.

"The seal is on its way," Ash continued, to Frastfil. "But there are other ways out of here. Ways that aren't sealed, I think."

Ash flicked her fingers and Frastfil's mouth reappeared. He jingled the coins in his pockets and looked puzzled. "What?" he said.

Ash lowered her voice, and Tadpole had to lean over to hear her.

"Roffle doors," she said. "I could escape that way."

Frastfil took his hands from his pockets and grasped his tunic, in the pose he used when he lectured students. "That will never work," he said. His voice grew more confident as he spoke. "Because all the roffles have taken to the Deep World. And, anyway, even if there were to be a roffle Up Top, he would never show us the roffle doors. They're a secret no roffle will share. As it happens," he added.

"Oh, shut up."

"What?"

Ash spat a half-chewed beetle into his face.

"I had a roffle here, once," she said. "Megatorine."

"Megatorine. I know him. Nice, helpful chap."

Ash turned her back on him.

"Not helpful," she said. "He wouldn't tell me where a door was."

"I told you so."

"Shut up!"

Frastfil stepped back.

"He was about to. He was just going to tell me where there was a door. But he didn't manage to get the words out in time."

"Why not?"

"He broke."

"What do you mean, broke?"

Ash smiled. Tadpole rested his cheek against the stone wall, to draw comfort from its coolness.

"I mean," said Ash, "that I had to encourage him to tell me. And, perhaps, I encouraged him too hard. He broke before he could say."

Frastfil beamed at this, as though he didn't think about what had happened to the roffle, only that he could prove himself right. "I told you," he said. "They never tell. And, anyway. There are no roffles here now. No more to ask."

"No?" said Ash.

"What do you think?" Ash asked Smedge.

Smedge smiled.

"Tim thinks he scented one," he said.

Tadpole felt a rush of fear. He drew his face away from the squint. He stepped back, and a cold, wet nose brushed against the back of his hand. He jumped, and nearly cried out in fear.

Tim's eyes looked up at him.

Mattie sprang back and pressed himself against the stone wall, so thin that he disappeared against it, like lichen. Only the shield stuck out, a metal sconce.

Tadpole turned to run upstairs.

"Kill."

"Eat."

Kravvins blocked his way.

He ran down.

"Smash."

"Rip."

"Eat."

Kravvins again.

Tadpole swung his staff at them, the star-flecked end crashing into a head and splitting it open. The grumble of hate swelled into a roar. They surged at him.

"No," said Smedge. He elbowed his way through and stood between Tadpole and the kravvins. "Eat him later. Ash needs him first." He put a slim hand to Tadpole's cheek. "I need him first," he added. "Make way."

There was no way to escape his escort. In minutes, Tadpole was back in the cell with Khazib.

Smedge chained him, ankles and wrists, to the wall.

"It's getting dark out," he said. "I'll be back tomorrow. With Ash. You know what we want. Be ready to tell us."

Tadpole rushed at him, and the pain of the iron restraints made him call out. Smedge hissed a spell, and the fastenings tightened, pinching his flesh.

"Tomorrow," he said. ‖

Sam woke early, the sun capturing the house

and holding it prisoner. He got up, looked out of the window and was shocked to see Tamrin approach. So near, only yards away, and he had no sense of her at all. No shock of joining. No impulse of her.

They saw him at the window, so he had to wave. Cabbage waved back, always ready to greet, always open to meeting. December raised a cautious hand. Jackbones nodded. Tamrin looked away.

He could see that she felt it, too. She felt the same. There was no overlap of their minds.

The door clattered open and Sam heard the greetings, hearty at first, and then astonished. He climbed back into bed and curled up.

The voices rose and fell. Loud pleasure. Silent wonder. Murmurs of question. Silent embraces. Soft stories. An awkward pause. The clank of metal on pan. Buzz of friendship. Sam screwed up his eyes and tugged the blanket tight.

When the door opened he made himself still as stone.

Whoever came in said nothing. Moved to the corner. The chair creaked. Sam strained to hear the voices downstairs, trying to work out which one was missing.

He knew anyway. It was the voice that had hardly spoken since they had entered the small house. He relaxed his grip on the blanket, kept his head covered.

"Where have you been?" he asked.

Tam didn't answer.

"Are you all right?" he asked. Stupid question. The sort you ask a stranger. Anything to make her speak.

She remained silent.

Sam pushed the blanket aside and sat up. He didn't look at her.

"How did you get here?" he asked. "Did you know we were here?"

He wondered where they had found bacon in an empty house. The scent wafted up the stairs. The voices were happy now. The sound of any family meal. A small spell was enough for him to be able to hear everything they said.

"If you don't answer me," he said, "I don't know what's been happening."

"That's the trouble," said Tam.

He looked at her for the first time.

"Anything?" he asked.

She shook her head, and raised an eyebrow. He shook his head.

They stared at each other.

"What happened to us?" asked Sam.

"The mirror."

"What?"

"When the mirror broke. I think that was when it happened."

"I was losing you before that."

"I know. But that was panic. Distance. Wild magic. I still had glimpses, moments. You?"

"Flashes of contact," said Sam.

He thought about it.

"You're right," he agreed. "Since the mirror smashed, nothing."

"What about Starback?"

Sam hunched and plucked at the edge of the blanket.

"Nothing?" she asked.

"Flashes. Sometimes. Nothing real. He stayed longer than you did. But he's fading now. Leaving me."

He turned a wet face to Tam.

"I'm going to be alone, Tam."

"I know."

They didn't speak again.

When a small tap came on the door Sam had settled his face again, and Tam was ready to speak.

"Yes?" she called.

"Can I come in?"

"Come in," said Sam.

Dorwin looked in. "We saved some breakfast."

"I'm not hungry," said Sam.

"That doesn't matter," she said. "We've all got work to do, and we need to be fed. Tam's having a second breakfast, aren't you?"

Tam managed a smile. "At least there isn't a roffle," she said. "Otherwise there'd be nothing left for us. Come on, Sam."

Sam could feel the puzzlement in Dorwin's mind as Tam encouraged him off the bed. She didn't understand their need to talk now.

They waited for her to go before Sam asked, "Are you sure Tadpole went home?"

"I think so."

"What if he didn't?"

"Then he's dead," she said.

The looks on the faces in the kitchen told Sam that they knew something was wrong. They were too gentle to ask.

The bacon was good, salty and thick. Cabbage served up the food with a generous hand. Sam found that he was hungry after all. He ate in silence. The others carried on a sort of conversation, avoiding anything important, saving it till later, when he and Tam had eaten. They had all caught up with each other's news while Sam was in bed.

"Look at us," said December, when Sam had reached the stage of mopping up the last of the egg yolk with a crusty bit of bread. "Do you think we're all that are left?"

"All what?" asked Sam. "Sorry." He swallowed his bread and continued. "What do you mean, all?"

"All that's left of magic," said Flaxfold.

Sam spread butter on a new slice of bread.

"There's Ash," said Tam.

Sam could feel that they were looking at him to see if he was saying it. He ignored them.

"Yes, Ash," Flaxfold agreed. "I mean, all that's left of real magic. Old magic. There's Ash and the wild magic. And there'll still be Frastfil and the college and their school magic."

"There's plenty of good magic there," said Cabbage. He finished his work at the stove and sat next to Sam. "It's where Jackbones taught me."

The old librarian smiled at him, and Sam saw how tired he was, how thin and empty.

"Jackbones has been a good master," said Flaxfield, "but he was apprenticed, as well as college-trained. As were you, Cabbage."

Cabbage raised a hand in acknowledgement. "You and Jackbones together," he said. "You're my masters. I know. And I'm forever grateful." He looked sad. "I missed your Finishing. Pretending to be Vengeabil, at the college."

Dorwin took Sam's plate and put it on top of Tamrin's. "What about your other apprentices?" she asked.

"All dead, I think," said Flaxfold. "Ash has been busy. Her kravvins have worked their worst."

"Are you sure?" asked Dorwin.

"No. Not sure. But I think that if any of them survived they would have been drawn here today."

"I'm sure of it," said Flaxfield. "All the magic that came from the mirror, to me and Flaxfold, and that we passed on to apprentices, is here in this room, now. We are the old magic. All of us."

Sam felt a thrill of pleasure run through him at this. He pushed it aside, ashamed.

"What's wrong, Sam?" asked December. "What are you thinking?"

Sam shook his head. Tamrin spoke for him. "He's thinking what a fine thing it is to be one of this small group," she said. "He's thinking that it's the greatest thing in the world to be a wizard. And not just any wizard, but one of the wizards of the old magic."

They nodded at this, one in agreement.

"But he's ashamed," she said. "Ashamed to be proud of the smallness of the group. He thinks he should be like Flaxfold and Flaxfield. That he should want more and more magic, more and more wizards."

Sam felt himself tremble at her words.

"It's over, isn't it?" he said.

Flaxfield put his hands together and rested them on the table. The confusion between him and Flaxfold resolved into a single, double person for a moment. Where there had been an old man and an old woman there were two, younger people, identical and neither one nor the other. "Over?" they said together.

No one could speak.

The moment passed and they were two again.

"I don't know," said Flaxfield. "I really don't know."

"All I know," said Flaxfold, "is that we're what's left. And whether we start now or end now, we may as well enjoy it."

"Just a minute," said Sam.

"What now?" asked Flaxfield, signs of his old impatience tearing at the edges.

"Dorwin," said Sam. "If we're the last of the old-magic wizards, why is she here?" He opened his hands to her in apology. "Sorry. I don't mean I don't want you here. I just want to know."

Dorwin didn't smile in return. "I understand," she said. "And it's a fair question." Now she smiled. "And let me give you a wizard's answer."

"What's that?"

"Another question, of course."

"Ask it."

Dorwin looked Sam straight in the eyes. "What came before the magic?" she asked.

"Tell me."

"The fire. The iron. The anvil. The smith. The swords. The shield. The mirror."

"And what comes after the magic?" asked Sam.

Silence fell on them like silk. ‖

Flaxfold banged her fists on the table,

stood up and gave the broadest smile Sam had ever seen on her face.

"Come on," she said. "If we're going to die, we'll have some fun first."

"What do you mean?" he asked.

She swept past him and out of the door.

Tamrin was first after her, then Jackbones, surprisingly alert and keen. The others pushed through as fast as they could.

"Magic attracts attention," said Flaxfold. "Is that right?"

They agreed that it was.

"So we've hidden it, rationed it, hugged it close? Yes?"

"What's the point of all this?" asked Sam.

"You know," she said.

She opened her arms wide, lifted her face to the skies and called out, "Butterflies. I want butterflies."

With no pause, no arriving swarm, no wait, she was surrounded by coloured wings. Blue and powdery yellow. White with orange tip. Red and black. Colours that blared out like trumpets. Colours that shyly peeped from between their fingers. Subtle browns and startling scarlet. Wings that had eyes like owls'. Wings like the bark of a beech tree. Wings like the fur of a tortoiseshell cat. Wings of veins and feathers and dots and swirls.

They flew around Flaxfold, tickling her face. Settling on her shoulders, her arms, her hair. Primrose-coloured wings made a halo round her head.

"Come on," she said. "Magic."

Sam felt as though he had been bound and gagged for a year. The fastenings fell away from him. He couldn't stop himself from running off, away from the house, into a clear space and jumping, high, high as the window he had looked through, high as the top of the apple tree beyond, high as the top of the old elm by the field edge. He spiralled down, whooping till his throat hurt.

He landed, gentle as a dry leaf, and grinned at them. Without thinking, he moved straight on to another spell. Rapping his staff on the ground he called out a charm. Pointy-nosed moles popped up all around him, their eyes tight against the sunlight, their little hands pushing aside piles of earth.

Tamrin ran over, laughing. "Don't," she said. "You'll frighten them. They're supposed to be asleep." She rapped her staff and the moles covered themselves with earth and were gone.

"What, then?" asked Sam. "What shall we do?"

"Try this," she said.

She lay on the grass, pushed her cheek against the ground

and whispered to it. Meadowsweet and clover. Vetch and ox-eye daisy. Celandine and buttercup. Orchids of all sorts, and foxglove and campion. Wild meadow flowers, in and out of season, sprang up. They ran out from her in all directions, glorious in scent and colour and form.

Sam hugged himself in delight. He whispered a new plant into being. A jasmine, evening-scented, yet pouring its sweet aroma into the fresh morning.

Tam sat up, plucked a sprig, fastened it in the neck of her cloak and smiled at him.

They held each other's gaze for a moment, until they were broken by the sound of Flaxfield, drumming his staff on the trunk of a willow. They looked across. The upstretched arms of the tree burst open and a thousand birds flew out. Every songbird and warbler that Sam had ever learned about in his studies. They invented themselves in song and spread out, filling the sky. Everyone raised their heads and looked at them in sudden joy. Sam looked to see how Flaxfield liked them. He couldn't see him at first. He moved forwards, taken with a swift fear that Flaxfield had been attacked or taken, that the magic had brought a sudden response. The tree trunk bulged and narrowed. Flaxfield stepped towards Sam. Like a moth whose wings mimic the bark, Flaxfield had seemed to be one with the willow, and then he was himself again, his cloak the colour and pattern of the tree.

"What happened?" asked Sam.

"You like them?" said Flaxfield, indicating the birds.

"The tree," said Sam. "What happened?"

"Look at Jackbones," said Flaxfield.

Sam turned to see the old librarian conjure up a field of faces. He surrounded himself with a company of people of all ages, men and women, like an audience in a vast arena, with himself at the centre.

"It's his library," said Flaxfold, joining them. "He misses them all."

"Have you ever been there?" asked Sam.

"Oh, yes. Of course. We're very old friends."

"Why hasn't Cabbage made himself a storeroom?" asked Sam.

Cabbage and December stood together, hand in hand, looking away from the others.

"He hasn't made anything," said Tam, moving close to Sam.

"Nothing you can see," said Flaxfold.

They stood and watched the two, distant from them. Sam turned over in his mind what it might be that they had made.

"Hey, look at this!"

Dorwin, who had no magic and had not joined in, had wandered off. She rejoined them, leading a memmont. Not so much leading, as walking beside. It trotted happily along with her.

Sam crouched and looked at it. "Is it Tadpole's?"

"Yes. I'm sure."

"How can you be sure?" asked Tam.

"We work with roffles. At the forge. I know memmonts. This is Tadpole's."

They all stood around, united again.

"Where's Tadpole, then?" asked Cabbage.

"I didn't see him. This fellow just came up to me. He was hiding in the bushes." She pointed.

"If Tadpole went home, he'd have found the memmont," said Flaxfold.

They looked at Tam. Her face reddened.

"I ran away," she said. "Drawing the takkabakks after me. I told you. He ran into the woods."

"But not back to the Deep World," said Cabbage, "or he'd be with this memmont."

The memmont leaned forward and tied Sam's lace.

"If he didn't go home, where did he go?" asked Sam.

He knew the answer, as well as they did. He just wanted someone to say it.

"He could only have gone into Boolat," said Tam. "There wasn't anywhere else."

"Then we'll have to go there for him," said Jackbones. "I'm responsible for him."

Flaxfold clapped her hands. "Too much magic," she said. "We're wasting time."

The assembly of scholars melted away. The birds flocked back into the silver-green leaves of the willow tree, leaving silence. The butterflies dissolved back into air. The wild-flower meadow drained into a single spot, like water circling into a drain.

Sam could never remember who said, "It's time. We're going to Boolat." ||

Part five

STARMAGIC

As armies go,

it wasn't much of one. Two young wizards, Sam and Tamrin. An old wizard, Jackbones, half-faded away. Two old wizards, Flaxfield and Flaxfold, who walked apart from the others, talking to each other in low voices, sometimes smiling, not often. Two other wizards, a woman with a face destroyed and a storeman from a college that was rotting away.

And there was Dorwin, leading a memmont. Sam noticed that she strode out confidently, making easy ground without the handcart to push.

"Who will protect Dorwin?" Sam whispered to Tamrin. "If there's fighting. She hasn't got any magic."

Tamrin had been looking up, scanning the sky as they walked.

"We'll have to watch out for her," she said. "Have you seen Starback?"

"Where?" Sam looked up.

"No. I don't mean, can you see him. He's not there. I mean, have you seen him? Today. Since we set off."

"No."

"No."

They walked on in silence. The nearer they drew to Boolat the more damaged the countryside. Fields black with burned crops. Orchards uprooted, the trees lying ashamed, their roots uncovered, their branches snapped. Streams running with the filthy effluent of slaughter.

"It's worse than ever," said Tamrin.

"The kravvins have been busy," said Dorwin.

She came alongside them, the memmont trotting next to her.

"But where are they now?" asked Sam.

Flaxfold and Flaxfield dropped back, to make five.

"They're waiting," said Flaxfold.

Jackbones slowed down and added to their number.

"I'll go ahead," he said. "You hang back and I'll see if they're lying in wait, or if they're in the castle, getting ready to attack."

"You'll do no such thing," said December, as she and Cabbage approached.

Sam felt a wave of pleasure wash over him as they all joined forces. He smiled at December. She smiled back, a broad, welcoming smile, and Sam noted that she had not drawn her shawl across her face since they had set off. Her eyes met his.

"No more hiding," she said. "No more covering myself. I am this. And Ash, Slowin, can confront me as I am, if she dares."

"She can. She will," said Flaxfield. "Slowin never had any shame. Not even as an apprentice. He, she, will look on you and gloat."

December smiled again. "Not for long," she said.

"Ash is very strong," warned Cabbage.

December took his hand. "Then I'll have to be stronger," she said. "Or be killed."

Jackbones made a little moan. "Death isn't so easy," he said. "Death has been hiding from me for more years than I know."

Tamrin stopped without warning and Dorwin bumped into her.

"Sorry," said Dorwin.

Tamrin shook her head, dismissing the apology. She raised her arm and pointed. "Look."

The topmost tower of Boolat poked above the trees.

"I didn't think we were so close," said Sam.

"Are you all right?" asked Jackbones.

"Fine," said Sam, feeling sick. "I'm fine. How did we get here so soon?"

"Things are shrinking," said Flaxfold. "Time. Journeys. Choices. Powers."

"All drawn towards Boolat," said Cabbage.

"We're stronger together than apart," December said to Jackbones. "We go on as we are. No acting alone."

Jackbones turned his head away from her, ignoring her.

"She's right," said Sam. "If you go off without us, we'll

only have to follow to find you. We'll split up. We'll lose our concentration."

"Anyway," said Tamrin, slipping her hand into Jackbones', "I want you to be with me."

He nodded. "All right. But I feel guilty about Tadpole. You know? I was told to look after him."

"I know," she said. "I was supposed to look after him as well."

"So what's next?" asked Sam. "Should we rest up here and get ready? Make a plan? We can't just go running in without anything in mind. I suggest that we—"

"Hang on," said Tam.

"What?" Sam snapped at her. He didn't like to be interrupted, and especially he didn't like not knowing Tam's mind any more.

"The memmont," she said.

"What about it?"

It had broken free of Dorwin and was loping off, towards the trees, fast, in the direction of the Castle of Boolat.

"As soon as you said 'Tadpole', it ran off," said Dorwin.

"That's it," said Tam. "We'll have to follow it. It knows something."

"We haven't chosen a plan yet," said Sam.

Tam put her arms around him and hugged him tight. She stepped back, laughing. "Don't you remember anything?" she said.

Sam scowled. "What?"

"We're not choosing to run straight at Boolat," she said.

Sam stopped scowling and laughed. It was simple. Obvious. And it took away all need to worry and plan. "It's chosen us," he said. "Come on."

Sam and Tamrin ran off after the memmont.

"Young legs," Jackbones complained, hitching up his cloak and running after, leading the rest.

Tadpole only knew it was morning when Smedge came into his cell. No light penetrated that deep. Only the greasy flame of the rush torch that Smedge held lit the gloom. The roffle sat up, his back against the stone wall, and stared at him.

"You slept well?" asked Smedge, as though Tadpole had dropped in as a guest.

Tadpole stretched and scratched his shoulder. His chains clinked. He had slept well. He couldn't believe it. No nightmares or sudden waking up. He slept right through. He looked around. Khazib was still sitting in the same position as before, staring ahead.

Smedge came right into the cell, kicking the door shut after him. He fixed the torch into a wall bracket, folded his arms and looked at Tadpole.

"It will be so easy for you, and for everyone, if you show us the roffle door," he said. "Then we can let you go. Back to your friends. Back to the Deep World. Anywhere you want."

Tadpole squirmed to get comfortable on the slimy straw. He hugged his roffle pack to his chest, and gripped his staff.

"Look at you," said Smedge. "You're a joke. Dressed up as a wizard, with your cloak and your staff." He moved towards Tadpole. "Let me tell you," he said, "the cloak doesn't make the wizard. You can dress up all you want, but unless you've got magic, you're not a wizard."

Tadpole tried to stare him down. He found it hard to keep his eyes on Smedge's face.

Smedge advanced, his expression growing more malevolent with every step.

"And what are you?"

Smedge stopped. He turned to Khazib. The man had not moved. Still he stared straight ahead.

"What?"

Khazib ignored him.

"What did you say?" asked Smedge. He turned his attention to the wizard.

"You're not a wizard," said Khazib.

Tadpole wriggled up to a more upright position, to pay closer attention. It was easier now that Smedge had turned away.

Smedge clicked his fingers and a thousand tiny needles dropped from the roof of the cell, showering Khazib and piercing him all over.

A spasm of pain crossed Khazib's face. He shook it off, unmoved.

"Oh, you've got magic," said Khazib. "And you've been to the college with the weak idiot Frastfil, but you're no wizard."

Smedge drew back his foot and kicked Khazib, hard, in

the ribs. The wizard rocked to one side, steadied himself and returned to his position.

"You're made of bad magic," said Khazib. "You're a waste product, not a person. Any magic that spills out of you is like the outpouring of a sewer."

Tadpole hugged his cloak round him, trying to disappear at the sight of Smedge.

The boy shimmered again, and shifted shape. He lost the form of the uniformed soldier and became all forms and none. Rat and slug, toad and cockroach; all overtook him. Worst of all, they melted into each other, making new-formed horrors. And, under it all, the persistent emergence of green slime. Tadpole felt that Smedge was struggling to push back the form of slime, to clamber into real shape, real body.

Khazib smiled and moved his head to look at Tadpole and nodded.

Green smoke poured out of Smedge, stinking and damp. Tadpole tried not to breathe too deeply. Smedge was still trying to regain shape. Little by little he emerged from the mess, until he stood before them again, complete, uniformed and stable, save for a dribble of green slime at the corner of his mouth.

"We've kept you too long," he said to Khazib. His voice was damaged from the changes and it squeaked and slurred. More slime oozed out as he spoke. "You're no use to us now. We've got the roffle. We can get rid of you."

Khazib sighed. "At last," he said.

"No," said Tadpole. "Don't. Please. Don't."

He hated the look of joy that crossed Smedge's face.

"So sweet," said Smedge. "You care about each other." He paused. "I wonder what that's like?" he said. "Oh, I know. It's useless. It makes you weak." He kicked Tadpole's leg gently with the toe of his boot. "You don't want to show me a roffle door?"

"I won't."

"Even if I hurt you?"

"No."

Smedge leaned down and whispered in his ear, wet and foul. "I think you will. If I encourage you." He touched Tadpole's cheek. A flash of pain shot through him. His back teeth filled with a hurt so intense he thought he would faint. A moment later, it was over. "Oh, I think you would, eventually."

He stepped away, leaving Tadpole gasping in memory of the pain.

"But I think it will be quicker if I make you watch me destroy this one," said Smedge. He kicked Khazib again, hard. "He's going to die today, anyway, so I may as well make use of him."

"No," said Tadpole. "Leave him alone."

"Then show me the door. It's easy."

Tadpole heaved himself to his feet, using his staff. He shouldered his roffle pack and stood glaring at Smedge. Smedge laughed. Tadpole raised his staff and swung it at him. Smedge stepped back. Tadpole tottered and slipped to his knees. Smedge aimed a kick at him and sent him halfway across the cell.

"This is better," he said. "Come on, roffle. Try again."

Tadpole found his feet again. He clenched his staff, wanting to point it, rather than swing it, wanting magic to pour from it, wanting to hurt Smedge, to stop him. He hesitated. Smedge laughed again.

"There's no magic there," he mocked Tadpole. "Here's magic."

He clapped his hands. The roof of the cell came alive as hundreds of bats dropped down and flew round and round over their heads. They swooped and crackled. They veered into Tadpole's face and dived away at the very last second.

Tadpole liked bats. He knew they did no harm, yet he waved his arms to keep them away. He staggered back and banged into the wall, the impact making his pack boom like a drum.

"Here's magic," said Smedge.

He clapped his hands again, and the bats were tiny crows, with savage beaks and ripping claws. They circled Tadpole, dipping and cawing. This was different. They would have his eyes out if they could. He covered his face with his cloak.

"That's right," said Smedge, raising his voice above the calling crows. "Hide away, while I deal with this one."

Tadpole heard another kick land on Khazib. He peered over the hem of his cloak. Smedge was preparing for another kick.

"Stop," said Tadpole. "All right. Stop. And get rid of these."

"Are you sure?" Smedge's foot was still raised, ready for the kick.

"Yes. Stop now."

Smedge clapped his hands. The crows flew up and melted back into the stone vault of the roof.

"Don't," said Khazib. "Don't show him the door. I'd rather die."

Tadpole hopped from one foot to another. "I have to. I can't let him hurt you."

"If you show him, they'll hurt many more."

Tadpole leaned against the wall and groaned.

"Now," said Smedge. "Come with me, before you change your mind." He held out his hand.

Tadpole moved away from the wall towards Smedge when a dark shape appeared in the doorway. A kravvin. It looked straight at Tadpole.

"Kill."

"No," said Smedge. "Leave them."

"Eat."

"What do you want?" asked Smedge.

The kravvin paused. Its mouth struggled with an unfamiliar word.

"Durgon."

"What?"

"Dargon."

"Dragon?"

"Dragon. Come. Ash. Dragon."

Smedge gave Tadpole a reluctant look. "I'll deal with you later," he said.

He pushed his open palm towards Tadpole. The roffle staggered back, slipped and fell against the wall. Chains cut into his wrists and ankles.

"Ow."

"Too tight?" asked Smedge.

"Yes. They hurt."

"Good."

He pushed the kravvin aside and ran off. The kravvin hesitated in the doorway, looking at Tadpole.

"Eat."

Tadpole huddled against the wall.

The kravvin turned and left. ‖

The memmont first,

then Sam and Tamrin. The others had caught up with Jack-bones by the time he broke clear of the woods. They ran into the open field sloping down to the castle and looked up.

Starback was circling ahead. Over the ramparts. High, and huge. Blue and green wings knifing the sunlight.

Kravvins and takkabakks surged through the great gates. Sam tensed himself for fight. Jackbones hissed and started to run towards them. Flaxfold grabbed his arm and drew him back.

"Wait," she said.

The red-black beetles formed a circle round the castle.

"Do they know we're here?" asked Tamrin.

Flaxfold lifted a hand and pointed to the jagged walls. Ash looked back at them.

"They know," she said.

"Why aren't they coming to us?" asked Sam.

Starback circled the skies.

"Smedge is with her," said Tamrin. "Look."

Smedge, black-suited, smiling, walked along the ramparts and came to stand next to Ash.

"They're alike," said Tamrin. "I never saw that before."

"He's a shape-shifter," said December.

"Yes, but under the shape, right in the centre of him, he's like Ash."

"I don't like it," said Sam. "Why aren't they doing anything? Why aren't they attacking?"

Starback continued to fly overhead. Sam reached out to him. He tried to flip his awareness to be Starback, to fly above Boolat. To look down on Ash and Smedge. To feel the sky beneath and around him.

Nothing.

His feet were firm on the earth.

"She's afraid," said Flaxfield.

"What?" Sam looked up at his old master.

Flaxfield smiled down at him. Sam drew closer, letting his shoulder brush against Flaxfield's cloak. He drew his breath in and enjoyed the scent of herbs and magic that Flaxfield always trailed after him — clouds of comfort.

"That feeling you've got now, Sam," said the old wizard. "The tumbling in your insides. The soft edges round your vision. The sense of the ground moving slightly beneath you, confusing your balance."

"How do you know?" asked Sam.

"Is it true?"

Sam nodded.

"That's how she feels," said Flaxfield. "She's waited for this moment. Worked for it. Planned and plotted it. Prepared for it and wanted it. And now that it's here, she's afraid."

They all looked at Ash and knew that Flaxfield was right.

"Her beetles are gathered around her for strength and protection," he said. "Now that the moment's here, she's afraid of it. That works to our advantage."

Flaxfold stood the other side of Sam and Tamrin. "It would," she said. "If magic were normal. But it isn't, don't forget. Not at Boolat."

The memmont broke free from the group and ran down the hill. Tamrin called it back.

"Leave it," said Cabbage. "It knows what it's doing."

"We're more than Ash," said Sam. "More magic. More strength. More power."

"We'll see," said Flaxfold.

"Flaxfield," said Sam. "Do you feel that way? The way you just said?"

Flaxfield smiled down at him and rested his hand on Sam's shoulder. "No," he said. "No, I don't. Not today. Not now."

"So we'll beat her?" Sam's face relaxed into a smile.

"I don't know," said Flaxfield. "I really don't know."

"You'll soon find out," said Dorwin. "Here they come."

The kravvins and the takkabakks turned their backs to the castle and, as a single army, intermingled, scurried up the hill towards them. Ash raised her arms and laughed.

"Spread out," said Flaxfold. "Stand your ground."

Starback, swift as a hawk, ceased his circling and dived at the beetles. When he roared fire over them they popped and sizzled. He swooped so low that he gouged a path through them, skimming the ground, crushing and slicing them in his path. Rising up, he banked, swooped and dived again. More fire. More ripping them apart.

They didn't falter for an instant. His attacks were deadly and damaging, but they were too little to overwhelm the red-black army of Ash's troops. There were too many of them. For every one he killed ten more poured out of the gates to join the others.

"They're getting closer," shouted Flaxfield. "No one do anything until I say."

Starback attacked the vanguard, scything down the leaders, slowing their advance. Still they came on. Still they gained ground. When they were twenty feet away Flaxfield flung his staff high in the air. "Now," he called.

The staff lit up.

Sam turned his face away, blinded for a moment by the glare. The staff became light itself, the essence of light. Blinding. Burning. It showered down on the kravvins and the takkabakks. For a second, they halted.

Sam's eyes recovered. He saw the army stall and stagger. He waited for them to pop and scorch. He relaxed his grip on his staff and began to enjoy the protection of Flaxfield's power.

The takkabakks twitched and recovered. They ran on. The

kravvins clattered and cried out.

"Kill."

"Eat."

"Kill."

The staff died, paused, and fell useless to the ground.

The memmont had reached the castle walls and was hunting alongside the stones.

Sam felt a sea of pain wash over him. He dropped to his knees, gasping. He looked up for help. The other wizards had also fallen. To their knees. On their sides. They writhed in pain. Flaxfield alone still stood, old, frail, staring at Ash.

"Boolat magic," he said.

Flaxfold struggled to her feet and stood next to him. "It reflects on the user," she said. "Things fall apart."

Sam reached out a hand found Tamrin's. He squeezed it.

The kravvins and the takkabakks were almost upon them.

"It's over," he said.

They held tight, waiting for the end.

Tadpole's wrists hurt under the iron grip of the manacles. He watched Khazib. And he watched the door. And he gripped his roffle pack. And he wrapped himself in his cloak. And he tucked the hawthorn staff at the back of his bent knees.

Khazib's eyes never moved. He stared ahead, ignoring Tadpole.

"What's happening?" the roffle asked, at last.

"Don't ask. Don't wonder. Just take it when it arrives."

"Take it?"

"Take it. Fight it," said Khazib. "You will know when it happens."

Tadpole fell back into silence.

Nothing moved.

No sound.

No sign.

"What are you doing back here?" asked Khazib.

"Eh?" said Tadpole. The damaged wizard had started to fall apart at last. He had forgotten.

"Not you," said Khazib, still not looking around.

Tadpole turned his head to the left.

Mattie was half-out of the entrance to the hidden passage. He grinned at Tadpole, stepped right out and waved the shield at him. Tadpole was so pleased to see him that he forgot his chains and tried to stand up. He called out in pain and fell back.

As though summoned by the shout, a kravvin appeared in the open doorway.

Tadpole edged back, pressing against the wall.

Another kravvin.

They stared at him with smooth, blank faces.

"Kill."

"Eat."

"Stab."

"Leave us alone," Tadpole shouted. "Smedge said to leave us alone."

The first kravvin took a step inside.

"Kill."

The kravvins halted.

Sam stared up into the smooth, blank faces. "Something's holding them back," he said, squeezing Tamrin's hand.

She stared up at the kravvins.

The army had surrounded the wizards. Sam and Tamrin had their circle of attackers; the others, singly and in pairs, had theirs. Like the rings that raindrops make on still water, the army formed itself into a pattern of circles, with wizards at the centre of each.

"Kill."

"Stab."

"Kill."

"Eat."

The kravvins, held back as they were, still barked out their longing for death.

Jackbones was trying his hardest to make them kill him. He flung himself against the wall of red-black carapaces that held him close. The kravvins trembled with a passion for attack. Sam thought to make a calming spell, to subdue Jackbones, to stop him from hurting himself. He covered his face with his hands and conjured a cloud of patience for the old wizard.

At least, that's what he tried. Nothing happened. Not even a trickle of magic.

"Tam?"

"What?"

"Make a spell for me."

"What?"

"Anything. A spring of water. A cloud overhead. Anything you like."

He waited.

Tamrin said nothing.

"Well?" said Sam.

She made no reply. Which was a reply. Sam uncovered his face and looked up.

Smedge had left the ramparts and was strolling through the host of beetles. Takkabakks clattered as he brushed past them. The kravvins tossed sharp shouts of killing and death. Smedge inspected the groups, one by one, arriving at last at Sam and Tamrin.

He looked down at them.

"You came here at last," he said. "You have no idea how pleased I am to see you."

He poked the toe of his boot against Sam. "You and I have some matters to settle," he said.

Sam started to answer, but Smedge sealed his voice with a sudden spell, and cast a net of magic over him. He turned his attention to Tamrin.

"But you," he said. "You've been such a trouble to me." He kicked her. "Such a nuisance." He kicked her again. "With your hiding and your secrets." Kick. "And your look-ing down on me." Kick. "Your nose in the air." Kick. "Your

clever magic. Your cheek. Your laughing behind my back."
He kicked and kicked, lost to himself in his revenge. Tamrin
made no move. She didn't cry out. She didn't resist. Sam felt
that she had found a way to ignore the kicks, to be somewhere
else.

When he saw that Tamrin wasn't showing any pain,
Smedge recovered himself. He stopped, panting from the
effort. Tamrin turned her head and looked up at him. She
smiled. It filled Smedge with a new fury. He raised his foot.
Sam, still silent and netted, struggled to move to attack him.

The foot never kicked. Smedge hesitated. Listened. He
lost the edges of his shape for a second. With a sly, startled
look he stepped back.

"We're wanted in the castle," he said. "Where there will be
so much time to deal with you."

He walked away.

Sam looked up at the castle walls. Ash, her face carved
with rage, summoned them.

The kravvins moved their captives down the hill, towards
the great gate of Boolat, as dogs herd sheep.

"She wants the seal," said Sam.

"We have to stay out of there," agreed Tamrin.

The leather thong with the heavy seal hopped from neck
to neck. First Tamrin, then Sam. Then back again, and back,
and again.

"If she gets the seal, then it's all over," said Sam.

"For ever," said Tamrin.

The kravvins bumped against them and sent them staggering down the slope, ever closer to Boolat.

And to Ash.

The kravvins halted in the doorway.

Tadpole hid as much of himself in the cloak as he could, only his eyes peeping out.

Mattie crouched next to him and rested his hand on Tadpole's shoulder. He kept to the roffle's left, ready at any moment to slip out through the hidden door.

"What are we going to do?" he whispered.

The kravvins struggled to come closer.

"I don't think they can get us," said Tadpole. "I think Smedge put a spell on the door to stop them."

"It looks like—" said Mattie. He stopped, as the walls boomed and shook.

"What?" asked Tadpole.

Another boom, like a great bell, muffled, shook the room. The walls shook. Mortar dribbled from the joints.

The kravvins became excited.

"Kill."

"Stab."

"Kill."

Boom.

Tadpole hugged the cloak right over the top of his head. The noise was even louder in this personal darkness. He looked out again.

Boom.

The wall split open and a black, shiny face peered through the fissure.

"They're coming through the walls," he shouted. "Khazib. Help. They're not using the door. They're coming through the walls to eat us."

With a mightier crash than ever the wall fell apart and the gap filled with faces. ||

Sam stared up

into the pale blue of the sky.

Starback, his attack defeated, flew off. A tiny figure, blue and green, disappearing from sight. Sam stumbled and fell. He grazed his knees on sharp stones. The blood comforted him. He wiped his cloak over his eyes and carried on, towards the great gates, stretched open ahead.

"Sam," said Tamrin.

He leaned to hear her.

"The memmont. It's going inside."

Sam turned his head to follow her gaze. There was no memmont.

"You missed it," she said. "It just dodged in. Maybe a roffle door?"

"Stab."

"Eat."

The kravvins hurried them on.

Jackbones was still hurling himself against the kravvins,

shouting at them, taunting them. December and Cabbage were together. As were Flaxfield and Flaxfold. Dorwin was ahead of them all. Refusing to be driven by the kravvins, she strode on, making them scurry to keep up with her. Upright and unafraid, she seemed in control, rather than a prisoner under escort.

She was the first to pass through the gate. Jackbones was second. The kravvins had hurried him on. Sam and Tamrin were third.

As they crossed the threshold, the seal settled itself around Tamrin's neck. It glowed bright.

"Look," she said. She stopped. The kravvins bumped into their backs.

She looked down at the ground just on the margin of the castle.

An exact copy of the carving on the seal glowed back at her in response.

"That's it," said Ash.

And there she was.

Right in front of them.

She waved her hand for the kravvins to stand aside.

The three of them looked down at the glowing imprint of the seal.

Tamrin and Sam were one side of the barrier. Ash the other.

They looked up, into each other's eyes.

"Welcome to Boolat," she said, stepping aside. "You'll never leave."

The kravvins pushed them forward, through the gate.

And they were inside Boolat at last.

The others followed.

"Flaxfield," said Ash. "My old friend. How much I've looked forward to seeing you again."

The kravvins melted away to the sides of the courtyard. The takkabakks stayed outside the gates, running up and down the hill, swarming.

Smedge stood in the gateway, his arms folded, waiting for Ash's orders.

Sam made sure that he looked at everything as fast as he could. Walls, turrets, doors, windows. He needed to know where everything was. If there was to be a fight, then Ash had the advantage of knowing the ground. He needed to learn as much as he could.

As he was looking, a door opened and a thin, shabby figure stepped out. His lined face and hooked nose were unmistakable. As was the sly way he walked towards them, smiling foolishly, hands in his pockets, jingling loose change.

Frastfil. The principal of Canterstock College.

"Ah, well," he said, beaming at them with apparent delight. "Here we all are. Who would have thought it, eh? Who would have thought it? What a pleasure to meet up like this, eh?"

He put his hand out to shake Sam's. Sam turned his face away in disgust. Tamrin stepped forward and slapped him, hard.

"Take that stupid smile off your silly face," she shouted.

Frastfil reeled back, steadied himself and smiled again.

"All this," said Tamrin. "All this ... this ... evil. It's you that did it. It's your fault."

Frastfil stammered a reply. "I don't think ... I mean, I don't know why you ... that is, it's not me that made, er..." He waved his arm, indicating everything around them.

"She's right," said Ash.

"Oh?" said Frastfil. He put his hands back into his pockets and jingled the coins.

"Whatever it is," said Ash. "Evil? I don't think so. It's power. My power. But whatever it is, I could never have done this. Never have brought them all here. Never have destroyed Canterstock College without your help."

"I did nothing wrong," said Frastfil. "Not really. I only meant to do good. I didn't destroy it. I made it better."

Tamrin shouted at him. "You stupid, stupid man."

Ash patted his arm.

"That was all I needed," she said. "Now, Flaxfield. Let me see you better."

She faced the old wizard. Sam felt his shoulders grow tight. He waited to see what Flaxfield would do. How he would fight her.

Ash stroked Flaxfield's cheek. He didn't move or show any sign of knowing that she had touched him.

"Do some magic for me," she whispered. "Please. Go on."

Nothing passed over Flaxfield's face. His thin fingers gripped his staff, the bones hardly covered by flesh. Flaxfold touched her shoulder against his. And Sam knew that Flax-field's magic was no more.

"No?" said Ash. "What a pity."

Sam couldn't look at the old wizard's face any longer. He turned away.

Ash walked back to Tamrin. She put her hand to the girl's throat, touched the heavy, iron seal.

Tamrin stepped back. Ash grabbed the seal. The leather thong tightened round Tamrin's neck. Ash pulled her back and put her face close. Her hand closed around the seal.

"This is for me, I think," she said.

She tugged, and the thong broke.

Sam rushed at her. She put her hand out and he fell like a hailstone, gasping for breath, pain like a knife in his side.

Ash, her excitement betraying her, crossed the courtyard with swift steps. She pushed Smedge out of the way and knelt at the edge of the barrier that had held her prisoner for so long.

"Stop her," said Sam.

He stared at Flaxfield, at Flaxfold. They did nothing. Jack-bones had collapsed on arrival at the castle and was sitting, forlorn and alone. Cabbage put out a hand to stop December. Sam noticed now that she had covered herself with her shawl again. Her head and face hidden. She shrugged off Cabbage's hand, stepped over to the kneeling figure of Ash and tapped her shoulder.

"Leave me," said Ash. She clicked an impatient hand to repel December.

"Slowin," said December.

Ash looked over her shoulder. Sam saw that she was surprised her spell had not affected December.

December unwrapped herself from the shawl.

"Slowin," she repeated. ||

Ash looked at December's wasted face,

the skin puckered and drawn, the lips nothing but a line, the eyelids hooded and heavy.

"What?" she said.

"It's been a long time, Slowin," said December.

"Ash. My name's Ash."

She stood, her hand slow to leave the mark of the seal on the ground. Sam noted the contrast between Ash's long, elegant grey robe and December's serviceable clothes. He was startled to understand that the difference between them was a deceit. Ash, slender and perfect, her fine features unmarked by age or damage; she looked like the princess of the castle in a tale for children. A beauty. December, damaged and destroyed. A face to scare birds. A face to fear. A cruel joke played on the flesh by ancient fire.

For a second he was deceived. His eyes tricked him. Looking again, he saw only beauty in December's face, only horror in the perfection of Ash.

"No," said December. "You're Slowin. You stole a name from me, and now I give you back your own."

"Who are you?" said Ash.

"I am Flame," said December.

She drew in a deep breath. Her hair became fire. Ash put her hand over her face to shield herself from the heat.

December stepped towards Ash and was halted by a deep, resonating boom. She stopped. The flames died down. Ash lowered her arm and looked at her.

Boom.

Sam felt the stones of the courtyard shake beneath him.

Boom.

The kravvins moved forward, alert to danger.

"Kill."

"Eat."

"Stab."

Boom.

Smedge ran over to Ash and took her arm.

They all looked down at the ground beneath their feet.

December and Ash confronted each other. Sam watched as each held the other's gaze. December, ignoring the booming beneath her, began to kindle her hair again and invoke the fire magic. Smedge stepped between the two of them.

"You're Bee," he said. "You're not Flame. Flame was taken from you, and you can't take it back. Not now."

Smedge's face began to melt and drip. His skin turned green. He oozed slime as he spoke. Flecks of it spattered over December.

"You're just a girl called Bee, who got burned into an ugly woman. And I'm the real child of the magic that damaged you."

He put his hand on her head and he melted over her. He sizzled, and the flames died out. His hand dribbled slime so that her head and neck and face were covered.

Ash laughed.

"Good lad, Smedge," she said. "I nearly believed her. Hold her there while I free the gates."

"December," Sam called. "Come here. Move away." He looked for help. "Cabbage. Come on. Do something."

Ash crouched down, putting the seal to its impression on the ground.

Boom.

The earth shook.

Boom.

The gates split and toppled.

Boom.

The arched, stone entrance shattered and fell.

Ash stood and looked through.

"Free," she said. "At last."

The faces surged through the broken wall of the dungeon. They had bodies, and arms and legs. Human bodies. Not the hard shells of beetles.

They ran straight past Tadpole, heading for the kravvins.

Faster than Tadpole could follow, they swung out. Axes

and picks, iron clubs and spades. They slammed into the hard black bodies, splitting them open.

More and more of the men clambered through the breach in the walls. Their faces black with dust and grime. Their sleeves rolled up. Their arms thick with work.

When Smith stepped through the gap Tadpole tried to get to his feet again, and again was pulled back by the chains.

"What's happening?" asked Tadpole. "Who..."

"The Finished Miners," said Smith. "I made tools for them. There's work to do. Come on."

"I can't. I'm chained."

"Then free yourself."

Tadpole shook his arms. The heavy chains rattled.

Smith pushed aside Tadpole's cloak with his hammer, revealing the small dagger.

"Come on," he said.

Tadpole drew the dagger and looked at Smith for help.

"Quick about it," said Smith.

Tadpole, feeling foolish, held the blade of the knife against the chain on his other wrist. It cut through the metal, like a boat through water. The chains fell away.

"I made that knife," said Smith. "Use it. Now, come on."

"Wait," said Tadpole.

He crossed the room to Khazib. The wizard had not moved from his spot. Tadpole put his hand under Khazib's forearm.

"May I?" he asked.

And he helped him to his feet. Khazib swayed and his knees buckled.

"Sorry," he said. "I've been kneeling like that for many years. Please. A moment."

More miners streamed through the gap. They ran through the dungeon and out of the door, following the first ones through. Khazib stepped forward, just one foot. Then the other. He swayed, righted himself and smiled.

"Let us see what is happening," he said.

They left the dungeon and made their way up the steep steps. Tadpole looked over his shoulder to check, and was reassured to see Mattie bringing up the rear, the shield on his arm. ‖

Part Six

STARBORN

Clouds ran off, chased by a strong wind
that cleared the vast emptiness overhead. The sky was growing
dark. Sam watched December as she sank down to her knees,
swamped by the green slime pouring from Smedge's hand.

Ash shone like a glowing coal, the grey of her robe flecked
with gold and silver light.

The ground shook under Sam. He struggled to keep his
balance, using his staff for support.

Deep booming echoed round the courtyard.

First the supports of the gates then the rest of the walls
shattered and split.

Ash turned round and round, in a slow survey of triumph.

"Free of this place," she shouted, above the noise.

The kravvins threw themselves against the falling walls in
a frenzy of hunger, shouting for murder. They turned on each
other, stabbing, lunging and biting.

Ash stopped turning. She crossed to Flaxfield and Flaxfold.
The two old wizards, helpless against her, waited in silence.

"Time for you to go," said Ash. "Do you want to die in fire, or shall I feed you to my kravvins?"

Sam ran over and stood shoulder to shoulder with Flaxfold. Tamrin, just as quick, stood next to Flaxfield.

"Kill us all, if you can," she said.

Sam looked over at her and nodded.

"All of us," he agreed.

And he threw himself at Ash, grabbing her throat and driving her to the ground.

As she fell, Ash slid away, a sliver of grey, righting herself and looking down at Sam where he fell. She touched his shoulder with a single finger and he felt a current of fire wash through him.

"You first, then," she said.

Sam looked up and saw Dorwin stand behind Ash. She took her arm and turned her away from Sam.

"Get out of my way," said Ash.

Another, greater crash shook the ground again. Sam rocked where he lay. The turret, high above him, teetered and Sam thought for a second that it was falling on him. The last of the dusk clouds raced past it, leaving the darkling sky clear.

Black faces and iron tools emerged from the cracks in the stonework. Like ants from a nest, the Finished Miners clambered up. They flung themselves on the kravvins, smashing them to pieces.

"Smith," said Dorwin. "About time."

He grinned at her. His hammer rested on his arm, ready for use.

"You found the iron, then," she said.

"And worked it," he said. "Worked it deep underground, with roffle fire. I made their axes and picks, their spades and shovels."

He leaned down and lifted Sam to his feet.

"All right, lad?"

Sam nodded, breathless, shocked at the violence all around him.

Boolat was crumbling. Every stone, every wall and door, every turret and tower, falling, under the blows of the miners. The kravvins, what was left of them, fled away, up the hill, to join the crazed takkabakks running in senseless circles.

Just as Sam began to recover his balance and start to take in the victory, Ash lifted her head and screamed out.

"Let it be fire," she shouted. "Let it all be fire."

A circle of flame blazed up where the castle walls had stood.

"Wild fire. Wild magic," she shouted.

The circle contracted and advanced. It swept towards them, consuming everything it touched. Smedge and December disappeared into its flames. Cabbage, his mouth wide open in some sort of challenge or cry for help, was eaten by its approach.

Sam's cloak scorched and then, before the flames even reached him, burst into fire, wrapping him in burning wild magic.

Ash alone was untouched by it. She stood in the centre of the blaze, her face alight with pleasure. Her arms upraised to welcome it.

Sam made one last attempt to conjure some magic to protect, to fight, to resist. His staff kindled in his hands and was swallowed by the fire, all magic spent. ‖

The host of Finished Miners

swept Tadpole up the staircase. They lifted him off his feet like a wave, carrying him with them. He looked over his shoulder for Mattie, comforted somehow by the frail boy with his shield.

They burst through the doorway, into the courtyard. Fanning out, they stopped supporting Tadpole and he dropped to his feet. Smith gave him a huge push away from the wall, which crashed to the ground behind him. Stone dust and mortar, shattered blocks and shards fell around him. Smith carried on, smashing kravvins out of the way with his hammer.

"Mattie," said Tadpole. "Are you there?"

The sensation of lace brushed his neck.

"No," said Tadpole. "Not this. I didn't leave the Deep World for this."

He lowered his head and closed his eyes against the killing and the wreckage.

Mattie leaned closer to him.

"Go home," he whispered.

Tadpole opened his eyes and looked at him.

"What?"

"Go home, then. There are roffle doors, aren't there? Take one. Go home."

Tadpole looked to his right. Just there. Only a few feet away. A roffle door. All he had to do was walk through it, and it would be over. He could leave Up Top to its troubles and go home. He stepped towards it. A small, furry nose peeped out.

"You," said Tadpole. "Come here."

The memmont's head appeared.

"Come on," said Tadpole.

The creature didn't move.

"It won't come here," said Mattie. "Not to this. It's waiting for you to go home."

Tadpole stood still. "I want to go home," he said.

He shrugged his roffle pack to make it easier on his back. He pushed the edges of his cloak to one side. He planted his staff firmly. His hand went to his dagger, closing over the handle, comfortable as ever.

"Are you going back like that?" asked Mattie.

"What do you mean?"

"You'll look odd, in the Deep Worl 1. Looking like that."

He fingered the hem of Tadpole's cloak.

"You could give that to me," he said.

The noise around them swelled and sharpened. Tadpole leaned in to Mattie to hear him. The shrieks of the kravvins made his head hurt. The booms and crashes shook him. Only sudden flares of flame broke the advancing darkness. He looked up at the sky. The moon edged above a broken wall. A single star shyly broke through the blackness.

Tadpole took a deep breath.

"The first one," he said.

He felt the memmont nuzzle against his leg.

More stars stepped forward as the darkness thickened.

"I'm staying," said Tadpole. "I'm joining in."

He took in the details of the battle in front of him. Smedge, drowning December in slime. The wizards, trapped by their helplessness in the midst of Ash's magic. Dorwin, greeting Smith with a smile. Sam and Tamrin, his new friends, either side of their old tutors. Frastfil, terrified, jingling his coins and calling out to Ash for help.

The Finished Miners were winning their battles with the kravvins, but Ash still had weapons.

As Tadpole started towards Ash, she shouted, "Let it be fire. Let it all be fire."

And all became fire.

"You're too late," said Mattie.

He buckled on his shield and held it in front of him, in a hopeless attempt to keep the flames away.

Tadpole saw the roffle door disappear, melt away in the furnace of wild magic.

He looked up again. The sky was black now. The moon glowed orange through the flames.

"The stars," said Tadpole. "I can't see them."

The fire raced towards them, building strength as it engulfed the two boys. Tadpole's hair began to singe. Mattie, closer to the flames, lit up like a torch. He still brandished his shield. The fire licked it, making a circle of flame.

As Tadpole looked, the fire stripped paint and age away from the shield, burning it back to the beaten metal. It began to glow, silver and bright. The curved surface looked back at Tadpole with a lustre from inside, no reflected light. Tadpole looked back at himself in the shield, his head surrounded by a field of stars.

His cloak and his hair stopped burning. He could breathe again through the choking smoke and heat. His staff, which had started to smoulder, grew cool. Without a thought of why, he raised it above his head.

A circle of ground around him became still and free of fire. He raised it higher, and the circle grew larger.

Mattie stopped burning. And he grew more substantial.

"Come on," he shouted. "Come on, Tadpole. Hurry up."

Tadpole strode out of his circle, right into the heart of the fire. As he passed he left a path for Mattie to follow. Wherever he trod, the fire spluttered and died. Smedge lunged to stop him. Before Tadpole could resist, Smedge lost shape, melted and disappeared.

"Say something," said Mattie, trotting alongside Tadpole and squeezing his arm. "Do something."

Tadpole stopped, tilted his head back and called out, "Enough fire. Go."

Without a pause the fire died. The courtyard became silent. The Finished Miners put aside their tools. December lay where she had fallen, shocked, but alive.

The wind streamed through the broken walls, blowing Tadpole's cloak away from his shoulders, revealing his roffle pack. He stood, legs braced, arm flexed, holding the staff. A nose nuzzled against his leg. He put his hand down to stroke the memmont, to comfort it. His fingers touched scales. He looked down. The memmont's familiar face looked up at him, disguised, but not hidden, by the thick skin and shining body of a new-made dragon.

"Who would have thought it?" said Tadpole.

He smiled. He lifted the cord from around his neck and examined the tooth. Sharp, white, pointed. A dragon's tooth.

"He was right," he said.

Tadpole took another look at the reflection of his face in the shield. Delver's precious present. Smith had recognized it. Tadpole prepared himself for the next thing. His head raised, he could see the courtyard and the people, but he could also see the skies over him.

"Look at them," he shouted. "Thousands and millions of them. Look at the stars."

Sam put out his hand, and Flaxfield took it, holding him as he had when Sam was a small boy.

Sam felt no embarrassment or loss of dignity. He just let himself enjoy the memory.

The pain had passed. The burning. The choking. The stinging eyes. The furnace in the lungs. All gone. In an instant.

He leaned a little and looked sideways, to see Tamrin. She was holding Flaxfold's hand and the two old wizards held each other's. All four of them, joined in much more than a single line of handclasps.

"It's all over," said Sam.

Flaxfield squeezed his hand and replied, in a soft voice, "Not quite. Not yet."

Sam secretly clicked his fingers. Nothing happened.

"Oh, that's over," said Flaxfield. "Our magic. That's all finished, now."

"Don't you mind?" asked Sam.

The moonlight cast strange shadows in the courtyard. Cabbage ran across to December and took her in his arms, lifted her half-upright. Sam saw that the slime had vanished from her.

"She's all right," said Flaxfield.

"Have they really known each other since they were children?" asked Sam.

"Yes, but look. Here's another."

Sam watched as a boy, frail, yet growing more substantial with every step he took, approached December. Sam let go of Flaxfield's hand and moved closer, to see what would happen.

The boy stood next to December. He was complete now, all frailty gone. A normal boy. He put his hand out to the figure in Cabbage's arms. Closer now, Sam could see her clearly.

"Bee?" said Mattie.

December took her eyes away from Cabbage and looked at the newcomer.

"It's Bee, isn't it?" said Mattie. "Remember?"

A small girl, pretty, shy, with shining hair in the moonlight, looked back at him.

"It was," she said. "I was. I remember."

She took Mattie's hand in hers.

"Mattie," she said. "You've been here, all this time."

"Waiting for you. What happened to you?"

Cabbage moved away. Sam, though he felt uneasy listening in, stayed where he was.

"All my life happened to me," she said. "But look at me now."

Mattie put his arms around her neck and cried. Sam knew he had to move away now.

"What's happened to December?" he asked Flaxfield.

"She took her name back from Slowin. And the fire burned away its own damage. She's the girl she was on her twelfth birthday. The day the wild magic was set loose by Slowin."

"Slowin," said Sam. "Ash. Where is she? He?"

"Don't worry."

Smith and Dorwin stood by a small man in a tattered grey cloak. He glared out at the wreckage of the castle.

"That's Ash?" said Sam.

"What's left of her. It's Slowin again, now. Now that Bee's taken her name back."

"But how could she do that? Why now and not before?"

Flaxfield turned Sam's attention to the lone figure in the centre of the courtyard. Tadpole had not moved since he had quenched the fire.

"Something slipped," said Flaxfold. "The old magic was dying with us. The new magic was preparing itself for now. Bee slid into that gap and reclaimed her own."

"And Smedge?"

"Smedge is gone."

"For ever?"

"I watched him, most closely. When Tadpole emerged from the flames Smedge just boiled away, like water. He was only ever the excrement of Slowin's work."

"But he did all that harm, all that wickedness."

"All Slowin's doing."

The Finished Miners had formed a cordon around the broken walls of the castle. They stood guard, facing out, defying the takkabakks and kravvins to come near. Though, Sam admitted to himself, the beetles showed no desire to approach, no sign of threat. They ambled or stood, as though dazed, drugged. A lost, lonely man wove his way through them, heading away. Frastfil. On his way somewhere safe.

"What shall we do now?" asked Sam.

"Don't you think we should welcome Tadpole? He's all alone Up Top."

"Except for that dragon," said Sam, kicking a lump of broken stone.

"Come on," said Flaxfield.

"I'll go and talk to Jackbones," said Sam. "He looks terrible."

He did. No worse than before in shape, but somehow destroyed from within.

"He needs to leave," said Flaxfield. "He risked his life for us once, years ago, and his punishment was to keep it for far too long."

"I'll go and see him," said Sam.

"No. Come with me. See, Cabbage is going to Jackbones. And Tam and Flaxfold as well. He'll be all right."

"I'll help Smith, then."

Flaxfield put his hand on Sam's shoulder, resting against his staff. The magic had gone, but not the old authority. He was still Sam's master.

"Our magic has gone," he said. "We have to accept that."

"But you were the first magic. You and Flaxfold. The two of you *are* magic. It can't just end."

"It hasn't. It's just beginning. It's Tadpole now. Look at him."

They looked together. Tadpole, alone, in the starlight, his head still raised to the sky.

"Starborn," said Flaxfield. "New magic. It's the turn of the Deep World."

"I don't want him to have magic. I want it," said Sam.

"I know." Flaxfield took his hand from Sam's shoulder. "I know. But you have to be his friend. Come on." ‖

Tadpole could see the loss in Sam's face

as the boy approached him with Flaxfield.

Loss, and dislike. Sam wasn't looking like a friend. Tadpole tried to smile at the two of them. Flaxfield didn't hesitate. He strode up to Tadpole and embraced him.

"Well done," he said. He stepped back and looked Tadpole up and down. "I never thought to see a roffle wizard."

"Thank you," said Tadpole. He smiled at Sam. "Hello, Sam."

Sam nodded and looked away.

"What are you going to do now?" asked Flaxfield.

"What do you mean?"

"You've got work to do," said Flaxfield. "Where will you start?"

"I don't know."

Tadpole looked around at the destruction, the people remaining, the clumsy, confused beetles on the hillside.

"I don't know," he repeated. "What can I do?"

"Sorry," said Flaxfield. "I think Flaxfold's calling to me. I'll leave you two to sort it out."

Sam started to follow, but Flaxfield gently stopped him and turned him to Tadpole. "Talk about it," he said.

Sam glared at his back. Then he glared at Tadpole. The roffle was afraid he had made an enemy.

"What can I do?" asked Tadpole.

Pages from an apprentice's notebook

OF MASTERS AND APPRENTICES

Longer ago than anyone can remember, there was a carver. He had the way about him to take a lump of wood and to brush his knife against it, so fast that it was hard to follow the movement. So gently that it seemed to caress the grain. So powerfully, that it bit into the hard oak as a pin pierces cloth. So truly, that when he had finished, the wood was a face, or a hand, a leaf, or a fish, or anything he wanted it to be. His name was Fica.

People who had his work treasured it, and, as the years passed, the pieces became more valuable than gold. Every piece was signed with a small ash leaf cut into the wood.

Many, many years after Fica had died, a skilful woodcarver, Guildgood, chanced to find an old knife on a market stall. He took it in his hand and recognized that the wooden handle bore Fica's signature. He held it and tested it and knew that it was Fica's own knife, for carving wood. He bought it, and he used it himself for many years. His work improved and he grew prosperous and sought-after.

When his hand grew unsteady and he could no longer use the knife, he took it to another carver, Orelver. Guildgood explained the story to him and gave him the knife.

More years passed and Orelver's hands grew tired and stiff. His joints ached, and he could no longer carve wood. He put the knife away, and, when his age was more than he could carry, he told his family to put the knife in his pocket when he was Finished. They did as he said, and the knife never carved wood again.

A WORD TO WIZARDS

You did not choose your apprentice. Your apprentice chose you. Sometimes, a wizard may refuse to take an apprentice. Sometimes, the wrong person will ask you. Not every apple in a barrel is sweet. So be careful never to turn away the right person or to accept the wrong one. But, when you have been chosen and have accepted, then the indenture binds you as firmly as it binds the apprentice.

Never refuse a new apprentice because you are tired, or busy, or happy to be alone for the while. Never refuse an apprentice because you are sad, or angry, or hurt.

Magic is not your property. It is your responsibility.

A WORD TO APPRENTICES

You did not choose your wizard. Your wizard chose you.

You may have knocked on the wizard's door and asked the wizard to teach you, but the path to the door was laid for you. When the paper is before you and the pen in your hand and the ink in the inkpot and you are ready to sign, you are not choosing your wizard. Your wizard is choosing you.

You bring magic with you, to learn from older magic. But your magic and your wizard's magic are for the next apprentice, who will be yours to train.

You will not choose your apprentice.

Your apprentice will choose you.

Don't refuse, unless you are sure

it is the wrong person.

*

"I don't know," said Sam. "What can you do?"

Tadpole put his hand down to stroke the dragon.

"How did this happen?" he asked. "Why a dragon?"

Sam's eyes filled with tears. "I think there's often a dragon for a new wizard," he said. The words clambered up from his throat.

"Will you help me, please?" asked Tadpole.

Sam nodded.

"What can I do?" The same question.

Sam cleared his throat, squared his shoulders and gave Tadpole a hard look.

"Is that the right question?" he said.

"Question for question?" asked Tadpole.

"It's the wizards' way."

"It's the roffle way."

"Let's do it that way, then," said Sam. "Is that the question?"

Tadpole thought about it.

"Has the dragon got a name?" he asked.

"Where do dragons' names come from?"

"What's your name?" asked Tadpole.

Sam stumbled at this question.

"Sam will do," he said, at last. "No other names now. Wizard names are over."

Tadpole thought about this.

"Then I'm Tadpole," he said. "That'll do for me."

Sam frowned.

"Flaxfield called you Starborn," he said.

"No. Tadpole will do for me. It's simpler."

The dragon stretched like a cat, stood up, rubbed against Sam's legs. Sam put his face in his hands and began to shake. The dragon twisted round his legs and almost made him fall. Sam almost laughed, choked and put his hand down to touch the dragon.

"Starborn?" he said.

Tadpole grinned. "Starborn," he agreed.

The two boys looked at each other straight for the first time since magic had filled Tadpole.

"What can I do?" asked Tadpole.

"Is that the question?"

Tadpole nodded, firmly. "It's one of the questions," he said. "What should I do? What shall I do? What may I do? What shall I refuse to do?"

"How do they sound?" asked Sam.

"Good. They sound good."

"All right, then."

"Which one first?" asked Tadpole.

"Where do you want to start?"

Tadpole considered this.

"I'd better find what I can do, first."

"All right. Do I know the answer to that?"

"No."

"So why are you asking me?"

"I've got a lot more questions. Most of them I don't even know about yet. Will you help me?"

"If you like."

"Yes."

"All right. And I've got a question for you."

"What is it?" asked Tadpole.

"What can you do?"

"Let's see," said Tadpole.

He stepped to one side, took his staff in both hands and drew in a deep breath. Before he could speak, Sam interrupted him.

"Wait," he said. "Before you try anything else. What are you going to do about him?"

"Who?"

Sam pointed at Smith and Dorwin and their prisoner.

"Him," he said. "Slowin. Ash. We can't just leave him here. Not after what he's done. Not with what he might still do."

"Why have I got to do anything?"

"Why do you think?"

Tadpole knew that the question was a challenge, a test. He resisted telling the truth. He could see the hurt on Sam's

face, the anger. He looked for a roffle reply. He searched his
mind for an answer to turn away the difficulty.

"I think..." he began.

"Yes. I'm waiting."

Tadpole held Sam's gaze. "Because I'm the only one left
here with any magic to do the job," he said. "Your magic is
spent. All of you."

Sam held his breath. Tadpole could see the boy's effort to
control his voice.

"That's right," he said, at last. "That's the truth of it."

"Is it right? I didn't answer the question with a question.
Was I right?"

Sam gave Tadpole a small punch on the shoulder. "Sometimes," he said, "it's up to the wizard to tell the truth, direct."

Tadpole punched him back.

"Now," said Sam. "Let's see what you can do."

Tadpole started to walk towards Ash. He stopped. Thought
better of it. Started again. Stopped again. Looked up at the
stars. He clenched his staff with both hands and leaned on it.

A river of light ran out from the end of his staff, flowing
over the stone slabs of the courtyard. It spread out, glowing
silver in the moonlight, joining light to light.

It reached Sam first. The boy reflected back at himself in
the surface. Flaxfield and Flaxfold, Jackbones and Mattie.
All, in their turn, were surrounded by the spreading pool. It
lapped against their shoes, and when they looked down they

were delighted to see themselves looking back.

A small island of black stone surrounded Slowin and his guards. The silver lake drew nearer with effort, repelled and then advanced, resisted, yet overcoming.

Tadpole fought to make the tide surge to them. He concentrated his effort, beginning to understand that magic was like lifting, or pushing, or doing a hard sum in your head. It needed effort.

Something was pressing back the surge of the silver tide. Either Slowin was resisting, or some other force that protected Slowin.

Tadpole braced himself, gripping the staff ever more strongly. He strove against the impediment.

The flow covered Smith's feet. He bent down and touched it with his finger. When he stood, his whole hand shone. Dorwin next, who allowed the small waves to lick her feet.

At last, Tadpole made one, strong effort and the island disappeared. The sea of silver light was complete. It reached Slowin and bubbled up around him. Tadpole walked towards him, holding the spell tight. He looked at Slowin. He looked down. Ash reflected up at him. Tadpole looked up again. Ash looked back at him, and Slowin was reflected in the silver.

"Which are you?" asked Tadpole. "Who are you?"

Slowin's face was hard with effort. He struggled to work a spell.

"Careful," said Smith. "There's a little magic left there. Enough to hurt."

Tadpole nodded. He stepped closer to Slowin, and could feel the wizard's breath on his face, smell the rank odour from his mouth.

"What are you?" he asked.

Slowin jabbed his fist out at Tadpole, catching him off guard. The roffle staggered. Slowin pushed past him and tried to run towards the ruined gate.

"Stop him," shouted Sam. "He's getting away."

Slowin's feet splashed in the silver light, scattering droplets like stars. Each one bored through him, leaving a gap. The more he ran, the more they tore him away.

"Stop," said Tadpole. He flicked a spell at the wizard, and halted him. "Look at you," he said. "You're destroying yourself. Stay there. I'll make you better. I'll help you."

Slowin beat his fists in the air, against the spell. "Leave me," he called. "Let me alone."

Tadpole held him in the spell. "If you run again, you'll die before you reach the gate," he said. "You'll destroy yourself. Stay where you are. I'll come and help you. You've done me no harm, not really. I'll help you, as long as you do no more harm to anyone else."

He let slip the spell and walked towards Slowin, his hand out.

Slowin's fists stopped meeting resistance. He felt the holding spell disappear.

"You'll help me?"

"Yes. Stay there."

Slowin became Ash. "We can work together." She smiled. "Both of us. Now that Smedge has gone." Her face radiated joy. "You've got new magic. We can share."

"No. Not that. I'll help you. But magic is over for you."

As quickly as she had appeared, Ash became Slowin again. Slowin glared at Tadpole. He looked around at the others.

"No," he shouted. "No."

He raced for the gate.

"You'll destroy yourself," said Tadpole. "Don't run."

Each step, each splash, each spray of silver pierced him more and more. His legs, corroded away, snapped. He fell on his face.

"Stop now," called Tadpole. "I'll help you."

Slowin snarled and choked. "I don't need help from a roffle."

He tried again to stand and, looking down at his ruined legs, began to shout out a spell. The words turned to ash as they left his mouth and scattered in front of him. He choked again and tried to spit, but only more ash sprayed out.

Using his arms to crawl on, he neared the edge of the courtyard, until, raising himself up one last time, he made a strangled howl, then, all power spent, fell forward and exploded in a shower of stars. ||

Tamrin had never felt more alone.

All those years at the college, hiding away, pretending to belong and not to belong, pretending not to belong and belonging. All those times alone, waiting for Sam, waiting for friendship. All the days and nights on the roof of the college, looking out, waiting, wanting. Even in all that loneliness, she had never felt so alone as she did now.

She backed away from the others, her feet leaving ripples of light in the silver lake.

She moved with stealth and silence, until she felt the broken stones of the wall on her back. She leaned against it, letting her knees bend until she squatted on her haunches, watching Tadpole confront Slowin.

She saw the wizard resist Tadpole's help. Saw him run for the gate. Saw him destroy himself in the silver. She watched Sam walk across to Tadpole and put his hand on the roffle's shoulder. She watched Dorwin comfort Tadpole as he melted into tears at what he had done. She watched Flaxfold take

Flaxfield across to Jackbones and Cabbage, clasping hands and reflecting on the end of their enemy. She watched December and Mattie walk aside together, hand in hand, heads close, whispering. She watched the dragon, Starborn, try his wings and, new-made, take to the air, spinning round overhead, never letting Tadpole out of her sight.

So, it was over.

The war with Slowin was over.

Boolat was over.

Smedge was over.

"Canterstock," she said. "What's happened to that?"

What if the college should be over, too?

She looked at Sam.

Sam was over as well. As far as she was concerned. The other half of who she was. Over. She had to be complete to herself now.

She had never felt so alone.

Tamrin put her head into the folds of her cloak and let silent tears soak into it.

"They forgot me as well."

Tamrin wiped her face and looked up.

"What?" she said.

"They forgot me as well."

She looked to her left, at the remains of a doorway to the cellars. A dark face, and kind, looked back at her. Khazib moved out and sat next to her, his legs straight.

"They all seem happy," he said.

Tamrin followed his gaze. Sam and Tadpole were testing magic together. Tadpole, comforted now, sent sprays of coloured stars high into the air, where they burst and showered down flowers and butterflies and bright ribbons.

"What are you going to do?" he asked.

"Who are you?"

The man put out his hand to greet her. "Khazib," he said. "Apprentice to Flaxfield. Wizard. Prisoner of Ash. Locked here for longer than I know. Released at last. Good to meet you."

Tamrin ignored the hand. He withdrew it.

"Wizard?" she said.

"Wizard," he agreed.

"Not any more."

Khazib's face became solemn. "I think that's right," he agreed.

"You've tried?"

"Yes."

"So what are you going to do?"

Khazib laughed. "Question for question," he said. "The magic's gone, but the wizard ways are still here."

He stood up. "I'll remind them I'm here," he said.

Tamrin watched Khazib greet Flaxfield. Her tears began to flow again as she saw them embrace, watched them smile, and talk, and hug Flaxfold. It wasn't long before she saw Khazib lean forward and whisper something to Flaxfold. The woman nodded, looked across the courtyard and saw Tamrin. She moved away from Khazib and started towards her.

Tamrin didn't wait. She slid round the broken wall, into the open space. She ran a zigzag path, avoiding the beetles, and found the cover of the wood.

"Back to Canterstock," she said. "See what's there." ‖

The stars looked back at them,

Tadpole and Sam, lying side by side on their backs, staring up.

"Are they always this noisy?" asked Tadpole.

Sam screwed up his eyes and pretended not to care.

"I thought they were points of light," said Tadpole. "No one told me about the sounds."

"They don't know," said Sam.

Tadpole propped himself up on his elbow so he could look at Sam. "What?"

"They don't know about the sounds. Only wizards hear them." Tadpole saw the sadness in Sam. "And not all wizards," he added.

Tadpole decided not to embarrass Sam by looking at him any longer. He lay back and put his hands behind his head.

"Can you understand what they're saying?" asked Sam.

"Can you hear them?"

"No."

Silence covered them. Tadpole waited.

The stars whispered to Tadpole. He listened with care and some difficulty. He picked out one voice and tried to fade out the others. It wasn't easy, like listening to someone in a busy inn parlour. At last he managed it. It was time to trust the silence.

"Could you hear them, before?" he asked.

"Yes. I could. Not now."

"Do they tell the truth?"

He had to wait for an answer. The stars laughed.

"You'll have to get to know them," said Sam. "Listen and watch. Make up your own mind."

They looked up again in a long silence.

Starborn sliced through the night sky, crossing overhead.

Tadpole propped himself up again to look at what was happening.

The wizards and the others had fallen into pairs and groups. Some slept. Some talked in low voices. Smith had left the courtyard. He walked round the perimeter, stopping now and then to exchange a word with one of the Finished Miners, who formed an outward-facing circle, protecting the castle and those inside.

Kravvins and takkabakks were still, only a few of them making a confused effort to walk.

Tadpole stood up and walked over to Smith. He climbed the low mound of stones that were all that remained of the walls. Smith saw him approaching and waited for him.

"Soon be dawn," he said.

Tadpole gave the sky a regretful look.

"The stars will be back again tonight," said Smith. "They're always there."

They walked slowly together, within the cordon of miners.

"You'll be going back home, soon," said Smith. "To the Deep World."

"I suppose so."

The sky began to catch a small suggestion of blue at the edge of the horizon. One by one, then in thousands, the stars withdrew behind the cloak of dawn. Tadpole kept his head turned up, trying to write the memory of the stars in his mind, until only one was left, gleaming alongside the fading moon.

"Look at that," said Flaxfold.

Tadpole hadn't heard her approach. Her sleeve brushed his cheek as she stretched her arm out and pointed to the hillside.

In the early sunlight the takkabakks and the kravvins started into action. They darted about, bumping into each other. The Finished Miners brandished their spades and picks, ready for battle.

"Things are righting themselves," said Flaxfold. "See."

The monstrous beetles shrank and splintered. They reshaped themselves and changed colour. Some had wings and took flight. Some grew horns and scuttled away. Greens and blues and reds. Stripes and spots. They buzzed and bumbled along. A cloud of jewels hanging in the sunlight. A stream of ripe fruits pouring down the hillside.

"They're beautiful," said Tadpole.

A great, flying stag beetle, half the size of the roffle's palm, flew towards him. It circled and landed on the shoulder of his cloak, folded its wings into the hard carapace like an elderly roffle tucking herself up in bed. Now it was the size of his thumb.

They watched it run down the cloak, pause at the hem, spread its wings again and fly off.

In minutes the beetles had dispersed, into the woods and long grass, under dead logs, up among the leaves, flying away, scurrying for cover.

"I've always liked beetles," said Flaxfield. The whole company was together now, assembled to watch the transformation. "Lovely little chaps," he said.

He put his hand on Sam's shoulder. "Thank you," he said.

"What for?"

"Are you ready?" Flaxfield asked.

Flaxfold came and took his hand. "I'm ready," she said. "Say goodbye to Tam for me," she told Sam. "When you see her."

"You tell her," he shouted. "Tell her yourself."

"Tadpole," said Flaxfield. "Look after Sam."

"Yes," said Tadpole.

"And you, Sam. Look after Tadpole. There's a lot to do."

"Shut up," shouted Sam. He pushed himself at Flaxfield and grabbed the old wizard's cloak. He buried his face in it and hugged him. Flaxfield put his arms around the boy and they held each other.

"The last and the best," said Flaxfield. "Thank you."

Flaxfold helped Sam to move away. She hugged him and kissed his cheek.

"Thank you," said Sam. "Both of you."

"There was only ever one," she reminded him.

He nodded.

"Say it, please, Sam," said Flaxfield.

"No."

"Please," said Flaxfield. "You have to."

"No."

The two old wizards walked away. Five paces. Ten. They stopped. They put their staffs on to the ground, side by side, and clasped them together with their hands.

"Say it now, Sam."

Sam took one pace towards them. He stood upright, hands clasping his staff.

"You have done all things well," he said, quietly. "Go where you must."

"Thank you."

They drew close to each other. Their cloaks wrapped together, blended, became one. The staffs grew, rose up, thickened and spread over their heads. The cloaks melted into the upright trunk of a tall willow, its leaves silver green in the morning sunlight.

Sam sat down and wept until his throat hurt.

He was thirteen years old. ||

The sun was hot, beating down

on the ruins of Boolat. Sam, hunched inside his cloak, grew uncomfortable.

He pushed it aside.

He said one of the words that Flaxfield had told him never to use.

"That's no language for a wizard," said Dorwin.

Looking up, Sam saw that all the others had moved away from him. Only she remained.

"I'm hot," said Sam.

He pushed the cloak right away and leaned back with the palms of his hands against the grass.

"Why wouldn't you be?" she asked. "It's a hot day. You're out in the sun."

Sam shook his head. Dorwin sat next to him. She touched the hem of his cloak with her fingertips.

"It's a Cloude cloak," she said. "And a wizard's cloak."

Sam looked away.

"It won't keep you cool in the sun any more," she said. "Nor protect you in the cold, any more than a good cloak would. Remember?"

Sam didn't turn his head to face her.

Tadpole was talking to Jackbones. Sam felt a surge of anger again. They had their heads close, as though exchanging secrets, as though they were old friends.

"You have to help him," said Dorwin. "No matter how difficult it gets for you."

"I know."

"Why don't you sit in the shade? Cool down."

The willow was full-grown, almost. Sam shook his head.

"Why not?"

"I don't mind the sun."

She squeezed his shoulder and left him there.

Sam watched the activity. The Finished Miners had left their guard posts and were gathered around Smith. Tadpole and Jackbones still spoke. Mattie and Cabbage and December seemed to be arguing. Khazib stood apart. Sam couldn't be bothered with any of them. He edged along the grass until he found himself in the shade of the willow boughs. He rested there for a while, in the cool grass. Standing up, he made his way to the tree. The trunk was a swirl of movement from root to branch, as though twisted in its growth. Not quite two strands, like a plaited loaf, but somehow conjoined, embraced. Sam leaned his face against the bark, enjoying the roughness against his cheek. He stepped closer and pressed against it.

It was hard to move away, but he managed it, without looking back.

"We're going," shouted Smith, waving to Sam.

Sam made his way towards them.

"Where to?" he asked.

"We don't have to go, yet," said a miner. "We can rebuild this."

"What?" asked Sam.

"As it was," he said. "We remember it. We're from long ago. Some of us worked the iron for the door hinges and the sconces. We mined the metal for the nails, the locks, the chains. We can rebuild it."

Sam laughed. "Never," he said. "Not this place."

The miner glared at him. "You think we couldn't?"

Smith stepped between them.

"It was a place of great beauty, once," he said to Sam. "It would be wonderful to have it back." He turned his attention to the miner. "And, of course you could, Bearrock," he said. "Before the sun sets tonight, you could do it. You're the Finished Miners. There's nothing you couldn't build."

Sam and the miner still stared at each other.

"Bearrock?" he said.

The miner held out his hand. Sam shook it. "Best you don't rebuild," he said.

"See," said Smith. "The others have made up their minds."

The Finished Miners had started to swing their picks. They prised up the flagstones and lifted them away. They pushed their spades into the earth and flung the soil aside.

Like beetles, they scrambled below the earth, climbing down and disappearing.

"Back to the Finished Mine," said Smith. "They're going back."

Bearrock took his hand from Sam's.

"Goodbye, Sam," he said.

"Yes. Thank you."

Bearrock shook hands with Smith and walked away, joining his friends. In minutes they had all gone.

"Everything is finishing," said Sam. "Everything."

"Changing," said Smith. "As iron changes in the furnace."

"What now?" asked Sam.

"For me? Back to my forge. Farmers still need billhooks and ploughs. Kitchens need pots and pans. Plenty for me to do. And Dorwin."

She came and stood next to Smith.

"We'll see you again?" she said to Sam. "You'll always be welcome at the forge."

"We'll see him again," said Smith, interrupting Sam. "With that roffle, I expect."

They took their leave of the others and walked away.

Sam, Khazib, Cabbage, December, Mattie, Jackbones and Tadpole stood together and watched until they disappeared into the trees.

Even as they were watching Smith and Dorwin depart, Sam couldn't stop himself from stealing glances at December. Her face, smooth and lovely, still glowed from the renewing fire.

Sam tried to think what sort of age she looked. Twelve or twenty? One hundred or older? It was no good. She was the only one of them who still carried the muddling imprint of magic.

It was December who spoke first.

"I'm going, now," she said. "Back home. To the mines."

"What for?" Mattie demanded.

Sam saw that there was trouble between them.

Cabbage spoke softly to the boy. "She may go where she pleases."

"What's it to do with you?"

"I can still heal," said December. "I know herbs and infusions. I can set a broken leg. I can cool a fever and deliver a baby. These are things that overlap with magic. They remain."

"What about me?"

December touched Mattie's cheek.

"You can come with me, if you like," she said. "I'll teach you."

"I don't want to go to the mines."

"But I must."

"I waited hundreds of years for you."

"Was it that long?"

"It seemed that long," he said. "Longer, perhaps. Or not quite as long. I wasted away."

"And now you're back," she said. "But I'm not the person you waited for."

"Of course you are, Bee," said Mattie. "You're just the same."

"No. Not at all. Not the same person at all." She put her

hand to her own cheek. Her face grew sad as she stroked the perfect skin. "I have one more little magic in me," she said. She lifted her shawl from her shoulder and wrapped it around her face and over her head.

Sam felt a wave of panic as he started to know what she was doing.

December shuddered and her breath came out in a deep sigh.

She unwrapped the shawl and settled it back on her shoulders. Her face was as it had been when Sam had first met her. Ravaged and ruined by fire. Skin puckered and pulled. Her hair burned away so that it grew only in patches on the shiny scalp.

"This is me," she said. "Time and magic have done this to me. I'm not the Bee you met. I'm December."

Mattie looked down and walked away. Khazib caught him by the arm.

"Mattie," he said. "I'm going as well."

Mattie stared away from him.

"Come with me. We're old friends now. Aren't we? You and I? We survived the dungeon and the walls, the beetles and Smedge. We got through it. Come with me."

"Where are you going?" asked Mattie. "What are you going to do?"

Khazib turned Mattie to face him and laughed. "I don't know," he said. "I have no idea. But look. Look at you. A boy again. And me. Back from the lip of death. And look up there. Not the slimy ceiling of a dungeon. Look at the sky. And there." He grabbed Mattie's shoulders and span him round.

"Trees and grass, and roads, and rivers. There'll be villages and towns. We might even go as far as the end of the land. I've never seen the sea. Come with me."

Mattie looked at the others.

"Go," said December.

"Go," said Sam.

They made their farewells.

"You whipped me, once," said Sam.

Khazib looked abashed. "Only a little chastisement, to make you work harder," he said. "Am I forgiven?"

Sam paused and thought about it.

"Are you sorry?" he asked.

"I'm sorry."

"Then you're forgiven."

They embraced and laughed.

But when Mattie and Khazib had gone away in one direction and December had gone in the other, his laughter had fled with them.

"Four of us left," said Cabbage, who was trying to recover from a difficult farewell to December. They had cried and promised to see each other again soon. "What's next for us?"

"Back to Canterstock for me," said Jackbones. "There's nowhere else."

Cabbage agreed to go with him.

"What about you two?" he asked.

Sam began to answer. "Back to Flaxfield's, first," he said, when Tadpole interrupted him.

"Look at that," he said.

A sliver of blue and green approached them, high in the sky. It flew with the speed of sparks from struck steel.

"Starback," said Sam. He hugged himself with joy. "Starback."

The dragon swooped down and made a smoky draught of air flutter their cloaks. He rose up and circled overhead. Then, there were two of them, two dragons, chasing each other in a jubilant circle. Starback and Starborn.

"Come down," shouted Sam. "Come down."

"Do dragons come when you call them?" asked Tadpole.

"No," said Sam. "Of course not."

Starback broke free of the circle and flew away. Turned, flew back, turned again. Three times, before Cabbage said, "I think you're supposed to follow him, Sam."

"All right."

"And he's going that way, at present," said Jackbones. "Let's go. I've had enough of Boolat."

They strode off.

Boolat, its broken stones and torn turrets, sank back into silence and waited for the grass and trees to cover it.

Sam took one last look back at the lone willow, but it had gone.

"That's good," he whispered. "Boolat was never the place for you."

"Come on," called Tadpole. "We need you." ||

It took several days

to get to Canterstock. Tamrin didn't hurry.

"What's the point?" she asked. "What will be different when I get there? I'll still be a wizard without magic. And what's that? It's not a thing at all. It's a river without water. A forge without fire."

She hit her staff against an innocent beech tree. "Shut up," she said. "Shut up. Talking to yourself. Like some loblolly."

So she was silent for a while and then began her mumbling again.

She didn't eat. She drank from clear streams. She chewed the end of a sweet stalk of grass to freshen her mouth. But she didn't want food.

She wasn't alone. She could tell that Tim thought she had not seen him. Sometimes he was ahead of her. Sometimes to one side. He kept in the shadow. He skirted round and tried to stay hidden. But she saw him almost as soon as she left Boolat.

Let him think he was fooling her. She didn't care. Didn't care what he did.

She kept a careful look out for kravvins. Just in case. She didn't know how far from Boolat they would wander.

She hadn't seen them transformed into ordinary, harmless beetles.

So she slept little, always alert for attack.

By the time the walls of Canterstock appeared, with the tower of the college rising over them, she was tired, hungry and bad-tempered.

She left the road, found a sweet meadow and sat, her chin on her hands, and stared at the town.

It looked wrong. Something about the way the sun hit the stone of the college made it seem softer, kinder.

She forgot herself for a moment and clicked a clear-sight spell, to help her to see better, further.

Nothing happened.

She grumbled out loud. "I suppose I'll have to walk there if I want to see."

Drawing close to the gate, she saw Tim slip in, ahead of her.

There were no guards. Tamrin kept her wits about her, ready for a trap. The narrow street to the main square was clean and swept. A flower shop spilled blooms into the street. Blue and green and red. The fresh, sweet aroma delighted Tamrin as she passed.

And the square itself.

People smiled at her. They stepped aside to let her pass, and called out hellos and greetings.

Tamrin ignored them and crossed towards the college. She stopped in the centre of the square and stared long and hard at it. Golden stone drank in the early-afternoon sun. Slender turrets and graceful arched windows. The glass gleamed.

"Going in?"

"What?" said Tamrin.

A friendly face smiled down at her. A woman with a basket full of fresh bread, apples, a cabbage and a pack of sausages.

"Are you going in?" she said. "You look as though you belong there."

"Oh," said Tamrin. "Yes. Yes. I'm going in."

The woman smiled again and went on her way.

The gate was open. Tamrin dodged past the porter's lodge, but there was no need. It was empty. She relaxed and checked if there was anything to see there. Letters stuck out of the pigeon holes, uncollected, unread.

She left them and made her way into the lower corridor.

There was no stink.

The globes had risen and they bounced against the high ceiling, glowing with a clear, white light. The ceiling, she saw clearly for the first time, was blue, alive with bright stars.

Tamrin stopped and stared around, not knowing what to do, where to go first.

She hesitated at the stairs down to the basement and Cabbage's storeroom. Not there. Not yet.

A small boy appeared at the corner of the corridor. He stopped, stared at her, ran up and grinned.

"It's all gone," he said. He bounced with joy. "Horrid magic. All gone. I'm going home."

"You do that," said Tamrin. "Where are the others?"

"They've gone. All of them."

He gave her a wink and ran off. Turning to look over his shoulder, he shouted, "You can go as well, if you like."

Tamrin waved him goodbye.

She drew in a deep breath and made her way up the winding stair.

"Not quite all gone," she said.

The library door was open. Dr Duddle came through, backwards, dragging a box of books. He was red and hot. Dribbles of sweat ran down his fat face and into the folds of his neck.

He pulled the box clear of the door and made ready to go back in. He took out a handkerchief to mop his face first and saw her watching him.

"What are you doing here?" he asked.

"What are you doing with those books?"

"Is Smedge with you? Where is he? I need some help."

Tamrin pushed past him and went into the library.

"What are you doing?" she said.

"Getting rid of these old books," said Duddle. "They're useless. Help me to find another box and fill it."

Tamrin folded her arms and looked up at the endless galleries overhead.

"All of them?" she said.

"All of them, of course."

He didn't seem to hear the murmur from the galleries. Tamrin struggled to work out what it signified. Laughter? Anger? Distress?

"What will you do then?" she asked.

Duddle's face became blank, then sly.

"Does it matter?" he asked. "As long as we clear away all the old stuff, we can work out what to do next."

Tamrin listened to the galleries. She waited, alert, concentrating.

Duddle left her and tried the door to the librarian's room. It was locked.

"Can you open this?" he asked.

"Why are you getting rid of them?" said Tamrin.

Duddle gave her another sly look.

"It's because he's no good at it," said Sam. ‖

Sam was still talking

about how different it all was as they climbed the stairs and approached Frastfil's study.

"But it's exactly as the guide book describes it," said Tadpole. He twisted round and pulled the book out of his roffle pack to show them.

"The book's right," said Cabbage. "It's how the college was, before Slowin and Frastfil. I thought I'd never see it like this again."

"But it's empty," said Sam.

"No use for a college for wizards, when there's no magic," said Cabbage.

"Here we are," said Jackbones. He kicked the door open. Sam marvelled at how robust the old librarian had become since the fall of Boolat.

Frastfil jumped up from behind his desk. His face was a diagram of fear. He raised his hands as if to protect himself. Seeing who it was, he lowered them and glared.

"You should knock," he said. "Don't you know that?"

Jackbones led them in and pushed Frastfil away from the desk.

"You don't belong there," he said. "You were never fit to be principal of this place."

Frastfil tried to force his way back. Jackbones pushed him, not even hard, and the man cringed and slid to the open window, half-turned away from them.

Sam couldn't decide whether he wanted to put out his hand to comfort him or tip him out of the room altogether. In the end, he did nothing and just watched.

"Did you make this mess?" said Frastfil. "Look at it. My study. Ruined. I don't know where anything is any more."

Sam inspected the room. The desk was tidy. The bookshelves were neatly ordered. The rug was clean and fresh. The rows of jars and small pots, candle holders and little, curious objects that wizards collect were arranged with care. Only one thing remained of Frastfil's filthy study: the armchair that his great-great-something-ancestor had once owned. It squatted, torn and squalid, to the side of the desk.

"And it stinks," said Frastfil. "I can hardly breathe in here."

A vase of stocks sat on a small, oak table. Fresh freesias in a blue and white jug on the corner of the desk breathed out the gentle scent of summer.

"Did you?" said Frastfil. He jingled the loose change in his pocket. "Did you make this mess? I should never have let you into the college. I knew you would be trouble."

"Do some magic," said Jackbones. "Go on. Make it how you like it again."

Frastfil looked back at him. Hesitated. Shook his head and looked out of the window.

"No magic?" said Jackbones. "Eh? What's that? Speak up."

"All gone," said Frastfil.

Jackbones looked at Tadpole.

"Show him some magic, boy," he said.

Sam felt a stab of regret and anger at Tadpole. He smothered it almost before it could hurt him.

Tadpole looked confused. He shook his head.

"A roffle?" said Frastfil. "A roffle? Do magic?" He gave an unpleasant laugh, reminding Sam of the real man behind the cheerful smile.

Tadpole rapped his staff on the floor. The armchair became a thick, yellow fog, filled with maggots and slugs.

"Stop!" shouted Frastfil. "Stop. That's my armchair. That was owned by a great wizard, my great-great-great—"

Tadpole rapped the staff again and Frastfil fell into the armchair. The wet creatures covered him, his hands, arms, face.

"I can't breathe," Frastfil gasped. His face turned purple and his tongue stuck out.

"No," said Sam, horrified at the sudden power and violence. "That's not what magic's for. Stop it."

"It's all right," said Tadpole. "Watch."

Frastfil struggled to get out of the chair. His legs waved

like an upturned cockroach. His arms flailed. He choked for help.

The fog melted away. The chair emerged. One leg collapsed. The stuffing disintegrated. The frame split and fell apart, leaving Frastfil sprawled in the wreckage. Tadpole rapped the staff again. Frastfil, unharmed, lay in the debris.

"I didn't hurt him," said Tadpole.

"Should have killed him," said Jackbones. "Get your knife and finish him off."

"No," said Frastfil. He smiled up at Tadpole. "Good chap. You can stay on here as a student. I'll teach you myself."

Jackbones made the most unpleasant sound that Sam had ever heard. "He still thinks he's worth something," he said. "He hasn't learned a thing."

"No," Cabbage agreed. "Not a thing. But I don't think he can. He's one of those who's been taught to think so well of himself that he can't stop, even when it all goes wrong, and it's his fault."

Frastfil hauled himself to his feet, change jingling, smile broad as ever. "We'll make the college great again," he said to Tadpole. "Build it up. You'll see."

Jackbones shrugged his shoulders. "You really should kill him," he said to Tadpole. "Just one little spell."

"Jackbones," said Sam.

Jackbones nodded. "You're right," he said. "It would make us as bad as he is. What shall we do with him, Sam?"

"Kick him out," said Sam.

"Just kick him out?"

"Why not? He's not worth anything else."

Cabbage sighed. "All that harm he did. All that damage to Canterstock College. All the people whose lives have been lost and ruined by him. It seems too little, just to kick him out."

"Tadpole?" asked Sam. "What do you think?"

"New start," said Tadpole. "Better not begin with a killing. Kick him out."

"Off you go," said Sam.

And, to his surprise, Frastfil didn't argue. He even looked relieved to be off. With a beaming smile and a last jingle of change in his trouser pocket, he left.

Tadpole rapped his staff on the floor. A wind seized the debris of the armchair and swept it out of the window. The room was clean and ready for someone new.

"I'm going back to my library," said Jackbones. He shrank again, the confrontation over. Sam could see through him for a moment.

"I'll come with you," said Cabbage. "Then I'll go and check on my storeroom."

"You can't stay here." said Sam. "It's empty. What will you do?"

"We'll see," said Cabbage. "You never know."

The bright corridors and brilliant globes delighted Sam all over again on their way to the library.

"And the stars," said Tadpole. "On the ceilings. Are they made up?"

Sam checked them. "No. They're the real patterns in the sky."

"And they have names? The patterns?"

"Yes."

"Will you teach me?"

"Perhaps. They may need new names, now. New patterns. We'll talk about it."

"What's that noise?" said Cabbage. "Voices?"

"In my library?" said Jackbones. "My library? Who would dare go in there?"

"Let's see," said Tadpole.

They held Jackbones back and listened outside the door.

"Duddle," said Cabbage. "I'll see to him."

"And Tamrin," said Sam. "I knew we'd find her." He grinned at Tadpole.

They listened a while, and Cabbage pointed to the box of books that Duddle had dragged out.

"Come on," whispered Sam, and led them in.

Duddle was by the librarian's door.

"Why are you getting rid of them?" said Tamrin.

Duddle gave her another sly look.

"It's because he's no good at it," said Sam.

Duddle spluttered a reply. Tamrin frowned at Sam, then, with a shrug, smiled and crossed over to him so that the two of them faced Duddle together. When they spoke, it was as though they were one again.

"He's a bully."

"And no good at his job."

"Poor at magic."

"Useless at teaching."

"Envious of the past."

"Resentful of others."

"Ambitious without ability."

"A dead, dud loss."

There was silence.

The silence of shock.

The silence that follows the truth.

Duddle tilted his head to one side. Thought for a moment. Looked at the others.

"Ah, Jackbones," he said. "Can you open that door for me, please? I want another box."

The galleries exploded. A shower of paper tumbled down on them. Paper willow leaves, slim and small. The whole space above their heads was filled with them, as the sky is filled with rain.

Voices followed, whispering, urging, washing over them.

"Jackbones. Jackbones. Jackbones."

The old librarian raised his arms. The storm of paper leaves thinned and stopped. The voices subsided. The air filled with the sweet silence of a library. The faces appeared around the rails above. Row upon row, rank upon rank. Waiting.

Jackbones walked over to Duddle, took his elbow and led him to the door of the library.

"You're the last of the disease that rotted this place," he said. "You have three minutes to leave the college. If you're still here after that, I won't need magic to deal with you. Understand?"

"What shall I do?" said Duddle. "I've nowhere to go."

Jackbones turned Duddle till he faced the door, drew back his foot and kicked him on the behind. The chubby doctor lurched forward, found his balance and ran.

The galleries rained down laughter and applause. Jackbones looked up and laughed and spread his arms again.

Sam and Tamrin, separate again now, looked on. Sam saw the joy trickle from Jackbones' face and his arms slowly fall to his sides.

The laugher diminished.

A slender foot appeared round the iron stair.

"Springmile," said Sam.

The woman let her eyes rest on him for a moment, but she didn't hesitate on her path to Jackbones.

"Well done," she said. She reached out her hand and took his. "Well done, Jackbones."

The limitless faces appeared around the galleries high above them. They gazed down, with solemn welcome. Sam expected a noise. Applause? Or shouts? Or the strange, disturbing whispers he remembered from before when the faces appeared. But there was silence and soft smiles.

Jackbones held Springmile's hand tight.

"Is it finished?" he asked.

"It is finished," she said.

He didn't look back.

Sam tried to put out his hand to touch Jackbones, a farewell. Springmile stood between them and guided the librarian to the step. She pressed her hand to his back and he walked up.

"I'll be with you in a moment," she said.

She faced them and put out her hand for Tadpole.

"Come here, roffle," she said. ||

Tadpole didn't move at all,

fixed to the spot with some feeling he didn't understand.

"Come," said Springmile. "I won't hurt you."

Tadpole took a single step towards her and stopped.

"What do you want?" he asked.

She smiled.

"I want to see a roffle who's a wizard," she said. She made a sweeping gesture with her arm, the shimmering dress catching the light as it moved with her. Indicating the rows of never-ending galleries high above them she said, "All the past magic of all time is here. Collected on these shelves. Going on beyond going."

Tadpole felt a shudder of irritation as Sam interrupted.

"Can we use it?" he said. "The magic stored here. Can we take it out again? Because if we can, we—"

Tadpole tapped his foot and silenced Sam.

Springmile waited for Tadpole to speak.

"Please," he said. "Carry on."

"Don't you want me to answer Sam's question?"

"Do you want to?" he said.

She laughed out loud, and the whole gallery laughed with her. A laugh of simple delight, not mockery.

"A wizard's question," she said. "Better than a roffle riddle."

Tadpole laughed, too.

"I can show you," she offered. "All that's up there, beyond where the college readers go. High up, with the Finished Magic. If you'd like."

Sam tried to interrupt again, and Tadpole's spell kept him silent.

"Let him ask," said Springmile.

Tadpole tapped his foot again.

Sam shouted at him. "Don't you magic me. Don't you dare."

"Sorry," said Tadpole.

Sam pointed a finger at Springmile. "She's going to take you away. Into the galleries. And you won't come back. Ever. It's a trick."

"Sam," she said. "Sam. Don't you know me better than that?"

"No," he said. "No, I don't."

Cabbage took Sam's arm. "Let Tadpole go with her," he said.

"Will you bring him back?" said Sam.

"Yes. I promise," said Springmile.

Sam gave her a sideways look. "Today?"

"Today. Within the hour. Minutes, perhaps."

Tadpole gripped Sam's shoulder as he passed him and followed Springmile up the winding iron stair.

Tamrin hadn't watched much of this. She kept to the shadow and the corner. It was as it had been before Sam had arrived. Back in the days when she was the college disgrace. The girl, expelled for naughtiness, who wouldn't leave. The girl who stole food from the kitchens and hid in the rafters. The girl who had more magic in her toe than all the other pupils put together.

She welcomed the feeling of loneliness and being different from the rest. It was an old friend who never let her down.

Whatever else happened she had the comfort of not belonging. So it didn't matter if they didn't care.

She wondered if she could make her way to the door and slip out before they remembered her. There were plenty of places in the college where she could hide. They'd never find her. In the end, they'd have to give up and go away, back to their own lives.

She edged along the side of a bookcase and towards the open door.

Just before she reached it, Tim came in and went straight to her. He barked.

The others looked at her, turning their faces from the stairs.

Tamrin sighed.

Tim barked again.

A curious, disturbing sound, because it wasn't a dog's mouth, it was a boy's. The body was the same, furry and brown. The legs were the same. It was the head and feet. A boy's hands. A boy's bare feet. A boy's face.

"What's happened to you?" she asked.

Tim barked. This time it was a sort of word.

"Worn!" he barked.

"What?"

"Worn off."

The more he barked, the more clear the words became, until his own voice returned.

"The spell. It's worn off."

"Some of it," said Tamrin.

"Help me," said Tim. "Please. When Smedge disappeared, the spell began to wear off. I'm almost myself again. Please help me."

"Why?" Tamrin's face was blank.

"You're my friend."

Tim tried to rub himself against her legs. She nudged him away, quite roughly, but not enough to hurt.

"No," she said.

"You won't help me?"

"I didn't mean that. I mean no, you're not my friend."

"I was."

"Yes. I know. And when Smedge and Frastfil attacked me and lied about me, you could have helped. And you didn't. You're not my friend."

Cabbage began to speak, and Sam stopped him.

"I was frightened," said Tim. "I couldn't help you."

"I was frightened," said Tamrin. "I needed a friend. And you weren't there. You turned to Smedge. And this is what you became."

"Please," he said. "Help me. I can't stay like this."

Tamrin shrugged. "You know," she said, "if I could help you, I would. You're not my friend. You never will be. But I'd do it for you, if you promised to go away and never bother me again. But there's no magic left. So I can't, can I?"

Tim's tail disappeared between his legs. He crouched low and shook.

Sam patted him. Cabbage put his arm around Tamrin and she shook it off.

"What's happening?" asked Tadpole.

"You're back," said Sam.

"Sorry I've been so long," said Tadpole. "I wasn't sure you'd still be here."

"What do you mean, so long?"

"Hours, at least. It might have been days. It's amazing up there. There's a whole—"

Springmile touched his shoulder and shook her head.

"Anyway," he said, "I'm sorry I've been so long."

He saw Tim and blinked.

"Is that…?"

"Yes," said Tamrin.

"What happened?"

"It's a long story," she said. "But he wants the spell removed. And I think you're the only one who can do it."

Tadpole frowned. He looked at Sam. "What do I do?" he asked.

Springmile touched his shoulder again and whispered in his ear.

"Sorry," said Tadpole. "I forgot. Tam, please, tell me what to do."

Tamrin felt a glow of pleasure that she tried to suppress.

"Why are you asking me?"

Tadpole looked at Springmile.

"Go on," she said.

"I need lessons," said Tadpole. "From Sam. And from you. If I'm to be a proper wizard. And I think it has to be you, as well as Sam. You made this staff for me, didn't you? Please, will you help?"

Tamrin looked at Sam. His face was set, hard, until he caught her eye.

"Sam?" she asked.

"I can't do it on my own," he said.

"What do you want?" she asked Tim.

"To be myself," he said.

"Say that, then," she said to Tadpole.

Tadpole rapped his staff on the floor.

Before he could speak a spell, Sam said, "You'll have to stop doing that. It's going to be really annoying."

Tadpole blushed. He put his hand on Tim's back and said, "Be yourself."

"Thank you," said Tim.

"What's happening?" said Tadpole. He span round and looked at Sam, then Tamrin. "It's gone wrong. I got it wrong. Stop it."

Tim yelped and ran across the library.

"No," he barked. "Nuff."

The head and hands and feet melted away, and Tim was all dog again. With paws and a lolling tongue and floppy ears.

He barged into Tamrin's legs and looked up at her.

"It's nothing to do with me," she said. "I needed a friend when you were there. And you weren't my friend. Smedge didn't make you a dog. It's what he found in you."

"You'd better go," said Sam.

"Come on," said Cabbage. "I'll take you down to the storeroom. At least you needn't starve." He looked at Sam and Tamrin. "I'm not going to say goodbye," he said. "I'll see lots of you, won't I? And you, Tadpole. I make the best breakfast for thirty miles. All right?"

"All right," said Tadpole.

Cabbage walked away, clicking his fingers for Tim. The shadow of a small, grey cat slipped out after him.

With a last, reproachful look at them, Tim trotted off.

"And that leaves just you three," said Springmile.

"I want to show Tadpole the roof," said Tamrin.

"A good idea," said Springmile. "Then find somewhere to sleep. It's getting late."

She embraced all three of them.

Sam watched her disappear up the winding stair, and felt lonely, lost.

"What's it like up there?" he asked. "I mean, right up? I've been to the lower galleries, where the readers go. But what's it like higher up?"

"Come on," said Tamrin. "The stars will be out." ||

There was no moon

and Tadpole stared into the slow, black sky.

"How many stars are there?" he asked.

The three of them lay on their backs, on the sloping slates of the turret roof, Tadpole in the centre.

"Millions," said Tamrin. "More than can ever be counted."

"There are books about them," said Sam. "In the library. Maps and charts, but more are not counted than are known."

"I remember," said Tadpole. "There wasn't time to look at them, though."

He sensed that Sam had moved away from him a little, and he remembered Springmile's advice to be careful in what he said.

"Please will you teach me the names of the patterns?" he said. "I don't think we'll need new ones, after all."

"It's all right," said Sam. "You're the first of the new. I know that. Don't be careful around me."

"We'll get used to it," said Tamrin.

"Can I be your apprentice?" he asked. "Both of you."

The silence climbed all the way from the top of the tower to the furthest star. Sam and Tamrin looked up into the night, not at each other. At last, Tadpole answered his own question. "I can't, can I?"

"I'm sorry," said Sam.

Tamrin took a deep breath before she said, "That's all gone for us. It's you, now."

"But we'll be your friends," said Sam.

"Will you tell me things? About magic?"

"Everything," said Tamrin. "I promise."

She let Tadpole take her hand and squeeze it. He had never been so happy. Two friends and a sky full of stars. And magic. He shifted, ready to make a spell, remembered himself and stopped.

"Go on," said Sam.

"Please," said Tamrin.

Tadpole propped himself up on his elbows.

"It's just that I want to do it," he said. "Like you want to sing when you're happy, or run, or swim."

"Or eat," said Sam.

"That's it. Roffles love to eat."

"Go on, then," said Tamrin. "Show us."

Tadpole stood up and raised his staff.

"But don't rap that thing, all right?" said Sam.

"Sorry."

Tadpole clicked his fingers. The stone top of the turret

bloomed into a glowing line of jasmine that lit his face and breathed a mist of delicate perfume into the night air.

Sam sighed.

Tadpole pursed his lips and blew. Green and blue and silver-grey lizards crept silently from the jasmine. Each as small as a fingernail. They darted among the dark-green fronds and rested on the white flowers, licking black tongues across their cheeks, reflecting beauty in the starlight.

Tamrin propped herself up and looked at Sam. He nodded.

When Tadpole had turned the whole of the rooftop and the turret into a garden, full of colour and scent and tiny creatures, Tamrin sat and enjoyed it, until Tadpole saw that it was hurting her to be there.

He blinked, and it was all gone.

"I'm tired," he said. "Let's sleep."

Tadpole and Sam slept in Sam's old dormitory.

Tamrin wouldn't stay. "I never slept here after I was expelled," she said. "I have a comfortable place. I'll see you in the morning."

They spent the morning looking all around the college.

"I want to see everything," said Tadpole. "Starting with the kitchen."

The pantries and larders and cool-rooms were stocked with every sort of food.

"And it's all fresh," said Tadpole. "How?"

Tamrin and Sam were one voice in reply. "Magic. Don't

forget. This is no ordinary place."

So they ate a breakfast fit for a roffle.

"We'll wash up later," said Tadpole.

"We'll do it now," said Tamrin. "Wizards still have to wash up."

She cleared the dishes away, and caught Tadpole tapping his staff on the ground, gently, so they wouldn't hear.

"None of that," she warned.

"Why?"

Sam washed the plates. "Because magic's not a short cut. It's not a cheap way to miss work. It's for something."

"What about the flowers last night?"

"Sheer, simple joy," said Tamrin. "That's good. But the rest of the time, well, here's a towel. You can dry the things. No magic."

"And then we'll look at the college?"

"Yes."

Classrooms and laboratories, the dormitories and the studies, corridors and kitchens; Tadpole followed them round in astonishment.

"It's so huge," he kept saying. "But so small, as well, the tiny rooms for the older pupils. The teachers' studies. I love it. What's through here?"

He pushed open a wide door and entered the great hall.

"Oh," he said. "Oh. That's just ... I mean, it's..."

"Yes," said Tamrin. "Make sure it fills with pupils, will you?"

"What do you mean?"

"She means," said Sam, "that if you're the first of the new, and Boolat has been destroyed, there must be a reason why this place is as it was before. I think you're supposed to use it, for new wizards."

"But there aren't any new wizards," said Tadpole.

"Wait and see."

"The garden, next," said Tamrin.

"And then it must be time to eat again," said Tadpole. "It's after noon."

"We'll see."

Tadpole refused to believe the garden when he saw it.

"It's bigger than three towns of Canterstock," he said. "It would never fit inside the walls."

"How do you think the library fits inside the building?" asked Sam.

Tadpole saw Sam's face and apologized. "This is very hard for you," he said. "Please be patient with me."

"It's all right." Sam rested his hand on Tadpole's shoulder. "We'll get on all right, the three of us."

"Shall we eat, now?"

"Not yet," said Tamrin. "There's the entrance quadrangle and the porter's lodge. Then, after all that, you need to find Cabbage's storeroom."

"Quickly, then," he said. "I'm starving."

"Roffles," said Tamrin.

Overnight, the letters had vanished from the pigeon holes and the porter's lodge was clear and neat.

"Ready for the new start," said Tamrin.

"Let's eat," said Tadpole.

"Try the gate, first," said Sam. "It can be heavy."

Tadpole unbolted it, turned the huge key in the lock and grasped the round, iron handle. It was bigger than both his hands together. He turned it to the left.

"It's not bad," he said. "Fairly easy."

The gate swung open.

"It's not Canterstock," said Sam.

Tadpole stepped through.

A small crowd of people gathered round the gate. They stepped back in alarm as it opened. Tadpole saw Delver and his neighbours, and his father. He turned to look at Tamrin. She and Sam were gaping in wonder.

"The Deep World," she said.

"Hello, Tadpole," said Delver. "I thought you were going Up Top?"

Tadpole's father advanced. "What are you doing in there? And where did it come from? And it's nearly time for dinner. And what's that roffle pack? Where did you get that? You're not going Up Top. It's too dangerous. And what are you all dressed up like that for? Wait till your mother sees this. And," he said again, "what are you doing in there? And what is it anyway?"

Tadpole looked at the gate. A bright, brass plate said, *Starborn College*.

He looked up. High overhead, so far away it looked like a skylark, a dragon circled. Tadpole smiled and sighed. That was going to take some explaining. "How long have I been away?" he asked.

"You just left," said Delver. "I came after you to give you a parcel of pies for the journey."

"What journey?" asked Tadpole's father.

"It's a long story," said Tadpole.

"And it's only just begun," said Tamrin.

Sam stepped back inside and closed the gate.

"What's happened?" he asked.

"It looks like the Deep World needs a college for wizards," Tamrin said.

She turned the handle to the right and opened the gate again.

"Canterstock," she said. She closed it.

"How will we find Tadpole, to help him?"

Tamrin studied the gate handle. She turned it right and opened the gate.

"Canterstock."

She closed the gate and turned the handle left.

Tadpole's startled face stared at them, and the puzzled faces of the roffles.

"Help me," he said.

Tamrin grinned. "Later. Enjoy your dinner. You know where to find us when you need us."

She closed the gate again.

"Well," she said. "It's like Flaxfield's study."

"What now?" asked Sam

"I'm going to find Cabbage. They'll need stores when the new pupils start to arrive."

Sam smiled.

"Back to Flaxfield's for me," he said.

"Flaxfold's," said Tamrin.

"Ours, I think," said Sam.

"I suppose it is."

"Will you come and see me there?"

Tamrin didn't need to answer. She walked away and waved with her back to him.

Sam took his time returning. The inn was still there, and, to his astonishment, so was the room that linked it with Flaxfield's house. A little piece of magic remained.

"Perhaps it will seep back, slowly," said Sam, as he closed the door and found himself back in the familiar study.

The ash tree brushed its branch against the window. The sunlight broke up into patterns through the glass.

Sam walked down to the stream. The old willow was there, and, a little way off, a new one, which hadn't been there when Sam had left. High-pointing, silver-green leaves and swirling trunk.

"That's better," said Sam. ‖

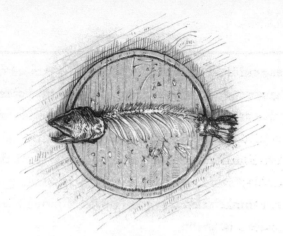

envoy

It was a Friday, and the old man thought it would be good to have a trout for his supper. Like old times.

He strolled down to the stream, glancing over his shoulder to take a look at the house. A flash of blue and green caught his eye, high against the sky and the woolly white clouds.

"Oh, you're back, are you?" he said. "It's been a long time."

He smiled and carried on to the stream. Halfway there, he paused, and looked at the two willow trees, their tall trunks, their silver-green leaves catching the light.

He sighed.

Turning away from his path, he walked towards them. The first, the older of the two, he stood beside. He looked for the scars of the branches he had once cut away, to make a woven basket. The years had covered them over. Perhaps there were one or two. "Probably not," he said. "Probably not."

At the second willow he paused for longer and looked up

at the sky through its foliage. The shadows danced on his face. He closed his eyes and smiled. Taking another step he put his arm around the trunk. It had grown too wide for him to encircle it. He traced his finger ends over the pleasing bumps of the bark, and noted, again, how the trunk twisted and blended two strands. The divisions had almost disappeared now, as growth knitted them together. He rested his cheek against it for a moment.

"This won't catch a trout," he said.

The stream ran clear and fast. He could see the pebbles at the bottom, and, in the shadows of the alders on the bank, he could almost see the flickering trout.

He found a length of twine in a fold of his cloak, and a hook fastened in the collar. Rigging a line, he sat on the cool grass and cast into the water.

After five minutes of casting and waiting he pulled the line in and laid it by his side.

"Not biting, Sam?"

He didn't look over his shoulder. He didn't need to.

"What are you doing here?" he asked. "Come on out, so I can see you."

"Over here," said the voice.

Sam looked over his left shoulder and saw the roffle climb through the roffle door into the sunlight.

"Tadpole, come and sit with me," said Sam.

The roffle joined him and they sat in silence for a long time, until he looked up and said, "Starback."

·

"Yes," said Sam. "I see him about once a year. I don't know. Maybe every couple of years. You know how it is."

"I know," said Tadpole. "Always on a Friday?"

"Always. You know?"

"I know."

"Sometimes he comes down. Mostly he flies over for a while and then he goes."

"He's coming down today, I think," said Tadpole.

Sam took the line again and cast for a trout.

"They're not biting today," he said.

"I've got a new apprentice," said Tadpole.

"That's good."

"It's a girl," he said. "I didn't expect that. And she's so good. Her magic is something quite new." He shook his head.

Sam poked Tadpole's side with his finger. "You don't choose your apprentice," he said.

Tadpole grinned. "I remember."

"Don't forget to show her how to make a good notebook."

Tadpole brought out a book, handmade in dark-red leather. "How could I forget?"

The dragon glided gently overhead, crossed the stream and came to rest on the other bank.

"How many trout were you fishing for?" asked Tadpole.

"One. Until you came along. Now I'll try for two."

"Make it four," said Tadpole.

Sam raised his eyes.

"More visitors?"

As he asked, the sunlight caught the blue and green folds of a soft dress.

"Springmile?" said Sam. He hauled himself to his feet to welcome her. "You've left your library?"

She hugged him and touched his cheek for a second before she greeted Tadpole.

"Look at you," said Sam. "Just the same as ever. And you, Tadpole. A young man. Well, just leaving youth behind, perhaps." He spread his arms out for them to look at him. "And me," he said. "Older now than Flaxfield was when I met him first. Older, that is, to look at. Not as old in years. But he was a wizard."

He turned away from them and looked into the stream until he was ready to catch their eyes again.

"What about that fish?" said Springmile.

"They're not biting."

"Oh, I should try, if I were you," she said

The first one took the hook at the first bite. Sam laid it on the grass and cast again.

"What have you come for?" he asked Springmile.

"We're sorting out the library," she said. "It needs doing, you know. As books arrive and shelves become full. We're short of one book for a full set."

"Oh, yes?"

Sam brought in the second fish and cast again.

"Yes," she said. "It's the full set of apprentices' notebooks from everyone taught by Flaxfield. We need one more to complete it."

"Mine?"

"Who else?"

"Well, Tam was his apprentice, too. Half and half with Cabbage. They both taught her."

Springmile nodded. "She was," she said. "Her notebook's ready to shelve. I wanted her to come with me for you, but she doesn't like to leave the college. She's waiting for you."

Sam landed the third fish. He knelt over the water and cleaned them into the stream.

"Do you have it?" she asked.

He wiped his hands on the grass, stood and felt in his cloak. From within the folds he produced a small book, leather bound, the corners rubbed, the surfaces bright with age and handling. The leather glowed in the afternoon light.

"That's it," she said. "We've made room for it on the shelf. I need to put it there."

"Now?" he asked.

"After dinner," she said. "If that's all right?"

Starback sprang up, took flight and circled over the house.

"Shall I cook?" offered Springmile.

"My guest," said Sam. "I'll cook."

They made their way up the slope to the house. Starback followed them in.

Sam put the frying pan on the range, dug his fingers into

the butter and took a piece as big as a walnut, let it bubble in the pan and fried the trout, dusted with flour, salted, and, just before the cooking was finished, sweetened with flakes of almond.

Starback got under his feet a little. Sam reached down absently and scratched him.

Sam didn't know what to do with the fourth fish. He left it in the pan. As they began to eat a shadow fell across the door. A woman entered and crossed to the cooking range.

Tamrin helped herself to the fish and sat next to them.

"It's good to see the house again," she said. "One last time."

Tadpole was the first to finish. He leaned back on his roffle pack and wiped his lips with the linen napkin.

"Wonderful," he said. "Thank you, Sam."

"For the fish?" said Springmile.

Tadpole blushed. "Don't tease," he said. "Anyway, thank you," he said again. "And Tam, thank you."

He almost ran out of the house before they could reply.

"You've got a key?" Sam shouted after the roffle.

Springmile cleared the table and washed the plates against Sam's argument that she was his guest.

Starback rubbed against Sam's legs and slipped through the door and up into the sky.

Sam tidied the table, complaining about his back. "Fishing always makes it ache." He fussed, getting everything into place. Taking longer than he needed. Tam waited outside, looking across to the river, the willow.

"We need to put your notebook into the library. Are you finished?" asked Springmile.

"Finished," said Sam. ||

About Toby Forward: If you were to fold the twentieth century in half and open it out again, you would see that I was born on the crease, 23rd February 1950, the day the second Attlee government was elected, led by the greatest Prime Minister of the twentieth century. Before that, the century was marked by two world wars, a general strike, Gracie Fields, the depression, bad haircuts, rationing, and the terrible winter of 1947. After that, it was peace, prosperity, Sandie Shaw, the welfare state, the white heat of the technological revolution, the flourishing of the grammar schools, the end of apartheid, the new universities, and rights for women and gay people. Modesty prevents me from saying that this new age was entirely because of my arrival in the world, but it looks like more than just a coincidence, don't you think?